Skillfully written, with abundant heart and insight.
—Charles Yu, author of *How to Live Safely in a Science Fictional Universe*

In this sharp, sensuous, powerfully observed novel, a handful of human beings in an embattled Missouri town struggle to make sense—to make lives—of what's given, bringing scrappy ingenuity and, ultimately, love to the arena. Tough, lonely, soul-scouring Sally LaChance is someone we never want to leave. Howling loss is here, and desperation—but so is nerve, curiosity, bittersweet sex, and hard-bargain-driving luck. It doesn't take long to recognize pieces of ourselves, and (turning pages faster) to worry and cheer in equal measure.
—Joan Frank, author of *Make It Stay*

Trudy Lewis is that rare, fearless writer who is unafraid of revealing the shadow side of our culture. In her new, master-fully-written novel, The Empire Rolls, she invites the reader into the heart of the heart of the country, to a mid-sized Midwestern town, where intimate relationships, and even love itself, are twisted out of shape by the forces of war, greed, and inequality. Written in electric, page-turning prose, Lewis turns her exquisitely tuned ear to the private lamentations that trickle down from public woes. In the tradition of her contemporaries, Russell Banks and Richard Russo, Trudy Lewis tells a compelling story that conveys with consummate insight the depth and texture of ordinary lives—how personal identity is profoundly altered by public events. This bracingly intelligent novel is a book for our times.
—Dale Kushner, author of *The Conditions of Love*

From the first scene at the roller derby I was whipped into the jam of The Empire Rolls. You will be too, as Sally and Jared, all-too-human, fight industrial polluters, the body's frailties, and their own self-destructive tendencies in this compelling, touching and humorous quest to find their way.

—Allison Amend, author of *A Nearly Perfect Copy*

The Empire Rolls

TRUDY LEWIS

For Heather,
Keep Rolling!
Best,
Trudy Lewis

MOON CITY PRESS
Department of English
Missouri State University
901 South National Avenue
Springfield, Missouri 65897

First Edition
Copyright © 2014 by Trudy Lewis
All rights reserved.
Published by Moon City Press, Springfield, Missouri, USA, in 2014.

Library of Congress Cataloging-in-Publication Data

Lewis, Trudy, 1961–.
The empire rolls: a novel / Trudy Lewis.

2 0 1 4 9 5 3 5 6 0

Further Library of Congress information is available upon request.

ISBN-10: 978-0-913785-48-5
ISBN-13: 0-913785-48-2

Text edited by Karen Craigo & Michael Czyzniejewski
Cover and interior designed by Charli Barnes

Manufactured in the United States of America.

www.mooncitypress.com

To Mike Barrett for holding everything together.

To Eddie and Jude Barrett for taking everything apart.

I

I still patrol Karst Park, days, a gun on my belt and a diet soda in my cup holder. But on Saturday nights I work the rink calling roller derby, trying to match my crackling new radio voice to the beat of the bout. I do a creditable job of it, too, for the sake of these hometown girls who may never reach stardom in any wider arena, if not for the benefit of my mom, who shows up regularly with her cane and earpiece to watch her favorites get knocked into the wall. I do it for my sister Sharee, who died in the seventies and who cruised this same track backwards under the disco ball and insisted on taking the male role in the couples skate, her narrow hips swerving like a rudder under some boy's sweaty class ring. When I think of her now, the long red hair parted in the back with her own motion and streaming forward into her face, I wonder if it was courage or fear that made Sharee proceed this way, backward into her destiny. I wonder if I am taking the same route, childless and divorced, veering into the midpoint of my forties, still rushing backward, raising my own wind. I look down at the rink and nod at the girls in their camouflage team shirts, their bright hard helmets, and their skimpy skirts. The youngest is eighteen, the oldest thirty-seven, and they shimmer with sex and suppressed aggression. They are students and mothers, nurses and teachers, war vets and veterinarian's assistants, policewomen, waitresses, insurance claims adjusters, and clerks. They have spent the week cleaning up blood, submitting data, and disposing of shit, all to the music of canned motivation and various forms of bad news. I take a long sip of clear soda and prepare for the onslaught. Chaz Enright, the manager of the Boonslick Bombers and owner of the Empire Roller Rink to boot, was emceeing the bouts at first. But some of the girls thought his comments were too disrespectful, referencing body parts on which he had no authority. Then one night my niece Reenie—Raven Pillage to the fans—broke down and told me she'd rather skate topless than have her tits called "tickets" one more time.

"'Tickets, tickets,' it's not a random obscenity," Chaz said, when I took up the matter with him. "That's what they called the sacred boobs of the founding mothers. Joanie Weston, Ann Calvello, they all had these big beautiful tickets. You know, that's what gets the fans in the door."

"No, that's what pushes your talent out the door," I told him. "If you don't stop embarrassing these girls, they're going to get disgusted and move on to the next fad down the line."

So after some consultation with his iPhone and his conscience, Chaz decided to let a woman do the talking for a change. That way, he would be free to take care of more pressing details. There he is, in the middle of the rink in street shoes with one of the refs hanging over him. The ref, a gangly guy who wears a pleated skirt and bat wings along with the traditional black-and-white striped shirt, leans down to say something, and Chaz begins a long response, squaring his shoulders and chopping at his open palm, looking up sideways every few beats to see if the kid is actually listening.

Myself, I don't have to hear what Chaz is saying to know what is on his mind. Ever since the war broke out, Boonslick has been in a boom. Labor and housing are cheap, there is plenty of land for development, the city doesn't appear too particular about zoning or environmental regulation, and the population is young. Every day, I drive past subdivisions creeping up on the Karst like big ugly barracks advancing into the bush and wonder if they will reach the park entrance before I retire. But for a guy like Chaz, it is all expanded opportunity and eternal diversification. Even before the boom, he owned two businesses in the little struggling downtown with its hopeful awnings and historical plaques. And now, the man is a regular mogul, part owner of a bakery, a piano bar, a cable station, a barbeque joint, an electronics franchise, and an Internet café. Of course, a few of these are chain stores out in the far reaches of the city limits, places where folks can park quickly and buy in bulk. They bring in the revenue for Chaz's more esoteric projects, the fragile masterpieces forged of local connections, high-concept marketing, youth culture, vanity investment, and buzz. It keeps him young, it keeps him sane, this constant influx of wrinkled bills pressed into the palm of the hand, the fresh lust of twenty-year-olds, the desperate hip-seeking frenzy of the middle-aged. After all, if capital is the raw stuff of life, he says, then commerce must be the purest form of creativity.

I see him climbing up the stairs to my perch above the rink, his black leather bike shoes pounding a rapid-fire rhythm on the flimsy metal structure. I have only maybe five years on the guy, but I've seen teenagers with less testosterone. He has one pant leg turned up, for effect, to let you know that after his ten-hour work day and a strenuous stint at the gym, he still had the energy to climb onto his bike and hump all the way out to this automotive mecca on the wrong side of town where the Empire Roller

Rink sits like a queen in her fresh coat of red and blue paint amid shabby muffler shops and peeling strip joints. He wears a tight knit shirt, burnt orange cloth with a badge-like insignia over the left breast pocket. His hairline recedes in twin inlets bisected by a widow's peak, and behind them, his dark hair is slicked into crests.

"Looking good, Sally," he says, sitting down on the railing in front of me with his crotch too close to my face. I don't mistake this for a come-on or a threat, because I'm too old for the one and too mean for the other. He just wants to let me know what he's packing, so I'll be impressed enough to stick around.

I shy away and lean back on the two hind legs of my chair. My hormone levels are shifting, too, and I feel the sudden need for more territory.

"Well, it's another night of sin and desecration at the old Empire," he says, looking down over his shoulder. "You've got your slumming frat boys, you've got your single moms on power surge, you've got your fat girls and transvestites thinking this is a place where they might get actually stand a chance of getting laid. Look at this pierced war dude in a wheelchair, playing up the hardware for all it's worth. And there's your sweet little Raven, adjusting her butt pad and thinking that with any luck she will see my wife's teeth get knocked out of her face."

I look down and see my niece, her skinny braids as long as jump ropes, her cat-eye glasses gleaming with pink rhinestones, her team shirt cut off mid-abdomen to reveal a flock of raven tattoos swarming the left side of her stomach and heading down toward her crotch. She's got both hands on her athletic bustle, which she's pushed down very low to accommodate the dipping waistband of her skirt. When she turns, I can see the lower curve of her spine and the evidence of teenage scoliosis.

"And why would she want to see that? They're on the same team."

"Maybe you haven't noticed, but the little deviant is developing a taste for older men."

Below, Reenie revs up and sinks into a curve, her sharp knees bending with the motion and her braids sailing back behind her. She looks like she could take on any older man, with no trouble. But the thought of Chaz enjoying her favors makes the soda burn in my craw.

"So what's the story with you?" I say, refusing to bite, and watching his body assume an expectant stiffness out there on the rail.

"I'm thinking of putting together a cable extravaganza to introduce the public to the talent, revitalize interest in the race. What do you think? You want to be the Judge Judy of the Roller Rink? You definitely have the dominatrix thing well in hand. All this could be yours," he tells me, making a sweeping gesture over the rink, then framing the vista with his hands.

"What do I want with an old roller rink?"

"Let me put it this way," he says, slipping his hand onto my knee and gripping the kneecap like a gearshift. "What else do you have going on? I mean, you have no kids of your own to chase around. Your husband, who, let's face it, was not a consuming interest in the first place, left you with nothing but a mortgage and a habit. Your only other boyfriend in living memory has fucked you over with practically every girl down there on the rink. And you're going to tell me what, you're too busy? You're too stressed? You've got too much chopped liver on your plate?"

"When you put it that way," I say, "it's not much of a pleasure working with you, either."

He beams, his smile pushing up incongruent dimples in his narrow face. "That's why you love me, Sally. Because I'm the only guy you know who will give it to you straight."

"Besides," he adds. "I've got a surprise. We have a special guest artist in the house tonight, someone who is sure to shake up the at-home viewers and cut to the chase."

He points down at the edge of the rink and I see Jared Mayweather, my only boyfriend in living memory, threading his way through the crowd in a pink bandana and an eyepatch, holding his camera close to his chest.

2

Jared Mayweather swigged from a bottle of Beam rinkside and lifted his camera from its case, hoping he wouldn't run out of whiskey before he ran out of battery juice. He had gotten a last-minute text from Chaz, instructing him to show up at the Empire Roller Rink at nine-thirty on a Saturday night to collect a little footage for a commercial venture. Jared, just home from a futile four-year stint in Chicago, unemployed, discouraged, and cash free, felt he had no choice but to haul ass out of his mother's basement, where he had been immobilized for three months amidst abandoned exercise equipment and an odd assortment of emergency provisions collected in the last orange terror alert to appear at the rink as requested. After all, he owed Chaz something, more than he liked to admit, which was probably why he had hardly seen the guy since returning to Boonslick.

The whiskey burned pleasantly in Jared's gullet, illuminating his aspirations from within and helping him forget the various favors, monetary and otherwise, he had accepted from his benefactor. What did he have to show for it, after all, the loans and encouragement, the dinners and indulgences, the drug money and advice? A couple of awards from local film festivals, a few on-location camera credits, an adolescent ambition, and a middle-aged gut. He leaned into the flimsy plywood barrier, turned on the camera, and shot the girls gliding by in black skates and short skirts, striped tights, black fishnets, garters, armbands, kneepads, and demolition helmets. Some of them had painted their faces white, blackened teeth, or applied dark smears under their eyes. They each wore a camouflage Boonslick Bombers team shirt, and on their backs, homemade name placards were slashed on in Sharpies: "Marilyn Monsoon," "Annie Warhaul," "Gigi Haddist," "Raven Pillage," "Courtney Foxhole." He wondered, idly, if he had ever hooked up with any of them, and decided that he couldn't be sure, what with the extreme makeup and costuming.

Then Ellen swooped by in a team shirt ripped down to the navel, revealing a tight black leotard silk-screened with a skeleton, her substantial rack swelling up out of the nest of bones. From her shoulders hung a harness of plastic body parts, noses and fingers and skulls, even a dildo with a bright red spot on the tip of its shaft. She caught his eye and winked. Then she changed direction, her short wrap skirt lifting with her own momentum as she executed a perfect turn and stopped on a dime, hand resting on her thigh, to reveal her own placard. "The Bawdy Bagger," it read, in glitter marker that looked like it had been selected by a third-grade girl. Ellen herself, although she must be at least thirty-five, was holding up well, her long athletic legs suggesting a familiar succulence only at the very tops of her thighs. Her face showed a few extra folds at the corners of the eyes and mouth, and her white-blond hair gleamed under her helmet, mocking the distinction between silver and gold. Jared couldn't believe Chaz had put his own wife on the roller derby team. But then, given the man's basic business principles, why shouldn't he? Ellen pulled a string from around her neck and inserted her mouth guard, giving Mayweather, for one fleeting instant, a view of gum and tongue.

Chaz himself stood at the partition, patting the girls on the arm or back as they passed, muttering directions and encouragement. Mayweather couldn't help but notice that Chaz had kept his gut in shape, and that the narrow panels of his pecs pressed aggressively into the cloth of his tight knit shirt, which suggested some variety of sports gear without giving away the game. Jared pretended to be absorbed in filming the girls as they passed. But by the time he felt the familiar dry touch on his back and the heel of the hand grinding into his muscles, he really was absorbed, zooming in on a mouth guard as it bit into a cleavage.

"How's the returning hero?" Chaz said. "You get my text?"

Jared felt his chest swell and his balls contract. Having never known the luxury of an on-duty dad, he didn't see why he should report back to any authority, no matter how casual. But he responded to Chaz's interest in spite of himself, the taste of camaraderie as sweet as the blackest and stickiest hash on the tongue. "I thought I'd scope the scene," he said. "You're the owner now?"

"Owner, producer, manager, promoter, and sales rep," he said. "I'm a versatile guy. What about you? You have any luck with the auteur biz?"

"A little action, you know, some movies on location in Chicago, and a few local art house gigs. Mostly I'm just saving it up to spring my magnum opie on the world." He held the bottle out, tipped toward Chaz, so the amber fluid glowed under the fluorescent track lighting. They were selling watered-down Bud on tap at the concession stand, a surprising development, given Chaz's well-publicized beer snobbery, and Mayweather was happy he'd had the foresight to import his own refreshment.

"No thanks, jarhead," Chaz said, running his hand over his belt. "I'm watching the waistline. Looks like you are losing your girlish figure, or else I'd have your ass out on the rink here in fishnets and pearls."

"Aw," Jared said. "An artist without any fat on him is like a corndog without the corn."

"Just watch out for the carbs, man. Anyway, here's the deal. I need you to score some footage of the Boonslick Bombers we can use on my cable channel. Maybe hook us up for a podcast, too. Probably twenty-two minutes, we can do some voiceover, splice in a few commercials, and call it a show."

"More diversification?"

"When the divorce didn't pan out, let's just say I had to find other outlets for my energies."

"Oh, yeah, what ever happened with that?"

Chaz raised his eyebrows and flicked his eyes from side to side. "Mission aborted," he said. "Too much drama. Besides, no matter what happens, you always need to keep a home team."

Jared shrugged and blew on the lens of his camera, feeling the air raise the hairs on his knuckles. What did it matter to him, anyway? He had never wanted to break them up, only to feel Ellen's compact ass in his hands and get an unobstructed view of her large, pale breasts elevated above him. "So what are we going for here?" he asked. "New Wave? Dogma? Altman? Hartley? LaButte? The girls have got a kind of Tarantino vibe out there. Anyway it's giving me the *Kill Bill* thrills."

"We are going directly for the wallet, jarhead. History shows that television coverage was the key to developing an audience in the seventies, and we need to replicate that if we want to clear a profit. We need to reach the guy drinking alone in his apartment complex and stimulate him into shelling out the cover charge."

"So, basically, it's back to old-school exploitation, a Spielberg-style visual enema."

"Old-style exploitation, old-school paycheck," Chaz said. "How about twenty bones an hour? Better than living off your mom."

Just then, something bumped against Mayweather's knee. He looked down and saw it was a kid. Ellen's daughter, maybe, who was always trying to horn in on adult conversations. But no, she was probably over ten now, ready to embark on the adventures of middle school. This one was still a preschooler, bunches of bright yellow curls held back off her face with velvet bows, deep brown strands of ribbon dangling down her neck.

"Daddy," she called, in an oddly adult voice, perfectly articulated, with silver strands of soprano and an undertone of twang. Chaz slid an arm under her butt and transported her to eye level, holding her face to his so that Jared could see the resemblance, or the lack thereof. This girl was Ellen all over, high forehead, wide mouth, blond hair, and slight nose, but the extreme curls and brown eyes were a dead giveaway to anyone who'd done time in high school biology. Jared felt his throat swell. The girl smiled and he saw his mother's long dimples; she turned her head and he noticed a flicker of his favorite cousin's pretty outthrust jaw.

"Etta, Mayweather. Mayweather, Etta," Chaz said. All Jared could think about was turning on his camera, but the little girl squirmed and twisted, threatening to fall to the floor, and he couldn't move. Etta, he thought, remembering the blues show on Boonslick Country. Sunday afternoons from two to five, the smells of meat and citrus, and Etta James' deep maple drawl. It was the sweetest and dirtiest music he knew, the vocal grind of sexual boasts and commands giving way to honeyed strains of gospel rapture, as if the singer were continually getting herself lost and saved. He visualized her broad girlish face: pale skin and African features under a bleached blond flip. Just like this little girl, he thought, her genetic identity exaggerated by its concealment.

"Daddy down," the girl said, and Chaz conveyed her back to the floor, where she grabbed Mayweather's leg with a light but possessive touch and pushed off him as she went, leaving ligaments slackened in her wake.

3

The Boonslick Bombers have been on a roll lately, defeating teams as distant as Bloomington and St. Joe's, spawning brawls that have resulted in casualties, on and off the rink, and bestowing bragging rights on a town badly in need of something to boast about. But even these victories can't distract me from my troubles out at the Karst. All summer, we've been finding construction materials dumped in the creek at the south entrance. Normally, we anticipate that we will have to do a little litter control: beer cans, candy wrappers, the occasional abandoned bandanna or sweatshirt. But this is far beyond our capacities. Added to that, my husband and partner Mason Whitehall left Boonslick in early June to wander off into parts unknown, and we're still short a man at the station. And after more than three months, I begin to suspect that we aren't going to be allocated the funds to replace him anytime soon. I don't know which is worse, the silence in the house or the echo in the woods. But right now, in this gulley between summer and autumn, I am content enough to commune with the forest. I look through the pale green leaves, dogwood to sycamore, and toward the chalky limestone cliffs with their broken faces. One clump of bright red leaves hangs down in front of me, extended like a torch to remind me of the coming winter. I can't say why Mason left, any more than I can understand why I let him go. We had been peaceful together. He needed a place to land and I needed a man who wouldn't torment me. For five years, that was enough, and then it wasn't. I started to wake up earlier every morning; he started to stay up later every night. We stopped speaking of anything but the bills and the park business. We walked the dogs separately. Though we continued to sleep in the same bed, we did not touch, and when we accidentally brushed up against one another, there was an unpleasant rush of sensation that threatened to dissolve the discipline of my body and wash my identity away.

I try not to despair as I turn back to the refuse in the creek, wade in up to my boot tops, and pick up a piece of flimsy plywood, about two by three feet, and, according to industry standards, too short for regulation use. This is the trash they are building houses out of these days. The outrage fills my veins and pulses with evil energy in my forehead. As long as I'm angry, I know I will be fine. In that way, it is convenient to live in difficult times, a war in the Middle East, crumbling public parks and school systems, rising gas prices, shrinking ice caps, universal greed. Because despite diminishing resources on all other fronts, there is no shortfall of fuel for rage. As I drag the board to the bank, I grit my teeth and think to thank the president, the senators, CEOs and developers, in a clipped Satanic prayer to those who have preserved me from becoming a sad, lonely woman abandoned on the cusp of old age. This, not his honesty, is why I love Chaz, I realize, because when I am with him I am always filled with the electric power of my own contained violence.

I look at the creek littered with wood and carpet scraps, bloated plywood, pieces of tile and metal tubing, a whole houseful of garbage damning up the flow. On a good day, the white limestone is visible through the water, rising up and extending like a sandbar halfway to the other bank. Just beyond, there is a series of irregular outcroppings, stepping stones in high water, resting places to accommodate hikers and their packs in the current drought. The water is not entirely clear, but murky, the color of herb tea, and there is a pervading smell of algae and spawn. I notice that the cattails along the bank are going to seed, the brown velvet showing silvery gray at the tips.

I fish an odd end of linoleum out of the water, getting the sleeve of my uniform wet, so that it darkens to a deep green and sits cold and clammy on my skin. It's still too warm for this to be a real discomfort, but I am annoyed that I didn't bother to roll my sleeve up first. How did I forget? I am experiencing the sensation of disembodiment that I get at pressure points in my life, when I bump into doorframes and coffee tables as if I can't distinguish my own borders without the illumination of pain. I first remember feeling this way in the weeks after Sharee died, my senior year of high school, when I would slam my body into any available surface, as if it were a heavy backpack carrying homework I would prefer to ignore. Was I trying to mimic the experience of her accident, the bruises on her body, the gashes in her head, so horrible that my mother would not let me see? Or was I simply trying to feel the space where she had broken off me, like a phantom limb? As the older sister, I was supposed to experience everything first. But Sharee was always getting ahead of me: She learned to tie her shoes first, learned to ride a bike first, developed small but distinct breast buds before I even saw the shadow of a pubic hair, started dating a full six months before Seth Davis asked me to accompany him to a friend's base-ment, where four boys and their chosen female counterparts gathered to watch an early episode of *Saturday Night Live* and drink sacramental rum and Cokes. Sharee had even lost her virginity before I did, only weeks before her death, and left, she claimed, a bloody stain in a deer wallow in the vacant lot behind the movie theater. I always thought I was just biding my time for a big growth spurt, at which point I would surge ahead and assume my natural leadership role. But once Sharee was gone, there was no maintaining the illusion that I would ever catch up.

I sense a disturbance in the forest behind me, and remember Mason's quiet ways. Perhaps he has returned to solve my problems. Or, with my luck, it's the polluters come back to finish off the job. This is one of the few occasions when I'm actually moved to check the gun at my side and to feel its snug heft at my hip. My hand is already resting on the holster when I turn and see Mayweather standing there with the forest behind him. He is visibly older now, with the sun in his face, pores coarsened, hairline pushed up higher so that I see the sharp uneven lines in his forehead, tiny bits of stubble lodged like stubborn seeds in the cleft of his chin. But he has managed to keep himself alive somehow and that shows, too, gives him a kind of authority he didn't have when I first felt his hand on my gun belt and gave into his advances as if he were the last free man on Earth. Is it almost seven years ago now? I haven't seen much of him since he returned to Boonslick, though one day in the spring he asked me to drive him down to Meramec Caverns, where he used to work giving tours as a kid. We made the trip in a hailstorm, came home in the sunshine, and ate a dinner of slaw and ribs on the deck, all without inappropriate touching or sentimental recollections. Now, I don't know if I ever need to see him again.

He is wearing paint-spattered shorts, this late in the season, and a pair of pointed red cowboy boots without socks. His blue Krispy Kreme shirt is unbuttoned to mid-chest, revealing a hash spoon on a leather string around his neck. He has on a brown hunting cap, and beneath it his hair has grown long enough to separate into two matted tails, the curls indistinguishable from tangles. He holds his camera bag as casually as a canteen, and I take my hand off the gun and back away.

"What gives, Ranger Sally?"

"Do you believe this?" I say. "The city council has opened the legs of the whole county for the developers and they still can't leave the park alone."

But even before he replies, he is already filming the carnage, the carpet squares bloating moss-like on the limestone, odd pieces of plywood jammed together in the middle of the creek to form a demented beaver dam. I can see, from his perspective, that all this is just an interesting study of textures, not a travesty of justice and a violation of natural law.

"Don't worry," he tells me, kneeling down to get a closer look. "I'm on assignment. I'm not stalking you or anything."

"Oh, that's right. You are back on the payroll with Enright Associates. How does it feel to be back where you began?"

"Ever notice how the creek is the color of a negative?" he asks me. "If I shoot from this angle, I can actually get the reflection of the trees, and it looks like all this crap is stuck in the branches." Now that he mentions it, I can see what he's talking about, but I'm more interested in watching him kneel there like a child about to launch a toy boat. His shoulder blades poke into his shirt, and his thighs tense as he leans back for a more distant view. I see the extra weight he's carrying and marvel that it doesn't affect his balance. Twenty-nine years old and still he hasn't assumed the defensive stance of a man. It's like he can't figure out that he has something to lose and has never learned to hold a little power in reserve. This, of course, is why women will crawl on their bellies over hot coals and broken glass to lie under the guy, a kid with no money and no prospects, middling looks, underemployed intelligence, questionable motives, and dirty fingernails. What can I say? I know it's worth the trouble because I've crawled there, too.

"So you got involved in this roller derby how?" he asks.

"You know, my niece Reenie is on the team. Raven Pillage. Girl with the cat-eye glasses and long braids? She's one of the star jammers, actually. My brother and sister-in-law, let me tell you, were not too pleased when she decided to put off law school for another year so she could deliver depositions out on the rink. I figured the girl could use some family support."

"She the one with the crush on Chaz?"

"That's his line, anyway. But I haven't noticed any such thing. In fact, last I heard she was begging me to get him off her case."

As long as Jared's occupied, I figure I should keep working, too, so I snag a scrap of carpet with a stick. But it's absorbed so much water that I can't drag it up the bank. I try several times before I give up, pull out my Swiss army knife and cut the carpet into smaller pieces so I can retrieve them. We work for several minutes like that, him filming, me sawing through the offensive orange nap of the carpet and into its thick rubber matting like a Native woman salvaging a carcass. I feel myself relaxing into a rhythm and Mayweather working up into frenzy at my side.

"Hey, do you know anything about the kid? I mean, does he treat her OK?"

"You mean Etta? Did you see her?"

"No question," he said "No fucking shadow of a doubt that she's Mayweather stock. I can't believe Ellen did it to me. I thought we had an agreement. Then I left town and she screwed with me."

"She screwed with you by giving birth to her own kid?"

"I told her not to do it. I told her I wasn't up for that sort of thing."

"Honey, you already did it, and she just took care of the cleanup. Anyway, what's it to you? No one's asking child support. No one's interested in naming names."

"It's just, now I feel like that fucker has a piece of me."

So we sit here on the bank of the creek together, watching the reflection of the trees waver in the water and feeling the same thing.

4

After weeks of drought, it had finally rained, and when Jared left the house for the Springfield bout, the gutters were still running. The gray pavement had turned black with rainwater, and wet leaves lay facedown in the street, exposing their veins. A bloody show of sunset appeared in the sky, while night scents of spice-bush and ditch weed invaded his nostrils, leaving Mayweather with the feeling that hadn't smelled anything but street food and garbage for years. Mayweather's mom, who had developed an unfortunate sense of propriety with her new fully employed boyfriend, was pacing the yard in bright blue clam diggers and collecting fallen twigs and branches before stuffing them into a plastic bag.

When she saw Jared, she rose to her feet and made the sign of the cross, her hands stiff in gardening gloves, though she was not, and had never been, to his knowledge, Catholic. "You put on shoes," she said. "You took a shower. It must be the end times."

"I'm going to work, you'll be happy to know," he told her.

"It's after six. What's the job?" She had definitely aged since he left home, her spare figure thickened at the waist and the freckles on her thin, triangular face beginning to merge into amorphous brown patches. But even so, she looked happier now that she had reached the age where other women's husbands had left them, too.

"It's a commission," he said. "I'm going to do a little publicity flick for the roller derby in town."

"Roller derby? They still do roller derby? I haven't seen a bout since '72 when Raquel Welch bombed Kansas City braless. "

"It's a revival, mom. Stick around long enough, and you get to see everything return."

"Like you, I guess? Like that ratty T-shirt from the eighth grade? "she said, pointing to the pink "Jesus Craves" number so tight that it showed his ribs and an insolent swell of belly just under the Savior's beard. "In my opinion, nostalgia is overrated."

"But what else is there, buddy?" Jared said. He kissed her on the cheek, which was damp with sunscreen, and left her there in the yard, sitting on the steps and breaking for a cigarette. She hadn't lost her zest for nicotine, at any rate, and it cheered Mayweather to look over his shoulder and see her puffing away, her face relaxing into deep introspective curves and her hand dribbling ash into the flower bed.

He didn't have a car, and so he walked down the street, past dogwoods and mimosas, elms and locusts and elderberries, half of the pea-sized fruit still green and half a muddy purple. Boonslick had been suburbanized since he left, its outskirts spawning a huge satellite system of subdivisions and strip malls protecting the city from the outliers of Missouri, like a medieval city walled in stone. But the center of town, newly released from the strain of gentrification, had gone back to seed; here Missouri reasserted itself like the ocean filling up a hole dug in the beach. The air was rich with the smells of barbecue and reefer, cigarette smoke, evening primrose, stale beer, and fresh mulch, even some murky suggestion of the Missouri River some ten miles distant. "The District," they called it now, like some kind of urban crime zone. Jared breathed in deeply as he passed the sex shop, the yoga studio, the mosque with the quarter moon impaled upon its spire, the alternative theater in an old bakery, the tattoo parlor, and the comic book store, all dwarfed by City Hall on its vast plaza of white monument and greenish stone.

Mayweather moved like a ghost in his former hunting ground, where he had once scored weed and ecstasy at will, taken his pick of daring girls and careless women, speculated relentlessly and esoterically about the probable course of his film career. He wondered if anyone would recognize him now, four years older, humbled by manual labor and urban poverty. It came as no surprise to him that Ellen had another kid, which he had heard through gossip and rumor and worse, but he had never really believed it until now. He felt the memory of Etta's touch on his leg and bent down to brush off the sensation. As he did, he bumped up against the unpleasant roll of fat at his gut, a reminder of the years of debauchery and procrastination. The girl was definitely his kid—she had the Mayweather jaw, and a cocky lopsided grace that Mayweather recognized from the outside in. But now, after all this time, she was Chaz's kid as well. There had been days, Jared knew, when he wished Chaz was his father. The guy, it had to be said, was the perfect blend of responsibility and perversity, calming you with his stability even as he egged you on with his constant speculations and digs. Could you score hash in the dry season? Could you name the first five Cronenberg films? Could you hook up with two coworkers in one weekend? Could you make it as an artist? Could you do it without introductions, capital, equipment, or friends?

Jared knew that he had benefited from Chaz's goading, without which he might have become yet another slacker about town, a self-satisfied Lothario content to drink cheap beer and feed his own head. But instead, he had become a freak of nature, someone too irregular to mount a real career but too stubborn to give in.

He turned toward the liquor store to replenish his supply of Beam, but he couldn't help stopping outside to film a lanky blond gangbanger carrying a skateboard over his shoulder like an M16 as he encountered a severely groomed African brother in regulation camouflage at the door. The two men nodded as if they had expected to meet, and the gangbanger held the door open for the soldier. Despite professional setbacks and romantic entanglements, Jared had improved his craft in Chicago and now felt a new ease in framing the shot. He thought of the WWII photograph of a soldier kissing a nurse and wondered what images might survive the current crisis. At least these guys could say they had done something in the last year. He felt as if he had dropped his life into Lake Michigan to let it drown. Strange how his abilities had waxed stronger, in waves of time-delayed mastery, even as his confidence was eroded by years of menial labor, underemployment, and intermittent commercial gigs. Somehow, he anticipated the men's jagged movements as they bobbed at one another a moment too long and engaged in an inaudible exchange. Then he shut off his camera, went in for his liquor, and kept moving on.

Beyond this point, it was public housing all the way out to the strip. But Jared had little fear of the area and maintained his usual jagged pace, occasionally stopping to take a swig from the bottle of whiskey he had just purchased or film a bit of scenery.

The lot at the Empire was swamped, with a few vehicles

doubleparked along the residential street just beyond the highway. Outside, a few stragglers stood passing a pipe: a bald guy
with huge ear gauges that made him resemble a robot, a pretty
girl in an antique sweater and a net hat, a tattooed biker with
multiple chains hanging from his belt loops. They stood there
next to a poster for Christian skate night, oblivious, even though
a few teenyboppers in jean jackets with crosses embroidered on
the backs stood there, too, practicing the moves to Soulja Boy
while they waited for their parents to pick them up. Jared hesitated on an island of grass at the edge of the lot. He dreaded
going in, having to assume some sort of attitude toward Chaz
and Ellen. He hated himself for agreeing to serve as a lackey
in their small-time entourage. But what else could he do? They
had everything and he had nothing. Or rather, he had only the
one thing, this dirty, precious, irregular talent, and in trying to
develop his single gift he had wasted everything else he might
have attained.

Just to delay, he looked around and saw that he was standing
next to a honey locust in full fall color, bright yellow fronds of
leaves, twisted brown seed pods hanging down in between. As
he stood staring up into its golden canopy, he felt a break in his
chest, like a snapped rubber band, a foreboding of pleasure and
dread. What was it? Yellow curls, brown ribbon. Etta Enright.
Etta James. He dropped to his knees as if shot, only half in jest,
and picked a pod up off the ground. It was maybe a foot long
and twisted like a snakeskin; as he held it in his unsteady hand,
the seeds shook inside, approximating the sound of a rattler.
Though the pods appeared brown on the tree, this one looked
almost purple close up under the streetlight. He broke the pod
open and used a long fingernail to dig out the flat brown seed
embedded in a sticky substance like the filling of a pecan pie.
Taking a whiff of the pulp, he decided it was closer to mincemeat,

really, with an insistent undertone of green. He picked out two more seeds and slipped them into the side compartment of his camera case for good luck.

The foyer of the roller rink looked like the entrance to a prison: thick brick walls, a cement floor, a tiny glassed-in ticket window where you had to shove your money under a grille. Jared noticed that some leaves had swept in and lay stranded on the cement floor. He gave his name at the window, got a funny look from the attendant, and was admitted free.

Inside, the air felt tinny with excitement, something metallic in the air—wheels grinding against one another to produce an ionic charge. He heard Sally's voice, a low familiar suggestion of sex underneath a glaze of maternal pride and civic responsibility, as she introduced the Boonslick Bombers one by one. Out on the rink, the girls skated in a troupe together, tossing a plastic skull from hand to hand, the tallest carrying a pirate's skull-and-crossbones on a pole. As each girl's name was called, she skated out in front of the group, raised her hands for applause or flipped up her skirt to display a message printed on her panties. Ellen, the Bawdy Bagger, tossed off her harness, a fishing net with body parts entangled in its meshes, and threw it to Chaz, who stood by proudly, stroking the grotesque garment as if it were a lady's evening cape.

The Springfield Stingers, meanwhile, sulked in wearing striped black-and-gold T-shirts, studded chokers, and wristbands until they, too, were introduced. Sally spared no detail in her characterization of their wiles: their reputation for muscle out on the rink, their combined weight of 2,106 pounds, the havoc they had wreaked in Bloomington the week before, leaving one girl with a broken collarbone and another with a fractured kneecap. They had brought a contingent of fans with them, Jared noticed, a few strange ladies with naked foreheads, penciled-in eyebrows, and bouffant fifties hairstyles, along with the usual tatty long-haired bar chicks and scruffy local boyfriends.

Once the bout began, Jared stood turning his camera from side to side as the girls skated around the rink. There were so many girls in motion, he hardly knew where to rest his gaze. He had dutifully consumed the literature and understood that the players in the star helmets, the jammers, needed to break through the pack of blockers skating in front of them, and do so repeatedly, in order to accumulate points. Sally, delivering the play-by play in a driving alto above, offered a bit of welcome guidance. It was true that her niece, Raven Pillage, was some sort of prodigy. As the first Boonslick jammer of the evening, she stood behind the pack, a star on her helmet, her legs bent, her rump in the air and her fingers pressed to the floor in front of her, preparing to race the Springfield jammer through the pack. Once the whistle sounded, Raven took several quick strides and caught a girl by the waist, rode on her back for a couple of beats, and pushed her out of the way. She turned sideways, slipping through two other blockers like a shadow. She pushed out one hip to bump the pivot player off track.

Meanwhile, the Springfield jammer, a big, sexy blonde in a gold lamé skirt, struggled to break into the pack. She knocked into an opponent, lost her balance, then regained it, but swerved out of control, her legs slowing as she struggled to realign her body. Now Raven was the "lead jammer," according to Sally, who claimed that the girl had soared through the pack like a hummingbird on speed. The jam ended when Raven was pushed off course, skimmed the partition by Jared, and began frantically slicing at the air over her hips, her joined fingers pointing toward her crotch, thumbs raised, jaw outthrust, and braids thrashing.

"And Raven Pillage calls the jam, she might be fearless, folks, but she is not foolish. This compact little cookie knows when to quit.

What a start for the Bombers, eight points only minutes into the bout. You can bet the Stingers are down there feeling the sting."

Then Reenie pulled at her scalp in a luxurious gesture, as if removing a wig, peeled the knit star cover off her helmet, and tossed it to Gigi Haddist, a dark beauty with kohl around her eyes and a dark scarf visible underneath her helmet, its ends trailing halfway down her back.

As he was filming the transfer, Jared felt a touch on his leg and looked away from the rink to see Etta staring up at him. Tonight, she was dressed in a ruffled lavender blouse and purple overall, matching purple ribbons in her hair. Her features were more distinct than he had remembered. When he dreamed of her, he realized, it was always a chubby idealized face, like that of a baby. How often had he had the dream? She gestured for him to give her the camera, which he did without thinking, kneeling down to show her how the mechanism worked. His knees pressed into the carpet and he felt the pressure of the hard cement floor underneath. From down here, you couldn't see anything but legs and shoes, crushed plastic cups and popcorn kernels scattered over the green-and-pink paisley carpet. The effect induced a kind of closeness, as if the two of them were isolated in a forest. The smell of sweat and beer, the shadows of spectators above them, the proximity to genitals rather than faces. He felt the most surprising form of desire rising from his abdomen and filling his ribcage with light. What could he want from this little girl? Perhaps he should film her so he would be able to study her face at home alone without distraction. That's what he would really like. When he placed his hand over hers to show her how to hold the camera, it was smooth as old-school celluloid and he could hardly bear to move away.

"You need to comb your hair out," she said, a superior expression on her sharp features. "It's just a rass nest, boy." And then, handing the camera back to him, she dug in her little purple purse to produce a doll brush with pink plastic bristles. "Here, I'll do it for you,"

She pulled off his hat, a green cap with earflaps emblazoned with the name of a fertilizer company, and set it on her own head. Walking around behind him with the ease of a professional stylist, she pressed her hand over the cap of his skull while she engaged a few of the tangles with the ineffectual plastic brush. The feel of her hand was calming and explosive. The brush passing through the tangles tickled at his scalp, and he remembered his mother combing out his hair, the hard yanks of frustration, no money for haircuts, no time for micro-managing his hygiene, no one to care if she didn't or she did. Etta's strokes, though less painful, were just as futile, and Mayweather felt an unaccustomed pressure behind his eyes. At first, he thought he was going to sneeze, but then he recognized the strange otherworldly aura that might, on some rare occasion when he was caught off guard or sober, announce the onset of tears.

Before he could give in to the sensation, he heard an abrupt roar and shout. A universal gasp rustled through the crowd, shading gradually into an audible silence. Jared had no desire to stand up and determine the cause of the commotion. Then he saw a bicycle shoe descend on the eye of the pink paisley pod in front of him, a turned-up pant leg, and a sharp pleat of black gabardine.

"You getting this, jarhead?" Chaz said. "Now this is what the working stiffs pay to see."

Standing up, he saw a group of skaters gathered against the wall and three figures in white streaming into the rink. Someone brought in a stretcher. A body was lifted onto it, and the crowd clapped, a polite patter of palms, more like the applause in a theater than any sound generated in a sports arena.

"Woman down," Chaz said. "High drama. Blood and guts.

Life and death. A surefire setup for narrative cinema, if you get my drift."

"Who is it?" Jared said, filming blindly away.

"Looks to me like the Haddist has been apprehended." And Sally's voice, above, confirmed the speculation. How was it that he had not heard a word of her spiel all the time he was talking with Etta?

Ellen skated by out of breath and grabbed the rail, her face flushed and her tits rising and falling in her shirt. When she saw Mayweather there with Etta climbing up on the bench behind him, using his shoulder as a handhold, her expression changed from fear to anger, and she turned away from the camera, so that he saw her face in profile, like a quarter moon.

"Head injury," she said to Chaz. "Could be serious. Look, I know it's business and all, but could you try to keep this pervert away from my kid?"

5

The next day is Sunday; I don't have to go to work, attend worship services, cater to a grumpy husband or a spoiled child, and so it's me who gets assigned to sit by the girl's hospital bed and wait for her to recover from the coma. Her face is dark against the pillow, and her nose seems almost Egyptian, its steep, elongated slope suggesting some ancient funereal frieze. There are still black smudges around her eyes, the smears of makeup indistinguishable from bruises. The lower half of her face, by contrast, is rich with baby fat, round cheeks, full lips, both upper and lower, in no need of lipstick to draw attention to their curves. Although she is unconscious, she is not entirely still; every few minutes she jerks forward, as if startled in her sleep, and a tremor passes through her body, the memory of a harsh blow or a violent spill. Gigi Haddist, in her civilian form, is really Gabriella Hernandez, whose parents work in a meat-packing plant in North Platte, Nebraska, and can't get here for a few more hours yet. Gabriella had joined the National Guard to help out with tuition at Boonslick College, where she was on a partial scholarship to play volleyball. But the Army called her up for a two-year tour in Iraq before she could finish her sophomore year.

When Gabriella returned to town, she tried to pick up where she had left off, but found herself too disoriented to figure out her benefits and re-enroll. In the meantime, she has been working at the UPS loading packages, a job with good wages, and one that requires mercifully few interpersonal skills.

Last night, when we admitted her, they went through her papers and the clerk insisted Gabriella had to be transferred across the street in order to collect on her government-mandated insurance. That's why I'm sitting in this fusty veterans' hospital instead of the modern University Hospital with its open vistas and Impressionist reproductions. I stare at the glossy framed photographs of the Vietnam Veterans Memorial and Mount Rushmore, all the presidents eying me with suspicion.

To Chaz's credit, he oversaw the transfer, contacted Gabriella's parents, and insisted on a private room. Now he is running around doing damage control while I man the hospital room. I open my book, *The Botany of Desire*, but can't seem to reattach to the fiber of the argument. I can't believe I have to witness this type of waste again. Gabriella is a gifted athlete who cannot accustom herself to the idea that her competition days are over, even if her education has been stalled. On the rink, she is pretty rough, quick to body-check and slow to call a jam. Off duty, she will talk with nonchalance of the beheadings she has witnessed, the rapes she has cleaned up after, the men and women she has killed, and becomes quickly enraged if anyone suggests these are poor topics for casual conversation. At other times, she becomes agitated for no reason, takes off her skates, and walks around the neighborhood only to return in a half-hour with a blank expression on her face, fists clenched in her front pockets or wrapped in the folds of her skirt. As a jammer, she is the muscle to Reenie's skinny trickster. Raven is the queen of contortion while Gigi is the dervish of speed.

A nurse comes into the room, a new one. I guess their shifts have changed by now. She takes the girl's pulse, checks the level of the coma cocktail in the IV bag, and calls me "Mom—," as in "Hang in there, Mom. She could be back with us any time." Something within me bristles at the mistake, but I don't bother to correct her since I know her job leaves little room for nuance and complication. Doesn't she notice that the girl is clearly Hispanic and I am a faded blond? However, this distinction means little in a world of adoption, intermarriage, divorce, and blended families. A bitter taste floods my mouth as I realize that this is the only way I am likely to hear the word "mom" applied to myself. I wonder if Sharee would have had children if she had lived. She was always the one to play with dolls, dressing them up in elaborate costumes and bestowing on them weird food preferences and exotic allergies, while I was drawn, even as a child, to puppies and turtles. Animals of course, are easy to satisfy and difficult to ruin. My labs Orion and Diana—Rye and Di for short—are thrilled to be walked three times a day in the woods by our house, to be allowed to lick the milk out of a cereal bowl when I'm done with it, to occupy the furniture with abandon and to sleep unabashedly in my bed. If only humans were so easily fulfilled. Look at this poor girl; her parents have done more for her than anyone could have expected, raised her strong athletic body to its peak of physical perfection and trained her psyche to withstand the onslaughts of an alien environment, despite their lack of money and influence and their no doubt demoralizing meat-packing jobs. She has survived childhood illnesses, teenage temptations, and full-out war. Now all their labor might be wasted with a single stroke of bad luck. I feel my stomach drop out from under me at the thought, a fully formed person suddenly vanished, undigested emotions with nowhere to go.

I stand up and move over to her bed, touch the air over her hand, which is warm with life. I am afraid to actually make contact as I think that perhaps this will endanger her recovery in some way. Surely she will live to skate another day, or at least to finish school, enter a profession, and provide for her parents in their old age. Since I am afraid to touch her, I begin to talk, the kinds of things I say just to cleanse my head of excess verbiage: random thoughts, lines of songs, phrases I have collected through the last several days: Probable cause. Green grow the rushes there. Watch me crank that soulja boy. Boonslick Bombers. That fucker has a piece of me. My whole personality is dissolving into a series of unrelated utterances. Then I say what I always say for luck, "Jared Mayweather" three times, very quickly, and then I add the girl's name, Gabriella Gigi Hernandez, for good measure.

As I am babbling, someone comes in the door and I see the person I have been expecting and dreading all day, my mother Lorraine LaChance, striding into the hospital room with her cane. It is a rustic item, unvarnished wood with birds and flowers carved into the sides. Lorraine moves at an angle, her head tilted to one side in a tentative gesture that someone else might mistake for frailty, but which I understand as stealth. She has taken to wearing a cross on her lapel, made less somber by the fact that it is constructed of tiny green and red bulbs that light up when you pull a red string at its base, an action she will perform, without compunction, at any dull point in a conversation. She picked up this ornament at the Lake of the Ozarks, where she attends a faith-healing service once a month. The worship is held in the home of a middle-aged couple who lost a teenage daughter in a sensational rape and abduction case that had the news media in a lather for half a year back around the time I started working at the Karst. Now they claim the girl—Celia

Adair—appears to the mother in visions and commands her to write. The poor woman has filled a bookcase full of composition books with automatic grieving. She prints up flyers each month, with snippets of her writings: doggerel verse, epistolary outpourings, Bible verses gone bad. The father has, at the specter's instruction, constructed a couple of pillars in their yard and instituted a regular Bible service, held under the dogwoods in the summer and inside next to a perpetual Christmas tree from November to March. And folks arrive from all around the state with their cancers and afflictions, their sons, daughters, and husbands maimed, disabled, or crazed in the war. Lorraine, too, with nothing much to complain about, attends on a regular basis, often bringing me evidence of her trip, some walnut crucifix or born-again refrigerator magnet. I have found myself wondering lately if she is experiencing early symptoms of dementia, but her baseline personality is so erratic that it's difficult to say.

She approaches the bed without speaking, pats the mattress hard enough to make it shake, untucks the sheet and pulls on the girl's bare toe, painted, I notice, a carmine red, a blue bejeweled toe ring sitting insolently on the digit next door. Lorraine, now satisfied that Gabriella is not faking, points to an empty chair with her cane and stands waiting for me to push it up to where she stands just a breath away from the bed. I watch her sink and settle down into the orange molded plastic as if it's a throne, sighing and creaking as she goes, wriggling her butt around to get comfortable. Meanwhile, I remain on my feet, just to stay ready for anything she throws my way.

"Did you see what happened?" I say to keep the emphasis on the facts before us. "That beefy Stinger locked skates with her. I can't believe the ref let it slide."

Lorraine folds her hands, extends two fingers as if she's about to make a church and steeple, and props her chin up there instead, her face a maze of elastic wrinkles. There is a resilience to the very old, as if they are able to withstand the inroads of time that wreak such havoc on the rest of us. Lorraine has looked the same way for fifteen years, tamped down into her final form. "I guess the poor mom has to be pretty broken up. She can stay at my place; there's plenty of room. I got the word out in the *Boonslick Beacon* and the *Herald*, too. Seems like folks would want to commiserate. And don't you think the girls should do some kind of prayer service? I picked up a CD of the music they play down at the Lake. Real gospel rapture, let me tell you; you wouldn't believe the notes some of these gals can hit."

Gabriella's toe still sticks out from under the sheet. I hate to see her exposed this way, and so I move forward to cover it, but not without a shiver appearing at my neck, the sensation of hair dye dripping down my nape.

"Mom, not all of these girls are Christian, or even religious. We can't ask them to participate in a faith-based event."

"The Lake's nondenominational. It doesn't report to any earthly authority. Face-to-face with the Almighty all the way."

"Frankly, that's what scares me. The operation is mongrel Pentecostal at best, and more than a little cultish, if you ask me."

"What's wrong with healing people, Sally? Do you have something against life? Or are you just dead set against any little thing that brings me peace?" Here she lights up her cross and beams. It's not the first time I've seen a religious icon being used as the social equivalent of a fuck-you. But when it's your own mother performing the gesture, there is an extra element of humiliation in the exchange.

"What's that?" she says, "I can't hear you." Then she turns the hearing aid on her left ear toward me, so that I notice it too is already decked out for Christmas with a sparkly snowflake decal. "You want me to make the arrangements? Thank you, miss, I already did. Mariah is willing to make the trip up and I thought it would be nice to have it over at your place, with the fall colors and all, out by that pretty little gazebo your hubby built for you just before you chased him off into the pines."

It is at this ticklish moment that Jared Mayweather appears. He slinks around the corner in a pearl-buttoned cowboy shirt and a purple hoodie, ripped jeans, and a cap with a couple of fishing lures pinned to the brim. As usual, he's leading with his camera, and I have to wave my hand in front of him to get him to turn it off.

"Mom, this is Jared Mayweather. He's, well, he's the videographer for the team."

Lorraine looks up sharply, her blue eyes chips of lapis in her wrinkled face. "Videographer, hmm. Hear you can get arrested for that," she says. "I hope you are careful, young man."

Jared laughs, a rich tenor, the pitch of his speaking voice, with a few dark bars of bass.

"How long you known my girl here?"

Jared has already begun filming Gabriella in her hospital bed, which I'm pretty sure is immoral, if not illegal. He works as dispassionately as he did while filming the refuse in the creek, trying for every angle, and I wonder if anything makes an impression on him. "Maybe seven years," he says, "Met her out at the Karst when she first started and I was in film school."

After he has some closeups of Gabriella's face, he moves out for a wider view "Say lactose-intolerant," he tells Lorraine, and she flashes her gums, in an eerie display of coquetry that looks more like aggression than flirtation. She actually enjoys being photographed, even at her age. There's some essential outline of femininity in her face that remains photogenic. Meanwhile, I am shying away from the camera and Jared tells me I need to paste one on for the team.

"Given the circumstances, don't you think I should have a more serious expression?"

"Sally never would smile," Lorraine says. "And this is even before, God save us, sorrow showed its ugly mug in our lives. Wouldn't smile, wouldn't wear a skirt, wouldn't pull the hair up off her face. You'd think the girl had something to hide, instead of being one of the prettier gals in her grade."

She stops and leans forward on her cane, as if she has been walking, working up a sweat, instead of just running her tongue. Then she knocks her cane against the floor, and starts to laugh at a joke she hasn't told yet.

"Actually, for years, I was afraid the ranger was a lesbian. Not that I would use the word back then. Still, I had some idea there was a kind of girl didn't allow just anyone to pull her wishbone."

Mayweather appears to be paying no attention, moving up close to Gabriella to film the hospital bracelet on her arm.

"Now, Sally's sister was another story, talking boys all day, every day of her life. I had to keep an eye out for Miss Sharee or she'd have gotten herself into some serious trouble before she was fourteen."

And now that my anger is really worked up, a tear falls from her eye and makes its slow way through the maze of her wrinkles that is her cheek, hesitating, every now and then, deciding which path to take. The old woman is crying and it's too late for me to defend myself. She stands and goes to the bed again, looks at Gabriella's strong and helpless form on the bed, smooths her hair away from her face.

"Maybe I shouldn't have been so strict after all. A teenage pregnancy doesn't seem like such a tragedy these days. Then at least I would have a grandbaby to remember her by."

Mayweather, who appears to have been ignoring her all this time, puts down his camera on the bed beside Gabriella and gives Lorraine a full frontal hug, just like she is his own granny.

But she keeps talking through the hug. "Now I have to wait 'til judgment to catch up with that girl and give her a piece of my mind."

I wonder which piece this might be, since they are falling away from her with such speed and regularity, like desiccated chunks of the Berlin Wall. Just when I think I can't contain myself any longer, a dark woman in a red windbreaker walks in the door, her loose curls disarrayed in the wind. She has on full makeup, jeans, and heels. She is clearly Gabriella's mother: the long nose, the full lips, the wiry body that might have proved athletic in other circumstances. She is, I am certain, younger than me, and when I see her eyes light on Gabriella, my gut pulls out from under me. Why do I feel more sympathy for this stranger than my own kin? The woman covers the room in three strides without acknowledging us and begins rubbing Gabriella's hand, rubbing and rubbing it, as if the girl needs to be warmed in this overheated hospital room. She speaks, too, crooning and keening in Spanish. But when the nurse comes in for a chat, the mother's English proves to be more than competent.

6

Mayweather left the hospital room intent on getting back to his film. He supposed that he should have more sympathy for Gabriella, but it was not as if he had ever slept with the girl, or even engaged her in substantial conversation. In fact, by now a whole generation of Boonslick's female population had passed into womanhood without benefit of Mayweather's intervention. Although he wished Gabriella the best, he couldn't help but think of her more as a subject than a living being. What caused a veteran to take up roller derby? And why would she choose the persona of a terrorist, the very character she had been waging war against? He wondered if he had any footage of Gigi Haddist in action. He was certain that he did, and visualized the flimsy silk skirt over thick black tights and brown leggings, leather lacings crossing and recrossing to well above the knees. He thought about the demands of dogma cinema: no Hollywood effects, no sets, no elaborate costuming. But if the effects were indigenous, weren't they fair game? If a person costumed herself in real life, wasn't filming that masquerade a type of cinéma vérité? Before he had left the VA hospital, he was already visualizing a full-length feature, a documentary about the trials of a girl soldier who travels from the Middle West to the Middle East and back again without a clue. Maybe there was some way he could excerpt a few unobjectionable bits for Chaz's infomercial and still live up to the bruising demands of his own aesthetic.

But as he walked along the hall he was stopped in his tracks by two men in hospital gowns moving very slowly ahead of him, taking up the whole breadth of the hallway. Over their gowns, they wore black leather vests with white lettering on the back. "Marines" pushed an IV pole and "Army" struggled along behind a walker, although neither had any visible injury. And although they were young men with full heads of bristly hair, Army's slightly blonder than Marines', they had the slow, retrospective speech of old-timers.

"I already got one kid," Army said. "That's why I had to sign up in the first place."

"I got a kid sixteen years old," Marines replied. "And I'm only thirty-three. When I left home, I told Aaron he was the man of the house, but now that I'm back, I don't know what I'm supposed to be."

Mayweather figured as long as he was stalled behind the guys, he might as well film them. It occurred to him that he had a kid, too, that he was of these men's generation and situation. But they seemed decades older, already accustomed to their own decline. What was it that separated Mayweather from such a fate? Not money or privilege or parental protection, Jared thought, only art and the camouflage it provided. He had chosen the narrow path into manhood, evading war and sports and commerce so long that he was in danger of never attaining full adult status at all. And yet, as far as he could tell, manhood had little to recommend it, so that he was better off pursuing his childish ambitions to their various dead ends.

Ahead of him, Army and Marines rounded the corner to the lobby and veered toward a glass case full of Native American regalia, so that Mayweather was able to capture the image of their hospital gowns juxtaposed against a magnificent beaded robe standing empty as if cloaking a ghost. From there, Jared swept out the front door, past a poorly executed watercolor of George Bush, his squint and smirk miraculously preserved against a wash of undistinguished pink flesh, and down a long row of American flags lining the parking lot. In the midst of this red-and-blue pageantry stood one lone black flag, a man's profile looking down in dejection. The caption read, "POW/MIA: You are not forgotten." But the desolate figure suggested otherwise and Mayweather left the scene depressed, the bright vision of his full-length feature and enigmatic heroine dimmed by the dismal atmosphere of the VA and all it represented.

In spite of his sour mood, Jared was able to hitch a ride with a guy in a silver Chevrolet with a red door. The guy who seemed to believe that his passenger was a fellow fly-fisherman, an impression Jared took care not to dispel as they drove back to his mom's house in a modest neighborhood of shotgun shacks and small brick bungalows near the center of town.

At home, his mother's boyfriend Wade Tanner was sitting on the front porch playing video games on his cell phone, crossed khaki leg blocking the door. Wade worked at Red Rock Insurance, carried an ID card and pager on his belt, wore hard shoes and sport shirts even on weekends, drank cheap beer in moderation and Diet Pepsi without restraint. He had an associate's degree from a community college, and claimed to be a Methodist without ever attending worship service and a Republican without ever darkening the door of a voting booth. In short, he inhabited that hazy demographic of disagreeable guys you could not get it up to actively hate. He was not a deadbeat or an addict, a pervert or a bully. He was not fat or bald or ugly or mean. In fact, he was a few years younger than Mayweather's mom, his cheeks pink with clean living. He had divorced his first wife, three years previous, and seemed to have no lingering investment in the short, childless marriage. And after dating Mayweather's mom Deidre for a respectable nine months, Wade had just given up his luxury condo, i.e., an institutional unfurnished squat near work, and moved his PC and stereo system onto the premises. Without looking up from his game, Wade asked Jared when he thought he might be getting his first paycheck

"Speed Dial, I hate to remind you, but it's my house, not yours."

"I don't see your name on the lease."

"I don't see a ring on my mom's finger, either."

"OK, OK, point taken," he said, finally making eye contact, his watery blue irises flaring with what might pass for temper in his pale workaday world. "I just think all of us should be chipping in."

"You'll get my chip as soon as I see it," Jared said. "The sooner you let me get about my business, the sooner the coin will be pouring in."

Wade tapped the sole of his shoe and swerved his leg away from the door, letting Mayweather pass without further comment.

Jared slinked into the house, planning to avoid speaking to his mother, who was paying bills at the kitchen table. She sat there behind a blue vase of late-blooming asters, her elbows resting on the flowered tablecloth, a calculator in her hand. She was humming as she worked. Mayweather recognized the tune of "Crimson and Clover," an ancient lugubrious melody which must have sounded some arcane association in the far reaches of her memory. Humming, paying bills? Well, if for some reason this loser Wade Tanner made her happy, Mayweather figured he owed it to her not to interfere. After all, he had no actual dirt on the man, and from what he saw, Wade appreciated his mom, buying groceries, taking her to the estate sales which were his hobby, and bringing her practical gifts—a food processor, a TiVo, a digital alarm clock—with some regularity. Jared did not feel morally entitled to fuck with that. He was relieved, however, that Deirdre had waited until middle age to hook up with a plodder, giving Mayweather the full benefit of a young hungry mother and a charismatic deadbeat dad. For the first time, he wondered if his mom had any idea about Etta. If she did, she hadn't even hinted at it.. But she had always been a great one for keeping information to herself, never fully disclosing, for instance, the exact circumstances of her divorce from Jared's dad, and only occasionally mentioning the man's whereabouts. Mayweather thought of Sally's mother and what she had said about not even getting a grandkid before her daughter had died. Maybe Etta would actually be a comfort to his mom, make up for the world of worry and misery Mayweather had caused her, justifying his sorry existence in the end.

"Jared," she called. "Are you home for dinner tonight? Wade's nephew is coming over and I thought maybe you'd let him use your DVD player. You still have any of those *Star Wars* videos? You used to love those things."

Jared cringed, his very sinews shrinking in protest. "Mom, I threw those out years ago. George Lucas is a blight on the face of American cinema."

"Still, you used to be a whiz kid with a light saber," she said and Mayweather blushed, remembering how many hours he had spent entertaining her with his grudge matches, and knowing, only now, the force she must have had to exert to sit watching patiently while holding her worries at bay: the bills, the laundry, the groceries, the nitpicking boss at the real estate office where she worked as a secretary, and most of all Jared's father, his drunken voice mail messages rich with pet names and obscenities, his freak appearances at inopportune moments, his intermittent child support.

Of course, Ellen had none of these problems. She was, if anything, too insulated from the world, and this, he supposed, was why she had relished rendezvousing with Mayweather in his basement apartment, laughing at the mismatched tile, the exposed pipes, the mattress on the floor surrounded by a magic circle of roach powder. It was only there that she could escape Chaz's benighted hipster circus and find something of her own with which to ruin her life—namely, the surprising product of their illicit fucking, Etta Enright. Why should the girl be branded with Chaz's label, like just another one of his business ventures? But then, "Mayweather," the parting territorial piss of his own absent father, would be no better. In any case, it was not Mayweather who was the heavy. Mayweather was not an exploiter of women; in fact, he was their liberator, he thought, and just to prove it, he went downstairs and dug up some Batman and Spider-Man disks to pacify his mom.

7

Once I'm dismissed from my post at Gabriella's bedside, I rush out to my truck, hoping to get in a brisk walk before dealing with the usual household business of a Sunday afternoon. After hours of enforced passivity in a closed space, my face feels stiff and my brain is freeze-dried in my head. Outside, there is a strong wind, so insistent that it blows my jacket open and pushes my hair into my face. A long strand of bleached blond gets caught between my lips, offering up the unpleasant soapy flavor of mousse. The edges of the parking lot are covered in leaves—yellow, red, and even purple—that weren't there when I arrived only hours before. And as I drive, I see more leaves flocking together in the street ahead of me, streaming out from under tires, flickering along at the ankles of the pedestrians, gold leaf outlining the motion of the whole day like the gilt in an illuminated manuscript or a medieval painting. The trees by the side of the road are emptying out quickly, and I can see dark knots of sticks and weeds, secret nests that were invisible only yesterday.

I barely stop to pick up my dogs and listen to a voice mail from Chaz, who seems to be upset about the newspaper coverage of the accident and even more annoyed that I never turn on my cell phone. But I am too occupied to take much account of this; instead, I immerse myself in the thick coats of Di and Rye as they mob me on the sofa. Di is the deep brown of the darkest and bitterest chocolate while Rye's coat resembles caramel in the sunlight and bronze in the shade. I bury my nose in their musky fur, the texture of bearskin and the strangely pleasant odor of feta cheese. This is the height of sensuality for me, and once again, I thank whatever gods might exist for Mason's humanity in leaving both dogs with me. I throw on my uniform shirt, and my gun for good measure, and because I know our resources are spread so thin that the ranger on call will be doing double-duty staffing the Visitor's Center and patrolling the trails.

I have some trouble managing both dogs by myself, but once I determine that the parking lot is empty, I let Di and Rye off leash and they rush into the weeds and natural grasses, iron-weed and blazing star, so that only their tails are visible. The prairie soon gives way to old-growth forest, and here, too, the leaves are blowing, catching in my long hair and crunching underfoot, giving me a feeling that I am not alone in the park. At the Natural Bridge, I look back over the trail behind me and see the broad wingspan of a bare sycamore, white as bone, stretching its ghostly limbs against a background of red and orange and green. It gives me a shiver, as if a great white beast were stalking me. And at the same time, I am drawn to its beauty and stand looking while my dogs run on up ahead. At this time of the year, the woods seem transparent, and I feel that I can step through them into another reality, perhaps one where my life is going to turn out to be worthwhile after all.

As I turn toward the creek, I see some unusual activity, a group of people pacing back and forth, lifting and bending as if maybe they are setting up camp in a non-designated area. This portion of the trail is backed right up against a country road, and sometimes people enter from that direction rather than driving past the Visitor's Center and official parking lot. It's public land, after all; we don't need a fence to keep people out, or a police force to patrol our borders. Or not generally, I think, getting closer and seeing that a truck has been literally driven into the forest, and three men in boots and heavy plaid work shirts are unloading the vehicle and throwing its contents, without ceremony, into the creek bed. One even has a dolly, and I watch with disgust as he maneuvers it skillfully over the rough terrain. This isn't a newly acquired skill for the guy. I think to check the logo on the truck: "Bailey's Construction," one of my suspects, although not the most prominent, since they are a newer company and haven't yet had the time or opportunity to thoroughly trash their own good name. But apparently they are well on their way. They don't even have the decency to come in disguise, and the men themselves give off no hint of furtive activity, probably feel nothing but a smug satisfaction in having snagged some overtime on a Sunday afternoon. I stand there frozen with rage, just watching them dump wood and sheetrock and carpet scraps into the creek. The carpet is a sickening shade of turquoise, and in spite of the biodiversity of Missouri, a place where three ecosystems meet, I am sure there is no natural occurrence of this particular color in the entire state. I wish I had a video camera. This is one time where Mayweather's obsessions would actually be useful.

But, lacking the tools of his trade, I take up the tricks of my own, reach for the semi-automatic pistol at my side, bring it out of its holster, and fire into the air, the kick of the butt and the rich stink of gunpowder giving me some satisfaction, freeing me from my paralyzed state. My limbs are newly alive, tingling with an electric charge, as if I am an extension of my weapon. However, the shot does not appear to faze the polluters much; it's hunting season, after all, and this area is filled, from September to January, with the sound of gunfire, the forest floor littered with cartridges, hooves and wild turkey feathers left behind where animals have been dressed in the field. I move up closer and make my presence known. Maybe it's true, I think grimly, that people just can't see a woman past forty until she commits a violent crime. So I fire the gun again, this time from twenty-five feet away, and the men finally look up from their work.

"Park Ranger here," I call out. "Don't move."

And they don't move, exactly, but they don't come out with their hands up, either, or freeze in place or look ashamed. Instead, they act as if they have been invited to take a welcome break from their labors. One tears off a hat and leans intimately up against a birch tree. Another spreads his leg and sits on the stump of a fallen sycamore we haven't gotten around to removing. The one with the dolly just clamps and unclamps his hand on the handles, like he is keeping himself in shape.

I remember that I am officially off-duty, too, and this complicates matters if I have to take further action. Of course, I can file a report as an independent citizen. But I know, from experience, how little impact such a statement is likely to have. As I'm standing there, it also occurs to me to wonder about the location of my dogs, and to worry that they might come within range of any random gunshots.

For the moment, I am going to have to work within the parameters of voice control, and so I remember Roller Derby, summon the moral authority, my new persona.

"What are you fellows doing here?" I say. "Don't you know any better than to take a dump on public land?"

"No offense, ma'am, but we're just fulfilling the terms of our contract," the man with the dolly says.

"Bailey's Construction," I read off the truck, very slowly like I haven't noticed it before. "That your outfit? You have more faith in your boss than the U.S. government?"

"At least he's in the black," the seated man says, and they all laugh, a dirty laugh that reminds me of locker rooms and alleyways you enter at your own risk.

"Look, you caught us, Ranger. Ranger Sally," he says, making a point of squinting as he reads my badge. "You want to give us a little slap, I'm sure we'll take our punishment like good old boys."

"On the other hand," the man by the birch says, "Your park is looking pretty punk. Maybe you'd get more bang for your buck if you just come to a little arrangement with our boss." As he speaks, he peels off a bit of birch bark and uses it to scratch at the back of his neck.

The man on the ground begins to laugh, opening and closing his legs. "And get some decent signage, while you're at it. It took us a good fifteen minutes to locate this dump." I look at the whitened inseams of his jeans, the smug set of his lips, and feel my teeth clamp together hard.

Meanwhile, Diana and Orion have come back to find me. They jump and writhe against each other, as flexible as fish, and I wish I'd trained them to be attack dogs rather than simply good company. Once they re-establish their place in my affections, they set out to investigate our present company. They sniff at the seated man's legs and he kicks them away with a sudden motion, just to display his bad temper.

That does it for me. I don't need to wait for any more evidence. I hold the gun right in front of the man's head and say, "Take off your pants."

"I don't think your badge entitles you to the privilege, ma'am."

"I said, take off your pants." I wonder what it is I plan to do. Perhaps I only want to say this, to feel the power of rough language, the only real power I have ever known. I think of Gabriella and what she must have done in Iraq. If she is prepared to kill for her territorial privileges, what am I prepared to do for mine? Of course, I have to remind myself, the park is not literally my property, even if I do treat it as my back yard. But then I don't own my house either, just the mortgage. I don't own my truck, but only the note from the bank. I'm not even in full possession of my own life, according to Lorraine, but will be indebted to her until the day she dies for every ragged breath I manage to tear out of the atmosphere.

The man stands and unzips dramatically, like he's prepared to take a leak in the forest. He's not scared yet. "Seen enough?" he says, a lewd and brave smile on his face.

But there's too much dignity in this pose for me—just the way a man most likes to picture himself, in full armor with only his weapon exposed. I want the legs unwrapped, the thighs naked, the underpants in view.

"No, take the pants completely off," I say.

The two other men look stunned, confused about whether this is a humorous or horrific scene. I would like to strip them all down and abandon them like that in the forest—leave them to the mercy of the Karst on their own. In this temperate fall weather, I wonder how long would it take for them to die of exposure. To ensure the desired result, I'd probably have to tie them up and I don't feel quite willing to make that type of commitment.

The man skims his pants down to his boot tops. He wears plain white cotton briefs, very clean, and although I can't see the elastic at the top, I imagine it is decorated with the traditional blue-and-red stripes. His legs are muscled with hard work, but unlovely, the shins a ghostly white under dark hairs and the thighs a mottled purple. There's puckered pink scar over the kneecap and an old yellowish bruise on the right thigh where he must have whacked himself at work. He probably has kids at his age, just past thirty, I'd guess, although thirty on a man like this sits harder than forty on the likes of Chaz.

"Now get down with your butt on the ground," I say, and before he can decide whether to take his boots off, I push him down there with my hand, firmly but gently, the way you might train a recruit. He is effectively hog-tied in his own jeans. "All of you sit, and take a good long think about what you're doing."

The other two men slowly ease down, kneeling rather than sitting, perhaps preparing to make a run for it when my back is turned.

"Look, I don't know you fellows. Maybe you are destitute or desperate or morally impaired. Maybe you were actually brought up to defecate in your own bathwater. Maybe it doesn't matter to you, what's happening to our country. Or maybe you just think democracy's all over and any asshole with a logo and a spreadsheet is now the law of the land."

At this, I dig a Liver Snap out of my pocket and toss it into the seated man's lap, perfect aim, balanced on the fly of his underpants. But he squirms a bit and it drops between his legs. So I toss another one for good measure and call to my dogs.

Di digs in and Rye follows, their snouts pushing the man's legs open, their fur dark against his stippled thighs.

"But I am done puzzling out the complications, guys. It's just too much work for me, given my heavy responsibilities and my sorry pay. Still, I can tell you this: if you ever touch my park or my dogs again I won't feel too shy to shoot you."

Of course, I'm sure that the dogs won't hurt him, but he has no way of knowing this, and I have to admire his control, even though the white underpants stain a little with moisture and his lips thin with fear. He doesn't make a sound, this guy. As a man of practicality rather than principle, he realizes that silence is the wisest course in this particular circumstance. Perhaps Diana and

Orion will scratch him a bit, as they often mark me in play, but any evidence of violence they leave will be minor in comparison to the wounds the man has already sustained.

I toss another Liver Snap, and another, until I am sick of myself, and my stomach turns to ash and tobacco inside me. I know these men are not the real cause of my grief although they are certainly guilty enough, reeking with the smug stench of borrowed power. Still, I am sorry that it takes me so long to feel any human empathy for them, lower the nose of my gun and place it back in the holster. The Karst, however, is still not placated and the wind blows even harder, thrashing branches, blowing leaves, and raising pale purple goose bumps on the seated man's thighs.

8

Sitting in the darkened basement with his legs propped up on a crate of freeze-dried emergency provisions, Mayweather reviewed the relevant footage on the outmoded video camera that seemed to announce its obsolescence along with his own. As he stared into the illuminated square, he attempted to visualize the roller derby blown up on the screen. The problem was, he had no computer, no editing equipment, only the camera itself and his old DVD player. He supposed he could ask Wade to borrow his PC, but that was a conversation he did not relish. Or he could pull in a favor from Chaz, who had a little more interest in the outcome. But then he would have to come into close quarters with Ellen, and who knew what kind of drama that might entail. In Chicago, Jared had regularly broken into a community college editing room with the ID of a girlfriend and used the equipment from midnight to four. This convenient arrangement came to an end when a security guard outed him and took away the ID, putting an abrupt halt to both the relationship and the project de jour, a documentary following the intertwined fortunes of two insurgent country punk artists in the Chicago area. Just as well that he never finished that one, since the subjects themselves had dwindled into obscurity, one lost to an all-absorbing love affair and the other self-destructing in a balls-out crack addiction. What had happened to his own girlfriend, he had no idea, but he remembered her sleek glossy hair and slightly plump limbs, her playful turns like a dolphin in bed, her love of New Pornographer lyrics and Hal Hartley films.

Mayweather rewound and located Gigi Haddist's last jam. What a look, a helmet over a scarf, like a fundamentalist super-hero. You would never know the girl was Mexican. Her long dark face spoke of veils and mysteries, harem conspiracies, and Kama Sutra moves. Her golden slave bracelets glimmered in the light, suggesting both bondage and the possibility of brass knuckle-style assault. He wished he had gotten to talk to Gabriella before the accident. All he had to go on was her body, its pronounced broad shoulders and wide-spaced breasts. The ripped sleeves of her camouflage team shirt revealed the mus-cles of a soldier, while her hips shifted with feminine fluidity. Unlike Reenie, she started her jam from an upright position, just slightly bent at the knees, not entirely turned over and touching the floor in front of her. Gigi Haddist did not flip up her skirt to expose her panties or turn expectantly to ask for the crowd's applause. Instead, she stood moving her bracelets up and down her arms, sliding a finger under her leather leggings, rubbing her thighs. When the ref blew the whistle, she went from complete stasis to high speed in an instant, picking up the momentum in only three strides, and slicing her way through the pack, throw-ing off skaters in her wake without ever seeming to touch them.

Jared reversed the film and watched the opening pass again. He watched it several times, until he felt the shift of Gabriella's weight in his own body and saw the moments of contact that changed the configuration out on the rink. He played and

replayed the fifty-second clip until it was a video game and he
had the illusion of controlling the action himself, that bit of
mercury that was Gabriella, the surprising way it transformed
the colors and shapes on the rink. He thought of the cheap kalei-
doscopes he had loved as a kid, the colored pieces realigning to
form new patterns, their constant recombinations a promise of
life's possibilities ahead.

When he looked up, it had been over an hour, and he figured
he might as well move to the next phase of his plan. He hitched
a ride to Chaz's new place in one of the old established neigh-
borhoods, Little Dixie, where slaveholders had once flourished
in their elm-shaded enclave. He had not been there before, but
figured, given what he had contributed to the household, that he
should have an open invitation. Although he could have easily
walked the mile and a half to the center of town, he felt some
irrational need to arrive incognito on anonymous wheels.

The place was a remodeler's wet dream: columns, bay windows, a big porch with window boxes and a porch swing. Chaz
and Ellen, of course, had painted the house mauve and done the
shutters and trim an electric blue, so as to set off their establishment from the dull white-and-gray schemes of the neighbors.
There was a tricycle outside, with long tassels hanging from its
handles, and when he saw it Mayweather felt his hollow gut
echo with some unrecognizable emotion. He had forgotten to
eat lunch. That's what it was. He reached into the pocket of his
sweatshirt and pulled out an emergency energy bar, demolished
it in three bites, and knocked at the door.

Ellen opened the door wearing a pair of turquoise shorts and
an oversize T-shirt. She was in the midst of painting, a wet brush
in her hand. Her feet were bare, revealing the pewter-colored
polish on her narrow toes, and her pale legs were dotted with
orange paint. When she saw him, she raised the paintbrush to

her face, as if to hide behind it—or was it just to keep the paint from dripping onto the floor? The shower cap on her head, a ridiculous thing printed with little fishes, made her look like a pretty nurse in an operating room. Jared, feeling lightheaded, was glad he'd eaten the energy bar at least. He reached into the house, took the paintbrush from her, and painted an orange cross on his chest.

"Paintball," he said. "You got me."

Ellen grabbed the brush away from him and he took the opportunity to pull her in for a kiss. Same smell of burnt oranges and lilies, same delicate body with a quicksilver current of will. He fingered the nuggets of her spine, taking in her scent, and wondered if he had the nerve to move his hand any lower. She still had not said anything. He stepped back to look at her face, an older face now, lines around the mouth and eyes giving the features more shading and depth, so that he wanted to get her in a good light and start documenting her gorgeous decline.

"Jared, you freak. I'm right in the middle of the dining room trim." And she moved away and looked down at the spot of orange on her own chest. She was not happy to see him, that much was apparent.

But even so, she could not resist walking him through the house, pointing out its features: the window seat, bay window, fireplace, kitchen island, and walk-in pantry. As if Jared gave a runny postcoital crap about architecture or real estate. He guessed she was just determined to show him how much her fortunes had improved. Not only was her husband willing to take in her bastard, but he had provided her with the ultimate dream house, deep in enemy territory, where they could flaunt their well-practiced bohemian eccentricity in impeccable upper-middle-class style. Jared was more interested in the visual appeal of Ellen's movement through the house, her thin shoulders framed by a doorway, her bust in silhouette in front of a window, the shock of her silver shower cap against a maroon wall. Along the way, he also noticed the paraphernalia of her two preteens. And here and there, amidst the older kids' toys, he found further evidence of Etta's existence: a big wooden puzzle, a push-toy vacuum cleaner, a bald-headed baby doll.

When they got to the back of the house, Ellen opened a big red sliding door and there sat Chaz in his war room, Etta playing with a dollhouse on the floor at his feet. A flat screen covered the entire west wall, and Chaz himself sat behind a desk as big as a bed, with a PC, two laptops, and an odd collection of plaques and paperweights. An exercise bike and an antique 33-millimeter projector occupied the back of the room, with huge speakers hanging from the walls above. Jared felt himself start to salivate, beads of moisture welling on his tongue and a medicinal emptiness filling his mouth. What couldn't he do with this kind of set-up? On the walls, he recognized some of the icons from Chaz's garage: an Edie Sedgwick poster, the framed album covers of Pink Floyd and the Velvet Underground, a couple of kayaking paddles crossed over the fireplace like a modern-day heraldic shield. In this new setting, the scrappy contents of Chaz's fantasy life took on a new significance, and Jared wondered if his own possessions, thus enshrined, would exude the same dignity.

When Chaz saw his guest, he looked back to the computer screen and typed a few more lines, sent off his document with a flourish, then walked around to grab Jared's shoulders. As he dug in, Jared felt a flicker of fear in his gut. Fear of what? He was reasonably certain that he could take the guy in a fight, in spite of the ornamental abs. Besides, he could never see Chaz lowering himself to exchange actual blows. No, what he feared from Chaz was far more insidious. He exerted himself to avoid looking at Etta on the floor, where she sat, he had seen, in doggy ears and overalls, her outline shimmering in his peripheral vision.

"Mayweather, my man," Chaz said. "Welcome to the command center. What do you think?"

Mayweather looked around, trying not to appear envious. "So where do you stash the brew?"

Chaz walked over to the minibar, grabbed two bottles of ale and popped off the caps with an Andy Warhol opener, the business end emerging like a thought bubble from the part of the artist's platinum hair.

Meanwhile, Ellen still stood in the doorway, one hip pressed seductively against the wall, her paintbrush lowered in her hand.

"You want to join us, El?" Chaz asked, extending a beer to her.

But Jared knew that the answer would be no. He remembered Ellen's extreme response to alcohol, which she seemed to imbibe only when in an amorous mood, so that her skin heated up to the temperature of a low-grade fever and gave off a metallic smell. Even then, her lovemaking was not a helpless passion, Mayweather thought, but a willed enterprise. Why did she will herself to fuck Mayweather? To regain Chaz's interest? Jared hated to think that he was just a foot soldier in their long-term war.

Etta spoke up, demanding a beer for her dolls and Ellen obliged by pouring apple juice into tiny shot glasses. Etta then presented Mayweather with a shot and demanded that he drink a glass along with her friends.

"Drink me," she said in a put-on voice that sounded like the song of the tooth fairy.

"Who are you, anyway, kid?" he asked her, not even hoping for an answer.

"I'm a little mermaid that got caught in the pipes," she said.

Jared felt a panic in his chest. But he lifted the glass and toasted. "To the Mermaid Princess."

"Aren't you going to save me?"

The bright taste of apple juice lingered on his tongue, painfully sweet, and he scanned his brain for an answer. Mermaids, fishnets, tridents, thrones. How did you go about saving a mermaid? He grabbed her hands and started swinging her around the room. She was surprisingly heavy, like a little ham or turkey, with a real smell—milk and canned peaches, Tater Tots and grilled cheese.

"Don't get your hair caught in the coral reef," he said. "Don't swat that stingray with your tail."

He did not even look to see Chaz's reaction. Instead, he found himself completely involved in Etta's game, until he feared that he would drop the little girl in the ocean and never find her again. Then he grabbed her back up again and held her still against his chest for two heartbeats, saying, "There, no problem, you're saved."

She reached over and kissed him on the cheek, a dry, matter-of-fact kiss that sent aches and chills through his jaw, even after Ellen took the little girl off to play in the dining room.

By then Chaz was sitting on his exercise bike, preparing to pick up speed. "Joys of fatherhood," he said. "You can't beat them with a paternity suit. Did you look at the papers? Not a very complimentary view of our operation. I need you to get some corrective images out to the community ASAP."

Jared picked up his ale by the neck of the bottle and took an experimental draw of the upscale brew, skunk and musk and chocolate in the mix. Then he went over to the computer to check out the news online, thinking that he would inventory the available editing programs along the way. The screensaver glowed at him with an eerie energy. He took a closer look and saw that it was a photograph of Ellen in her roller derby gear.

The screen flashed shot after shot: Ellen in her Bawdy Bagger cape, Ellen sailing around the rink, Ellen sitting on the bench topless, pulling her skate toward her chest, the right nipple barely grazing one of the wheels.

"I dabble," Chaz said. "You're the artist, I give you that. But you have to say, I have a good eye."

Jared looked back at the screen and waited for the porno shot to come around again. He had to see how it was done. He was surprised at the rage that he felt, metal shavings swarming a magnet in his head. He had not had a violent outburst for some time, but when they came, they wracked his ribcage and gave him migraines for hours afterward. He didn't want to have to go through that again.

So he sat there listening to Chaz spew about the local rags, one owned by the college journalism program and the other by an old blue-blooded family. "And where's the journalistic objectivity in that?" The op-ed in the *Beacon* questioned the patriotism of a team that would mock national security by naming its players after terrorists, while the blog in the *Sentinel* found the retro premise offensive, just a notch above a gentleman's club, the girl-on-girl violence and the cheesy costumes calculated to arouse dubious male fantasies. Both papers bemoaned the risk the girls were taking, young women who could do anything with their lives, but who chose to self-sabotage like it was still the seventies, to the possible detriment of their future careers as mothers, businesswomen, politicians, and wives. It was a slow news day, apparently, for the press to focus so much attention on a single sports casualty—not even a fatal one at that. Chaz was taking care of Gabriella and he wanted people to know it. Her mother was staying at a local motel, at his expense, and he had overseen her medical care. He had every reason to believe the girl would recover and be fine.

"So, just curious. How many people use this computer?" Jared said. The frontal action flashed him again, and he saw that the breast wasn't actually touching the skate, but only poised to do so. Remarkable that the nipple remained smooth and relaxed in that position. He had to admire Ellen's powers of concentration. A line of poetry passed through his head, on a banner like a subtitle. "And you returning on your silver wheels." Where did that come from? he thought. He hadn't looked at any poetry in years.

"Just family and whatever company or business associates I have around. Why do you ask?"

"You really want your wife's bare-ass rack out there for everyone to see?"

"Why not? She doesn't seem to have an objection."

"And the kids?"

"Nothing they haven't eyeballed before." He leaned off the bike then, picked up a couple of free weights from a nearby stand, and began to lift, bringing them up to his chest and back down again, even as he continued to pedal. His muscles slid around under the skin, sickening in their plasticity. "I don't think you're in a position to toss around moral pronouncements, jarhead."

"You were the one who was talking divorce."

"I admit, I was confused. I had too much of this—chi, life force—and I thought I had to spread it around. But I just reinvested all that lust and restlessness, poured it back into the family business, and look what it's got me. Look what it's got Ellen. Not to mention what it's done for you. "

"Me?"

"You got a free pass on this one, Mayweather. Now you just might get somewhere if you can avoid fucking up again."

Jared stared at the screensaver, clenching the mouse. But then the nude shot made its third round and he lost his concentration, picked up a pretentious black marble paperweight and threw it into the screen. He didn't stop to examine the damage, but passed through the house the way he'd come, reversing the action, rewinding his fate, not even stopping in the dining room where Ellen stood on a ladder painting the trim at the top of a window and Etta sat with a selection of Play-Doh at the big dining room table covered with a transparent plastic sheet.

Outside, he looked at the house, his lungs streaked with pain.

From there, he hitched a ride to Karst Park and jogged up the trail, his camera bouncing against his chest. At the turn into the old growth forest, he saw a honey locust, its yellow fronds all blown away and the seedpods hanging down against the bare branches, a tree of crooked blades swinging in the wind.

9

The men don't go peacefully and they don't take their trash with them. The guy pulling his pants up claims that he is going to file a suit, and the man with the dolly confirms that their boss Bailey knows a crackerjack lawyer who specializes in just this kind of thing. With the gun back on my belt, I have been transformed back into an ineffectual public servant. I can feel my legs shaking, the sweat prickling up like dew in my poorly shaved armpits. The man who has been scratching himself with birch bark spits in my direction, grips his crotch at me, and growls. At least when they pile into their truck, it is still about half-full of industrial waste: that much less garbage I will have to haul out of here. But they will probably go and dump their load elsewhere on public land rather than disposing of it properly. How long will it take me to get back to my truck, I wonder. Maybe seven minutes, five if I run. I'll let them think I am retreating, then surprise them somewhere up the road.

Not five feet down the trail, I fly right into Mayweather, who is filming me from a safe spot behind the trees. He is a surprisingly solid presence in his purple sweatshirt with orange paint stains. He gives me a look of disbelief, pupils colonizing his hazel eyes. Maybe I've finally managed to impress him. But there is no time for gloating. I just tell him to put away his camera and follow me back to my truck. Di and Rye run on ahead and Jared pants away at my side. I can tell he hasn't been getting much exercise. He's obviously stronger than I am, but my breath control is better and I'm sure my blood pressure is, too. I check my watch. Three minutes since we left the scene of the crime. I put on speed for the home stretch, streak into the stand of prairie grass, feel the ground beating under my feet. My lungs burn like they've been poured full of molten glass and my ribcage weighs me down, but I am determined to maintain my speed.

In the parking lot, I bend down, touching my thighs, to catch my breath, and take in air like huge droughts of cold water. Rye and Di are already there, waiting patiently in the truck bed. I get in the cab and consider my course of action, staring at my shaking hands on the wheel, the bare white band of skin on my ring finger, the pale moons populating my unpainted nails, until Jared arrives, jumps in, slams the door, and bends his long legs into the available space. His jeans, I see, are marked up with geometric doodles drawn in Sharpie, and his sweatshirt is covered in tiny, sticky seeds, which I know from experience won't come out in the wash and will have to be picked off by hand. As I drive, I watch out of the corner of my eye as he goes through the contents of my glove compartment.

"I don't have any gum, if that's what you're looking for."

"No, I think I left something in here," he says. "Yes," he shouts as he grabs the orange envelope of a long-overdue parking ticket, and shakes a fat bud out into his hand.

"You left your weed in my car," I say. "What, are you trying to frame me?"

"You wouldn't believe how that looked on camera. You are an action hero, man."

"Let's just hope it's not too gory," I say, and then realize that I have evidence, I have evidence of the dumping, but it is going to incriminate me, too. And given the current climate of high terrorist alert, what is going to look worse, a few guys quietly littering on a Sunday afternoon or an out-of-control public employee with a gun?

Jared, always prepared, pulls some paper out of his camera case and starts rolling a number on his thigh.

"Do you have to do that?' I say, turning a corner onto a gravel road. "I'm in enough legal trouble as it is." There are three back entrances to the Karst, and two other parks within a three-mile radius. I figure the polluters are headed for one of these spots.

"This is totally native, Ranger. You wouldn't believe how much of this pure Ozark ditch weed you've got going on right out here in your domain."

"So now I am going to have to fight with drug harvesters, too?" I decide to secure my own borders first and head toward the exposure out on route NN, where the road opens onto a wooded area with several sinkholes.

"Hey, it's your job; why not start enjoying it?" he says. "Look, I'm not really trying to be an asshole, but I have to get reacclimated before I go into full-out migraine mode."

I remember the night we went to the old Rialto Theater with its ornate banisters, crimson curtain, and multiple chandeliers for a special showing of *Spellbound*. At intermission, he ran into an old classmate from film school, had an argument about George Lucas and Stephen Spielberg that spilled out into the street. Although there were no actual blows exchanged, I had to nearly carry Jared home, cover his forehead with a washcloth soaked in cold water, and keep him in complete darkness for nine hours, feeling him sweat beside me, absorbing the acrid odor of battery acid and bad dreams. I had never heard him hold his peace for so many minutes in a row and it gave me pause; what was Mayweather, after all, if not a highly charged collection of chatter and hormones?

"Does that happen a lot now?"

"Only when I have to suck up to an asshole."

"You've been to see Chaz."

"Slaveholder Central."

"You didn't have to come back."

"Do you think she actually loves him?"

"Why not? They've been together, what, almost fifteen years? Admit it; you're a little in love with the guy yourself."

I look over to gage his response and he blows smoke in my face, reminding me of Mason and his constant sweet smell of marijuana, his deliberate movements, and his square, well-trimmed fingernails.

"I think I can manage to tear myself away from his sorry ass."

"Third time's a charm," I say and pull up to a bare patch of land at the side of the road, a few tire tracks in the mud from the recent rain. No sign of the polluters, though I'm happy to see that a family of five is returning to their car: boy with a hiking stick, girl with a border collie, toddler of indeterminate sex on the dad's back. At least someone is enjoying the park today. I wave out the window to encourage them in their responsible use of public land. But when I turn back to Mayweather, I see that he is still staring.

"Ranger, did you ever get yourself impregnated?"

"Maybe you are getting a little carried away with your sperm count."

"I'm serious, you can tell me."

"Not that I know of. There were some close calls, but I never had to make any grisly choices, if that's what you mean."

"Are you just as glad?"

I flick on my turn signal and pull onto the ZZ, take the smooth curve around the park and look at the rows of millet on the other side, green stalks and purplish tips, separated from the road by the long ditch swollen with rainwater. One of the farmers has put up a scarecrow, its blue plaid Carhartt shirt spilling straw. I picture Etta with her raggedy curls and familiar jaw line going through the contents of my purse. "Well, from what I can see, it's a whole lot of piss and plastic," I say. "But you know, if my life had been different, I might have given it a shot."

"That's what I think, too," he says and I look over to see the expression on his face, the strangely open gaze under the swarm of fishing lures pinned to his hat: long and feathered, smooth and speckled, fat and lean.

Maybe I am just stoned with secondhand smoke, but I feel calmer than any woman with a looming lawsuit and a criminal future has a right to be. I am actually happy, I realize, astounded to recognize the emotion as it appears unbidden out of my chest to fill up the sky. The clouds streak across the horizon in front of me as if some cosmic hand has reached into a cumulous mass and dragged its contents over the blue horizon, white trails of ether spilling out from between each godlike finger. What does it matter, how long this happiness lasts? It could stretch out to fill a whole lifetime in a few minutes. It could blow away in the next windstorm. Or it could just keep changing form and following me around.

Then I remember my polluters and my gut turns over, leaving a big bare patch of dread exposed.

"One more entrance," I say. "Do you have the camera ready?"

"Are you really going after these guys?"

"What do you think? Would you just sit around and let someone desecrate your domain?"

At the next turn, I look back and see Rye and Di's fur pressed back in the wind. They sit patiently in anticipation of yet another walk. We are headed for one of my favorite places in the park, where sinkholes and grasslands give way to a perfectly circular pond surrounded with cattails on one side, willows on the other. As I pull up, I look for the red truck, but there's not a single car in the lot. Then I see iy on the tire tracks leading off from the gravel lot and right past the trail. It takes a sharp curve around the signage and heads on into the park. The dogs are running out to the pond before I can even get my bearings and Mayweather grabs at my waist and pulls me close for an instant, so that I can smell his smooth homegrown marijuana, his breakfast burrito, and probably two days' worth of curried sweat, still sweet as a boy's. I disengage his hand and place it on his camera.

"You have to get the shot." I say.

"On the grave of John Huston, by the ghost of Robert Altman, in the name of all that's unhyped and unholy, so help me God. "

"You have to get the shot without me in it."

And then I start up the trail at a saunter, not walking, not running, just keeping pace with the wind as it slows to a light and steady breeze. I am sailing down the trail without impediment, my will lifted from me, and my body moving on alone. At the edge of the clearing, I stop and see the narrow yellow branches of the bare willows, like whips on the bright blue back of the pond. Closer to me, the cattails are molting, caught between gray and brown. And there, at the nether lip of the pond is the red truck, an eyesore in the midst of the gold and green day. Behind the vehicle, in angry curves, is a trail of trampled grass and upturned mud. They haven't taken a straight route to their destination, but have driven round in several intersecting circles, tearing up the entire field in the process. Near us, butterfly weed and blazing star lay flattened to the ground and closer to the pond, a whole battalion of cattails has been mowed down in the wake of the tires.

"They've gone mudding on your park, " Mayweather says and turns on his camera.

I stand fingering the gun on my belt, as solid and familiar as my own hipbone, but I know that the success of the maneuver depends on my silence. Happily, Di and Rye have disappeared into the woods, apparently uninterested in the men they have already so thoroughly investigated. I'm guessing the guys were too absorbed in their hate crime to notice two dark blotches pass at the speed of sound. Jared and I move closer, lurking along the tree line, filming as we go. The men have already started dumping their load into the pond, shouting curses, driving boards into the water like spears, cramming mats of carpet between the reeds. Further out, the dried lotus pods sit like sentinels in their straw hats, observant but unmoved, and my own rage stills at the sight. But when I look over at Mayweather, he is sitting down on a stump, the camera running blind, and his head down in his lap, the lures on his cap gleaming in the sun. The migraine again. I need to take him home, get him in a darkened room, and pass him some painkillers. I move over to put my hand on his forehead and he hands me the camera without looking or speaking. When was the last time I used a camera? I am, after all, without a use for one: no kids to brag about, no significant vacations to record, no desire to fix my own image and project it back to the world. The thing is unsteady in my hands, lighter than I expected, and cool to the touch. I try to find the polluters in the lens. The men wander in and out of the frame and I can't seem get the destruction of the field and the culprits in the same shot. How can I prove causality here? It's as much as I can do to film the open tailgate and some of the broken field. I zoom in close and as I do, I notice what I haven't seen before: the damp earth on the tires, the crushed stems of milkweed spilling fluid, a dark seed inside the pale lotus head, the leaf scars on a sapling torn out by the roots, even the polluters themselves, one freckled, one sun burnt, the third with curling chest hair like a graying ascot in the V neck of his shirt. Once the truck is emptied out and its dusty red bed exposed, they all unzip and piss onto the evidence, three separate streams catching the light of late afternoon and meeting in the middle like the blades of the Three Musketeers.

For just half a second, I can't help but see the beauty of the three liquid shafts of light. Then I break down in disgust and shut off the camera. Even an animal knows better than to foul a water source. I can't believe I'm not running out to stop them. I should be used to this by now, standing around silently while everything I love is desecrated and all natural law is left abandoned like so much inconvenient kill on the side of the road. I should be an expert, I think, seeing how I've been practicing all my life. I reach down to Mayweather and help him up. His body is pliable and he leans on me as we walk down the trail, his weight a calming ballast, his breath sour with fever, his head bent down to shield his eyes from the light.

IO

Mayweather's migraine had a life of its own. It sat on the left side of his head and vibrated. It gathered colors and rolled over, crushing synapses like so much clover as it went, so that he had to grit his teeth and cease all internal movement. The migraine grew restless, nevertheless, reverberating in his eardrum, walking the tightrope of his corpus callosum and threatening to split the connecting cable of his consciousness with its weight, severing Mayweather into a man who had no memories and a man who only longed for such a convenient deficiency. He opened his eyes to see where he was, flashed on a mandala hanging on the wall: red, yellow, blue, brown. But before he could make out anything further, the migraine beamed him with its disapproval, shooting into his optic nerve and forbidding him to focus. He closed his eyes again in submission, feeling dampness between the lashes. The world without focus was a misery for Mayweather, random sensations bumping into half-formed thoughts and unidentifiable emotions, the fear that had been nailed down under something visually interesting now free to wander wherever it might want to go.

He'd read that it was unusual for a guy such as himself to experience migraines. Generally, sufferers tended to be type A perfectionist women, people like Ellen, for instance, who kept their houses and fingernails neatly painted, their children in the proper nuclear containers, and their marriages intact. Mayweather was too chaotic and evil for such suffering; it was hardly fair that he had to endure the trials of the straight and the dissipated, too.

He rolled over and felt a body at his side. Sally or one of the dogs? He curled into it, not caring about its identity, but only drawn toward the warmth that emanated from it and formed a channel of thaw in the midst of his dissociation.

Somewhere, a phone rang. His cell seemed to be implanted directly in his ear, but there was no way he could reach it. He would have to go in through his nostrils, he thought, the way they extracted brains from Egyptian corpses in order to mummify them. He only wished he could be mummified. That was the ticket. Suck the sucker out of its hiding place in the left frontal lobe with a straw. The body next to him rose, walked into the other room, left him alone with his migraine, arguing aesthetics. Should a film replicate the chaos of life or attempt to carve its random materiality into a totem with which the viewer might banish the specter of nihilism for ten to two hundred minutes? Should the blue go on the left or on the right? He pushed the colors around in his mind, as if manipulating a palette on the computer. If only he could get the proportions right, he was sure the migraine would magically depart. He pushed the red into the nether region at the south of the frame, as he did, it formed an opening, a door into a pantry, through which Mayweather could see a cabinet packed full of tubular red objects: cells, eggs, twisted cloth napkins, rolls of old school film? The cabinet kept opening and opening, there was everything you needed in here, more than you could ever use, in fact, and no need to feel deprived ever again. Just as he thought this, a huge piece of his brain started to disintegrate, warming, melting, causing a landslide inside his head. The migraine escaped in a flash of white, and in the aftermath, Mayweather's pain became just diluted enough for him to be able to lose consciousness.

He awoke the next morning at four a.m., according to Ranger Sally's radio clock, after twelve hours of sleep, feeling better than he had for years. His head was fully operational, all kinds of room opened up for business, and his dick was hard, bobbing up under his hand. The Ranger slept next to him, still in her uniform shirt, he noticed, although she'd unbuttoned it to reveal the white cotton camisole underneath and slipped on a pair of ribbed blue rock-climbing pants that seemed to serve as her pajamas. The dogs slept curled into her, one burrowed into her stomach and the other resting inside the curve of her bent legs. Her long, sun-streaked hair fell over her face and her arms were flung out as if she had been practicing tae kwon do in her sleep. She was probably still dreaming of kicking that polluter's ass. He thought of waking her, but it seemed too cruel, after she'd tended to him through the night, so he touched himself experimentally, trying to find the right fantasy to fit his mood. He revisited an incident with two coworkers in a projectionist's booth, he imagined Ellen's breasts pouring out of a harness, he invented a scenario involving a pommel horse and a brunette. But although his imagination kept him stiff as a rake handle, he still could not come. The only thing to do was to get up and work.

He turned on the light and glanced up to where he'd seen the mandala on the wall. It was actually the Missouri state seal, a grizzly bear groping it on either side. This seemed odd, since as far as Mayweather knew, there were no bears in Missouri. But he recognized the red panel in the lower left-hand corner as the mysterious red cabinet from his migraine-induced dream.

He went immediately to Sally's computer, which, he discovered, had a rudimentary iMovie program. It was primitive, but then so was he, and he scorned the effects he might have achieved on Chaz's more sophisticated equipment, just as the Danish dogma cinematographers, with their dour view of progress, eschewed glossy Hollywood technique. Mayweather found his camera where Sally must have left it, on the end table next to a bleached-out turtle shell, and hooked up the cable to feed his footage in. After that, he did not look up for two hours, until the dogs woke and padded into the living room to check on him. This was his cue to stand up, go to the refrigerator, grab a few slices of lunch meat, feed some to Di and Rye and eat the rest himself, folding the remaining slices into a meat sandwich.

From there, he wandered toward the open door of the spare room to watch Sally sleep. She must have decided that it was too difficult to get him up the stairs to her bedroom and stayed to keep watch over him through the night. With the dogs gone, she had now rolled onto her back, taking up most of the room with her arms under her head and her legs spread. When had he ever seen a woman sleep like that, as if she had a right to the whole bed? The dawn crept over her face, illuminating its full lips and stark forehead, but revealing something else too, a private expression of grief or longing he had never seen. On film, she was more definite, anger lending color to her face and emphasizing the sharp line of her jaw.

Now his hands smelled like salami, spicy with pepper and tinny with additives. He went over to the bed, lifted the blankets from the bottom and warmed his hands around her ankles. Then he carefully worked his way up her legs until he arrived at the top of her rock-climbing pants and dragged them down her

hips with his teeth. He was climbing a rock, he thought, visualizing the limestone cliffs with vertical falls of ice frozen onto their
faces. Inside her clothes, Sally was warmer than he had imagined, yeasty with life. He moved his face downward to catch her
smell of grass and earth, her light brown pubic hair growing
low and wide over her pubis in a shallow V, some curly irregular
hairs escaping into the creases of her legs. Mayweather leaned in
and tasted the meat of her labia, the flavor of raisins and pemmi-
can. Mincemeat, he thought, remembering the pulp inside the
pod of the honey locust, and Sally said his name from above in
that authoritative roller derby voice, narrating the possibilities.

She pulled him up her torso, turned to face him, and wrapped
one leg around his waist, reaching for his cock like a vine to be
turned in the right direction. How different from the beautiful
entitled girls who expected you to worship them from below,
panting at their breasts, or the timid compliant ones with some
slight social stigma or physical irregularity who let you ride
them whichever way you wanted. Sally pushed at Mayweather,
as if to roll him over, then he gripped her legs around him and
pulled her, covers and all, onto his lap at the edge of the bed,
and they fucked face to face, their eyes fully open in the morning sunlight, his belly pressed up between them like a willing
third party. She was still in a dream, her pupils dilated in her violet eyes, and the skin of her right checkmarked with the raised
pattern of her pillowcase.

"I guess you're feeling better," she said.

"I've been worse."

"You've been much worse, Mayweather."

"Very, very worse."

"But now you're fine."

"Just right," he said. "How about you?"

"I will be even finer when I nail those malefactors."

Afterwards, she made the coffee and he packed a bowl; they sat out on the deck eating Frosted Flakes sprinkled over lime yogurt and looking out into the trees, red shading into gold. The fall morning smelled like gunpowder and bonfires; it fired his ambition, as if all of life was still ahead of him and he was just setting out to see what he could see. The thought of his new film was delicious, like a pastry waiting to be eaten or a cold glass of beer ready to be downed. He reached over and rubbed Sally's neck, felt the tension there, moved in and mapped the pressure points of her back: one knot for each of the polluters.

"Don't worry," he said. "We'll get those peckerwoods."

Sally shifted her expression from one side of her face to the other and poured herself more coffee. "What about the girl?"

Mayweather, through force of habit, started rehearsing denials in his head. But then he realized that Sally meant Gabriella, lying in some twilight state in a VA hospital bed. He remembered the footage of her long strides, powerful shoulders and hips, her form gliding around the curve, her skirt sailing out behind her and then, when she turned, pulling taut over her front, showing the bold outline of her pelvis like a coat of arms. He thought of how he might splice this image with shots of the bare painted toe in the hospital room, then the quote about, what was it, the cunts who run this country with their military contractors and their mind control. Of course, this wasn't what Sally meant, either, She meant the physical girl in the bed, and whether she would ever get up out of it and walk—much less skate—again.

"Never underestimate the power of a good shout-out prayer service," he said.

"While you were asleep, my mother set the whole thing up and invited half the city. Fortunately, I convinced her to have the well-wishers congregate in the park instead of my back yard."

Looking out at the environs, Jared could definitely see why. The gazebo Mason had built was sadly neglected, a few white splotches of bird shit staining the railing, and the surrounding grapevines drooped with purple fruit fermenting on the vine. Jared remembered meeting Sally's husband for the first time as he tended to the vines in his cutoff shorts, red bandanna dangling from the back pocket. She'd acquired the guy on a break and then married him very quickly, without any warning. Sally never did say how she hooked up with that graying loner, or why they split either, just like she'd never asked Mayweather himself to leave or stay. But when he saw the way she'd filmed his migraine, his head cradled in his hands, a reddish curl burnished in sunlight, he knew that she had missed him more than she would say.

II

I go to work that morning, the same as usual, and leave Mayweather in the house putting together his film. As I drive, I see the sun burning the fog off the horizon and feel just the slightest chill on the breeze. My body is liquid inside my uniform, nerves rubbing against all the seams. But I can't afford to luxuriate in the sensation. I try to harden myself into a recognizable being by rehearsing the many requests and instructions Chaz has texted me at intervals during the night. I need to contact the local papers. I need to order refreshments for the prayer service. I need to drop by the hospital to check on Gabriella and her mom. I need to see if Reenie can contact the girls and rearrange for practice later in the week. With all this labor, you would think I worked for the guy. My actual boss, the supervisor of all the state parks in the Boonslick area, is much less directive, and appears only in the event of a flood or government restructuring. Still, I anticipate that I will have to suffer some sort of official interaction with the man in the wake of my recent lapse of judgment.

I pull into the entrance and pass the Old Castle, a half-completed mansion built by an electricity baron before he went bankrupt and had to sell his land to the state, back before anyone anticipated that tourism would become one of Missouri's premier industries. However, the interest has now turned from untouched land to debased country music, water parks, and outlet malls. Before too long, I think, we could be selling the park back to the electricity baron's great-grandchildren. The white limestone brick wears well and makes for a popular backdrop for vacation photos, but I can't imagine an actual family agreeing to inhabit this hillbilly Taj Mahal. I see it more as a casino, really, either that or a banquet hall. A shiver forms like a fault line down my back and I remember that this was where I first saw Mayweather, seven years ago, balancing on the wall and trying to get a shot of the turret. At the time, he was just one more work-related obstacle. Back then, I was new to the job, fresh from a long stint as a government bureaucrat and frustrated other woman, and I was in no shape to recognize destiny when I saw it in the form of an overly curious and poorly groomed boy. I think back to the pleasure I took in the Karst during those first weeks and months, the precarious structure of the natural bridge, the creek's constant rush and sigh, a box turtle moving so slowly across the trail that I'd see him as I rushed off on some errand and then again, still toiling along, when I returned. But most of all, I loved the feeling of my own body in the midst of the sun and wind, the deep smell of spice and pollen in the summer, the sharp ale breath of winter, mud and frog spawn in the spring. And now, perhaps the best season of all, when every root and fruit gives up its essence before rotting quietly into the dirt.

I park my car at the visitor's station, sign in with the other ranger on call, and head out to view the damage. On my way,

I notice a red ear of corn, probably dragged across the property line from a farm field by some animal. I see a maple with its leaves still attached, ragged and resistant. I notice that the hedge apples have dropped to the ground, huge green globes the size of grapefruits, their exteriors mottled like the surface of the cerebellum. I kick one across the trail, pick up another and tear it in half, still surprised at the hollow innards of this oversized fruit. As I approach the site of the incident, I feel my breath quicken. The ground has frozen over in the night and the raised mud of the tire tracks is illuminated with stars of frost. I find a particularly high crest and stand on it, attempt to mash it down with my boot. No luck. Maybe later, I think, when the sun has done its work. I tramp to the side of the pond, stand there examining the boards and carpet scraps choking its far end, the cattails lying prostrate in the grass. Yesterday's wind has departed and the water is flat as a slate under the morning sun. I see myself reflected in its blue-gray surface, a vigorous blond, neither short nor tall, fat nor thin, young nor old, inhabiting the middle ground of my own existence like a shadow. It is too late in life for me to hope for whole cartloads of happiness but still too early for me to give up. What will I do for the next twenty or thirty years, as much time as it takes for a tree to grow from a sapling to a shade-giver or a human to progress from infancy to maturity?

Something stirs in the water, a largemouth bass or maybe a channel catfish, thrashing its way to the surface. I see its strong mobile shape and speckled skin, a slash of silver in the dull blue water. Then, on an impulse, I wade into the pond and reach out, as if to catch it with my bare hands, like some native woman in search of dinner. To my amazement, I actually touch the fish, feel its slick solid weight against my palm, though I don't of course, catch the creature before it descends back into the muck.

Then there is another reflection in the water, a tall man with a green hat and a leather jacket. His thick bangs are bright silver and white stubble is seeded into his rough narrow cheeks like grains of rice. I'm not surprised to see the park supervisor, Guy Dempsey, only amazed that he has found me so quickly.

"I can see why you were provoked," he says, taking off his hat as if to show his respects at a funeral and then sinking down onto his long haunches to finger the garbage at the side of the pond. As he speaks, his left eye twitches, a whorl of wrinkles appearing and disappearing at the side of his face. At times, it seems as if he is winking at me in amusement; at other moments, he appears to be wincing in pain. I wonder how much he has heard about yesterday's incident, and how quickly he is planning on reacting,

I back out of the water, wiping my hands on my pants. "I guess you have been getting some calls."

"A few," he says. "You have anything to report?"

"What can I tell you, Guy? I popped a few blood vessels on this one and I still can't see my way to apologize." My boots are water resistant, so my toes remain toasty, although my damp pants are clinging to my calves and chilling me all the way up the leg. "These three jokers from Bailey's Construction showed up to use our state's natural resource as their personal Dumpster. They seemed to think their boss had a bigger dick than mine. So I had to pull out a few party tricks to assert my authority."

"This the site of the crime?"

"One of them. Before they trashed the pond, they did a number on the creek, and that's when I got a little extra-curricular with the weaponry."

"It's a serious charge, Sally."

"Well, I have to point out that I didn't harm anyone, or damage any property, either, which is more than you can say for these malefactors."

"Bailey's Construction, let's see, the mother company is Dalton, the grocery store, the garden center, the gym. Oh, and they were also the primary benefactors for the new football stadium. What do you suppose are the chances of you winning that lawsuit?"

I feel my gut drop down into my female parts. My severance pay from my last government job is just enough to tide me over into retirement. If I am sued and fired simultaneously, I don't know how I'll survive. "So it's me who will be winning or losing the lawsuit on my own?

"I hate to remind you, but you made an executive decision to sling that gun around. Look at this place, Sally. Do you think that we can afford legal fees on top of everything else?"

"I know things are bad. That's why I was trying to defend our borders."

"Our borders are permeable, Ranger LaChance. Back when I started in the last century, we had a big issue with poachers. I had more than one ranger killed in the line of duty. Since you've been around, though, we've only had to deal with squatters, hillbillies, hobos, white trash. But now we are up against a bigger force. You know what will happen if the next tax levy doesn't pass? We will be looking at selling off the place, piece by piece, to the highest bidder. They want to manufacture feed out here, fine: build a shopping mall or prison, test biological warfare or detonate nuclear warheads, we don't have much to say about it."

"So why do I have this gun in the first place?" I say. "Just so I can carry around a little bling on my hip?"

Guy stands up slowly, his patience exhausted. I am so close to him that I can hear his bones crack, like branches in the wind. "Sally, when we hired you, we thought your sex was an advantage. You're the last one I'd expect to see hot-heading around, using your piece irresponsibly and letting your hounds go to town on some poor devil's scrotal area."

But when I hear about my inappropriate anger, it just makes me that much angrier. "You thought I was so beaten down that I wouldn't make a fuss?"

"Look, Sally, I have known your family for over forty years. I thought you were a peacemaker."

"Well, I'm sorry, Guy, I have worked for you almost a decade and I thought you were a conservationist. I guess we are both just laboring under major misconceptions."

His eye twitches again as he puts on his hat. "We'll discuss this later," he says in a weary tone. "Meanwhile, why don't you get a truck and clean up this holy crap?" And even he can't help kicking at a protruding two-by-four as he speaks.

"And deposit it where? Back at Bailey's lot?'

"The municipal dump will be just fine."

So that is it. I am not charged to protect the people and their land after all. I am merely being paid to clean up after the contractors and polluters. I am a ridiculous figure, prancing around in this uniform, pretending to be a lawman when I am really just a glorified maid. What is a woman of my age good for, after all, but to clean up other people's messes? It doesn't matter that I have scrupulously avoided accumulating any of my own: babies with their spit-covered paraphernalia, teenagers with their angst and addictions, men with their fiscal indiscretions and their sexual needs. I am just an empty pair of hands waiting for my next dirty chore.

I walk back to the ranger station, get my truck, and drive it out to the pond, retracing the route of the polluters. The frozen ground resists my tires, but even though I am careful, I am sure to mow down more weeds. I will have to do a controlled burn here, anyway, clearing out the whole area for new growth. It will

give me some satisfaction to rid the field of any signs of the tres-
passers, though the DNA of their piss will surely linger in the
pond for years.

This thought makes getting back into the water particularly
distasteful. By now, my damp pants legs have dried, but I have to
get wet again to drag the rubble from the pond piece by piece,
thinking, all the while, of the polluters and their fluids. I realize
that I am still tired from the night and then the morning with
Mayweather, my legs shaky, my breasts tender under my uniform, the nipples irritated and erect inside my sensible bra. I get
a splinter in my finger and tweeze it out with my fingernail and
as I look up to examine the offending wood chip in the light, I
see that I am staring at the reflection of Chaz Enright standing
tall astride his glorious red racing bike, his feet in their black biking shoes planted firmly on the ground. He is quite a sight here
against the fading organic matter in his tight polyurethane biking gear, black with red stripes. He looks like a scuba diver about
to take a dip in this modest pond, ten feet at its deepest, after a
record rainfall.

"Woman, what does it take for you to answer your phone?" he
says, dismounting with an agile kick.

"Maybe I'd turn it on if I was expecting good news."

"How about a tip? You check the morning paper?"

"Did they go after you again?"

"No, looks like you are the main course of the day."

He digs his iPhone out of his messenger bag, dials up the
local website, and hands me the item like I'm taking a call.
There's my name in the column all right, along with a descrip-
tion of a crazed park ranger pulling a gun on three unsus-
pecting workmen and subjecting them to tortures of a sexual
nature. "Ms. LaChance could not be reached for comment,"
the article concludes.

"Good Lord, they make it sound like Abu Ghraib," I say, flicking on my cell phone after giving it the night's rest. I have seventeen messages, most of them from numbers I've never dialed. I could spend the morning cleaning up my image or just clear out the pond instead. Of the two of them, I think the pond is more valuable and so I hand the phone back and return to my work.

"Too bad they didn't get a photo."

"Oh, believe me, I have all the visuals anyone could ever want."

"You can't buy this kind of publicity, Sally," Chaz says, pointing me down the column to where the writer mentions that I moonlight as an emcee for the Boonslick Bombers.

"I am about to get fired and all you can think of is your profit margin. If you're going to stand there blocking my sunlight, you might as well give me a hand."

Chaz puts the phone back in his bag and lifts a board, holding it as precisely as if he were going to frame a window with it, instead of just throwing it into the truck bed. Even now, his body has not lost the hang of labor, and this reminds me that he is not an entirely useless guy.

"My boss was just out here telling me how the state can't afford to back me in event of a lawsuit."

"Quit your job already, Sal. You could make more in my organization in a month than you can spending all four seasons out here in the heat and cold."

"Doing what?" I say. "Getting your latte? I'm too old to be your gofer."

"Well, now that we've got the dominatrix thing going, I think our cable show will really kick off. Then we can diversify with a little consulting—leadership and creativity workshops, nature and landscaping advice."

He throws another board into the truck as if it's a spear, his modest but shapely biceps showing to advantage, his face animated with the possibilities. Guy's face, by contrast, seems bland and unmotivated, as if he is gradually escaping from his own identity, leaving only his uniform and his wink behind. And which is more admirable after all? To become the most exaggerated version of oneself—the dominatrix, Madonna, trickster, shyster, bully, harpy, whore? Or to disappear into the rest of nature? In the pond, my image is shaky enough to give me pause, stretching out toward the lotus heads without quite reaching them. Can it be that I have survived this long without ever becoming an identifiable being? Or am I simply dissolving after reaching my final form? I look at Chaz for a clue, but he is intent on arranging the boards into a more efficient formation.

"Just think of it, Sal. Flexible schedule, great wardrobe, no money worries, all the opportunity in the world to meet eligible men."

"What makes you think I'm interested in that?"

Chaz has succeeding in dragging a square of turquoise carpet up the bank, where he squashes the water out by stomping on the nap, first one biking shoe, then the other, pressing the water out. I am surprised that he isn't more squeamish. But once again, he seems to have devised a way to work the system without dirtying his hands. "Well, if you ask me, you're scraping the bottom of the barrel with that overgrown kid."

"I thought Mayweather was your friend."

"Looks like he's your project now. You want to support the kid for another twenty years while he spawns bastards all over the county, be my guest."

My uniform feels too tight and the sun is warming up underneath the breeze. Probably, Chaz has already called Mayweather this morning and has filled in the dots on his own. "I guess it's better than supporting the bastards," I say.

But Chaz hardly blinks. "At least I can afford it," he brags. "And if you stick with me, so can you." He gives the carpet a final stamp and then lifts it, still heavy enough to strain his arms, into the truck bed. "If that's what you want, of course. Maybe you are really just a masochist, after all."

Then he hops onto his bike and rides off, playfully following the track the polluters have made. He has so much energy that his butt doesn't even touch the seat of his bike, and I wonder what it is that buoys him up, allowing him to maintain the optimism and heartlessness of youth this far into middle age.

In the meantime, we've hardly made a dent in the pile of refuse in the pond. For a while, I try Chaz's method of squeezing water out by foot. But my boots are far more unwieldy than his biking shoes, and I don't have the patience for the repeated hop and step, almost like a move on a dance video. So I go back to cutting up the carpet into smaller pieces light enough to lift without squeezing out the water. I have dismembered three squares and thrown them in the truck when I see another figure in the water, this one a woman, long hair, small breasts, heart-shaped face. At first, I think my eyes are playing tricks on me—or maybe it really is Sharee there, laughing at me mucking around in the dirt of this Earth while she has gone on to the high life somewhere beyond the clouds. Then I turn around and see Reenie—Raven Pillage—her long hair unbraided for once, kinky with the memory of restraint. She wears a pink vintage jacket with a pasteboard daisy pinned to the lapel, a pair of black toreador pants emphasizing her tiny waist and broad hips, strappy high heels with open flowers spread across the toes. Her heels are almost as elevated as her roller skates, in fact, so that she totters above me, though I am actually the taller woman. The wires of her iPod hang from her ears like ivy vines, and freckles shimmer in her dewy face.

"If you are looking for Chaz, you just missed him," I say.

She pulls out one earbud and I can make out the faint music of her iPod; it's Buddy Holly, not what you expect to find in the ear of a twenty-three-year-old.

"What?" she asks, though she clearly understood me, because she adds, "Why does everyone think I am trailing that geezer? No, I came to see you, Aunt Sal. I came about the prayer service."

"I'm sorry. Your granny just cannot be stopped."

"No, we're into it. I mean, it's a cheesy folk remedy, but couldn't hurt. Besides, this gives us something to do instead of just standing around and cleaning our skates."

"The girls really don't mind?" I say, studying her

"To tell the truth, I don't think anyone's really religious enough to care, one way or the other. But people want to do something, and Granny's friend seems like a pretty rad character."

"I'm warning you. It could get grisly. It sounds more like a séance than a church service."

"Even better," Reenie says, "People will be stoked." She takes the wire from her other ear and I notice that we've moved on to Jerry Lee Lewis—"Don't Put No Tombstone On My Grave." I catch a line—"All my life I've been a slave"—before she turns the music off and wraps the cord around the body of the iPod, holding it as primly as a girl used to hold a testament, everything she would ever need stored safely inside. This song in particular reminds me of Lorraine, with its mixture of martyrdom and bravado. Much more so than Buddy Holly, who certainly would not last even the standard two minutes and twenty seconds of a pop single with my formidable mother in a ring.

"So what do you want me to do?" she asks, stuffing the iPod in her backpack.

I am tempted to request her help with the garbage, but the shoes seem prohibitive. To my amazement, she pitches in without being asked, pulls a board out of the water, and drags it to the truck, careful to hold it well away from her clothing. Her heels make little hoof prints in the mud, so I know the day is warming up. If she stays here much longer, she won't be able to make it back to the trail without sinking in past her painted toenails.

"You know, Gabriella is semi-religious," Reenie comments. "She used to pray to the saints in the war, she said, one in particular, I can't remember which, someone who got her boobs chopped off for being a Christian."

"That sounds apocryphal," I say.

"No, this stuff is real. You can't get any more hard-core Catholic."

"You talked to Gabriella about this kind of thing?"

"She said God kicked Allah's ass before, back in the Crusades," she didn't see why he couldn't take the fucker down again."

"Then she is behind the war effort all the way?"

Reenie looks up and I see that Sharee is there after all, in the high forehead, the long narrow nose, the fiery determination to press her point home until it is lodged firmly in her opponent's chest cavity.

"Well, she was there, wasn't she? I'm telling you this because, you know, I think maybe she'd approve, even if the service isn't exactly Vatican II." Her face goes red and I recognize the familiar flare of her temper. But then she begins to cry instead, her frail eyelids all purple and tears caught like pearls in her long lashes.

"It could've been anyone," she says. "It could have been me."

I drop the square I'm working on, flick the blade of my pocket knife back into place, and stow it in my pocket, then walk over to try to give her the requisite embrace. I was close to Reenie when she was a kid, let her braid my hair and give me butterfly kisses, was known to hold her on my lap in a crowded back seat of a car or on the coffee-brown sectional sofa in her family room. But there is something about getting next to another adult woman that makes me uncomfortable. I think back to Mason's college-aged daughter and the trouble I had living with her for just a couple of months, the abrasive bright perfume of her pimple cream and tanning lotion, the drone of her relentless optimism, the pumped-up sales pitch of her voice.

When I touch Reenie, though, I feel something else, a sense of her frailty under all that bright skin. She smells of licorice and coffee, and her tightly muscled body is shivering, as if it can't contain its own energy.

"I didn't want to tell anyone," she says. "But me and Gigi were together, at least I think we were."

"You were involved with Gabriella," I say and guide her to the open truck bed, where I push back the wet boards and carpet snippets to offer her a seat.

"Just maybe the last three weeks. We hooked up before the exhibition bout. That one night we went out to the Beehive after practice and she started going on about the war, how no one who hadn't been there should be allowed to vote, how the towel heads smelled of diarrhea, how the women were really all nymphomaniacs under those veils and bedsheets. Then everyone else left. I think they were kind of pissed, actually. I mean, I hate that racist bullshit, too, but when someone's actually been there, what can you say?

"Then she asked me over to her place. You know, she lives over by the freeway in one of those duplexes. She took out this book of photos and she kept asking me which ones I liked, girls with veils over their faces and their tits exposed, blonds in harem costumes, belly dancers feeding their bangles into their twats. Her hand was next to mine on the book and when I saw it there, I realized how dark she was in comparison to me. I'd never get that brown if I tanned every day all summer. She asked me if I'd ever eaten a fig, and I said no, just a Fig Newton. Then she laughed and said she knew just what I needed to loosen me up for the season. She went into the kitchen and came back with a plate of these things that looked like tulip bulbs. 'Try one,' she told me, and knelt on my chair with one knee to split the fig open. It tasted like a mix of dates and caramel, sticky and sweet as the filling of a pecan pie. But before I was even done eating it she started to kiss me. 'Not much like a Fig Newton, is it?' she said."

While Reenie is telling me this, I feel the enclosed spaces of my body—groin, underarm, back of the knee—moisten with desire and anxiety. I had myself all aired out with the practical concerns of the day, and now I'm back where I started with Mayweather. I try to concentrate on Reenie. What is she telling me? That she's gay? That she's in love? That she's guilty? That she's suffering?

"The worst is, I can't even tell her mom or act like her girl-friend. I mean, I'm really just her teammate, like everyone else."

I put my arm around her shoulder and pull her tight with all my strength. "I know what you mean, honey," I say and stare into the pond, round as a rink, its surface dotted with lotus heads and shot with irregular rays of sun. It's painful to think of Reenie in a sexual situation, but I realize that at twenty-three, some experimentation is better than a protracted autoerotic vir-ginity. And to tell the truth, Gabriella is better than Chaz in my book. I'm uncertain, however, whether this is a matter of gender or sheer personality. Both are bullying, exploitative, and offen-sive, but Chaz is more proficient in his manipulations, by virtue of experience, if nothing else. Besides, Gabriella's current trou-bles reverse the situation, so that she is now the victim rather than the predator.

"You aren't going to tell Granny, are you?" Reenie says

"Of course not, but I wouldn't be surprised if she already knew."

"You don't think it's weird? I've never done that with another girl. I never even wanted to, but I don't know, Gigi is different. "

I move around restlessly and the gate of the truck bounces beneath us.

"You never did it, did you?"

I blink into the sun and scan my memory for the night over twenty years before, when I rolled around with a girlfriend on the floor of her dad's hunting cabin. For one weekend, we did it at every available spot in the vicinity: in a meadow of broom grass, up in the deer stand, in a cave by the creek. Then we never touched again, although we maintained a perfectly comfortable relationship when we were out with our friends. The trouble with girl-on-girl action, to judge from that weekend, is you never know when you are finished or when you began. I can't imagine living with that sort of open-endedness. Come to think of it, even my friendships with women seem to have drifted lately. The adultery that invaded my circle a couple of years ago didn't help, and now even Reenie's mom, who was a relative, after all, has begun eluding me. I seem to be shedding my patience along with my reproductive capacity, the elaborate rituals of womanhood dropping away from me like unnecessary petals, so that I can no longer remember which side the napkin goes on, why and when to apply makeup, what's in the recipe for red velvet cake, or how to politely decline an invitation to a lingerie party. I have no more time for discussing diets or Botox. I just want to live out the rest of my days drinking good beer, sticking close to nature, and running with my dogs, which makes me, I suppose, some kind of honorary man. The woman I should be growing old with, of course, never even got her full growth, I think, with

TRUDY LEWIS

a painful explosion of air in my chest. Sharee's pale freckled skin, like a piece of unbleached muslin; her small bare breasts shaking with laugher when she pulled down her shirt to display the broad bony gulley that was all she had for a cleavage; my hand on her hip, to show her the proper way to swing a hula hoop; her hand on my shoulder to illustrate the art of slow-dancing; our hands between our own legs, back when we were small enough to share the bathtub, peeling open the labia to reveal the damp, wrinkled pink buds hidden inside.

"Something similar," I say. "But it was just a blip on the screen. Still, I think of it as a valuable experience. Nothing to feel bad about, for sure."

"I guess you are going to tell me it's just a phase and I'm going to be married and pregnant and living in a subdivision in a couple of years."

"Honey, I have absolutely no idea. I don't know, is roller derby a fad or is it the defining moment of your physical glory? Is this thing with Gabriella a passing phase or the love of your life? God, maybe this whole benighted existence is just a painful growth spurt and we are going to be completely different creatures in the next life, people you wouldn't even talk to if you passed them on the street. Anyway, I'm kind of hoping that's the case."

And then something in the water moves, a fish flops out of the pond and seems to linger suspended in the air while the sun strokes its back with light. A turkey hawk dips and circles on the wind. Reenie pulls up the lapel of her jacket, wipes her face on the lining, reattaches her iPod, and gives me a kiss on the forehead. "Thanks, Aunt Sal," she says, and begins making her careful pigeon-toed progress back across the devastated field.

12

At four-thirty, there was a glare through the window, the computer screen bleached out, and Mayweather looked up from his work. He hadn't eaten for six hours, hadn't even gotten up to pee, and his bladder was extended to its full impressive capacity. He saved his work, stood up, stretched his wingspan on one side then the other until he heard his vertebrae crack, and wandered out the back door without bothering to look for his shoes. He had a superstitious dread of entering the bathroom with its frightening array of female products, so he just pissed right off the deck, into the herb garden, where a few bright leaves of basil were still recognizable despite the recent frost. Thinking of the crossed streams of the polluters, he adjusted his own spray so it caught the light, and glittered in a rainbow array of primary colors; he shifted the bright shaft from the herb garden to the grapevines, pretending it was a strobe. This was one hellishly long pee; it gave him time to think with satisfaction about the skill he'd employed in splicing the polluter's golden showers with the girls skating around the rink, Ellen tossing her cape in a heroic gesture, Reenie with her ass in the air and her fingers pressed to the floor of the rink; the Haddist calling off a jam, her insistent palms chopping into her well-outlined crotch. He even managed to get a gleam off the boards, so that they looked like they had been turned to liquid. Now no cable station in the country would show his masterpiece—he'd have to put it on YouTube or distribute it as porn. In fact, he had already started the process, separating out a clip to put up on his page, just to mark his progress: "Lady Park Ranger Goes Postal." In it, Sally looked like the Statue of Liberty—or to be more precise, the scaled-down replica Jared had seen in Cape Girardeau—her right arm raised to shoot her semi-automatic pistol into the air, her other hand dangling a couple of empty dog leashes. From this distance, her uniform had a military feel, clinging with authority to her breasts and hips. He wished that he could get a shot of one tit exposed, the fiery raw nipple pointed toward the viewer. In French iconography, Liberty was always at least partially top-less, but the Frogs had known well enough that America was too young and prudish to harbor gratuitous nudity in its public stat-uary, no matter what its private morals or its actual manhandling of the hungry and naked on its shores. Still, even clothed, Sally was formidable, her substantial hips planted on a slant and her long hair flying with static electricity. In the subsequent shot, he had the girls skating all around her, like the tigers in the Sambo story, faster and faster, as if they would churn themselves into butter if they could only pick up enough speed.

He looked down at his hand on his cock and saw that it was shaking. The editing process always filled him with adrenaline as he imagined himself in the position of Godard cutting *Breathless* down from two and a half hours to ninety minutes, each vio-lent stroke getting the guy closer to the radical aesthetic of the New Wave. Even the vanity projects Jared had done in Chicago had given him a thrill, as he sliced away at the incidentals and pretensions of overstuffed family movies and promotional shorts until he finally glimpsed the shape of some hovering avatar or brooding shade. Of course, not all of his efforts had been successful. The last guy, the owner of several tanning salons, had refused to pay Jared when he saw how the filmmaker had turned his business into some kind of joke: sunglasses affixed to the sunlamps, a row of orange girls straddling one of the beds as if they were riding a missile or conveyer belt, the owner himself posed in front of a "Get Away" billboard, so that it appeared a pineapple was growing out of his head. But most people, to tell the truth, were oblivious. They didn't care how they were represented; they just liked to see their own ugly mugs on film.

Jared zipped up, ran his hand under his shirt and over his chest, rubbing at his breastbone thoughtfully. Sally would be home soon, he figured, so he went to the fridge to check out the possibilities for dinner. The first thing to attract his attention was a beer, of course, a local brew from St. Louis, one that he'd sampled his first time drinking on Sally's deck. He wrapped his hand in his shirttail for leverage and screwed off the cap without an opener, then lifted the bottle to his lips, still standing there in open door of the refrigerator. Oktoberfest, reminiscent of fall camping trips and German philosophy. He thought of Nietzsche and Fassbinder, recalled his period of *Sturm und Drang* in film school, just at the peak of his affair with Ellen. Back then, he's had some idea that bagging his mentor's wife would elevate him to the status of an uberdude, when in reality all it did was turn him into a dick. He remembered distinctly the day that Ellen had announced that she was pregnant, and then the night, weeks later, when he told her she could edit out his love child for all it meant to him. He grabbed some lunchmeat, folded it over, tasted its tinny flavor against the yeast of the beer, thought of this morning's session, wondering if Sally was still on the pill.

Then he opened the defroster drawer and found a package of ground hamburger.

He turned on the oven, fished a pan out of the cupboard, opened the package, and rolled a wad of meat between his hands, relishing its cold raw pulp against his palms as he shaped meatballs after meatball and squashed them down into hamburger patties on the pan. On a whim, he cut up an onion and a couple of peppers, then added a few handfuls of frozen fries from the freezer. An indoor hobo's dinner for the road. He was just returning to the refrigerator for a second beer when the doorbell rang. He considered letting it go unanswered, but then decided it might be the UPS or a repairman of some kind, so he wandered toward the front of the A-frame, stubbing his toe on the wood-burning stove in passing and limping to the door.

Ellen stood there in a red leatherette coat belted over her neat waist, cleavage well represented in the open space between lapels. Mayweather's toe was still throbbing, but he managed to maintain his composure and ask her in. When he swung the door out, he saw that she had Etta with her. The little girl wore a leopard-skin hat, her yellow curls in doggy ears. She looked like Julie Christie in *Doctor Zhivago*; how could a four-year-old look like Julie Christie? She pushed into the doorway and grabbed Mayweather by the waist. He made as if to catch her, then realized that he hadn't washed his hands; the raw meat was still greasy on his palms and could cause something dire—what? Salmonella?—if transmitted. So he merely gripped Etta with his forearms as she pushed past him and began gliding over the floor. At first, he thought he was hallucinating as he saw her skim by without lifting her legs. Then he realized that her tennis shoes had wheels on them and she was actually skating across Sally's living room floor, dodging lamps and end tables, heading down the hall toward the guest room.

Meanwhile, Ellen was still standing at the door and staring at him. "What are you doing here?" she said, playing with the knot of her belt.

"The usual. Making a movie, I guess."

"If that's what you want to call it,"

"What about you?"

"I'm dropping Etta off for babysitting. I need to go in and visit Gabriella and I'm tired of waiting for Mr. Clean to reappear. God, Jared, I thought I was too old for you. Now I guess I'm just not ancient and horny enough for your taste."

"Either that or you missed your window of opportunity."

"Shouldn't Sally be home by now?"

"How would I know? You're the one who's exploiting her for free babysitting."

"And you're exploiting her for what? Free bed and board?"

"I wouldn't talk. Just because you've got a ring, it doesn't mean you're not a ho," Jared said, blushing. He remembered the screen saver, with Ellen's bare breasts hanging out over her skates, the nipples large as sand dollars and more relaxed than he had ever seen them.

Meanwhile, Etta had disappeared into the next room and Ellen pushed past him to follow the girl's progress. Mayweather hated the thought of Etta entering the bedroom with its scattered clothes and mangled sheets. He looked down to see whether he was actually dressed, which he was, thankfully, except for his shoes, which he still hadn't managed to locate.

"Sally lets me skate anywhere I want," Etta announced as Ellen grabbed her under the arms and pulled her away from the bedroom, not without making eyes at Sally's abandoned bra, a sensible nude number camouflaged against the wicker headboard.

To make amends, Jared offered Ellen one of Sally's beers, which, much to his surprise, she immediately accepted. Then they moved out to the deck, where Etta continued skating. Ellen couldn't sit still, standing up and continually steering Etta away from the stairs. She got her purse strap tangled in her belt. She stumbled off her heel and spilled a third of her beer. Then Jared told her to relax; he'd take care of it. He stood over the stairs like a goalie, leaning on the railing, his beer in one hand. Every time Etta would come near the stairs, he'd move in and nudge her with his leg, making a game of keeping her out of his territory.

"She's a wily thing, isn't she?" he said.

"Takes after her father."

"What's with that guy?"

"Can't seem to make up his mind about anything."

"So you really think I'm a pervert."

"Either that or just next door."

"You know, I'm sorry that I told you that about the operation. I didn't know what I was saying."

They both stared at Etta, her doggy ears swaying as she gripped the wooden slats of the railing and swung herself back and forth, like a prisoner behind bars.

"Well, I know you didn't mean it," Ellen said. "Really, how could you resist seeing how she would turn out?"

"Not bad. I like the thing you did with the mouth—very Scarlet Johansson. I like the name, too. How'd you get Chaz to agree?"

"That was hardly the sticking point."

"No, really, does he treat her OK? I mean, any different than the other kids?"

This was the first time Ellen appeared to worry about Etta overhearing them; she turned away from Jared and toward the girl, grasping the back of her neck as if to hide it from him, or, more likely, to emphasize its pale length inside the red collar of her coat. Etta was using a couple of deck chairs as an obstacle course, skating around and around them with increasing speed. She definitely had potential, Jared thought, and shivered to think what Chaz would make of it.

Jared paused, swung on the railing, moved up a step then down and lowered his voice. "I mean, he's aware?"

"We agree that it's a possibility," she said, turning back to face him. "But when we got back together, we decided to start with a clean slate."

"Which means I never happened, right?"

"Look, Jared, I'm exhausted. I'm going to sit down, all right? Roller derby is hell on the body. Even if I'm not one of the more aggressive players, I'm still hurting out there every night. Let me give you some advice: Don't wait until you're thirty-five to take up a contact sport." She slipped off her high-heeled clogs, rolled up her jeans, and showed him the bruises on her shins. One of them was as perfectly formed as a God's eye, with purple and yellow rays emanating from its dark center; another had the graphic pointillist dots of a comic strip. Jared badly wanted them both on film.

But before he could ask, Etta skated over and began to pat her mother's legs.

"Poor Mommy," she said. "Those bad girls hurt you."

"I'm fine, sweetheart. It's all part of the game."

"Yeah, your mom is super tough and limber. She can take the heat."

Etta looked up at Mayweather, yellow sparks flaring in the irises of her hazel eyes. "How come you never skate?" she asked.

"I'm not that tough," he said. "Besides, they tell me it's a women's team."

"I think you're scared," she told him, skating closer to his post at the head of the stairs and trying to catch him off guard. "My dad says you're too scared to play."

Jared felt his breath leave his body; his gut was punctured, the air escaping rapidly, a shred of dignity rising up in his throat and getting caught between his teeth. He ran his tongue over his incisors. He looked at Ellen laughing in the deck chair, rubbing at the backs of her calves with pleasure. How could he possibly respond?

"Take that back or I'll hunt you down and put dog poop in your skates," he said, chasing Etta from the stairs. She glided away, laughing, then crouched down to pick up a handful of leaves and fling it in his general direction. The smell of mulch and hay and spicebush rose in the air, and he couldn't help marveling at her coordination, remarkable in a four-year-old.

"You tell him," Ellen said, leaning back in her chair, as if her daughter had relieved her of the objectionable job of reprimanding Mayweather. She downed her beer, then let out a tiny hesitant hiccup and announced that she was off to the hospital. He could keep an eye on Etta until Sally returned.

Mayweather stared in amazement. Was this a test? "So, does she come with any kind of gear?" he asked.

"Nope. No stroller, no diapers, no sippy cups. She's all yours, Jared. A complete free-standing girl."

13

When I walk in the door at six p.m., Etta is smearing ketchup on Mayweather's face and Di and Rye are sitting up begging for hamburger. There's a game of Candy Land spread out on the coffee table, dimes and quarters in two piles. I go to the bedroom, rip off my uniform, and button myself up into my flannels, then come out and sit down at the computer without speaking.

"Hey, you," Mayweather says. "There's grub on the stove."

But I go straight to my e-mail and see with horror that 119 messages have accumulated in my account. Do I read them one by one or is it time to get selective? I recognize a few names: Chaz, my boss Guy Dempsey, the editor of the paper, and of course, Lorraine, who has taken to the virtual communication with a gusto rarely seen in senior citizens. I know I shouldn't do it, but I start with her. She has alerted the churches and the media, bought 150 vigil candles in cardboard holders, recruited church ladies to bring jars of sweetened iced tea and plates of oatmeal and refrigerator cookies. She wants to know if I'll say a few words to introduce Mariah, this charismatic gospel woman whom I have never met. She wants to know if I'll wear something decent. Can I put up signs in the park to direct people to the proper location? What is the location, anyway? The clearing by the natural bridge where we've held those prayer breakfasts in the past? I close the e-mail without responding. What a time for a high-profile event out at the Karst, when I'm not certain I'm even employed there anymore. Just to be sure, I open Guy Dempsey's e-mail next. It seems to take several years for the message to appear, as the Webscape logo at the right of my screen glows, mysterious multicolor matter swirling around inside its sphere like the currents inside a crystal ball conspiring to tell my future. In this long thirty seconds, I can hear Mayweather and Etta laughing on the sofa. She claims he owes her a quarter, and I realize that they're actually gambling over Candy Land. My head throbs and I am so thirsty that my tongue feels like a rye cracker in my mouth. I know I should reprimand them, but I can't even speak, I'm so exhausted from dragging trash and anticipating the legal repercussions of my actions. In the seconds before the message appears, I live a whole alternate life: a husband, a child, a respectable job in the private sphere where I'm never even tempted into believing that I'm doing something meaningful for the general good. Then the message appears and my gut drops into my lap. Dempsey apologizes, but he thinks he needs to dismiss me, effective next week. I may have noticed that there is a big stink in the papers, and an investigative blogger has posted a link to a certain incriminating video on YouTube. I turn to look at Mayweather, but there isn't the slightest bit of guilt on his ripe, unshaven face. He probably thinks he's making me into a folk hero, and expects me to thank him for the exposure.

I open up the other e-mails in a jumble, looking for the link. Most of them are actually letters to the paper, CC'd to me at my work address. The slow pace of the high-speed Internet connection is excruciating; I could move through them more quickly if they were just letters lying on my desk. One man in the first ward congratulates me for sticking it to the developers, who have gotten grabby lately. A schoolteacher takes the opportunity to deliver a lecture on gun safety. A group of Islamic women writes in objecting to the mockery of their faith in Gigi's roller derby costume and announces that they will be at the prayer service in full force to conduct a peaceful protest. A disabled vet writes in about the plight of returning warriors and post-traumatic stress syndrome. A police officer says this is exactly the reason park rangers shouldn't be allowed to carry guns. The president of the local Peace Coalition draws a parallel to America's toleration of torture, Lynndie England and Abu Ghraib. A representative from the growing Hispanic community on the north side of town expresses sympathy for Gabriella's case and claims that there has been scant media attention for the role of Hispanic Americans in Operation Desert Storm. An amateur soccer player writes in to say that he had to give up the sport because he had no health insurance and was afraid that that he'd suffer a serious accident like Gabriella's. Without universal health coverage, how can we expect Americans to be more active? I put my hands on either side of my head and rest my forehead on the computer keyboard, depressing several random keys. The whole world is screaming with need. And this is just one little town's worth of trouble. My limbs are shaking and I'm suddenly cold in the warm house. I don't know what I'm afraid of, since I've already been fired. I just keep moving through the e-mails, pausing only long enough to look for the link, so that I'm not really reading anymore, but only flashing through, glancing at a few words in each message. Zoning laws, women in the military, deterioration of the public park service, increasing use of police tasers, a lack of opportunities for women in sports. Then I see it, a line of blue code at the bottom of an e-mail about out-of-control law enforcement. One citizen, at least, has his eyes open. The link has an otherworldly attraction for me. I press into it with unnecessary force, confirming the letter writer's view of my unwonted aggression. There is a swollen pause, and the black YouTube screen appears on the monitor, scarcely bigger than a square of mirror in a makeup compact, 4.56 minutes of film, a tiny fraction of my life. I wonder if I can actually sit through it, in this state. I press for sound, and hear a crackling anthem sung in a black woman's voice, something I don't recognize, *You've got to roll with me, Henry, all night long.* And to my surprise, what I see isn't the park, but the roller derby, with the girls streaming past, Gigi Haddist in the lead in her star helmet, loincloth flying, her dark headscarf forming a shadow under her helmet as she veers into an opponent's orbit and elbows the girl headlong into the partition. At my feet, I feel Di and Rye fighting for the space beneath the computer desk. I reach down and touch them for comfort, and when I do, I feel another presence at my back, Mayweather, probably cued in by the music, stands behind me rubbing my shoulders, giving me some idea of just how bad this is going to be. My muscles didn't even hurt before, but now the pain ripples up in waves, and I touch his hand to guide him away from the worst of it.

"I wanted to show you first," he says, "But I was in a fevered state." He rubs my shoulder with more force, pinching a nerve, so that I have to stop myself from crying out. Meanwhile, Etta has come over and is trying to sit in my lap and he begins a disquisition on her spiritual godmother, Etta James, who is singing in the background. Etta was too hot for the airwaves, apparently, too sick for the for those FCC pricks, and the censors forced her to change the lyrics, so that "Roll With Me, Henry" became "Dance with Me, Henry," a disgrace to dirty-minded blues singers everywhere. On the screen, the polluters appear out of

context and pee over the rink. The girls keep skating, Chaz dis-
putes with a ref under the disco ball, his face awash with green
and purple, Ellen pops in a mouth guard then adjusts her cleavage, and I sit in my emcee booth and blow on the microphone.
Etta's tone becomes threatening as she instructs Henry on his
obligations to the flesh.

"Well, this is just a trailer, really."

"That's what I'm afraid of," I say, while the singer's little name-
sake sits, a pleasant weight on my lap, and neither of us stops
her from watching. Now I see myself in the forest, the green of
my uniform distinct amid the turning leaves, my gun pointed
toward the man on the ground and the dogs pressing their noses
between his legs. I can hardly stand to watch myself on film, in
the best of situations, and this time I have much more to worry
about than just my looks. It's not the gun that shames me, really.
It's the expression on my face, an inhuman rage that leaves my
features unrecognizable in a pure raw surge of indignation. And
even though I was there, I am afraid the outcome will be different this time, that the woman on the screen will shoot the
men, causing irreparable damage to her reputation and her soul.
Something about Etta's smooth cheek against mine fills me with
foreboding and I scoot her off my lap, ask her to go fetch my
purse, and find some mints in the zipper compartment. All without taking my eyes from the woman in uniform, who seems to
have bewitched me, her flying hair, her unforgiving profile, her
flushed cheeks. This must be why I've been such an isolationist
all these years, never gotten pregnant, had a close girlfriend, or
fallen hopelessly in love. From the proper distance, I am the best
of women: self-sufficient, respectful, good-humored, and kind.
But once my boundaries have been broken into, my carefully
constructed identity cracks open and this raging fury appears.
In these moments, I know a power I never feel in my ordinary

plodding existence. I am ruthless, like Chaz; promiscuous, like Ellen. I am careless, like Mayweather, as indestructible as an unattached young man out on a tear. Looking at the screen in fascination, I realize that this is the self I love, the angry woman with the gun, exuding a strange and otherworldly beauty. The other one, with her hesitations and insecurities, holds no interest for me, just as she never held much appeal for my mother or sister. It's the rage that makes me visible, and without it I am just a collection of indifferent body parts seeking an orbit.

I look behind me and see that Mayweather is fascinated too—with me, with the roller rink, with his work?—there is probably no distinction for him in this moment. That must be why he woke me up to screw this morning; he'd just seen the whole incident again, then pieced it into the shape of his own film. After which, he felt as if he might as well complete the fantasy of total domination of his visual field by occupying me too. If I lose the job and the gun will he ever be interested in me again?

"I'm fired," I say, and the rage flares up into my temples, obscuring the shame. After this, what will there be to separate me from other women? Only my failure to keep a husband, bear a child, or insert myself into some engrossing drama between powerful men. "Do you think it's a coincidence that this happens two hours and fifteen minutes after you post your pee party film?"

"Really, Sally. People always have to have some suspect reason for coming to art. You know, it's titillation, it's scandal, it's violence, it's porn. Do you think the Coen brothers are really interested in murder? No, it's just a crude mechanism to focus your attention so you'll sit there staring at the way the light drifts through the bullet holes in the door. What do we have, two hundred hits already?"

I log out and revert to the screen saver; he obviously can't focus when his own work is on the screen. "I said do you think this little piece of yellow journalism had anything to do with me getting the a?"

"Well, Ranger, you're the one who did it, aren't you? If you feel so bad about other people seeing it, maybe you shouldn't have let it rip in the first place."

"You seemed pretty excited about it at the time."

"Hey, I personally think it was righteous. I'm just saying."

"Jared, I don't know who is stupider, you or me. You keep plugging away at the film-making with no success or encouragement and I keep letting you screw with me."

His face turns pink under the stubble, but he doesn't miss a beat. "I'm definitely stupider," he says. "Because at least you are getting laid."

The nasal passages high up in my head fill with tears and I know I have to accelerate to keep myself going. "I'm telling you, your antics have consequences. The rest of the universe doesn't exist just to give you something to look at."

He flicks his eyes over me, like he is dismissing my visual interest with a wave of his long eyelashes. "Why are you here, then?"

"I don't know, Jared, because it's my house? Because it's my computer, because it's my job, because it's my time and my body and my fucking long-standing babysitting appointment and you are just a deadbeat and freeloader on the bare back of my existence?"

I look up with horror. This is almost as bad as pulling a gun on the polluters. I've never fought with Mayweather before, never asked him to vacuum the floor or accompany me to a boring family event, never upbraided him for his poor hygiene or his fluid sense of time and fidelity. This not asking, a gilded restraint painted onto my limbs and features, makes me feel brave and sexy, somehow aligned with the forces of youth and chaos instead of the stultifying strictures of ownership and age.

"You want me to take down the film?" he says.

In the next room, Etta is opening the refrigerator, looking for more treats. Her skating shoes clatter against the kitchen tile. She calls to the dogs to share her bounty with them, compliments their manners and their fur.

"Are you saying you'll do it if I ask?"

We must stand like that for thirty seconds, longer than the Internet delay, longer than the opening sequence of the film, longer, it seems, than it took me to decide I'd sleep with him all those years ago, when he was truly minor and not just a rootless young man foundering on his way to middle age. His beard is lighter than the hair on his head, glinting on his cheeks like a mask of pollen and mirroring the flecks of hazel in his brown eyes.

"Just ask already," he says. "And then we'll both know."

14

Mayweather didn't relish the moment of Ellen's return, but promptly at six forty-five, she stood in the doorway, swinging her purse on her shoulder and eyeing Sally up and down, as if to assess whether a woman of her age could still strike a spark. Sally, for her part, stared right back, remarkably unselfconscious in her blue flannel PJs printed with elks and pines, her hair twisted into a clip at the back of her head, odd tufts standing up here and there suggesting coital activity or restless sleep. She had been crying, her long green eyes rimmed in pink. There was a smallish patch of acne on her left cheek, probably aggravated by Mayweather's beard, he realized, as he inadvertently touched his hand to his chin, and a streak of white moisturizer or sunscreen clung to her neck.

"S or M?" Ellen said. "I'm taking a poll."

"You saw the YouTube," Sally offered, giving Mayweather a look.

"One of the girls had her phone at the hospital and she pulled it up for me. I didn't know you had it in you."

"Surprise," Sally said, and he couldn't tell if she was offended.

"What did they think?" Mayweather asked as Etta came up behind him and caught her mother around the waist, pulling at the belt of her red coat.

"Well, Marilyn and Courtney were impressed. Reenie decided she needed to adjust her form on the curves, Annie said she looked fat, and Sarah thought the thing ought to be on X-Tube, considering all the pissing dicks."

"And I thought it was tastefully done," Mayweather said.

"Mommy, Jared put me in his film." Etta told her, and Ellen raised a tweezed eyebrow.

"The music, the music, Ellen. You remember Etta James, don't you? Boonslick Country Blues Hour, Sunday afternoons three to five, red hots and whiskey, somewhere around the year ought three?"

Ellen blushed, pink flooding the sensitive area supported by her high cheekbones. "Not much," she said.

"Anyway, by some coincidence, Etta here has the same name. So I decided to dedicate the soundtrack to her."

"Sweet," Ellen said. "I guess that means she'll be collecting royalties."

"I'll be in touch about that," Mayweather said, wondering if it wouldn't be appropriate for him to start some nominal little fund for Etta, so that, when the time came, she would be able to finance her inevitable rebellion from Chaz. He hoped it would be a good one, something involving nudity and conceptual art on multiple continents. The thought startled him. How was he going to start a slush fund for his daughter when he could hardly stretch his budget to cover his own Beam?

"I think you may run into some trouble there," Ellen said. "The last time we tried to access the film, someone had taken it down. Maybe the censors got to you again, huh, buddy?"

Mayweather looked to Sally, whose face seemed to leap into

another dimension, her smile pushing her features into deeper relief.

"No, I took it down myself," he said. "That was just a sneak preview, anyway. I'm not finished yet."

"Oh?" Ellen said. "It's hard to imagine how much more damage you could actually do."

Mayweather was attempting to piece together an argument about the destructive nature of art when Sally interrupted his thoughts.

"What about Gabriella? Any news?"

"Still nothing," Ellen said. "Once she hits the three-day mark, her chances of full recovery are rapidly reduced."

"And her mother?"

"She's got a war room set up over at the VA, knitting needles, mariachi music, voodoo dolls, the works. Poor lady. She is in complete denial, talks to the girl in Spanish day and night. Luckily, Lorraine is hanging in there keeping her company."

"Well, that's got to be a distraction anyway," Sally said. "I guess we'll see you out at the prayer meeting tomorrow night?"

"Actually, Chaz and I are agnostic, but this psychic hoedown sounds too good to miss."

"Bring this little girl with you," Sally said, reaching over and squeezing Etta's shoulder. "I didn't get my fix tonight. "

"She rules Candy Land, by the way," Mayweather said, moving toward the girl, uncertain of the likelihood of a hug or kiss. The air all around her was bright with electricity. He could feel it on his skin. He could even hear it, a sound like locusts luring him to another reality. He hesitated, thinking that Ellen might stop him if he got too close. Then Etta grabbed his leg, swung around him, and peeked out the other side.

"I beat Jared," she said. "I beat him out of three quarters"

"Wow, sweetheart!" Ellen said. "And that's hard to do. I don't think I've been able to beat three quarters out of the guy the whole time I've known him."

Mayweather felt the blow in his solar plexus and looked to see if there was any forgiveness in her expression. Ellen's face had recovered its usual color and she was as beautiful as she'd been five years ago, before crossing the threshold into her thirties, only now there was a kind of sharpening of the angles, more presence and less glow. How could he blame her for being angry? He had never offered her anything, not a movie ticket or a flower or a massage. In fact, the only thing he had ever given her was Etta, and even that he had tried to take away.

"You got me," he said, remembering that he had said the same thing to her yesterday. In fact, he seemed to be saying it over and over, like a kid playing war, falling down and dying dramatically, only to get up and die again.

"Sweetheart, looks like everyone's got you. That's the problem." She turned to Sally, as if she had been waiting for this all along. "Look, you are a nice lady and I wish the best for you. But you don't seem to have any instinct for self-preservation. You just lost your husband and probably your job, too, and now you are ready to hook up with a dope-smoking deadbeat who will siphon the rest of your savings before he self-destructs or moves on to the next mother substitute down the line."

"Is that what Chaz is telling you?" Jared asked, quickly enough to spare Sally the embarrassment of responding and himself the pain of hearing what she might have to say.

"Chaz doesn't have to tell me anything. I've got no illusions. When I was pregnant with Etta, something just clicked, and I knew I would do whatever it took to get the best dad for my kids. And let's see, who has more to offer, you or Chaz? On the one hand we've got a historical landmark house, stock portfolio, great medical insurance, and stable family life, and on the other we've got, oh yes, a voyeur and alcoholic with an empty wallet and a heavy gut."

"Is that why you let him put you on the roller derby team and dress up in that ridiculous evil outfit? Is that why he's got your tits up on the screen saver for everyone to see? What kind of vibe does that send to Etta, do you think?"

"What's the matter, Roman Polanski, you suddenly develop a moral code? Anyway, look at what you did to Sally. That's about a hundred times worse."

"I took the film down. I took it down already. What more do you people want from me?"

"Nothing," Ellen said. "I want nothing from you, which is damn lucky, considering that's all you've got to give." Then she reached down and picked up Etta so that the girl's legs dangled, the wheels on her shoes spinning in air.

After they left, Jared just stood there, staring at the door and wishing it had some visible bullet holes for him to film through. He could feel Sally behind him, the warmth of her body on his back, so that he could sense her shape even though she came short of actually touching him. As much as he wanted to turn and pull her to him, he just couldn't do it. So he commented, in a tense tone without inflection, that he thought he would look in on practice at the roller rink.

"If you can wait ten minutes, I'll give you a ride," Sally said.

She disappeared upstairs and he went into the kitchen for another beer, idly wondering whether he was literally an alcoholic. He preferred to think of his current state as a general dissipation rather than a servile dependence. However, he had noticed that one benefit of his weight gain was an increased capacity, so that he could drink an entire six-pack without significant cognitive or motor impairment. If anyone asked, he could say that was the project he had been working on for the past four years. He sat on the sofa, crossed his leg over his knee, peeled a bit of rubber off the bottom of his shoe, and wondered if he'd made the right decision by coming back to Boonslick, where he had so much unfinished history. At first, the anonymity of Chicago had been exhilarating, the lake and the skyscrapers, the freaks and commuters; never a lack of visual stimulation, that was for sure. Then he lost one girlfriend and another. He made significant starts on sixteen films without finishing a single one. He ran out of vanity video gigs and had to look for a humbler means of support. He finally took a job prepping vegetables in a Mexican restaurant, but he cut his hand a week and a half into his tenure and had to quit on the spot, his blood dripping a surprising shade of purple on a translucent mound of onions. Because he didn't have insurance, he couldn't go to the emergency room, and so stitched the cut up himself with catgut provided by his roommate, a virtual stranger whom he had located through an ad in *The Reader*.

One night, his hand infected and his brain afire, sitting slumped and shivering by the radiator in a polyester cowboy shirt and a thin denim jacket, he decided he couldn't take it anymore; the bums in Boonslick had it better, warm weather nine months of the year, plenty of opportunity for temp labor, cheap rent, an excellent Salvation Army, friends who would feed you on a whim and girls who would fuck you in a heartbeat. He could always go back. Why not? He still had contacts, a mother, a father substitute, a couple of stable ex-girlfriends, and even, if rumor was correct, a daughter who must be walking and talking by now. The apartment building, in shady but cheap Humboldt Park, smelled of curry and sour milk and some powerful nuclear-strength pesticide. He was lucky, he guessed, that he only shared with one roommate. There were whole families of Mexican, Indian, and Arab immigrants living in some of the

studio apartments below. Mayweather was, at this point, surviv-
ing on refried beans and tortillas—cheese was a luxury he could
rarely afford—and he kept everything in the refrigerator with the
beer, since that was the only space free of cockroaches. He had
known cockroaches in Boonslick, of course, but they were of a
more genteel variety, respecting the boundary of roach powder
around his mattress and waiting respectfully until lights-out to
do their scavenging. Here, he felt the insects crawl over his face
and legs in the night, heard them crack underfoot if he got up
to piss, and watched them hard at work, shamelessly scrounging
crumbs in the clear light of day.

Still, he was able, in good moments, when the sun shone
through the windows and onto the bare blond floorboards
worn to gray splinters at the edges, to think of this place as his
Walden, where he had gone to live deliberately, and to discover
who he was while living in isolation from everything that had
ever known. He remembered one day in particular with special pleasure, it was summer and the little kids were playing in
the trashed-out courtyard, blowing soap bubbles that drifted
up on the wind and took on the colors of sky and cloud before
breaking against the pane of his open window and shattering
amidst the babble of unrecognizable languages. But the week
he cut his hand, it was February, and the snow still sat piled in
the courtyard, an ugly gray shade of graphite that defied the
inroads of light. In Boonslick, he knew, you could smell spring
by now, even if you could not yet produce any visual evidence
of its return. Chaz would be screening his annual classic film
festival, in protest of the declining quality of the Oscars, and
Sally would be clearing the trails of limbs and branches that had
fallen during the winter. He could almost see Ellen taking off
her sweater and shrugging into a particular red silk blouse with
gaps between the buttons; he could picture his mother sitting

out on the screened-in porch with coffee and cigarettes, flicking her lighter with satisfaction and watching for the cardinals and blue jays, who were already sending out feelers of song. Thinking of his mother, Mayweather experienced a tremor of guilt. He knew she would hate to see him in this state, the boy she had struggled so hard to raise, her only son, who, in spite of their basically solid connection, had rarely given her reason to be pleased. This place would seem like a deliberate mockery of her labor. But she couldn't stop him. Really, no one could.

His head and his hand were indistinguishable now, and in his mind little paisley modules of a sickly pink and blue broke, reconfigured, and broke again, like the fluorescent penicillin cells in his high school biology textbook. Penicillin, that was what he needed. He would have to go to the emergency room to get some, even if he couldn't pay. He remembered seeing a hospital somewhere nearby—Norweigan American Hospital. He found his red cowboy boots, now stained with the salt from the snowy streets, and struggled to drag them onto his feet with one hand. He finally had to stand up, and, leaning against the kitchen counter, and just stomp down hard.

His injured hand—the left—flared with a white-hot agony. He was sure, in his fevered state, that he could lift it to the doorframe and torch the whole apartment building with its flame. Could he possibly get a glove over the thing? He had been avoiding looking at it all evening, but there it was, the incision starting over his middle finger and stretching down into his palm, the jagged stitches, like the visual image of a sound track or an EKG. The flesh itself was pink and swollen, a few blue lines running all the way onto the back of his hand. He remembered reading that Henry Thoreau's older brother had died from a cut he'd gotten shaving. Otherwise, the guy would probably have been the literary genius in the family, with old Henry following as sloppy seconds several steps behind. That would just be Mayweather's luck, to die of some freak injury before he could completely piss away his promise. Of course, there was some glory in such a death, but Mayweather realized, with some surprise, that he would rather live and risk a long-term experiment with failure than die prematurely before riding out his fate. He winced as he pulled on a glove, each of its fibers seeming to ignite against his flesh. He didn't want to get frostbite, on top of everything else. As he passed through the halls, he smelled cigarettes mixed with coffee grounds and rich spices. His hunger rolled over into nausea, and he touched the banister to steady himself, imagining, in his fevered state, that the paint blisters were actually the corpses of cockroaches that had been painted over in haste. He reached into his pocket, lifted his el pass to the light, and realized that it had expired, and he didn't have a two twenty-five to his name. Of course, he could always hitch, but this was not so easy in Chicago, where drivers were more suspicious than your run-of-the-mill suburbanites and hillbillies.

At the bottom of the stairs, he saw one of his neighbors, an Arabic man with a heavy beard, holding his little daughter by the hand. The girl wore a pink quilted jacket patched with silver electrical tape and ate dried fruit out of a bag. Her head was covered with a black wool scarf, making a strange contrast with the fluorescent polyurethane pink of her jacket, which swirled, in his imagination, with psychedelic patterns of frost and dew. Mayweather held up his injured hand in greeting, then ripped off the glove to provide a visual aid, feeling as if his palm and fingers were being scoured with steel wool in the process.

"I need to get to the doctor's man, I need to get on the el. Do you have some change?"

The man reached into his breast pocket, as if he was pulling out a gun or a business card, and handed Mayweather his el ticket, the electronic strip gleaming in the dark, like some secret code.

"Thanks, man. Thanks, I owe you," Mayweather said, as he turned toward the station, where he read the card in the machine and saw that there were three rides left—a wealth of generosity, given the man's apparent cash-strapped state. Now that Mayweather thought of it, he realized that he had never seen the man and his little daughter again.

Sally touched his head, pushed his hair around, so that his scalp longed to be scratched clean of memory.

"Are you coming?" she said.

Mayweather looked at his left hand resting on his knee and turned it over to see the scar stretching down from the middle finger and into the palm, a white raised ribbon bisecting his heart line, and decided that he would.

15

After that, I have no idea how to brooch a conversation with Mayweather, so we just ride in silence until he switches the radio on to Boonslick Country and the Louvin Brothers' three-part harmony springs forth a cappella from the airwaves. I can see that this is an improvement, because he begins to sing along, pounding out the rhythm on his knee and then on mine. I look at him out of the corner of my eye, smile, take the turn back into town and wait until I hit the next intersection to touch his leg in return.

"OK?"

"If you don't mind harboring a deadbeat dad."

"I've harbored worse," I say, and wonder if this means he plans on staying.

At the Empire, I park in the lot, noticing that the honey locusts have lost all their yellow leaves, which are now scattered like shorn curls around the pavement, even though many of the long curved pods still cling to the trees. I pick one and sample its texture, its casing smooth as the skin of a leather pump against my fingertips, its point sharp as a blade on my palm. A small crowd has gathered in the lighted entrance to the rink, a group of women, their heads covered in hoods or scarves, some of them carrying large cardboard signs. As we approach, I see that they are, in general, very young, approximately the age of the Boonslick Bombers, and their scarves are bright with polka dots or geometric shapes, their long stylish tunics more futuristic than archaic, like the garb of science fiction queens. As we get closer, I can see the lettering on the signs: "People of the Book Unite!" "Don't Tread on My Veil and I Won't Step on Your Flag," "Make Hajj, Not War."

Behind me, Mayweather already has his camera out and I wonder if they will object. But they seem very comfortable, laughing and jarring one another, playing with their scarves like you would see a Western girl playing with her hair. One of them approaches me, offers me a flyer for an open house at the local mosque, all faiths welcome, and tells me that she wishes we would think more carefully about the political implications of our show. We may not be aware, but the FBI has placed their mosque under investigation, with no provocation but a few phone calls to old friends. Their computers have been confiscated and their imam is forbidden to leave the city, even to visit friends and relatives in neighboring towns. Now that she mentions this, I seem to remember some commentary in the paper a couple of weeks ago. Every negative image of Islam pushes the US closer to nativist hysteria and racial profiling, she continues, reminding me of the anti-German business policies and Japanese Internment Camps of WWII.

I admit that I harbor considerable skepticism about the prospects of a peaceful and politically responsible roller derby. But I take the girl's flyer politely, express my concern about the investigation, say that they are welcome at the prayer service, and apologize for any cultural insensitivity on the part of our team.

I look back to see how Mayweather is faring, and see him awash in swaths of bright-colored cloth. The women, although they do not actually touch him, swarm around asking to look at his camera, and the wind blows their long veils across his body and over his face. I feel an unaccustomed jealousy arise from my lizard brain and flood the sensitive area behind my ears. I hate to think that this will become a regular feature of my emotional repertoire. But Jared pulls away, grabs my hand, opens the door to the rink and pushes me through it, so that we are in a different space entirely, the heat and glare of harsh fluorescent lights, the sweet-and-sour smell of sweat mixed with popcorn and perfume.

Inside, the girls aren't skating, but sitting around on benches instead, their arms braced behind them and their skates restlessly pawing the ground at their feet. A few of them have brought their children, the younger ones walking around chewing toys or drinking from sippy cups, and the older ones playing on the video games in the far corner of the building. The disco balls over the rink are unlit, and the house music is off for once, so that the smallest noise is magnified between the high ceiling and the concrete walls. Raven Pillage wanders between the benches as if they are pews, holding a clipboard and wearing a whistle, her hair pulled off her face in a pink sequined headband, golden freckles glowing over the bridge of her nose. And Lorraine is there, too, passing out what appear to be homemade brownies on a big Mexican platter, a souvenir of my brother's Acapulco cruise a half-dozen years ago. She is in her element now, no cane in sight, her head bobbing with affirmation. When she sees us, she gives away the last brownie, holds the platter over her head, and starts waving it around like the silver trophy at Wimbledon. The girls cheer, for me or for Mayweather, it isn't clear which.

"We're talking committees," Reenie informs me. "Do you want to be on Regulations or Merch?"

Mayweather, who has moved from one sort of temptation to its opposite, stands directly above Britney Spearhead and stares deep into the negative space of her cleavage. The world, I realize, will never stop providing him with beautiful girls at which to direct his gaze. Do I really want to follow his camera wherever it takes me?

"Aunt Sal, we're making the break. We're going to join the Women's Flat Track Derby Association."

"When did this happen?" I say.

"Well, you know." Annie Warhaul replies. "Lots of free time sitting around that hospital room."

Lorraine nods her head energetically as she hitches up her pants legs and sits down on a bench, her tiny bowed legs hardly reaching the floor in their white tennis shoes with red-and-blue striped laces. Next thing I know, she will be wanting to get up on skates herself. I stare at the T-shirt she's wearing, an American flag pattern cut on the bias, so that the stripes run across her lumpy chest and the stars swoop down over one shoulder. The bright print overwhelms the pale speckled flesh of her complexion, making it look like she is already dead and lying in state. I have seen several people wearing these creations, all of them over sixty. I myself am old enough to remember when wearing the flag was an act of dissent, so naturally I'm confused about how it has become a badge of patriotism. Although in Lorraine's case, I can't tell if it is a political statement or just a random provocation.

"Besides, you are an inspiration, sista," Marilyn Monsoon adds. "Schooling the man like that."

"I hear you, "Megan Foxhole says. "Those guys definitely didn't know what kind of roller-bitch they were messing with."

"You're forgetting, I'm the man, girls," I say. "And it's these assholes who are the gangstas."

"Whatever, Ranger. You can lead my platoon whenever you want."

"Yeah, you are definitely a Mean Green Queen"

And one girl even asks me to sign her belly with a Sharpie, an act I perform as carefully as an appendectomy, while feeling Mayweather's eyes on my hand.

Meanwhile, Mayweather too comes in for his share of praise. Reenie says she had no idea he could actually film a movie that could attract so many hits and a number of the Bombers ask if he will make videos of them in action to put up on their Facebook pages. He agrees, good-naturedly, but warns them that he insists on having artistic control of the project, which may mean that they turn out looking a little more like *Ugly Betty* than Angelina Jolie.

While he is talking with them, Lorraine comes over and squeezes my arm with her claw, admiring the biceps, which had in fact grown considerably since I took the job with the park system. I can't help but wonder whether it will deteriorate back to its pre-law enforcement state once I've been dismissed. Even now, Lorraine's rough matter-of-fact touch fills me with a horrible love, and turns me back into the shy girl who watched her mother's young mobile face for signs of affection or temper, which often dovetailed into one other without warning or transition.

"I didn't know you had it in you, Sally," she says. And that may be it, all of the approval and delayed gratification that is due to me in this life. It sits on my skin like the glitter makeup all the girls are wearing, and I think it may well be worth losing my job and my savings, not to mention my morality and self-respect.

"Now I won't be afraid to meet my Maker when he rings me up," she declares. It's true, she's had "Bringing in the Sheaves" installed as her ring tone and so she really is ready to depart at any time.

Once the greetings are completed, Raven Pillage returns to her talk, explaining that the girls need to take control of their own labor if they want to get anywhere in life. It's not just about roller derby, she says; it's about taking responsibility and standing up to the powers that be. This is a new generation, after all, DIY all the way. As she talks, Reenie's ponytail bobs up and down and her hands mold the air like she is pulling arguments out of the ether, weaving them together, then cutting them apart with a sharp chop like the one she delivers to call off a jam.

The Bombers nod. One of them comments that she wonders why they are paying dues to the league instead of getting paid themselves. All they get out of the deal, really, is free beer and hot dogs along with their twenty-dollar costume allowance. Another says that Gabriella's accident made her think about the whole insurance issue. What would happen if Gigi didn't have the vet's insurance plan? Would her family be left to pay the bill on their own? Britney Spearhead lifts her deceptively delicate arm into the air, elbow first, as if she's knocking out an opponent, to lodge her own complaint. Chaz has told her repeatedly that she's not allowed to wear her roller derby costume without his permission—to the bars, for example, or to her Wiccan festivals. He keeps saying that he owns her image. How can that be?

"Point of law," Raven says. "If we join the WFTD, we have to be majority-owned by skaters. And two-thirds managed by them too. So that means more independence but more commitment, too."

After this, there is a general flood of complaints, some of them surely irrelevant: the quality of the beer, the bad lighting in the rink, the way that the Bawdy Bagger always gets to play pivot, even though she is too old and slow. They all agree that they hate the suggestive comments Chaz makes to them, the way he leers over them in the commercials, like they are his hos to distribute as he pleases, even though a third of them are lesbian, and most of the rest are married or otherwise engaged.

"It's not even like I think he's really interested in hooking up. I mean, if he was just horny, I could respect that. It's more this attitude where he wants people to know he can hit our trim any time he likes."

"Yeah, but he did get us that spot in the *Beacon*."

"And he convinced my folks that I wouldn't have to drop out of college to play."

"Still, that man is seven Sundays worth of bad news," warns Lorraine, who can't stand to be left out of any conversation.

"Would it be worth it to you to do all the work?" Reenie says. "You wouldn't get much of a paycheck, maybe ten bucks a game, and you'd still have to pay dues. I mean, we all know it's never going to be a career. But at least this way we'd be operating like a team, not a cattle call. That's how the girls do it in Austin and their league is getting all kinds of attention. TV appearances, articles in the glossies, even a gig at South by Southwest."

As she's talking, the music turns on—the Village People singing "YMCA"—and Chaz appears at the refreshment bar in his black-and-red gear. For a minute, I expect him to break into a dance routine. Instead, he trots over and starts passing out information sheets. His pecs swell inside his Lycra shirt, although he's not a large guy, and the cords of his neck show to advantage. If he's a dirty old man, I wonder what that makes me. He starts picking up trash off the floor, swinging the girls' legs around to get at the debris, straightening their bags, rearranging their straps and hair and pulling lint off their jerseys. When he gets to Mayweather, he bumps into his shoulder in a mock gangsta salute, and says, "Late again, jarhead."

Then he stands next to Reenie and puts his arm around her, his hand dangling perilously close to her right breast.

"I don't see much practicing going on," he says. "I guess you girls are on a break. So while you're sitting on your butt pads, I'm going to take the opportunity to get you all your little pre-op noses on the same page. Here are our operating costs and here is our take. You will note that, on average, we are currently making about three hundred and fifty bucks a night. This is what's known in the biz as a vanity project, i.e., undertaken for the sake of personal satisfaction without any anticipation of monetary gain. Maybe you are not aware, but we are on the cusp of a major recession—maybe even a depression, and I don't mean the kind where you start popping SSRIs and the bogeyman goes away. There is a drop in the housing market, there is markup in retail, and if I'm not mistaken, you are beginning to see some serious change drain at the gas pump. At this rate, girls, you better practice hard, because you may be roller skating to work before it's all said and done."

Reenie shrugs out of his grip and taps her whistle against her clipboard. "Exactly," she says, "That's why we need to keep going. You know, roller derby was actually developed during the Depression as cheap entertainment for the masses, sort of like reality entertainment one-point-oh. They were holding all kinds of marathons back then, dancing, walking, biking, goldfish swallowing. And so someone got the idea, why not start a skating marathon? It's the perfect sport for hard times. No extensive training, no expensive equipment, no special athletic skills."

Chaz makes a face like he's smelling something rancid. He turns away from Reenie and toward the other girls, who are sitting up straighter, now that they can feel the threat in the air. "Look, I know Gigi's accident has taken its toll on the whole team, and I really appreciate you all pitching in to show your support. That's to our credit. But I hate to see this situation lead to a drop in morale."

"What are you talking about?" Britney Spearhead says. "You just told us that we are headed into a major depression and that you're short on dough. Is that really supposed to boost our morale? Make up your mind."

"Correction, I did not insinuate that I myself am short on funds. I am simply warming you that our happy little real estate bubble is about to be deflated. Meanwhile, this novelty outfit is the merest trickle in my income stream."

Here, I have to interrupt. "Are you telling these gals that their services are no longer wanted?" Maybe I just have pink slips on the brain, but I sense some shift in strategy. Did he overhear Reenie's speech? Or has she already been hinting around about her scheme?

"I'm just saying, if there's any trouble, I am not averse to selling this place. In fact, there has been some serious interest in the old queen now that I've given her such a thorough makeover. I hate to tell you this, friends and fans, but the Empire may not survive as a roller rink, per se. Potential buyers are telling me she's the got the perfect shape and location for an electronics franchise or a beauty academy."

There is an unpleasant lull as we imagine these options.

Then Reenie speaks. "This development wouldn't have anything to do with the proposal that I sent you?"

Chaz laughs, and evenly spaced wrinkles radiate from his deep-set eyes, "You've got an exaggerated sense of your own powers if you think you can jack around the economy and stimulate growth opportunities all on your own. It's true, you are a teenage witch, but I don't think your magic has much bite above the belt." As he speaks, I can hear the tease in his voice, as if he's always just about to deliver a joke that never emerges, as if life itself is a joke, and he's the only one sly enough to understand its punch line. His delivery is quick where you'd expect deliberation and slow where you'd anticipate speed, with a generous sprinkling of ellipses, so that the listener is forced to pay close attention in order to follow his logic. And yet, as usual, in the end, you wish you hadn't heard what he had to say.

I am considering intervening, when Lorraine stands up, the Mexican platter pressed to her chest like a shield, and pokes Chaz with the upper edge of it, aiming, it seems, for the soft spot between his chest and gut. "I won't sit here and listen to you insult my granddaughter. This little gal is bound for great things. She's going to be a lawyer one day. Heck, she may even be a senator or judge. And you think you can humiliate her just because you're a grown man and she's a sweet young girl."

Chaz pulls her hand away from his chest and holds it in his own, exhibiting an odd sort of gentleness as he pats her palm. "Come on, Lorraine. You've known me, what, a dozen years, and I've never done any raping or pillaging yet. I just don't like to be disrespected in my own establishment."

Then Reenie herself steps in and puts her arm around Lorraine. "That's OK, Granny. He's is doing me a favor, really, toughening me up for the real big-time assholes down the road."

In the corner, of course, Jared is filming away and I see him remove his eye from the camera for just long enough to wink in my direction. I am kneeling on one of the benches, not sure, apparently, whether to sit or stand. My limbs still carry the memory of yesterday's attack and this morning's lovemaking, so that I am pulled between the poles of anger and languor. If Chaz is worried about his finances, why would he encourage me to quit my job and leap into his payroll? Was it a trick of some kind? I have been noticing the gas prices, higher, it seems, every time I fill the tank, and the markup on my favored brand of soda. I have been calculating the terms of my retirement package, and considering whether I really need to keep the house, now that

Mason is gone. The sale of the Empire may be no great tragedy; built in the fifties, it's too new to be a historical landmark. Still, the roller rink is one of the few local businesses that has survived my childhood, a place where I can still imagine Sharee at her best, skimming over the floor without appearing to exert herself, her slim figure awash in the red-and-blue lights of the disco ball while I linger by the pinball machines trying in vain to attract the attention of some oblivious boy. I hate to acknowledge the degree to which these bouts and practices have now become the focus of my social life. In fact, the Bombers and their entourage may be the only people outside work whom I encounter on a regular basis. And now both of my venues for human interaction could be closing down for good.

When I look up, Reenie and Chaz have wandered off to the refreshment stand, where he is checking out the beer taps, a towel over one shoulder, and she is standing behind him talking his ear off. Lorraine sits at one of the tables nearby, offering her protection as needed, fiddling with her cell phone and adjusting her hearing aid while she waits. The rest of the girls are now back the rink, where their usual spirits resume, as they race one another, execute turns, or smash into pileups and lie laughing on the floor. That leaves just Mayweather and me. He's stopped filming, for now. He comes over to where I'm standing and sets a hand on my shoulder, and I startle at the touch, not knowing whether I can afford to respond.

16

Apparently, Chaz was too urbane to bring up the matter of the computer monitor until he had Mayweather to himself. At least, this was Jared's read, as he watched the master of damage control work his magic with the team of disgruntled girls and disgusted women. However, every now and then, Chaz shot Mayweather a glance, lifting his eyebrows over their prominent ridge, just to remind his protégé that the matter would have to resurface eventually. It wasn't until after practice that Chaz mentioned he had the Beamer and there was no need for him to get home any time soon, since Ellen had gone to bed with a sick headache and he was taking the next morning off to work on the books. Mayweather processed the information quickly, told Sally he'd catch up with her and adjourned with Chaz to Corks, a dance club designed to resemble a wine cellar, with wooden casks arranged around the dance floor. Chaz may not have been the oldest person in the place, but he was close, and even Mayweather was looking long in the tooth amidst the black-clad adolescents with their pierced eyebrows and imaginatively shaven facial hair. The music was too loud and too generic, shoegaze at its worst, but there was no finer venue for people-watching, Mayweather's favorite occupation. Walking in, right off the bat, he saw a girl in a halter made of chain-link pop-tops and a group of guys passing around a hash pipe under the table. The smoking ban was clearly not enforced on the premises and clouds of cigarette and marijuana smoke choked the room. There had been several late-night shootings in the alley outside, but this seemed to only add to the establishment's appeal.

Chaz and Mayweather sat at the bar, watching the bartender go through his routine, tossing bottles of liquor as if they were batons and squirting seltzer with the panache of a firefighter. He was a handsome guy of about Jared's age, his sideburns looming dangerously close to his mouth, and his bare ripped arms tattooed with intergalactic battles. In spite of the noise, he took their orders without strain—a gin and tonic for Chaz and a shot of Beam for Mayweather—so that he appeared to have mastered the art of lip-reading as well. Now this was a man who had found his calling, Mayweather thought, a rare example of someone who managed to earn a living while keeping his dignity intact.

Jared, sleepy from the afternoon's beer, felt himself coming into a second wind as he downed the Beam in three swallows. The sweet burn purified his gullet, reminding him that his body was a vessel devoted to perception. He never wanted to become dulled with use, so stoned by routine that he lost his ability to see what was in front of him, the world that was new and seething with untapped significance on a daily basis.

This was his horror. But now it occurred to him, staring at the bartender, that perhaps he had passed the threshold, that he should stop worrying, because it was already too late for him to become mindless and respectable. He should be relieved, really, though what he actually felt, the music vibrating the barstool beneath his butt and turning to froth in his ear canals, was a kind of panic, the fear that he would be left alone, the only person of his acquaintance still seeing rather than doing, forced to suffer the curse of awareness on his own.

Beside him, Chaz tapped the glass with his onyx ring, signaling the bartender to pour another round. He looked at Mayweather with a smirk, put a firm hand on his leg and gestured toward the dance floor. Even with all the smoke, Mayweather could smell the product on the guy—cardamom and musk. He wondered if Ellen went for that bouquet or if it was something she merely tolerated. He turned his barstool away and pretended to look over the crowd. It was the usual—a big group of girls in the middle of the floor, shaking their tits at one another in an orgiastic frenzy; in Mayweather's experience, these were the ones who were actually quite frigid in bed. On the periphery, a black kid practiced step dancing, totally inappropriate for the music, though not half bad. A few couples made clumsy foreplay on their feet, while an Asian chick with a Hispanic partner ravaged the floor with what looked like a disco tango. Chaz's hand materialized on his back and steered his gaze in the other direction, where Britney Spearhead was doing a chicken dance, all elbow and knees. How could a girl who was so fierce on the rink be that clumsy on the dance floor? Her pretty delicate breasts and long hair extensions shook with the exertion. Next to her stood a hulking white guy with straight teeth and short hair—obviously slumming in his Guns 'N Roses T-shirt. He reached over and casually dipped his hand into her team shirt, like it was something he was entitled to. Obviously, Britney disagreed, because she wrenched her upper body away and kicked him in the shins. He responded by pinning her arm behind her back and continuing to paw at her breast.

Chaz rushed over to intervene and an argument ensued, the

guy shouting incoherently over the music and Britney screaming in his other ear. This was Jared's cue, he supposed, to get up and defend his pack. He didn't want Chaz to be too confident about his loyalty, though, so he took his time, halting the movement of the barstool, easing off his seat, and edging his long awkward body onto the floor. The light blinded him and he couldn't read the expression on the guy's face. Was he furious enough to throw a punch, but perhaps too inebriated to make the connection? Jared simply moved his body into position and waited for the blow. As it frequently turned out with these types, the guy was more into verbal abuse than actual physical confrontation. Once he saw that Jared was prepared to fight, he gave him the finger and turned back to the bar for another drink.

Meanwhile, Chaz and Jared managed to drag Britney out into the alley, where she claimed that she could take care of herself and didn't need their help.

"It's not that I actually give a frig about your questionable virtue," Chaz said. "I'm just trying to protect my brand." He pointed to her black Boonslick Bombers T-shirt, strategically ripped as if to facilitate the type of groping she had suffered on the dance floor. "I told you, I don't want you wearing your uniform outside the rink. It dilutes the drama of the bout. And besides it gives my organization a bad name. After all, the tickets may be yours, but the arena is still my property."

"Not if you sell us out," Britney said.

"If and when."

"Well, I'll smoke a bowl on that. No hard feelings, huh?" She pulled a pipe out of a tiny velvet pouch hanging from her shoulder and offered it around.

The weed was spiked with sticky black hash, the color and texture of melting tar on a summer street, and Jared inhaled it with pleasure, savoring the sweet complex flavor in the cool autumn air, the smell of opium amidst burning leaves, discarded fast food, and the spice from the Thai restaurant down the street. He stared at the bricks of the alleyway, which seemed to move into deeper relief for his benefit, the pizza boxes in the open Dumpster, the green and brown beer bottles at his feet.

Chaz held his body rigid as he brought the pipe to his lips and turned his head sideways to inhale. He would do exactly five hits, Jared knew, enough to prove that he was no lightweight, but not so much that he'd suffer any lapse in judgment or lose a single minute of the next day's work. Jared made up his mind to count, just to prove his theory, but somewhere after his own third hit, he lost track, absorbed in the fantasy of filming a re-enactment of a streetfight, the football player, the drug dealer, the encounter in the alleyway, their faces smudged with darkness, only their black and white hands visible under the streetlights. He could hear Chaz and Britney gossiping in the background, something about the best outlets for local grass.

So even though he'd known it was coming all along, he was completely startled when Chaz brought up the business of the smashed computer screen. "Speaking of fair trade. How you intend to reimburse me for that monitor you trashed yesterday?"

"I guess you can just put it on my tab."

"That's getting pretty hefty." Chaz said. "Are you really up for a life of indentured servitude?"

"Maybe you figured it wrong," Mayweather replied. "Maybe it's you who owes me."

Chaz looked intrigued. He blinked twice and then held his eyes very still, in anticipation. Even though they were on the small side, their dark blue rays exerted a powerful force in his face. Looking into them, Jared was reminded of the disconnect between these harsh flat disks and Etta's brown irises, drawing you in with their mysterious strands of amber and green. "How do you figure?" Chaz said.

"I gave you the most valuable thing you have."

"What's that? Your sticky fingerprints on my wife?"

"You know what I mean. I don't like to say in front of a third party."

"Fine, I'm sure that Brit has heard the rumors."

Mayweather took another hit and held it in until it seared his lungs, leaving sweet burnt spots like charred meat in his chest. "You took my daughter," he blurted out, blowing smoke in Chaz's face. "And I want her back."

The smoke cleared between them, and Chaz's features took on an eerie cast, his brow ridges distinct as horns, his muscled jaw pulsing. In the back of the alley, there was a rustling and then a banging. Perhaps the drug dealers had arrived to take another victim. But in that moment, Jared was more frightened of Chaz and how he would respond.

"I will pretend I didn't hear that," Chaz said.

"Why's that? Can't you admit it's true?"

"Even if it were, what difference does it make? I'm the girl's legal guardian."

"So she's your property, too? Your brand? The DNA is mine but the image is yours?"

"Jarhead, you are in no shape to put your name on anything—not a check or a car loan or a library card. Much less an actual person."

There was more rustling behind the Dumpster and a cat with a patchwork coat of brown and black and white emerged, its tail aloft. Britney turned toward the animal, as if relieved to remove herself from the vicinity of the conversation. She reached down to pet the little thing and Jared heard her calling it honey and sugar.

"I guess you have to ask yourself if this is something you actually want," Chaz said. "Or is it just attractive because it's currently mine to enjoy? Then, once you are convinced of your whole-hearted desire, what are you prepared to do for it?"

"What do you think?"

"I think you have many unexploited talents, my friend, most of them spoiling like tuna salad in the sun."

17

I go home alone to my dogs and sit on the sofa riffling through a wildflower field guide: columbine, jack-in-the-pulpit, shooting star. Now that the season is over, I'll have to go back to animal tracks and geological formations. It's too early for me to go to sleep, so I get up and make myself some tea, throw a couple of pieces of bread to Di and Rye, count the beers left in my refrigerator. I look at Mayweather's purple sweatshirt on the floor. At least he will have to come back to retrieve that, I think, but then I realize that he will probably discard it like everything else in his life. The orange paint stain accuses me: What have I ever done to keep him here, anyway?

I walk out onto the deck and see bare tree branches wavering in the violet light, hear a few caches of ragged leaves rattling in the wind. There's one lone pine in the yard, its dark irregular boughs bobbing. The moon is obscured behind milky veils of cloud cover, but I stand there long enough to see the heavenly body emerge from the haze, a yellow half lozenge with the center sucked out of it. A waning moon, no time to start anything new. I stand there for almost ten minutes, waiting for something to occur to me, long enough to get chilled in my denim jacket, long enough to hear a dog bark, a car drive by on the interstate, an owl have its say in the woods behind my house. Then a warm wave passes over me, like a gentle hand on my brow. My neck drips sweat into my cleavage, activating the lust that lies in wait for me every time I let down my guard. A vent seems to open at back of my knee, blasting hot air into the crevice. My back is running with perspiration as if I've been walking in a desert all this time instead of just standing immobile in the forest. I am melting into the atmosphere; I am disappearing into the current of time. At this moment, I feel close to Sharee, and what she has become, an impulse, a shade, a packet of energy? But it's not over yet. I'm only halfway there, if Lorraine's longevity is any indication—or three-quarters, maybe? How to live half in and half out of mortality? Why invest in anything—a house, a job, a love affair—if it is only temporary, anyway? This question has plagued me since adolescence, and I haven't found an answer yet.

As I stand there, inhaling the leafy mulch of the yard and the vinegar of my own sweat, I think I see the moon turn, its face emerging from the bare space at its center. I swear that I hear a voice speak. "Daughter," it says, then something indecipherable. Free? Flee? Feed? My temperature drops twenty degrees in an instant and I am chilled to the bone again, the sweat cooled to ice droplets on my skin and goosebumps pulling themselves up from every part of my body so that my entire surface is a raised grid.

I look down at the deck and see a brown ribbon, pick it up and rub the velvet between my thumb and finger. It has the feel of a molting cattail. Something has escaped me, I know, but I am just as certain that something else will come to take its place.

I go inside, shed my clothes in a pile on the bathroom floor, and examine my body in the mirror. My breasts, always smallish and widespaced, have dropped a bit, so that they are now more prominent, pear-shaped, the nipples broadened and lightened with time. There is a small pouch at my belly, far down over my pubic bone. I imagine that this is what the belly of a pregnant woman might look like just as she is beginning to show. My arms and legs are essentially what they have been all my adult life, muscled, brown, reliable, but now they are lightly speckled with white like the coat of a fawn. Could this body still be loved? Could I love it? My face is fuller than it once was, but it still has the shape of my mother's lovely young woman mask. How odd that as I get older and tougher, my face has grown softer and more approachable.

I am a showering woman by nature, but I surprise myself by opting for a bath, preparing the water as if it's for someone else, the temperature as hot as I can bear. I pour in mineral salts from a carton I got as a gift from my nieces the previous Christmas and have never used. Lavender and lilac, the smells of youth and old age. I sit on the edge of the tub, both legs immersed, my butt cold on the porcelain rim before I take a breath, ease in and lie at full length. I sink in farther, pulling my hair into a makeshift knot on my head. I rest my feet up on the tiles above the faucet; I put both hands on my abdomen and squeeze, as if trying to push something out. I finger the hard shell of my pubic bone, open the folds beneath, feel the space inside. Plenty of space, I think, plenty of time.

I practice bringing myself to orgasm without picturing any human being, only the universe pulsing, the stream running, the leaves pressing up against each other, the rugged limestone rock face slick with rainwater, two black snakes with radiant green stripes mating in the middle of a path. Can I get there without resorting to my own erotic history or the intervention of cultural porn? If I actually touch the clitoris I will short circuit the process. I know from long experience that the best method is to work the surrounding area until the nerves deliver the news of ecstasy on their own. I want it to happen slowly. I want to spread this out over the whole evening, over my entire body, over my thinning outworn identity, until I am nothing but a vibrating current on the stream of time.

But before I can get there, Mayweather appears in my mind, a stubborn Mayweather, his sweaty curls, his soft sideburns, his curved penis hard as a tusk of carved ivory in my hand. Mayweather, who has brought me so much by way of physical enjoyment, is now nothing but an obstacle in the path of my pleasure. Just thinking of him, my nipples, already erect, contract to a point of painful compression, and my nerves swim off in different directions, minnows disturbed by a splash in the pond.

The water is growing cold and I am too discouraged to heat it up and try again. So I get out and dry off, toweling my body in a way that I hope will blunt any residual shivers of desire. I walk into the living room naked, a perk of living alone in a deserted A-frame in the woods. But is this pleasure of isolation really worth the worry of the upkeep, I wonder, the mortgage to be paid on a single salary, the worry that the whole thing will come tumbling down on me or simply devalue itself to the point of no return before I can cash it in for my retirement? They tell me, for one thing, that an A-frame will never sell in a town like this; you have to wait for some out-of-state eccentric to come along and take the bait. I see the brown ribbon where I've left it on the coffee table and, on a whim, pick it up and tie it in a bow around the banister as I make my way up the stairs.

In my room, I find a sports bra that will squeeze my tits into a state of temporary paralysis, a pair of yoga pants, a long cotton blouse. Still, I am too alert to even attempt sleep. So I go downstairs again where Di and Rye are lying circled around one another, like a single being with two heads. I begin patting

Di's black coat, which disturbs Rye so much that he gets up and nudges my leg, pleading for attention. His bronze face is marked with a few dark brown streaks. His pink tongue hangs out in solicitude; his speckled gums show. I ruffle his fur, slightly coarser than Di's and with a muskier smell. I pet both dogs at once, and they are so encouraged that they jump onto the sofa with me and we are now a single three-headed beast. I lose myself in the hypnotic motion of grooming them until I start to feel hot and crowded, then disentangle myself, and sit down at the computer to see what's happening with my career.

The e-mails have accumulated like dew in my absence, but I don't bother to open more than two or three. Instead, I find the iMovie program and click on to Mayweather's work. I only hope he hasn't destroyed the footage of the polluters in the process of splicing it into his precious art film. But while I'm there, I can't stop myself from viewing the video again. The butts and legs of the skaters as they move around the rink. My stiff arm holding the gun above my head. The polluters by the side of the pond crossing streams. Is Mayweather really a talented guy? More to the point, does he actually have the determination to see his work through every stage of creation and distribution? And if he doesn't, what will become of his ambition? Will it shrink inside him until it is nothing but a few dry seeds rattling in an empty head or, on the contrary, swell him up like a waterlogged corpse washed up on the bank? It's not lost on me that the thing that makes him so appealing is also what will probably destroy him in the end.

I move to the file of the polluters with relief, seeing that Jared's saved the unadorned footage after all, no doubt antici-pating making a large-scale full-length feature. It's a lucky thing I have no comparable ambition. I only want to solve the prob-lem directly before me, find some satisfying pathway on my own. As a result, I'm pretty lonely at times, caught between the folks seeking contentment and those chasing glory. In fact, my friends and family are always asking me, in one way or another, what it is that I want. Lorraine thinks I should find and keep a husband. Chaz thinks I should cultivate a career and bank account. Mason always thought I should go back to school for an advanced degree in biology. Only Mayweather seems to have no suggestion for my future. Perhaps that's because he sees me as someone too old to have a forward trajectory of my own. The thought sinks into my gut and fills me with despair. Even though I know the proposition is false—Lorraine has lived several lives since she was my age—the idea that Mayweather sees me as a static object, unmoved and unmoving like a tree in the forest, causes me to lose face with myself.

In order to prove to him otherwise, I have to act. I pull up the footage and watch it over again, letting the images feed my rage. I focus on the deep ruts of the tire tracks, the fallen cattails, the men's ugly members, one long and brown, one red and stunted, one white and misshapen like a mushroom. I feel the anger reawaken from my chest and radiate outward, until my limbs are electrified with it and the hairs on my arms are standing on end, my face hot, my teeth clamped tight. Is this actually a feeling I want to cultivate? Perhaps this is the key, to be able to access my rage at will, and bend it toward some recognizable goal.

I may not have much computer savvy, but I know how to send a mass e-mail and I know how to find the information I need. I spend over an hour tracking down addresses: local environmental groups, the park service, the city government, the EPA, the police chief and the county sheriff, my boss, even Bailey himself, along with my old married boyfriend from Jefferson City, who is now conveniently settled as the assistant director of Missouri Natural Resources. I know that the battle will be thankless and endless, but I need to stay in the game just to keep myself alive.

When I've assembled the addresses at the top of the page, I compose a brief message, something about the desecration of public land in the service of private greed and sign with my full title. Then I sit rereading what I've written for several minutes, sounding it out in my head. Outside, the night noises congregate: the crickets, the dogs, the intermittent traffic, and the insistent owl. I look out the tall window and see the moon glowing with all her might, throwing off a white luminescence like a cloak around her. Is this what she is telling me to do? Or is she warning me to stop while I'm ahead, to enjoy this blessed solitude for as long as I can? For years, I haven't listened to anyone's advice, understanding only too clearly the particular bias of each party, and distrusting any authority imposed from above. But now I have come to a place where I long for some direction from outside myself. Is there any trustworthy counsel to be had? In the end, I can only guess. I hover above "send" for five minutes, considering whether I want to reenter the world. Then I press down with conviction, sending an electric charge into my elbow, and casting my stone into the pool.

18

Chaz led Mayweather directly from the alleyway to the Beamer, even though they'd both left full drinks at the bar and Jared's mouth was still watering. Britney tagged along, providing eye candy if nothing else, Jared supposed. He couldn't help but notice her physical resemblance to the woman—or girl, really—Chaz had been screwing in those months before Etta was born. And yet Chaz treated Britney with none of the respect with which he'd endowed that little prick-tease wannabe who'd jumped ship the minute Chaz pronounced himself prepared to leave Ellen and take her on for good. Jared had even had a brief fling with the girl on her way out of town for parts unknown—most likely some other mid-sized Midwestern city where she could reprise her aching-to-be act for a new and willing audience of rubes.

The black BMW glowed under the streetlights, its curves outlined with shine. Inside, the leather smell was overwhelming, a cross between an old school library and a biker's bar. Jared deliberately avoided getting in the front seat with Chaz, but was surprised when Britney joined him in the back, slinging her leg over his, so that her fishnets snagged the seam of his jeans and he couldn't get disengaged for some seconds of uncomfortably close contact. Jared had ceased to be amazed by the consistency with which women sought him out.

"Jared, will you get your leg off me, dude?"

"All I ask is that you refrain from dripping fluids," Chaz said, resting his arm on the seat beside him as he backed out, his profile outlined in the soft glow of the dashboard. "This leather smells like a mother when it's wet."

"No worries, " Mayweather said, managing to gain an inch between Britney's thigh and his own. He wondered whether he did this out of actual distaste or in deference to Sally. No words had passed between them on the subject, and yet he felt, after dropping back into her life like this, some short-lived loyalty was probably in order. The affair with Sally was the rare exception to his usual modus operandi; he had actually sought the Ranger out, when, at the age of twenty-two, he was trying to make a film at the Karst and needed a reliable research advisor. Something about the Ranger's authority drew him in, and although he hadn't deliberately intended to seduce her.

In the front seat, Chaz was narrating the scene on the street before them: skateboarders downing cheap beer on the steps of the Methodist church, a young couple checking out the band posters on a kiosk, a lonely foreign student playing himself in a game of chess inside the window of the coffee shop (no doubt desperately hoping to be interrupted), a fiercely decorated band of goths smoking outside the tattoo parlor, waiting for marching orders from their suicidal leader. These were the only people out this late on a Monday night. Far from resenting the role of chauffeur, Chaz seemed to relish it, looking back occasionally to check the positioning of the hands and limbs in the backseat.

"Where are you taking us?'

"You want to get your daughter back," Chaz said. "I guess you'll have to earn it."

"What do you have in mind?"

"Watch and learn, my friend."

"I'm all eyes," Jared said.

"All eyes and talk," Britney added, indicating that perhaps she was not so dim as she appeared.

Chaz took a turn onto the main drag of the District, where there was a bit more action, a few bands of college-aged guys trolling the street, and girls in groups of two or three looking top-heavy in their denim jackets or sweatshirts over long bare legs in the briefest of miniskirts. The Beamer was smoother than anything Jared had encountered, dreamlike and stealthy, gliding close to the ground. Although he had never been the type of guy to lust after a motor vehicle, he had to admit it was a fine ride. Beside him, he felt a stirring, the tickling of soft hair under his elbow. He was afraid that Britney was now moving toward his lap. But when he looked, he saw it was the kitten that she had somehow managed to stow away on her person.

"Whoa," he said. "You don't know where this little guy belongs. Now he's going to get all turned around and never find his way home."

"Little girl," Brittany said, pointing toward the pink underparts.

The kitten settled into his lap, on his right leg, really. Its whole body fit under his hand as he rubbed the silky fur, amazed at the tiny bones inside, much more compact that the airy packaging would suggest. The kitten licked his palm, the texture of its tongue surprisingly rough, like athletic tape, as if it was urging Jared on to some feat of bravery. He picked up the pace of his petting and the cat started purring, a sound that vibrated through the length of its body.

"I call her Catastrophe," Britney said.

"You brought an unvetted beast into my Beamer?" Chaz said. "If I see one claw mark on the seat, you are off the payroll as of yesterday."

"What payroll? The twenty-bone costume allowance? I think I'll take my chances."

The pitch of the cat's purring grew deeper, a kind of full-body moan, as if in response to Chaz's protest. Mayweather stroked its ears and moved from there all the way down to its tail. The white patches in its fur glowed a ghostly gray and the brown ones receded into the darkness. Each creature, Mayweather thought, has its preferred neural pathway, like a thumbprint under the skin.

"You named a cat you just met?" he said to Britney. "Don't you think she's already taken?"

"There's no collar. Maybe she was born in the wild."

"Watch out," Chaz said. "The thing could have rabies." He pulled up to the curb without warning, moving the car to parallel in just three passes, and Mayweather thought that he had stopped to kick out Britney and her stowaway.

But he just opened the car door, pocketed the keys, then motioned for them to follow him across the street. Jared handed Catastrophe to Britney, who stuffed her into the purple velvet pouch of her purse, and they followed Chaz into another bar. This one, only too familiar to Mayweather, was identified by a pink neon cocktail, fizzing its three bland bubbles out into oblivion and then starting over again. Three of the bar's walls were full-length windows looking out onto the main strip, and the fourth was a watered pink taffeta covered with photographs of local heroes and folk lushes. Jared had been here before, of course, and knew that one yellowed photograph in the upper left-hand corner, near the pink marbled column, showed his father in his early thirties, not much older than

Jared himself, drinking directly out of a bowling trophy, a red-head, not Jared's mother, planting her tits into his back. Briefly, he wondered who the photographer had been, since the shot was not without some crude sense of proportion. Jared's father, it was said, excelled at every activity that did not lead to monetary gain. In that way if in no other, Jared had followed in the old man's footsteps. He hoped Chaz would not mention the photograph, but of course he did, walking right up and tapping it with his iPhone.

"Jarhead's dad," he said. "Not a bad-looking guy, if you don't mind the puke stains or delirium tremens. Of course, that was before my time. But you can still hear talk of him at AA meetings far and wide. What was the story about a keg and a ferret?"

"It's apocryphal," Jared said. "As long as you're asking." He tried not to look at the photograph—but what was the point, really, when it was already burned into his long-term memory, the sharp chin with its patch of reddish beard, the thin lopsided nose with a deviated septum, the hooded brown eyes fitted into his face with long strands of wrinkles. This was very close to the face of the man whom Jared remembered from his occasional visits, who would take him to rodeos and bowling alleys and dog shows and of course bars—probably every dump and watering hole in town—breathing alcohol and tooth decay into his face as he administered fond advice about Johnny Law and pussy.

On one occasion, he had insisted on picking up Jared at church camp in the Bootheel, three hours from Boonslick. He had just broken his leg in a construction accident and walked in swinging defiantly on his crutch with some story about Jared's mother coming down with walking pneumonia and needing him at home. Clark Mayweather was driving his own mother's van, upholstered with green-and-gold shag carpeting, a cooler of Bud riding shotgun, and a hotel ashtray full of loose weed in the well, a clay pipe sitting provocatively in the center. As Jared threw in his backpack, his dad kindly offered to move the cooler so Jared could sit up front, but he opted for the back, where he could watch the scenery in peace. From there, he could see his father's thick curls emerging from the back of his feed cap, his broad shoulders in the uniform of the most recent short-lived trucking job.

"They teach you anything about pussy out here?"

"Yes sir, these Methodists is all about pussy."

"First rule of pussy is, thou shalt not kneel down to any gods before me."

"Second rule of pussy is, thou shalt not forget to pull out before your time." Jared had been repeating the litany for years before he had any idea what the words meant. Only gradually had it dawned on him that this was an implicit insult to his mother, who clothed and fed him, took him to the doctor when he was sick and the pool or the movies when he was bored. And yet, this man, his father exerted, a strange fascination, promising some crude power from the world beyond.

"In my experience, church and camp do not mix," his dad said. "How about going on a real camping trip?"

"Whatever you say," Jared said. "But I hope you actually told mom what you were doing. She isn't really sick, I guess."

"No, the old girl is just off blowing my child support at the Home Depot." He turned the radio on to Boonslick Country, his favorite station, where the licks were sweet and the lyrics were God-fearing.

Jared sat in the back, counting his father's empties as he tossed them onto the floorboard. Even at eleven, Jared was not so naive as to believe that a man couldn't knock back a few and still keep his eyes on the road. Still, when his father reached an even dozen, he began to get nervous.

Clark pulled into a convenience store and left the motor running. Jared unbuckled and picked up the ashtray of weed, smelled its spicy green bouquet, placed a bit on his tongue, and chewed. It was not as extreme as he expected, no more than chewing on a blade of grass in a field, and there was no effect that he could tell.

When his father came back, he had two six-packs of Budweiser. He tore one can off the plastic ring and dumped the rest in the cooler, then threw his crutch into the passenger seat, where it stood at half-mast, looking like a rugged cross on the move.

The wheels wobbled on the highway, and Clark's head bobbed to the music, as Jared watched the greenery along the roadside. Every now and then, they'd hit a limestone pass, where the rock had been cut to accommodate the highway, asserting itself in rough layers of grayish white on either side. On top, there was just a thin cover of green, like the icing on a birthday cake, causing Jared to speculate that every childish pleasure he enjoyed might be the merest bright surface over some rough indigestible chunk of reality. Knowing it might be months before he'd see his father again, Jared alternated between wanting the terrifying ride to be over and hoping it would last as long as possible.

"You get any down there?" Clark said.

"No pussy yet," Mayweather said, recovering. "But I did catch me a couple crappie."

"That's my boy."

If he could just get his dad to stop somewhere, he knew they'd be fine. His panic seemed to be increasing, his head blossoming like a dogwood in May. Perhaps Clark had actually done something with Jared's mother, who always seemed to bring out his temper with her straight-faced defiance and her infuriating good will. Perhaps he really was here to kidnap Jared and to take him all the way to California. Jared imagined a series of days on the road, learning to drive, maybe, learning to drink and get high and curse with conviction. He considered the joy and fear of such a fate. He wished he had some way of contacting his mom. Another passageway opened in his head and he pulled his camera out of his backpack, started documenting his whereabouts: his hand against the shag carpeting, his father's body disconnected from his face, which leered eerily back from the rearview mirror, the crutch riding shotgun where a mother should have been.

He looked over his dad's shoulder to see that the speedometer was at eighty and the tank was almost empty. Finally, Clark pulled over into Indian Mound Park and circled the campsite like it was the Indy 500. A few campers, hanging out wet towels or smoking in their lawn chairs. stared in disapproval. Mayweather was out of the car and onto solid ground in seconds, the earth pulsing under his feet. When he opened the trunk he discovered to his surprise that the old guy had actually packed some camping gear—an orange tent, a lantern, a skillet and coffee pot, even a couple of Army surplus sleeping bags. Jared, who had learned something after all at church camp, pitched the tent in a matter of minutes while his dad pissed into the ashes of the last camper's fire, again attracting more attention than was desirable. Jared tried not to think about his father's cock, which he had seen all too often over the years. It was unusually large, dark purple in color, rising from a nest of wet-looking curls. Jared's own dick was nothing like it, pale and curved, with no pubic hair as yet. He remembered his dad's comments about his son's little banana and his mother's worry, sufficient to cause her to draw this peculiarity to the attention of the pediatrician, who assured her that it was an entirely normal variation of male anatomy.

Jared remembered his youthful pride and embarrassment in pissing beside his father, but now he wandered off on his own, toward the tall elms and woody vines. He walked past a patch of columbine with its airy arrowheads of yellow and pink, some blue chicory flowers close to the ground, then picked a patch of ground and aimed, wondering whether his briny stream would feed the vegetation or kill it.

When he returned, he found his father was passed out on a sleeping bag, his mouth open and his boots splayed. He looked more like a wandering bum or mental patient than someone to be feared. So Jared just grabbed his fishing pole and an old skillet and headed out to the lake where he caught three trout and fried them over a fire right there on the rocky bank. By then, the sun was going down, taking masses of red- and-orange cloud cover with it. Jared saw a dark form, a pillar in the distance, growing larger as it approached, and felt his throat constrict with tension. Then he made out the limp, the crutch, the determined vaulting stride against the red sky. Clark Mayweather was slow all right, but he was going to make it home for dinner before the sun dropped down and extinguished itself in a lake of fire.

Jared handed his father a fish and they both ate with bare hands, tasting the crispy skin, the flaking flesh and spitting out bits of bone as fine as feathers. It was still the best meal Mayweather had ever tasted.

"Looking pretty scrappy there," Chaz said, jarring Jared from his reverie. "Remind me to get someone to tear down these geezers and put some new faces up on the wall."

So Mayweather turned away from his father and back to the business at hand.

19

At ten-thirty, I give in, turn out the lights, lock the doors, and herd the dogs up the stairs. This is better than sleeping in the guest room and giving the impression that I'm waiting up for Mayweather. If he is sober enough to fuck, he can certainly venture as far as the second story to achieve his aim, and if he just wants to crash downstairs he's welcome to sleep in the spare bed on his own. Locking the doors, on the other hand, might be unnecessarily cruel. Still, why should I risk life and limb just because he's too improvisational to ask for a house key? Di and Rye chase one another to the bed and I turn down the red bedspread with its pattern of bears and pine trees. Underneath, the flannel sheets are the color of birch bark. I lift the top sheet, get in, and make a tent with my knees so the dogs can follow, Di settling in at my right thigh and Rye at my left. Flannel above and beneath me, fur on either side. What could be more pleasurable? I try not to visualize Mayweather's hands. I try not to think of the down at the nape of his neck, the harsh nubs of his whiskers against my thighs, the soft belly cushioning the hard cock and pushing it further out into the world. Here in my own bed, if nowhere else, I should be entitled to a little peace.

I pick up *The Botany of Desire*. I haven't made much progress since Gabriella's accident. I suddenly wonder how she's doing and think to check my messages. Lorraine's phoned in her next command all right, something about more magazines for Teresa, Gabriella's mother, who desperately needs the distraction. As Gabriella nears the three-day mark, all her bodily functions remain stable and most of the swelling of the brain has receded, but she is still unresponsive to external cues. According to Lorraine, however, she is making noises in her sleep, shouts and grunts and whimpers, even some garbled syllables that could conceivably be Arabic. Ten-thirty is a bit late to make a call, and so I'm off the hook for now. Reenie's also left a message. She says that she is going to the hospital on her lunch break tomorrow, if I'd like to join her. I surprise myself by dialing up her cell phone.

She sounds a bit groggy, but I can hear the hammer of hip–hop in the background.

"You're not out, are you?"

"At the Grope and Grind."

"I got your message. Sure, I can come to the hospital with you. Any time, really, since I'm suspended from my job."

"I can't hear you, Aunt Sal. Hold on."

I hear the phone pass through a veil of music, growing louder then softer, past the combative banter of male conversation and a shimmer of traffic to arrive at a patch of relative silence on the other side.

"What did you say?" Reenie asks.

I tap my fingers on the receiver and think about Reenie standing out on the curb with the smokers, talking into a pastel cell phone that resembles a pocket mirror. I can't imagine voluntarily wearing a tracking device, like an animal with a transmitter tied to its leg. Even though I have to carry a phone professionally, I keep my own cell on mute and reserve its use for emergencies. But for Reenie and her generation, it seems that being available is tantamount to being alive.

"I said I'm fired, anyway, or I will be in matter of days, so I'm pretty much free to meet you at the hospital any time you like."

"Shit, how did that happen?"

"You saw the deed on YouTube. I crossed a line."

"Fuck it, Sally. Sometimes it seems like the only people who get fired are the ones who're actually doing their jobs."

I appreciate the attempt at support, but I can't agree. To me, it appears that everyone is being fired these days, regardless of their service record or even the employer's needs. After I'm gone, will the Karst even hire a new ranger to replace me? Or will they just limp on, two employees shy of what it takes to keep the place decent?

"Anyone else out there with you?" I ask

"You're not looking for a hookup, are you?"

"I'll keep your secrets if you keep mine."

"It's hardly a secret that you have a thing for the guy."

"Or that you're in tight with Mr. Enright."

"Shut up. Hey, my ride is leaving. I love you, lady, but I have to go."

After she hangs up, I try reading again, but I have to keep going back to rethread the argument. What do I need to know about genetic mutations anyway? I'm already beyond that now, out of the game of reproduction and out of my job as biological advisor at Karst Park as well. I go downstairs again, turn on the lights, look out the window, and see my reflection staring back at me, a strange woman, neither young nor old, wearing loose clothes that disguise her muscles and emphasize her curves. When I was younger, the sight of my own face and figure made me restless;

what was the use of beauty if it didn't get you anywhere? But lately, when I imagine my body it is usually in motion; my looks are diminished, it's true, but I feel a perverse pleasure at disintegrating in the service of being, burning up with use. Now that I'm back to sleeping with Mayweather, however, that satisfaction is slipping away from me and I'm staring at myself like a girl again, worrying about how he sees me, making calls to clubs to track him down. It's shameful, I think, but I feel more alive than I have in some time. My reflection is blocking the view out the window. I can hear the trees blowing in the wind, but can't see the movement of their branches. Maybe I will unlock just one door. I go back out to the deck, open the screen, and feel the cool night air rush in at me with its smells of dried meat, campfires, powdery leaves disintegrating into mulch. Why is it that the smell of fall—the smell of death really—fires my veins with such ambition? Ambition to do what? To embark on another dead-end love affair? To start in on yet another career? To sell my house and take to the road? I leave the door unlocked, then walk back into the house, my shirt draping off my shoulders like a shawl.

In the living room, I sit back down at the computer, God knows why, to check my e-mail again. Maybe I am no better than Reenie, wanting every second to know that some other living being is thinking of me. To my surprise, I've already gotten a response to my mass e-mail. It's a note from Eric, my former love interest in the Department of Natural Resources, saying that he'd like to see me and that he has an open slot at eleven-thirty the next morning, dangerously close, I realize, to the habitual hour of our lunch-time assignations in the late nineties. I check the time on the message: 10:23. He responds to his mail after ten p.m.? Then the wife is still waiting up for him? Or has she already turned out the lights and resigned herself to falling asleep with nothing but her mindful nature sounds CD to keep her company? The wording of Eric's message is so clipped and astringent that it gives off no tone whatsoever, no indication of approval or disapproval, helpfulness, worry, lust, or outrage. You have to practice, I know, to reach such a state of Zen at the keyboard. I guess I'll just have to make the trip over to Jeff City to check out his expression for myself.

As I'm logging off, the phone rings. Maybe Reenie is calling back, I think, or maybe it's Mayweather deigning to inform me of his plans for the evening. It could even be Mason, who was always something of a night owl, phoning in to let me know where he has landed. But the male voice on the other end of the line is gruffer than Mason's mellow mumble and deeper than Mayweather's tenor rant, reminding me instead of the phone solicitations for the State Troopers, always made by some bullying bass with a thick Southern accent, threatening me with the full force of the law before softening me up for the kill. "State trooper here, ma'am. Oh, don't worry; there's no trouble. I'm just calling to remind you of the dangerous work the troopers do for our community and asking you to remember the widows and orphans left behind." I have always had trouble with the State Troopers, who do not hesitate to pull rank over a lowly Park Ranger at every opportunity. But it's getting close to midnight and even the troopers are giving innocent citizens a rest.

"Sally LaChance? Ranger Sally LaChance? You are one stupid cunt to mess with me and my crew."

And then the line goes dead.

I look out the window at myself looking in. How did these cretins get my number? Actually, now that I think of it, it's right there in the phone book for anyone to see, clearly the listing for a single woman, in spite of Lorraine's warnings. Even when Mason lived with me, he did so anonymously, without a listing of his own. Don't these guys even fear being traced? I look at the number, which doesn't tell me much; I try to remember the details reported in the paper, the bare facts of these three men, one twenty-nine, one thirty-three, and one thirty-seven. Really closer to Mayweather's generation than my own. Since when do I need to fear someone younger than myself? That is the real mark of age, I suppose, the sense that it's the younger people who now hold the power of moral authority and physical threat. One man is from St Louis, recently laid off by Boeing Aircraft; one is just back from Iraq and lives out in the country by the water treatment plant; another has an address on some floral court or arboreal lane in the warren of dead-end streets in the low-end subdivision at the northern edge of town. I've always been able to take care of myself; I've never been frightened of the forest or the dark, only the regimented and haunted spaces of the malls and subdivisions. But the fact is, this A-frame is mostly glass; if anyone wanted to get to me badly enough, it wouldn't be difficult to do. My nearest neighbor is over a mile distant. Even Di and Rye are sleeping upstairs undisturbed. I call them down, trying to modulate the high streak of panic in my voice; I am not one to leap to the worst-case scenario, but I like to be prepared. The familiar padding of the dogs on the stairs sends little shocks up my legs and spine.

Then the phone rings again. "Stupid cunt, you are going to be sorry you ever picked up a pistol. When we're done with you, you're never going to wear a uniform again."

I refuse to take this passively, and so instead of just hanging up, I start to argue. After all, it's not like I lack experience talking down redneck locals, who appear in the Karst bearing a bad mix of alcohol and firearms on a regular basis. Still, I have never encountered this degree of personal rage.

"Listen," I say, "We had a pretty negative encounter. I don't like what you did out there, and you don't like how I responded. Why don't we just let the law settle things from here?"

"Look, bitch, the law is too good for you."

Di and Rye begin barking as if in response to my outrage. And as I'm talking, the door to the deck clicks open. The sharp barking of the dogs simmers down into a warning growl. Could it be Mayweather standing there in front of the refrigerator, looking for another beer? But then are three more steps, and the intruder is well beyond the refrigerator by now. I look up and see a man in a ski mask, a bright green weave with yellow stitching around the eyes and mouth. How ridiculous, I think through my fear. Why wear a mask when the point is to let me know exactly who they are and why they are coming after me?

20

At the Neon Cocktail, Chaz indicated a corner table where two windows met, and Mayweather followed him to the familiar spot, from which, Chaz always said, you could see half of Boonslick stepping out on their spouses, meeting up with their suppliers, or stumbling home drunk. Along the way, they lost Britney to a middle-aged customer on the prowl, who, recognizing the costume, started chatting her up about the roller derby. From his seat, Jared saw the man pull up his polo shirt and hand Britney a Sharpie so she could autograph his belly. Presumably, he'd seen this move on television.

When Jared turned back to Chaz, he saw that they had been joined by another man, a guy in his mid-thirties, hair thin in front and thick in back, heavy sideburns nearly touching his chin. He wore a silk shirt with a black-and-green diamond print, an open vest with lining of a contrasting pattern. There was a dragon medallion peering out from his chest hair and a half-visible Chinese character tattooed on the side of his neck. He handed Chaz and Jared drinks without asking what they wanted—that accursed gin and tonic again, the quintessential antiseptic cocktail, no color, no taste, no connection to the Earth. Jared would rather drink pure grain alcohol, if it came to that, he thought, and pushed the drink away from him with two knuckles.

"How's it going?" Chaz asked. "You get my text?"

"He'll be here," the guy said. Only after several inscrutable exchanges did Chaz turn and introduce Jared.

"This is Mulligan. He was in the class of what, eighty-nine? We played in a band together, made one heartbreaking single and called it a career."

"You called it a career, Enright. I toured the Midwest sleeping in flophouses for another ten years, collecting debt and crabs."

"What's your sound, man?" Jared, class of '97, inquired.

"We were doing a kind of post-punk glam. Then Cobain bit it and no one wanted to hear anything that didn't feature a flannel snot cloth and a Neil Young whine."

"Bad timing," Chaz said. "Bad luck. But you landed on your feet. I think you've found your calling."

Jared looked out the window and saw short-haired, broad-shouldered fraternity brothers patrolling the street, a huddle of younger kids sitting smoking on the brick border of an urban flower garden, a homeless man with dirty blond dreadlocks collapsed next to a shopping cart. A professor-type walked by with his dog, oblivious, and the shorthaired German shepherd sniffed at the homeless man's cart, his owner barely managing to pull him back before he peed on its wheels. Looking at the dog's glossy coat, Jared thought of Sally and her Labs, the A-frame in the country where she was probably expecting him any minute. But he didn't know himself when he planned to return.

Back at the table, Mulligan had produced a lacquered pillbox. He opened the lid, and Jared stared at the white powder inside, like so much baking soda waiting to leaven and elevate a social interaction at any time. Mulligan held the box in the palm of his hand and gave Chaz a questioning look.

"Go on," Chaz said. "I'll join you freaks later."

Mulligan excused himself to the men's room and Jared followed. The walls were papered in stylized vaudeville nudes, and there was a chalkboard on which someone had written a dirty limerick in blue chalk. The room smelled of piss and smoke and urinal cakes. Mulligan stood inside an open stall and beckoned Mayweather in. Jared was not a habitual cokehead, but he wasn't one to pass up an opportunity for mental expansion, either. They stood in the stall and snorted out of a spoon. Jared's nostrils burned and his brain lit up from the central stalk outward to all the little tributaries seeking light and heat. The high was as clean as ammonia but it didn't allow for the introspective leeway of marijuana. Just a straight shot to ecstasy, no digressions along the way.

Mulligan now seemed far too close so that Mayweather could see the waxy wrinkles next to his eyes, the tiny pinpricks of blackheads on his nose, the raw pink skin under his nostrils, as if he had a bad cold. Was this how Jared would look in another eight, ten years? Dressed as a kind of clown of his former self? Was Mulligan even the guy's real name? Or just the ridiculous identity with which Chaz had bestowed him?

"Chaz tells me you are quite the lady's man."

"Whatever."

"But you are a well-connected guy."

"I do all right."

"Think you can pass some product for me?"

Mayweather remembered how Chaz had said that if he wanted his daughter back, he'd have to work for her. Was this the exchange Enright was proposing? Mayweather's brain iced up and he felt the deep crevasses of cortex expand so that he was in danger of falling into one and never returning. Was this all he was worth to Chaz after all? Would he have to buy back his own daughter ounce by ounce, with the constant threat of being arrested? With his luck, he would be thrown into jail and never allowed the slightest bit of custody after all.

There was a giggle at the door and Britney appeared in the stall, her bare midriff shaking with laughter. Mulligan directed her to open her mouth and smeared coke over her gums and lips and began to kiss her experimentally, as if to sample his own product. He pushed his knee between her legs and she grasped onto him. Mayweather wanted no part of this particular threesome, so he disentangled himself, slammed the stall door, and went back to the table, where Chaz was now sitting with another unfamiliar guy.

"Jared, meet Kevin Bailey."

A wave of recognition passed over Jared in his altered state. Bailey. The guy was around Chaz's age, with a deep tan that extended painfully into the part of his hair, one eyebrow interrupted by a scar and the barest mask of gray and brown stubble over his lower face. His lips were oddly pronounced, though not large, and when he smiled, Jared saw that his teeth were covered in incongruous tracks of transparent braces. On his right wrist, he wore several grimy braided cords, and on his left, a heavy platinum watch. He had been playing with a case of business cards as he talked, and Jared noticed that his fingers were severely callused, though long and nimble as the digits of a musician.

When the man stood to shake his hand, Jared felt the rough palm, smelled the fresh perfume of sawdust. Bailey, he now realized, was the name of the construction crew Sally had encountered out at the Karst. Was this the guy?

"Turns out, you and Kevin have some acquaintances in common," Chaz said.

Jared tried to make an inquisitive face, although in his gut he was already certain of the man's identity.

"I guess you are the daring young dude who put my crew up on the YouTube."

"That would be my opus. What do you think?"

"I think you might not realize the commercial value of your work."

"I'm strictly art house," Jared said. "No union card, no major studio credits, no agent."

"Well, I don't know much about art, but I know what I am willing to pay for," Kevin said, twisting his watch around on his wrist.

Chaz shook his gin and tonic, which has been drained down to a couple of ice cubes and nothing else. " Just to throw out a figure, what do you think of five thousand dollars?"

"That's more than a thousand bucks a minute," Bailey said.

"Fine's over ten thousand," Chaz replied. "And if you get sentenced, it could be as much as fifty."

Jared's gut jolted and he gripped the armrests of his chair, felt the heads of the little ornamental tacks that held the leather in place. Wasn't this worse than being used as a pusher? Here he was, trying to create art and all anyone could think about was scratch.

"So tell me, Mr. Bailey, what attracts you to the piece?" he asked. "Do you like the ensemble work or are you more into the handheld camera technique? I know, I know, reminds you of a bit of Godard, doesn't it? You don't think it's too derivative?"

Kevin Bailey pushed forward in his chair, gave Jared a serious look like a schoolteacher or minister. His brown eyes were unblinking in the dim light, and even though he wasn't an especially large man, he seemed to be ready to knock over the table. Jared already felt it press into his midsection, making him all the more aware of his extra weight. "Kid, if you're here to do business, let's get down to the Xs and Os. But if you just want to dick around with me, I don't have the time."

"Hey, slow down, brother. I was just drinking, like everyone else. But if you want to talk trash, I'm wondering why you had your guys dumping your load in a state park."

"Do you know where the municipal dump is? Clear out the ass end of Boonslick, as it turns out. Labor, mileage, it all adds up to a pretty poor business proposition. Meanwhile, all this state land is sitting vacant—not a thing going on. Oh, maybe you've got a kid or two playing Dungeons & Dragons in the forest or some Boy Scouts sodomizing each other in a pup tent. But what if they do run across a little garbage on the trail? It's hardly a tragedy. I know when I was a kid, I loved the vacant lot. But the most fascinating thing about the place was the junk sitting on it. Rusted out cars and lawn chairs—that wasn't pollution, man. That was our clubhouse. I did not tell my crew to dump in the park, if that's what you're asking. But they did show some initiative by figuring out a cost-savings benefit."

"So they get a raise, then, huh?" Jared said, feeling the coke fire his temper.

Here Chaz interrupted, put his hand on Jared's shoulder, and commenced kneading. "My friend is suggesting that he doesn't necessarily agree with the use to which you might put his property. In my mind, that's a good reason to raise the asking price."

"Do I ask how people are going to use the houses I build for them? Whether they're going to set up a puppy mill or abuse their kids or beat their wives? Hell, they could be keeping sex slaves in the family room or burying corpses in the basement. What's it to me?"

"That sure sounds like a far-out flick you've got going on in your imagination," Mayweather said.

Bailey looked up, surprised, then leaned back with his arm over the back of the empty chair next to him, easing into what appeared to be a well-worn track of conversation. "People think your average businessman is a pretty numb fuck. No imagination, right, no creative spark? Hell, I go through seven different scenarios every time I strike a deal. You have to, just trying to stay ahead of the game. Not like you pretentious bohemian types. Artists, right? Filmmakers, actors, jugglers, fiddlers, nose-pickers? The whole District stinks of it. You all think you are the bomb of creativity when you're really just little one-trick wonders stuck on some fixed idea that you can't even sell to yourself."

Instead of being insulted, Jared was suddenly struck dumb, trying to think whether he'd ever been accused of stability before. Inertia, maybe. Stability, never.

Britney and Mulligan appeared at the table, coke smeared on their lips like powdered sugar from a cop's doughnut. Britney's purple velvet purse was still at her side, but it was flattened out, and Jared wondered where the cat had gone. He guessed she wasn't into the ménage scene either.

Britney winked at the man whose belly she had signed and put her arms around Chaz's neck from behind. Then she passed the little black box back and forth in front of his nose.

"I hear the clean water violations can go up to ten thousand dollars a day," he said, ignoring Britney and swatting the box away. "At that rate, five grand is a steal."

Bailey glared at Jared as if he'd prefer to finish the conversation instead of reaching an agreement so quickly. The scar in his left eyebrow seemed to deepen as he flexed his brow, made a grimace and parted his lips parted to reveal the braces again. Clearly he had not come from money. Maybe it was true that the real businessmen were more interested in working the angles than in the sheer crass accumulation of volumes of cash.

"I can do five grand," he said, a bit of his lip sticking to his braces and delaying the relaxation of his smile. "If I get the film tonight and if I know for sure that you've destroyed all the copies."

Mayweather checked his gut. Five grand was more than he could earn in two months of manual labor or three of freelance drudgery. It seemed unlikely that he would ever be offered so much money for such a short clip again. But if he sold the film, he would lose the right to the most inspiring bit of camera work he had done for over a year and he was uncertain whether he could go on making the roller derby film at all without the images that had incited his imagination. Still, it was a challenge thrown out to him. If a businessman could consider seven different means of striking a deal, couldn't he achieve his vision by pursuing any one of a number of paths? He hated to have his hand forced, hated to see his work used for some unholy purpose. Not to mention what Sally would think if she ever found out. He looked at his hand to see that it was shaking. Did he really want money that badly? He hated Chaz, he hated Bailey, but more than that, he hated himself for ever getting to this point.

"How will I know if you've destroyed the copies, you wonder?" Bailey continued. " I will know because I took the trouble to look up your mother Deirdre Mayweather, her address and phone number, her place of employment, and her credit report. In fact, your mother's employer is an investor of mine, so it won't be any problem at all for me to check out the situation whenever I want."

Mayweather, on edge already, lunged across the table without thinking and grabbed Bailey around the neck. He felt an immense power, then, shooting into all his limbs, a direct link to all that was unstudied and instinctive. Maybe he had sat and listened to these pricks for too long. Chaz with his needling and Bailey with his offensive innuendo. Bailey's neck was thick and powerful, stronger than it looked. The guy was probably a former construction worker himself, Jared thought, as he tried somehow to bend the body double. He struggled until he had Bailey's head down on the table, as if to baptize him. Now he was staring straight into the open cup of the man's ear, and could not stop thinking, even then, of the strangeness of the vision: the rough lobe indented with an old piercing, the spiral of pink cartilage, translucent as a seashell, then the dark inner channel, smudged with a bit of reddish wax, opening and opening into the darkness of the brain. Then it was as if a spring had loosened and Bailey rose up again, threw Jared off so that he stumbled into the window, broke the pane, and fell out onto the sidewalk, spraying the homeless man with pellets of glass.

Jared, finding himself unharmed, took off his cowboy boots, sat down on the curb and shook the glass out of them, then continued walking down the street barefoot, his boots under his arm.

21

The man in the green ski mask is armed, I see, not with a proper pistol, but one of those police Tasers they've been selling like Tupperware out in the subdivisions. The weapon is purple and highly decorative, shaped like the ray gun on a *Star Trek* episode, just the thing for violence of a recreational nature. A C2, if I'm not mistaken, 500,000 volts, the standard domestic model. The man waves it around like it's a water gun, clearly unfamiliar with its use. Why not treat it like a water gun? After all, it's not much more difficult to obtain, available on dozens of Internet sites along with pepper spray and surveillance equipment, no license necessary, highly recommended for the personal safety of anyone over eighteen.

I feel my abdominal muscles give way and wetness seep into the crotch of my yoga pants, the smell of my divorcee's diet of coffee and broccoli rising to my nose. But I can't let my physical fear stand in the way of my ability to respond. I stand stock still, my spine straight and my feet firmly planted, taking up as much space as possible, as I've been taught to do when dealing with aggressors. I lift my arms into the air, to show I'm compliant, but bent at the elbows, to remind us both of my agility and strength.

"I'm unarmed, " I say. "You won't need the Taser."

Meanwhile, the dogs are all over him, leaping and barking, because after all, they don't recognize any weapon but claws or teeth. I call them off, but it's too late, he shoots Di in the neck, her beautiful form collapsing in mid-air and then dropping with a sickening thud onto the wood floor. The sound of her crying is terrible, agonizing and rhythmic, high-pitched as the wail of a much smaller animal, as she flails against the floor, hitting the leg of the sofa repeatedly. I can hear her skull knock against the wood and her teeth chatter like dice in her head. Even though I know the wound is probably not fatal, I feel as if the ribs are being pried off my body. I actually know something about the effects, since we went over Taser use in my law enforcement class. At one to two seconds, the subject experiences intense pain and muscle contractions, at two to three seconds, she may be momentarily paralyzed, then dazed and disoriented. But if the voltage is applied for much longer, or the victim is shot repeatedly, the action may result in brain damage, seizures, stroke, or even, in a few recorded cases, death by cardiac arrest. Unfortunately, the weapon is highly sensitive to human error because there is no stop device. And Green Cheeks is certainly a great candidate for error, since he doesn't seem to be aware that the gun isn't recommended for use on animals, or that the proper target should be the subject's hip or leg. Diana, recovering some small degree of motor control, attempts to scratch the probe out of her flesh with her hind paw, her movement frantic, uncharacteristically clumsy. Then she gives up and curls herself into a nest of pain, her muzzle on her paw and her eyes on me, as if asking for an explanation. She lifts her head up, a proud inquisitive tilt even in the midst of her agony, and then dips it back down into her paws again to resume her suffering without complaint.

As Rye approaches, the man looks like he will shoot him, too, and so I rush to intervene, thinking of my own pistol locked safely in the gun cabinet where I will never be able to reach it. I'd be well advised, in fact, to avoid drawing the cabinet to the man's attention. I order Rye to his spot by the sofa but I don't have time to look behind me and see if he has obeyed because I am bent over Diana, stroking her fur, saying her name, and looking instinctively for the wound. I find one probe just above her collar, protruding maybe half an inch from her thick chocolate coat. I jerk it out, as quickly as I can, feeling its resistance, a fishhook in the flesh. Diana's cries reach an unbearable pitch as she struggles against me, and I struggle to keep my panic at bay. It is horrible to think that she believes I am the one who is hurting her. But perhaps I really am the guilty party, I think, since it was my own knee-jerk aggression that provoked these assholes in the first place. I was the one who used my poor beasts to fight a battle that only humans are corrupt enough to wage.

The barb is as long as a dogwood thorn covered in blood. Keeping one hand on Diana's side, I bring the metal arrowhead close to my face, examine its sharp point against my finger, smell the rust of blood, the chemical burn of electricity, the sharp acidic reek of fear. The man moves away, as if to give me space. Perhaps he has some remorse, I think, for torturing a dumb animal, and then I hear the Taser again, the grotesque zapping beam of it, so that I imagine a lap of electricity landing on Rye's back like a lash. I can't stand to look, but I do, because I feel I owe it to Rye to somehow participate in his pain.

Incredibly, the man has missed, or maybe he's actually hit his target, but misjudged the effect, because Rye is more provoked than subdued. He growls and snaps at the man like a pit bull, rage sizzling deep in his throat. Now that he's certain the violence is intentional and not a mere accident of play, he shows his fine teeth, the result of frequent late-night brushing, leaps up at Green Cheeks and bites his hand. I am amazed, since I've never known him to attack a human in all the years since he came to me as a pup. Green Cheeks attempts to switch the Taser to the left hand. But it drops onto the floor, where I am conveniently positioned with Diana, and I splay myself across the polished wood, press my right foot into leg of the sofa, and push off from there, propelling my middle-aged body maybe six feet across the floor, and grabbing the Taser just before he gets there. So instead of grabbing the gun, he grabs my wrist, and I pull him down onto the floor with me, where he knocks into the coffee table and spills Mayweather's empties onto his back.

And just as I think I am in control, another man enters the room, this one in a navy blue ski mask with a band of red around the crown. What is this, trick-or-treat? You would think they would confine themselves to more standard criminal gear. But maybe they don't have the funds to devote to costuming and have to make do with whatever is on hand in their various homes or in the half-price bin at Walmart. This man has a Taser, too, black with yellow stripes, the model the police carry whenever permitted to do so. He holds his weapon at attention and I hold mine and we stand there for a long time without speaking. The Taser is wet in my hand, and I go through all the body fluids before I realize that it's blood. Green Cheek's blood from the bite Rye gave him, or maybe just the blood from Diana's neck. The fear of HIV occurs to me, a possibility I've been trained to consider it in all circumstances, but I concentrate on keeping my hand steady and my eye engaged. I remember how men hate eye contact and hope that this is one time the gendered disability will work to my advantage.

Diana's cries have quieted to a whimper and Green Cheeks is cursing under his breath, favoring the blasphemous, I notice, over the merely profane. Out of the corner of my eye, I see him tear a strip of cloth off the curtain and wrap it around his hand. Lorraine could never imagine that her handiwork could be put to such a use. Thinking of her, I wonder if she will mourn my death as she did my sister's, with obscene and tireless enthusiasm, finally granting me the status of a favored child that I have craved for so long. After all, if I die like this, there will be plenty of opportunity to play up my heroism, to petition the city for a memorial, to embroider my memory, and to hound the press. But the thought of my mother's grief makes me seriously weak, and I have to maintain my aggressive stance at all costs. After all, if Lorraine has done nothing else for me, she has certainly taught me courage. And then I realize they probably don't intend to kill me at all, but only to maim and debilitate me in such a way that I permanently disabled, my insult to their manhood avenged.

As I go over these thoughts, I keep staring at the man, watching him so closely that I see sweat drip from the neck of his ski mask. I imagine that it is my gaze that has forced this fluid from him. I imagine that he is racked with guilt, stewing in self-doubt. And perhaps this is true, because just as I'm thinking it, he caves, looks away from my eyes and down toward my hand, and begins to speak.

"Maybe you don't know who you're dealing with. I been all over this ground and back again in Iraq while you were playing cops-and-robbers in the woods."

I am surprised, in spite of myself, by the deep serious quality of his voice, gruff with cigarettes and testosterone, but still mobile with intelligence and inflection.

"Is that where you learned to maim the weak and torture the innocent?"

"This isn't about over there, is it? It's about a lady ranger can't keep her hands to herself."

"Don't tell me you think you are some masked avenger of vigilante justice." My voice sounds unforgivably prissy, even to myself. My hand is slippery on the Taser, my sweat mixing with Green Cheek's blood. I hear his breathing behind me, and wonder how long it will take for him to recover sufficiently to make another grab at me. At least I know how to use the weapon, which I've handled once or twice in target practice.

"Lady, I am not too concerned about saving trees or possums. I'm just trying to keep my family alive. Yeah, I got benefits, sure, but do you think they cover my kids' asthma or my wife's arthritis? Negative. Nada. Nada. Nada. That's what they tell me over at the VA. She can't even make coffee or give head, much less go to work, and they're telling me I've got to cough up ten thousand dollars for tests. Ten grand for tests! What are they gonna take me for when they actually find a treatment?"

"I don't see how polluting the Karst is going to help your family."

"I know you aren't so concerned about people, right? You dried-up old cunt. You got no one to look out for, no husband to worry about, no kids to support. Why not hug a tree and kick a construction worker? Why not pamper your ugly bitches here and treat them like the kids you'll never have?" The cruelty animates him, so that there is a rough rhythm to his voice, a singsong of accusation that cuts into my underbelly and makes my intestines groan inside their sack of skin.

"You actually think you're more of a person because you've managed to reproduce yourself?" I say.

"I do, yes. I became a much more important guy on the night my daughter was born, and when my son came along I was a regular goddamn prince."

"And so you're prepared to take away my rights?"

"Wake up. There are no more rights, you stupid cunt, just

whatever you can get away wtih." This seems to fire him up for movement, so that he lifts the Taser experimentally and takes aim at my shoulder.

I aim my Taser, too, at the man's lower thigh where I am convinced it will not do any permanent damage.

"Some things you can't let go. Being attacked within your own borders or being disrespected in front of your crew." Now he seems to be talking to himself instead of me. I wonder if I have it in me to use the Taser and I decide that I do. He fires or I fire, I can't tell which happens first, my shoulder shatters with a volt of electricity and I am thrown off my feet and onto the floor. It is a rubbery pain that reverberates through my body and will not stop moving so that I can take its measure. The force field holding my limbs together has been severed, and my physical being seems to expand with every new wave of sensation. I am slipping my boundaries. I am spilling over the living room. I am filling up the world. Is that my blood that I am leaking? Is it urine? Is it energy? Is it the weak electrical charge that is all that is left of my soul? Somewhere, a limb flails rhythmically against a hard surface, somewhere a female voice bleats out a primal scream—pulsing with life and revulsion. Even though it's a sound I've never heard before, I recognize something in the tone, the shape through which the scream passes. It is the voice of my sister, I think. She is trapped in the moment of her death, reliving her agony until someone can break the current and release its power over her.

Green Cheeks takes the Taser from my hand and kicks my hip in passing. I want to tell him to stop, but I cannot speak, cannot move, cannot form a coherent thought. And now I know that awful sound is actually emerging from somewhere within me, a wordless wail of pain, the deepest hurt I remember—has this always been there? I turn over on my belly and start to crawl, arm over arm, away from the source of the pain. And then he shoots me in the back again—please God—I think, *I hope he's missed my spine.* He is shouting now, his voice gathered up into an inhuman grunt, calling me a cunt and a pig and a whore. I can feel his spit on the small of my back where my shirt has pulled up. He kicks me in the buttock and then shoots me in the same spot, like an animal he is trying to subdue, as I keep pulling myself toward Diana and the door.

My landscape is flattened out, and all I can see is the shape of my own arms in front of me, the leg of the sofa, the huddled dark mound of Diana on the floor beyond. The shooting seems to have stopped, at least for now, but the whole room is echoing with its pulse.

I feel Rye approach, drop onto the floor and push up next to me, so that he is lying alongside me from shoulder to thigh, his fur touching my bare arm, an excruciating touch, every rough fiber of his coat a tongue of flame against my singed skin, but all that holds me, in the end, to this spot on the floor, the only piece of territory I can still claim as my own.

22

As Mayweather walked along the city street, bootless, he felt the cold textured concrete on his feet, dodged beer cans and broken bottles, kicked at a cardboard tub bereft of fried chicken, felt the occasional pleasure of a single waxy maple leaf lying flat and face up in his path. He had gone barefoot constantly as a child, so that his feet were often completely soled in calluses and mottled with the purple blood of mulberries. Mayweather thought about the ways in which children were actually tougher than adults, recovering more quickly from physical injuries and blows to their egos, their stubborn idealism forming a sturdy armor against corruption and cynicism. To a large degree, Mayweather had resisted shedding this resilience, remaining impervious if not oblivious so late into his twenties that it seemed either magical or perverse. But now he noticed that his feet had become more sensitive, scraping against the concrete. He could not abide threats to his mother or daughter; he could not pretend that art existed in a shadow land of perpetually suspended morality, or that his actions did not have reverberations in some reality beyond the lens. With one careless fuck, he had caused an entirely new being to form. A girl like himself, but not himself, her face recognizable but unique, her fate separate yet intertwined. And it occurred to him that the cock was not after all an instrument of torture and death, as jokes and hip-hop videos would suggest, but literally the implement of life. Or maybe that made it a tool of torture, after all. Because what could be more terrifying and sadistic than forcing someone to live, and, beyond that, to remain alive in the sorry circumstances of this ass-end, as-is world?

Was this the last of his youth, he wondered? Would he now be humiliated into living a rote existence, all joy and ambition forgotten and replaced with doglike gratitude for the poor plastic gratifications of capitalism and stability? Or would he reject that fate and follow his father in turning his back on his own child? Generations of children following and fathers turning away, whole armies of them, circling in on themselves, in a counter-clockwise spiral of rejection. Looking at the moon above him, he could hardly bear the weight of it, could not think why he himself had been born. The skyline of the little downtown was black against the bruised purple sky: the cupola of City Hall, the gothic clock tower of the university, the lonely spire of the mosque. He had lived here all but four years of his life; he had made two dozen short documentaries, fucked upwards of fifty girls, passed through several networks of street drugs, held any number of low-wage, unskilled jobs. And still he had no idea of how lives were lived here, of how people explained the horrible, meaningless beauty of existence to themselves.

He passed the pool hall, he passed the tattoo parlor, he passed the Internet café and the comic book store, a rush of wind behind him. Was someone following him? He heard the stealthy rustle of soft athletic shoes, a rustle of leaves, the harsh breath of a speedwalker. Finally, there was a hand on his back. Was he about to be mugged? If so, the mugger would be disappointed, because he had a total of six dollars and half a joint on his person. Perhaps, enraged by the victim's poverty, the guy would just settle for the satisfaction of a good beating. Well, Jared had already pinned one man tonight; he might as well take down another. He turned to face the pursuer, as if in a dream, and saw that it was a familiar person after all.

"Jarhead, you all right? You must be pretty fucked up to forget your piece." Chaz lifted Jared's camera by its strap and let it fall back dramatically onto his shoulder, where it looked more fashionable than functional against his tight-fitting orange shirt.

"I'm not going to hand over anything to that fucker."

"Come over here in the light so I can look at you."

Chaz pulled him toward a street lamp, where he grabbed Jared's shoulders roughly, as if to shake any remaining glass out of him, grasped his chin and looked into his eyes for what—signs of drug use, rebellion, brain damage? He pulled down the skin beneath each eye to examine the eyeballs.

"Quick, what's the year?" he asked.

"Two thousand seven."

"Who's the President?"

"George Bush the Sequel."

"Where's the fire?"

"In my brain. Man, did you hear that asshole go on about how he's going to get to me through my mom's credit report?"

"Listen, Jared, you don't have to do anything you don't want, but it looks to me like you've spent a lot of years trying to decide how to support yourself and you've come up with squat."

"So you're going to help me out by hooking me up with a blackmailer. Man, what do you think of me? Really, do I look like some small-time criminal trying to sell out his mother and his vision?"

"You look like a guy who needs to sleep it off. You've got a cut on your cheek." he said, collecting some blood on his finger and holding it out for Jared's inspection. "Why don't you let me drive you home?"

Jared hadn't even felt a scrape. Raising his hand to the wound, he thought of his mom and Wade awakened by the sound of the front door opening, making an even louder racket now than it had when he was a teenager due to years of the foundation settling and resettling in alternating seasons of drought and heavy rain. He hadn't been home for over forty-eight hours. But he didn't really want to show up now, bloody and high, around eleven-thirty, he guessed, when both of them would be in bed but still navigating the lightest phase of their sleep cycle, sure to get up and demand an explanation. Of course, there was some-where else he might be expected. He tried to think whether he had told Sally he would get back to her tonight. As far as he could tell, they hadn't made a plan, but he imagined her down-ing a brew out on the back deck in the moonlight, dragging a twig through the wax of the citronella candle, and waiting for his return.

"Maybe you could take me out to the ranger's place."

"That where you stashed the film?"

"That's where I'm staying for a while. You know, at the moment, I'm transitional."

Chaz nodded and knocked Jared in the shoulder. "What did I tell you about those older women?"

"Cut the crap, Chaz. Don't you ever get sick of yourself? Or do you really think it's cute, like I'm just a prize stud waiting to have a go at whoever gets thrown my way?"

"When you are older—if you ever get any older—you'll understand. After a while, you have to start setting things in motion just to stay alive."

"So you set me on your wife."

Chaz looked away at a couple of miniskirts passing down the street, as if to evaluate the thigh muscles underneath. "I guess I got carried away. Look, I love you, man. You are my soul. You are the guy I would've been if I hadn't gotten entangled in the meshes of responsibility. I love Etta, too, you know. She's an amazing hybrid, a real exotic, would never have occurred in the wild."

Mayweather, sickened by the analogy, interrupted before he had to hear any more. "And what about Ellen? What does she get out of the whole deal?"

"I don't know, a get-out-of-jail-free card, a new house, another kid."

"You think that's it? That's all she deserves?"

"More than you could ever do for a woman, isn't it?"

Mayweather blushed, his skin newly sensitive, as if singed with the light from the streetlamp. "I wouldn't be so sure," he said.

Back in the Beamer, Jared sat in the passenger seat and felt as if they'd forgotten something. Britney? The cat? The purpose of the evening? Chaz dumped the camera, without ceremony, into his lap, and he lifted it out of its case, set about examining it for signs of interference. No, the last shot in it was his own, a sequence of Raven Pillage lecturing the Bombers, her cat's-eye glasses flashing and her long braids draped in front of her like a priest's vestments, Lorraine holding up the Mexican platter, Britney raising her skinny arm. But somehow, his grasp on the material and the instrument seemed different. He wondered whether Chaz actually planned to sell the rink or if he was just bluffing. He wondered if this whole coup was merely Reenie's way of flirting. He wondered if Britney secretly enjoyed seeing her image bought and sold.

"What about Brit?" he said.

"I'm leaving her behind to soothe Bailey's bruised ego. For an artist, you are quite the pugilist. Maybe we could get you on the rink during intermission, have you take on a volunteer from the crowd."

Mayweather didn't reply, but just switched the radio from the aging hipster channel, now playing Elvis Costello's "Watching the Detectives" to Boonslick Country, where they were in the midst of a Johnny and June Carter Cash number, "I'm Going Down to Jackson." Maybe monogamy was a pipedream after all, only managed with large doses of infidelity or violent sparring. What was worse, the outright abandonment his mother had experienced, or the coy detachment of Ellen's marriage to Chaz? Jared had been around the two of them for years, seen their marriage from inside and out: Ellen biting her lip when Chaz appraised a girl at a party, Chaz raising his heavy eyebrows in dismay or encouragement when Ellen talked at length about her body or her admirers, the hurried call home in the midst of a sex session, the careful coordination of tasks at a dinner party, the bare breast on the screen saver, the possessive hand on a hip. What could it mean? People certainly threw around the word love. Mayweather felt it was more honest to avoid the term altogether and to limit himself to expressing appreciation for particular sex acts, social favors, monetary contributions, or body parts. That way, he was always above board and in the clear.

Chaz turned the music down so low that Jared could hear him chewing gum over the Cash duet. They drove out of the District with its lighted storefronts, past the used car lots and hardware stores and the Empire Roller Rink sitting pretty on a slight rise behind a dive bar. They glided into the dark of the country road. The moon was out, and the stars were prevalent under its beams. Jared thought he could make out Orion, and he remembered Sally standing inside his arms, as close as the lining of his coat, taking his hand in hers to trace the outlines of the hunter's constellation.

The trees were shaking in the wind, bending and rising, black against the sky. He cracked a window just to smell the country air and took in the dry pine and the deciduous rot, gunpowder, ash, and a distant spray of skunk. The creek was so close he could hear it moving, restless in its bed. He looked at the camera in his lap, the hole in the leg of his jeans, felt a chill and remembered that he'd left his purple hoodie at Sally's place. He was suddenly anxious to get back, to check his movie to see if it was as fresh as he remembered, to tuck his bare feet in the sweet spot under the sofa cushion, to feel a small but powerful hand moving with forgiveness over his belly and toward his groin.

Beside him, Chaz had turned inward, his profile pale and unrelenting against the night sky. Jared looked at him, trying to think what he needed to say.

"You know, she is a ball-breaker," Chaz commented out of nowhere, holding the steering wheel near the bottom with one hand.

"I think I can handle it."

"The last guy wasn't in such good shape when he limped out of town."

"What do you think I'm doing, proposing? I'm just going back to collect my stuff."

"I'm only saying, when you're thirty-five, she'll be over fifty."

"If I even make it that far," Jared said.

Sally's place was at a turnoff just past a couple of Asian massage parlors and the gentleman's club, Teaser's. They took the turn without further comment, drove down the gravel road feeling the wheels gristle and listening to the bits of rock fly off like hail behind them. It was a noisy approach, and Jared guessed that Sally would probably hear them drive up if she was still awake and sitting out on the deck. If not, she would probably sleep through it and wake up only when he lifted the covers to find her all warm and yeasty in her flannel sheets.

The mailbox at the side of the road was open, its long red flag thrown up in a salute. The house itself was hidden from the road, and the gravel drive was as long as a city block. After a couple of minutes, they saw the house emerge from the trees, a tall triangular shape like a treehouse, the upper floors darkened, but the front room lit a brilliant yellow, the same color as the moon. In front of the house, Jared saw not one truck but two.

"Looks like the old girl has company," Chaz said.

Jared remembered the night, years ago, when he'd come around and found her fucking her supervisor from the government job in Jefferson City, the car with the baby seat in the back, the gory view from the kitchen window. He'd saved her from a big mistake that time and he was ready to do it again, if necessary, in spite of jealousy and loss of face. Who could she be with at this time of night? He tried to remember the vehicle of her ex, but came up with nothing. Besides, the guy could be driving anything by now.

Chaz sat idling the engine, waiting for Jared's decision.

"Well, do you want to find out or no?"

Jared sat stick-still in the seat and gripped his camera, pressed his toes into the floorboards, felt the hot breath of the heater on his bare ankles.

"If you don't mind, I'll come in and take another look at that movie," Chaz said.

"We'll have to get her to the door first."

"What, you're telling me you don't have a key? What kind of man are you?"

But Jared was already half out of the car, his feet on the ground, stomping his boots back on. When he stood, a pellet of glass fell from the pocket of his jeans and he reached down to pick it up and stare into the crystal kernel: a cloudy of piece of hail, a bit of quartz, a misshapen marble.

In the yard, the grapevines swayed on their stakes, the tendrils making dark arabesques in the strangely pale evening. An owl had its say, and a small animal, a fox or badger, passed quickly through the garden. Jared stretched his long limbs, remembering the pleasure of unlimited space, his body seeming to fill the whole night, so that he couldn't distinguish himself from the objects around him. He could hear something in the house, a male voice, shouting rhythmically; he could feel the hairs elevating one by one on the back of his neck. Then by some instinct he went around to the deck and passed through the back door from there. The kitchen was empty, and the sound was coming from the living room, where there was a body stretched out on the floor with a man standing over it—some kind of bondage or role-playing? The prostrated form was clearly Sally, the long ash-blond hair covering the face and splayed out onto the darker floorboards, the rounded but muscular hips slightly raised, so that the waistband of her gray yoga pants dipped to reveal the pale in-curve of her back and a bit of bright pink cotton panties. He knew she was perverse, but this was the first he'd seen of this particular sport, and he felt the need to comprehend the parameters of the game before interrupting. His cock filled with blood and moved tentatively against his groin. For one second, he thought he would have to report back to Chaz empty-handed and ask, shamefaced, for a ride back into town. But he found himself paralyzed at his post in the doorway, forced to watch the session to its bitter end. He touched himself and even his hand felt the shock of pleasure, the nerve endings in his palm responding to the nerve endings in his cock and multiplying the sensation. Then he began to make out the man's words, saw the second man on the periphery and knew, with a deep sickening blow to his solar plexus, that it was something else entirely. He could not stand there looking and speculating any longer. He had to take his chances and go in.

23

I wake up, as if from a nightmare, and realize that it is true. I must have passed out, and in those seconds or minutes of unconsciousness, dreamt that I was viewing the violence on video, the bright colors of the attackers' masks, the dramatic shape of the Tasers, Diana's dark form twisted in air. But when I come to, I'm in the same situation, lying on the wood floor of my living room in a pool of sweat and piss, the Navy ski mask behind me, reciting horrors I have never thought of, children with their faces ripped off by bombs, rapes enacted on the bodies of mutilated girls, mothers trying to reattach the severed limbs of their dying children, men castrated in the streets, even dogs tortured with explosives up their asses and barbed wire around their necks. How can a pampered bitch like me even pretend to know enough to carry a badge and serve her country?

I can still feel Rye shivering beside me, the hard muscle vibrating under the fur. Diana is on the floor beyond me, perfectly still. I pray to any passing god or goddess that she is not dead, but only bluffing, holding her energy in reserve. Perhaps it is better to play dead, but something within me won't stay put and I struggle to get up, using my hips for leverage and finally pushing myself up onto my knees.

There is a boot in the small of my back, pressing me back down toward the floor.

"Bitch, I will blast you again if you move a muscle. And these mutts are going to be next. "

I freeze, unsure whether to take the risk of easing back onto the ground, so I just stay there on my hands and knees, my hair falling over my face so that I see Diana's dark shape through a veil of blond mane. How long can I possibly stay in this position? My muscles are cramping so hard they're making me nauseous, a menstrual ache running through my entire body. My bones grind against each other and I can feel the places where the darts have pierced my skin, radioactive spots singing back in on themselves. I try to remember my police training. This would not have happened if I didn't live alone, I think, and then I try to erase the thought, because feeling sorry for myself will only drain me of the aggression I might otherwise use to escape. Navy Ski Mask is moving in, dangerously close to my ass. I feel him nudge me with his knee and flinch away, protecting my sore spots. But I can't afford to think of my pain; I need to stay focused on my mobility. I can't let go and imagine myself a helpless thing to be manipulated by his will. And then, as I draw my attention away from my wounds, I am suddenly aware of my feet, agile in thick warm socks. My feet are in fact, very close to his, and he is slightly off balance, I realize, leaning over me. I check my balance in preparation and then just as he hits me on the ass with the butt-end of the Taser, I deliver a mule kick to his thigh or groin—I can't tell which—and knock him down to the ground.

In the confusion, he lands on my back and I throw him off, we roll around on the floor, the barbs pushing deeper into my

flesh. I have one split second of confusion in which to grab the
Taser from him, and I take the chance while I can, knocking the
weapon away from him so that it slides under a chair, then propelling myself forward to root under the dust ruffle and pull it
out by its nose.

Green Cheeks must be afraid to shoot, seeing that Navy and
I are so close together entangled here on the ground. I see him
moving around for a clear view of the situation. Then I am
aware of another man behind him, the third polluter, surely,
who has not shown up until now. Can I even pretend to contend
with three men, all younger than myself and seasoned with hard
physical labor? I will if I have to, I think, because I am not ready
to lie down and die. Where does this determination come from?
Up until this point, I was not sure I had a will to live at all, even in
the coziest of circumstances, and here I am fighting for a chance
to survive under any terms at all. Because regardless of the dubious value of my misspent life, I cannot let anyone take it away
from me by force.

I lift the black Taser, its yellow stripes mocking the idea of
caution. But my discipline is so strong that even in extremis,
the rules for the proper use of such weapons go through my
head: the suspect should be unarmed and uncontrolled, not visibly pregnant or disabled, a clear and present danger to others
or himself. Check, check, check, and check. I aim for the large
muscles in Green Cheeks' thigh. As I pull the trigger, I feel the
pressure of its release, not a real kick, since it is so much lighter
than a pistol, but a release and sigh like an arrow shot from a
bow. The man falls, and begins to yelp in deep repetitive curses.
It is harrowing sound and I want, with all my instincts, to go
and help him, to examine the wound, to make what repairs I
can. There is, already, remorse for an action I can hardly regret.
But I recognize this impulse for the womanly indulgence it is

and steel myself with anger: my dogs, my creek, my pond, my house, my body. I feel the rage quicken in me, taking over my limbs with frenzy, pouring fever into my brain, so that his cries become a kind of rageful music, the soundtrack to my altered state. I am back in fighting shape again; I feel my powers return, and remember the image of myself holding the pistol, my hair flying, and everything that is normally turned inward—making me awkward and tentative—released on the polluters in a single flowing gesture of destruction.

Then, without looking too closely, I shoot the man standing behind Green Cheeks, too. And just as the twin probes pass out of the Taser, I look at the face and see that it is Mayweather, home from some adventure, the fishing lures on his hat agleam in the fluorescent light, his expression still dreamlike with curiosity. I only hope that I have avoided the chest and heart. He falls to the floor, too, and his voice erupts, like sound passing through a cheese grater, so that my organs move inside me and my breasts ache with the weight of what I've done. I try to go to him, and as I do, I feel Navy Ski Mask grab my ankle, pull me down again. I am straining toward Mayweather, my body stretched out as far as it will go, convinced that nothing can prevent me from getting there. On my way, I grab Green Cheeks' purple Taser, gather it toward my chest, and keep crawling. Mayweather's eyes roll back in his head, so far back that I can only see the whites, like the blank stare of a marble statue. When the irises return to view, their hazel depths have been emptied out, exposing a detritus of green in the light brown pools. The darts have pierced his shirt, not in the chest, as it turns out, but in the stomach, and I pull them out, lift the thin cotton and see the twin marks they have left, like the fangs of a snake in the smooth elastic flesh with its light covering of brown hairs. He is rocking on his spine. I touch my cheek to his abdomen, smell the sharp singe of electricity, and imagine that I am a native woman who can suck the poison out of his wounds. But Mayweather has been invaded with a current, not venom, and its effects are invisible, unknowable, and probably long-term.

I aim both Tasers at Navy. I'm not sure exactly what I plan to do, but before I can decide, I hear someone walking up behind me, someone in light shoes, whistling a familiar tune.

His step stops just behind me, there is a pause, and he clicks on his iPhone.

"Could you get a couple of police cars and an ambulances out here at twelve-twenty Karst Road ASAP?"

Once he signs off, he takes one of the Tasers from me, directs the men to sit in straight-backed chairs, and ties their arms behind them with the sashes from the living-room curtains, telling me I'm lucky that he takes an interest in his friends' romantic entanglements. Otherwise, he would be halfway back to Boonslick in his Beamer by now. "But that's why you love me, isn't it," he says, "Because you know I've always got your back."

I would respond, but the adrenaline is draining from my body, and the pain is filling up all available space in my consciousness. I realize that the quills are still in me, how many, I'm not sure, but I must look like a porcupine here hovering over Mayweather. He is still groaning, but the frequency is decreasing, and his eyes are showing signs of recognition and intelligence.

Chaz strips the ski masks off the intruders and cocks his head at them, as if trying to get an angle on their motivation. "I don't know, but if it was me, I'd stick with basic black for illegal acts."

"It's the same guys," I say, struggling to regain my voice. "The polluters from out at the Karst."

Green Checks, as expected, is the older crew chief with the graying chest hair, and Navy is the sunburned redhead. They both curse at Chaz, but I can tell, too, that they are relieved to have the whole incident behind them. But where is the man I actually threatened? He doesn't seem to have shown up at all. I want to ask about him, but I find that I am unable to speak. Now that Chaz has taken over, I feel myself easing back into the circuit of my own pain.

His cell phone rings with the shout and siren of a hip-hop anthem that sounds like a police raid. But this time it really is the police, which I know because he has conveniently selected the speakerphone function, perhaps to intimidate the intruders. "Boonslick's finest, on our way. Everything under control?"

"We're all still alive, if that's what you mean," Chaz says. "But we could really use some immediate attention."

I see that Rye has walked over to Diana and is sniffing her. She lifts her head slightly and my heart jumps, a jagged motion of joy. If she survives, I tell myself, Mayweather will be all right, too, and I will live to make it up to all of them.

"Now," Chaz says, settling onto a footrest and crossing his knees. "You fellows look like upright citizens. What the hell are you doing? Your boss Bailey is busting his balls trying to make your last criminal act disappear from the record and you are out accumulating more charges. I tell you, the ingratitude of the working class, it's pretty astonishing."

Navy may be tied up, but he isn't gagged. "You grateful for what I did to those sand niggers? Or do you want to make that disappear, too?"

"That, my friend, is politics, about which I have no opinion. This is purely business. Very bad business, if you ask me. "

Meanwhile, Mayweather props himself up and begins to pull a dart out of my back. I think of the seeds sticking to his sweatshirt, the same ones that cling so steadfastly to my pant legs and sweat socks that I can't get them out in the wash. What does it take to rid yourself of guilt by association? The war, the contractors, even the government, not to mention the sexual and economic adventures of your lovers and friends. He twists the dart around to loosen it, like an unwanted staple in a document, and I wonder if he is taking relish in being a little rough. Why not? I'm the one who shot him, after all, while he was nothing but an innocent bystander for once. One hand presses sweetly on my back, urging my soul to return and re-inhabit my body, while the other roots the arrow around in the flesh, inflicting the most excruciating agony.

"Well," he says, "maybe you are the S-and-M type after all. If you wanted me back so bad, you just had to say so. You didn't have to take me down like a six-point buck."

"At least I brought you in alive," I say, and the dart comes away in his hand. He holds it in his palm and presents it to me, the way I show Di and Rye their ticks when I have uprooted them with my fingernails. It is just as bloody, and several times as large, but I am happy that I have someone to groom me for a change.

24

In the emergency room, Mayweather was forced, once again, to own up to his lack of insurance. He would not have even come if Sally and Chaz hadn't forced him. How much could they possibly charge for the visit? Sally had already removed the barbs, after all, and the only thing the nurse in the teddy bear scrubs seemed to offer was a quick blood-pressure check and a Breathalyzer test. His head was still singing with the rush of electricity, the sensation of being shut down mid-image and then rebooted without benefit of having saved his file. Sitting on the examination table, he lifted the gown and looked at the points of entry, two ugly holes to the right of his belly button, still smeared with blood. It looked like he'd been snagged with a huge fishhook, fought his way off, and then gotten hooked again. He was surprised, however, that the pain was not localized, but seemed to pulse through his entire body, as if he were a mosquito zapper, or actually, the mosquito and the zapper, too.

The resident on duty, a man with an alarming crop of thick dark hair, a beaked nose, weak chin, and huge Adam's apple, who seemed hardly older than Mayweather, came in and gave him a lecture about the amount if alcohol in his bloodstream, .15 percent, well over the legal limit.

"I wasn't driving, dude."

"Still, why would you want to do that to your body?" the doctor asked. What was it? Dr. Aznar? He looked like he could be Arabic, but spoke with no discernable accent. In fact, the perfection and formality of his language was a bit suspicious, in a guy so relatively youthful. Mayweather looked closer and saw that his skin was an exotic shade of amber with olive undertones, probably a bitch to film without going green, and his eyebrows were so thick they totally obscured the shape of the brow.

Dr. Aznar untied Mayweather's hospital gown and told him to take a deep breath, then listened to his heart thudding its reggae rhythm while Mayweather stared at his own pale legs in the short gown. Was that another bruise on his thigh? It didn't seem as if he had seen his own body in weeks and sat there gazing at the long blades of his calves, the knees knotted with muscle, the sparse hairs slightly darker than the oily curls on his head. When he looked more closely, he saw that the hairs actually curled off in different directions, as if they were drawn by competing currents, and couldn't remember if they'd always been this way. The doctor checked his reflexes, one knee then the other, looked into the depths of the eyes and ears. His touch was light but authoritative, and Jared, perhaps due to his weakened condition, found himself liking the guy, in spite of all indicators of to the contrary.

"How'd you get the cut?" he said.

"Oh, that. An unrelated incident. Long night, you know."

"I'll be up front with you, Jared. We don't really know much about the effect of these Tasers. If there is no immediate reaction, no heart attack, no seizure, you could be in the clear. But there are no studies on the long-term effects, which could, in some instances, include stroke, ongoing heart conditions, seizures, and memory loss. Generally speaking, Tasers are used on a class of people, who, let's be honest, often already have a host of other troubles, ranging from addictions of every variety to schizophrenia, diabetes, and AIDS. So there goes your control group out the window. Still, it helps us to know if there are any preexisting conditions. So—do you have any medical problems I should know about? Other than the extravagant alcohol intake, of course."

Mayweather sat with his gown open, a chilly wind down his spine, and pondered his physical history. It seemed that most of his life was spent coaxing his body to comply with the demands of his art. His gut, his appetites, his headaches and insomnia. "Well, I do get some wicked migraines," he said, finally, just to have something to offer.

The doctor's eyebrow perked up, and Jared could feel his excitement. "And what do you do when you feel one coming on?"

"Smoke a bowl, if I can. Then I just go to bed and sleep it off."

"Cannabis is a known deterrent. Although unfortunately illegal, so I can't recommend it." The fact that he admitted this surprised Mayweather and made him like the doctor more. "When's the last time you had one of these migraines?

"Seems like the day before yesterday. It's been a hell of a week."

"And how does your head feel now?"

"Muddled, man. I just got shot by my own girlfriend. So naturally I'm a little confused."

"I understand it was a grisly scene. Looks like ten to twenty shots fired, animals among the targets."

"Incredible."

"We are seeing more and more of these incidents. Of course, most of the victims up to now have been shot by the police. But with commercial accessibility, all that could be changing."

"You mean people will be zapping each other for fun and games?"

"You'd be surprised what people will do, even to their own relatives. We think that even the police shouldn't be using these weapons without further studies. After all, they're classified as implements of torture by Amnesty International. And now we are faced with the prospect of a whole population applying electric shock therapy to their friends and neighbors at will."

"Bad vibes, definitely."

"It gives a whole new meaning to the concept of social engineering." Dr. Aznar slapped the plastic padding of the examining table by Jared's leg. "So what does this mean for you? Migraines are still a mystery to us, but the depolarization theory, the more prominent one these days, says that a migraine comes along when neurological activity is depressed over a certain area of your cortex. The process begins up to twenty-four hours before you feel the incident peak. During that time, you'll probably get some warning signs, changes in smells or tastes, auras, sensitivity to light or visual stimulation, emotional dips and surges. And then, when the migraine crests, you go into complete lockdown, am I right? Believe it or not, some researchers have been applying shock therapy, very much like these Tasers, in order to cure migraine patients. What they do is restimulated the area, get traffic flowing, in that pre-migraine window before there's complete gridlock in your brain. So feasibly, you might have gotten a beneficial effect."

"Like shocked straight?"

"Something like that. On the other hand, the treatment is highly experimental. You've heard about all the shock therapy in the sixties and seventies, right? They blasted a whole generation of housewives and vagrants, the results not so good, to my way of thinking. Look, electricity is going on in your body all the time. That's how the synapses communicate with one another. So when someone says two people have 'electricity' between them, it's not just a figure of speech. But when we disrupt that flow, we take some big chances, chances with moral implications. Are we just speeding up traffic for a while? Introducing a detour? Or are we permanently rerouting the neighborhood? You're heard of people who get struck by lighting and develop a new tic or talent, lose their sense of taste or smell? We just don't know how it happens, and results vary incredibly from individual to individual. Frankly, our methods are still pretty crude."

As Dr. Aznar spoke, the sounds of the emergency room formed a symphony behind him—the beep of monitors, the ring of the phones, the intermittent cries of patients, the creaking of gurneys. It did sound pretty crude, Mayweather thought. They were not in a separate room, but simply a little nook with a bed and a few cabinets, a curtain drawn closed around them. Somewhere nearby, Sally was getting the same treatment. Mayweather wondered how she was faring. She'd always seemed fairly sturdy, but like Aznar said, you never knew. She had been zapped, what, three or four times, and still retained the will to save herself. That was a woman you'd always be able to depend on in an apocalypse.

"So, bottom line, you will want to watch yourself for symptoms for the next few days and let us know if there are any changes. Do you mind if I take a look at the wound?"

Mayweather nodded and the doctor dropped the gown from his shoulders, so that it fell onto his lap, exposing the broad bony chest and the belly rich with irregular living and the twin points of entry, looking swollen, the skin raised like anthills around them. The doctor palpated the wounds with his gloved hands, reached for a swab, and cleaned away the dried blood.

Mayweather felt himself relax under the touch that wasn't sexual, but not entirely dispassionate, either. What would it be to touch other bodies for a living—not simply to record their images, but to actually interfere with them, altering their physical existence in time and space, reconfiguring their being?

"Well, it's a clean entry. Any abdominal pains at all?"

"Nope. In fact, I'm feeling pretty hungry."

"Well, looks like you got lucky and your gut blocked the barbs."

"Saved by the belly, right? And they say that belly fat is unhealthy."

"We should keep you overnight for observation, though."

"Look, about that, I am not insured, so … I know a hospital stay costs a shitload and I just can't do that to my mom."

Dr. Aznar looked over Jared's head at the clock on the wall. "I realize that's an issue, but there's also a question of medical accountability."

"How about I sleep on a sofa in the waiting room and just give a shout-out to the nurse if start to get queasy?"

"Well, I guess that would be just as good."

"Thanks, man. You seem pretty flexible."

Dr. Aznar nodded, so that Mayweather saw the white part in his black hair, the pale scalp nearly blue with the reflection. "Most people think medicine is a hard science, but when you get all the factors in play—the environment, the individual, the rich array of genetic variations and chemical interactions—it's really more of an art."

So this was why Mayweather liked the guy, he thought. But then, he realized, he had heard Chaz use the same line about business being the highest form of creativity maybe two dozen times. So what was the difference? Was art really something sacred, set off from the concerns of commerce and industry, or was it an impulse that ran through every existence like a live wire in the pattern of the weave?

A nurse looked into the waiting room, a pretty woman with muted freckles and a sharp, compact chin. "Not conducting another symposium, are you Dr. Aznar? We've got a head wound in Area C."

Aznar looked up, startled, his eyes dilated and his Adam's apple agog. He pulled the gown up to Mayweather's shoulders and tied it back up again quickly, as if he had considered the body too closely, then offered his hand. "That's my cue, Jared. I'll check in on you in the waiting room before I go home. Oh, and let's follow up on those migraines. You know, you don't necessarily have to tough it out all alone."

Once the doctor was gone, Mayweather stood up, untied the gown again, and let it fall to the floor. He looked down at his body, its wounds and bruises, its crests and curves. His chest was broad and hairless, marked with a deep indentation at the breastbone, where Sally would often press her thumb with satisfaction. His belly sat stubbornly above his groin, so tightly packed that it appeared to be an entirely separate entity. And underneath, his cock hung draped over a cascade of hair and balls, at rest for now, a long pink tube with no juice running through it. His legs, unlike the rest of his body, were densely muscled from walking all around town and his feet were so large that he often had trouble finding shoes, the toes splayed and the knuckles as prominent as the ones on his hands. It was no longer the body of a very young man, or even a particularly healthy one. Mayweather thought about what Aznar had told him. He wondered if the make of his body—the migraine personality—was what caused him to want to be an artist, and if it was this same vulnerability to sound, light, and beauty that prevented him from fulfilling his artistic ambitions in the end. He'd always assumed it was something deeper. But could anything really go deeper than your own cortex and synapses? Mayweather touched one wound then the other, fitting his fingers to the entry points, and feeling for a sign.

When the nurse came in five minutes later to admit him for the night, she would find the white hospital gown abandoned on the floor of the emergency room, the body itself nowhere in sight.

25

After all that's happened, I'm surprised to find myself in the Department of Natural Resources, five minutes early for my eleven-thirty appointment. My ass is so sore that the thirty- minute drive to Jefferson City felt like I was riding bareback on an unbroken stallion instead of settled comfortably in the cab of my trusty Dodge truck. But now that I've arrived, I feel a resurgence of confidence. When I worked here years ago, I wore a different uniform: silky blouses in bright colors, sensible skirts, low-heeled pumps, a quick dash of color over my cheeks and lips. This morning I tried to replicate the look but couldn't bear to pull on nylons over my wounds, and so settled for a modified version: a white tuxedo shirt, rich brown velvet trousers just now coming into season, a pair of tooled boots with two-inch heels. I am nubby where I used to be shiny, and slightly larger around the hips and waist, but also more muscular from physical labor. I can't imagine that Eric has aged any better. And yet, somehow it will always be me who has to worry about slipping from the peak of physical perfection that characterized our three-year affair at the end of the last century, when we were both still able to keep senators' hours and engage in sexual congress more than once a day. Eric had a family at the time, one kid at first and two by the point when, at the insistence of his wife, he packed me up with my severance pay and sent me away to work at the Karst. I was ambivalent about marriage, anyway and had no desire to exchange my adrenaline-fueled affair for sweatpants and a minivan.

As it turned out, I did like the new job at Karst Park, which took me back to Boonslick and my family, reignited my passion for wilderness, and led to my marriage to Mason. So I have no regrets, really. But it is still painful to consider the disparity in our positions. Eric was appointed assistant director of the Natural Resources two years ago and is clearly being groomed as the director; he still has the same long-suffering and devoted wife, a beautiful half-grown family, and no doubt at least one or two convenient aspiring mistresses on the side, while I, though pretty well settled, look like someone who has missed out on life in all three major categories: romance, family, and career. And now I'm back in his office asking him for help. It's not a happy situation, and I search my mind for positive spins on my current fate: I'm mentoring my niece, I'm exploring new career options, I'm getting some young, unfettered ass with no strings attached.

I look down at my hands curled in my lap and regret not putting on more lotion before I left the house. I survey my high-necked blouse and wish it revealed some cleavage, the sexual attribute that seems to wear best with age, since, as the flesh of my chest loosens, there's more available meat to push up with a supportive underwire bra. I'm only too happy that I can't see my own face and the effects of outrage, torture and sleep deprivation on my complexion. To distract myself, I examine a map of Boonslick County on the wall, the red business zone in the middle representing the District, bolstered by long sidebars of strip malls on all sides. The yellow residential areas bleed into the city's center to form an orange ring and then become strictly segregated at the edges, some of them so new their street names have been written in by a practiced hand in a very fine black pen. And there along the northwest border is the Missouri River, its irregular blue cord poised like a lash, always on the ready to change course and wipe out everything the in the next flood.

I am seated on a brown sofa, trying to position myself so that my back doesn't touch the sofa cushions and reactivate my multiple Taser wounds. It's amazing how quickly the crisis has been sorted out. The ski masks are in police custody, Di and Rye are at the vet's for observation, Mayweather is out at the A-frame, sleeping it off. And I am visiting Eric's office with a story that has been dramatically altered in the past twelve hours since I sent my e-mail. I haven't seen Eric in years. He used to visit me out in Boonslick for the occasional courtesy call, then after I put a stop to that, I saw him a few more times at official functions But I haven't even caught sight of him for at least three summers now. I suppose he's had his nose to the Natural Resources grindstone. I wonder if he'll still have that defiant quality that set my teeth on edge. Or will the system have sucked all that out of him and left a competent bureaucrat with nothing to distinguish him but a taste for tail and gin?

It's too bad that I have to see him in these circumstances. I am still more than a bit shaky; in fact, I have had a severe case of the shakes since the incident last night. I can see my thigh vibrating, and even my thoughts seem to fly up syncopated and disconnected: Di in her deathlike stupor, Gabriella unconscious in the hospital bed, Navy's harsh voice shouting obscenities behind me, Mayweather, Mayweather, Mayweather, who I can't lay claim to and I can't forget. The night in the hospital, however, has done me some good, and I find that I am oddly soothed by the environment of the office, with its fluorescent light and its astringent smell. The receptionist, a plump but well-made-up woman of thirty-five or forty, is reading a romance novel marked with a Bible bookmark, which she patiently replaces, with a smile and a sigh, every time someone enters the room. The walls are covered with Missouri memorabilia: a sign from the old Boonslick Tavern, a university banner from the fifties, a Civil War plaque from the negro cemetery, theater posters from the Rialto, and of course maps showing the progression of each city's grid.

I have lived here most of my life and so I've seen some of these changes myself. Boonslick's simple downtown becoming a hippie hangout, then a punk scene, and finally a tourist trap for those seeking some safe belated bohemia on the plains, the cow pastures and soybean fields cut up, one by one, into subdivisions with rustic names for plain folks interested in rural living without the work or dirt. Even I have morphed inside my skin, from a shy girl overshadowed by her younger sister to a reckless wanderer, a hard-boiled bureaucrat, the other woman, the older woman, a lady ranger, a hippie wife, a roller derby dominatrix, and a vigilante cause celebre. For a moment, I marvel that all those manifestations have unfolded out of the pale, undeveloped identity that was my original self, and wonder whether the shifting roles are as shallow and disingenuous as those forced onto the land.

When the receptionist calls my name, I get up very slowly, unclamping my muscles one at a time and avoiding my Taser wounds. Eric stands there, as he still does in my dreams, his long limbs and mobile fleshy features, the body still showing the discipline of his high school swim team, and the face with that same smart-ass expression that always made me want to jump his bones. But his slicked-back hair is now engraved with silver and his unfashionable mustache is graying in two thick swatches over the sensitive center part of his lips. His wardrobe, formerly so slick as to suggest homosexuality, has become downright homey.

He wears a pair of navy suit trousers with a blue vest trimmed in leather, a modified work outfit that suggests a country lawyer, a shirt with cuffs rolled up to reveal his long articulated forearms, and a quite conventional platinum wristwatch. Perhaps this is merely the costume of high-ranking government official in a backward rural state?

"Sal," he says, without ceremony. "Good to see you, Sal." His handshake is rough and elastic, and I'm happy to note that he hasn't become one of those professionals who treat women with the exaggerated chivalry that always feels more like mockery to me.

Eric doesn't bother to disguise his sexual appraisal, as he looks me up and down. I'm actually happy, I decide, with my wardrobe choice, which shows my figure to advantage and suggests something of the rustic character of my new life in the woods. However, I can't help but wish I were seeing him under better circumstances, not after my body has been pierced, electrocuted, and manhandled and my mind has been torn into confetti by the strain.

But I still meet his eyes, just as I did in the old days, and don't shrink under examination.

"Are you satisfied with the upkeep?" I say.

"Not bad. What are you now, forty-five?"

"What are you, fifty-two?"

"Next birthday. We're on the down slope, Sal. But that doesn't mean we can't enjoy the ride."

And it is as if I never left, the sense of time turning over and taking off, the two of us on a bubble speeding toward some unknown destination and not caring what we might crash into along the way. I feel warmth suffuse my cleavage and a single drop of sweat fall through my bra, sliding down toward my belly and igniting the skin as it goes. Sweat thick and sticky with minerals, more like oil than water. Is this a belated volt passing through my system? A hot flash of warning? A memory of the exertion I've expended over this man whose love for me will never return? I've been standing here alone so long on the rugged peak of my life that I can't tell anymore.

"Well," I say. "It's been one hell of an uphill climb."

Eric's office is a holy disaster, just as it used to be over in the old place: golf clubs, piles of files and newspapers heaped on the floor, an espresso machine set up on a mini-fridge, a jar of striped mints and a bowl of crab apples on the desk, a half-played game of horseshoes lying in the corner. He has used the entire wall space as a bulletin board, legal notices, maps stabbed with stickpins, even a couple of items tacked to the wall with long dog-wood thorns, as if to emphasize their pressing importance.

I look around for the inevitable family photo and see it poised there on the desk in an oak frame—three kids now, good-looking grade-schoolers, and a pretty brunette wife who looks self-satisfied as the domestic goddess of her own cook-ing show. It occurs to me that the second child, a girl with thick sun-streaked doggy ears and Eric's sensual lips, could be mine—since I was regularly screwing her father for eighteen months on either side of her birth. The wife is only thirty-five, by my calculations, and the age difference between her and her husband is approximately the same as the one between Mayweather and myself.

"What can I offer you, Sal? Soda, coffee, a cigar?"

I make a dubious face and he laughs. "Nowadays, we actually have to go down to the boiler room to smoke the cigar, so maybe we should just stick to the beverages."

"A soda is good," I say. "I still like the clear kind, diet if it's available."

He gets a cold one out of his fridge and tosses it at me; after the night I've had, I'm surprised to catch it, my old softball skills appearing from out of retirement to come to my aid. But as the cool air of the office dries my sweat, I get the chills, and each sip of soda takes me deeper into the arctic zone, where I tremble for what's left of my integrity.

Eric motions for me to sit, and I spend some time positioning my limbs in the leather chair. Meanwhile, he is sipping from a Greenpeace mug, his mustache damp with coffee.

"Looks like you are having a rough time."

"You read the item in the paper?"

"I've been following your adventures. You are quite the local celebrity."

"And now things have gotten even more tabloid."

He sets his mug down. "Oh?"

"Last night those polluters, or at least two of them, broke into my house and shot me up with Tasers."

Eric looks at me in disbelief, his forehead wrinkling in uneven waves all the way to the shore of his receding hairline.

"I'd show you the marks, but the location is dicey. You can read all about it in the police report. Long story short, they are in custody, and I'm pretty thoroughly perforated and juiced."

"But you're still on your feet and in my office."

"Guy is saying he's going to fire me—or at the very least deny me legal assistance. If I was hired to protect public land, shouldn't he give me a free hand to go ahead and do my job?. Or if I'm really just a figurehead then maybe someone should make me aware."

Eric begins pushing items around on his desk, clearing a space between us: a magnifying glass, salt and pepper shakers shaped like a hen and rooster, a protractor, a set of colored pens, a stale bagel, and a bottle of salad dressing. For some reason, I have a vision of a settler clearing the land. Finally, I see a blotter with a map of the county, lines drawn every which way.

"Sally, I have labored for fifteen years to keep these parks clear. Do you know how many states of this size—and with this degree of ignorance and poverty—have twenty-three state parks? It is a little miracle in the midst of a massive land grab. And it's not just conservation. We've actually expanded the system. We're getting the bike trails connected to horse trails and hiking trails. As you know, last year we linked up Hungry Mother and the Karst." Here, he uses his thick finger to draw a line from my neck of the woods to the swampy patch on the other side of the freeway. He makes a flourish of tuning his wrist over, as if to show that he has nothing up his sleeve, then loops his finger around to the boot heel of the state. This spring we'll be putting in a trail from Elephant Rock to Meramec Caverns."

I tap my nails on the map with impatience. "That's the aerial view, anyway. What about what's happening on the ground? Did you really send me out there to do a job or were you just trying to get rid of me?"

He reddens, like he's in danger of losing his temper. "If I'm not mistaken, you got exactly what you wanted, a good severance package and a work assignment closer to home."

"Come on, Eric. You know I wanted more than that."

"Oh, and your distance from a certain unsavory situation with a co-worker."

I decide to ignore this comment and go straight to the point. "Who is this Bailey, anyway?"

"Bailey is a powerhouse. He built up a successful construction business from scratch, then got the Daltons—of Dalton Real Estate—to buy in. Now they are treating him like the spoiled and dissolute son they never had, and he's taking full advantage."

"Yeah, his minions took advantage on my ass."

"Look, Sally. Word is, the housing market is about to crash—not just a little tumble. We're talking heads rolling on a massive scale. And when that happens, we'll be in a position to get whatever we want from these people—nature centers, commuter trails, outdoor classrooms, cabins for youth camps. All on the cheap, because we'll be the only buyer in town. It's going to be like the old WPA, except with the details outsourced to the construction companies. In this job, you've got to be visionary; you can't get stuck in outmoded pieties. It's a new world now. The whole public/private distinction is a remnant of the past, like communism or disco."

"Do you feel that way about your family? They're just a public resource like anything else? How about your fishing spot on the Meramec River? That available for development by McDonald's or 3M?"

"You know what they say, Sally; if you don't like the way the wind is blowing in Missouri, all you have to do is wait a while."

"If you ask me, it's not just the wind that's blowing hot air in my face."

"What do you want? These guys who came after you have been apprehended, no? Do you want me to talk to Guy? Do you want me to provide you with one of our lawyers, free of charge? You want it, you've got it. All the resources of this office at your disposal. All you have to do is ask."

I lean forward on the desk and look into his eyes, which seem to have grown brighter as the wrinkles around them proliferate.

"And what do you want in exchange?"

"Have I ever asked you for anything?

I pause and let the weight of his question fall in on itself. "I assume we are excluding acts of a sexual nature?"

"Don't give me that, Sally. You weren't my fucking intern. You gave as good as you got."

Well, that was how I saw it at the time. But now I just don't know. Was it really a personal matter—a private affair, as they say? Or was there some type of public exchange involved, since most of the screwing actually took place in a government office?

Eric blinks, and I think I'm going to start shouting or crying. We both look down at the map, to give ourselves a minute, and I find myself staring at the cool green Karst, its irregular shape like a bird with only one wing. I gave up my sister. I gave up my lover. I gave up my husband. But I can't afford to lose this battle, too.

"OK, I get your point. Just leave Bailey alone, will you? Believe me, the guys who actually went after you are not going to walk away."

"The guys who went after me are underlings and victims. I want the person responsible to take the fall."

"Sally, look at the federal government. Look at the senators dancing with Beelzebub over there at the state capitol. Hell, look at any religious hierarchy of your choice. Evil doesn't really need anyone to spearhead its cause. It's just the natural state of things."

"Listen to you," I say. "Going on about good and evil like a Sunday school teacher. Isn't evil an outdated concept too?"

Eric reaches over and takes my hand, playing with the plain gold wedding band, which I have not yet bothered to remove. His touch is so tender that I feel my outlines dissolving. If he goes so far as to take off the ring, I may disappear altogether. "Don't look now," he says, "but that's what I've been trying to tell you all this time."

26

Jared was lying in Sally's bed, recuperating, when he heard his ring tone, which he'd recently switched from Ryan Adams' "Shakedown on Ninth Street" to "Tough Lover" by Etta James, go off with a bump and grind. He grabbed his jeans off the floor and pulled his phone out of the back pocket, dizzy from just the slight movement. The floor tilted beneath him, righted itself, and shifted in the other direction. He was not well, he realized; his heart was racing and there was a taste of rancid butter in his mouth that wouldn't go away. The delayed reaction the doctor had warned him about? The onset of another ill-timed migraine? The caller ID revealed a familiar number and he swallowed hard.

"Hey, buddy," he said.

"I know you are a capable adult, honey, but we haven't seen hide nor hair of you in a couple of days now, and I admit it, I'm worried. So I'm on my lunch break, and I just thought I'd check in."

"Sorry, Mom. Things got a little irregular."

"How's the new job?"

The job. Jared had almost forgotten that he was semi-employed. He propped himself up on the pillow and tried to retrace his steps.

What had he done in the past two days and which were the parts he could actually tell his mother about? He scrambled to produce the bowdlerized version and came up empty.

"The job? The job is good. But that's the last thing on my mind."

"That's what Wade said. He says a young man your age has trouble keeping his eye on the bottom line. But I'm proud of you, Jared. You came home, you got straight, you found yourself some gainful employment. Now if you can only stay focused, I know you are going to do great."

Just thinking about Wade, Jared could feel his cortex becoming depolarized, so he drew his focus back to his mom, sitting there at her desk in the real estate office, turquoise or coral crocheted sweater draped around her shoulders, eating slowly from her little Tupperware container of salad or leftovers after catering to those snobs and social-climbers all day. He remembered Bailey's threat, whether to his mother's finances or her person he couldn't tell. He wished he were a better son, or that he had some steadfast sibling to keep the pressure off his back. But he was all she had and so he had to step up to the plate.

"Mom, I'm OK now, but there's been an accident, a break-in over here at Sally's."

"Sally? Do I know this Sally?"

"She's a lady friend of mine, the ranger out at Karst Park."

"Not the one we've been reading about in the paper?"

Mayweather didn't even know she read the paper.

"Jared, how do you get involved with these people?"

"Well, those guys you read about, they started it. They broke in over here and shot my friend up with Tasers. Then just to make a point, they zapped me and the dogs, too."

Jared stopped and realized that in his mind, it was already these men, and not Sally herself, who had shot him, although the police report would show otherwise.

"Sweetheart, are you OK?" Her voice assumed that pitch of panic that had been the sound track to his every childhood accident, no matter how trivial. It was first annoying, then endearing, and finally frightening, because of the dependence and self-pity it set off in his head.

"It's you know, just a flesh wound, like they say. I got thoroughly probed last night in the emergency room."

"I'm coming over there right now. What's the address?"

"Mom, you can't come over."

"I'm coming over. No problem. I have plenty of sick leave built up, and it's slow today anyway."

"Mom, it's not my place. You know, Emily Post would not approve."

"Jared, you're old enough to know that all rules of etiquette are suspended when your child's safety is at stake."

Jared felt that one in the gut for sure. He took a breath, listened to his heart speeding and hiccoughing along. "OK," he said. "It's twelve-twenty Karst Road, a big A-frame down a long private drive."

Maybe he could get her in and out before Sally returned. Where did she say she'd gone? He remembered with an unpleasant crawling sensation: the Office of Natural Resources, where she had an in with one of the higher-ups. Though she didn't tell him this precisely, he knew the guy must be the one he'd caught her with during the summer when they first met. Later, Sally had explained that the man was her former co-worker—well, nominally her boss—from Jefferson City, someone she'd been screwing for several years without managing to grow tired of the guy, give him up, or snag him away from his wife. The move to Boonslick was supposed to enforce a definitive break, but the dude kept showing up whenever he had business in town. Then Sally would let him charge her up again. Mason he could understand, the guy had some integrity at least, not to mention killer weed that he cultivated as carefully as his grapevines. Anyway, no one could describe him as a sell-out. But this guy from Jeff City was something worse than a plodder or a slacker; he was a player in a suit, with the pretense of respectability, all the while he was pimping and whoring on the side. This was the type of guy Jared despised most—worse than Wade, even, who God knew didn't have the brains for deception, worse than Chaz, who didn't bother disguising his impulses, sexual and otherwise, and worse than his father, Clark Mayweather, who was, if nothing else faithful to the least-common denominator of himself.

How could Sally go for someone like that—the polar opposite of Jared? Why would she want to be some married loser's second line? And why was she going back again now, after finally getting free of the creep? Maybe there were women—just like guys—who really didn't want anything permanent, only as many different scenarios as they could imagine: older guy, younger guy, married guy, stoner, jock, musician, artist, mountain climber, gym rat, frat brother, banker, construction worker, thief. He guessed he could see the appeal, having done some grazing and sampling of his own. But he hated to think he was just one more type to add to the list. If he was a type, what would he be?

He got up to pee and as he walked through the hall, he heard the door rattle and someone walk into the house. Surely the polluters hadn't gotten out so quickly. But there was always the third guy, the one who hadn't appeared last night. Perhaps he was showing up to get his own belated hits in. Or maybe Bailey had sent in a few other goons to finish the job so badly botched by the ski masks. He thought about the guy threatening his mother. He thought about Sally lying on the floor on her belly like a rape victim. He didn't like the way he'd come off in the whole interaction, and determined to be more heroic this time around.

Downstairs, there was a bustle of something being dropped on the ground. He heard the computer boot up. Were they searching through Sally's files for his film? He looked around for a weapon, found a bizarre metal vacuum cleaner attachment of ominous suggestive power, and charged down the stairs with it raised in his hand, shouting a wordless war chant that unfurled from deep in his chest.

He felt his adrenaline kicking in higher with every step he descended, as if he were falling into his destiny. He was ready for anything—bullets, Tasers, slow merciless torture, or quick brutal death.

As he touched the bottom stair, he launched himself into the living-room in a single bound and practically fell onto Lorraine LaChance carrying a stack of Tupperware containers and a cardboard boxes, stacked so high, in fact, that she could hardly see him. The boxes fell, her cane dropped, and the cookies scattered, but Lorraine had the presence of mind to grab the chair behind her before she joined her cargo on the floor. Still, she looked pretty rattled, her glasses crooked and her skirt hiked up, revealing the tops of her knee-high nylons, the elastic digging into her pale flesh and the vivid blue veins raised in deep relief on her thighs and calves.

Mayweather was perplexed. Should he run upstairs and put on some pants or should he tend to Lorraine first? If she were actually on the ground the decision would be easier, because it would be a clear emergency situation. As it was, she didn't seem to be injured, but you could never tell with someone so ancient, who was always a candidate for a heart attack. Come to think of it, it was his own heart that was flying out of his chest. He pressed his clavicle as if to push the organ back into place, and then touched Lorraine on the shoulder.

"Are you all right?" he finally said.

"Well, aside from being scared senseless, I think I'll survive. What are you doing in my daughter's house? And what happened to this place? Looks like a twister touched down in here."

"You didn't talk to Sally yet? There was a break-in last night."

Lorraine tugged her skirt down and pointed a finger at him. "You're that videographer, aren't you? I knew I'd seen you before. Where's my daughter?"

"She's in Jeff City, trying to get some legal help."

"Oh Lord, not Jeff City. I thought we were done with that. You say she's ambulatory? Nothing torn up or broken apart?"

"They were using Tasers, so it was pretty gory, but she checked out OK at the hospital and then she took off this morning like nothing happened."

"Tasers? I haven't seen one of those gadgets yet."

"I can tell you they're not pretty." He lifted his shirt up over his underwear and showed Lorraine the viper marks in his stomach, raised and irritated there beneath the sparse hairs.

Lorraine readjusted her glasses and leaned in close, like she was examining some fine print or a particularly intricate stitch in a home-sewn garment.

"Hey, I'm not shy, Mrs. LaChance. You can touch it if you like."

She lifted a crooked finger, weighted down by its own wrinkles, and gave his belly a tentative jab. Mayweather was surprised by the energy running through her, a vibe as palpable as the breath of a video camera or speaker.

She made a *tsk*ing sound, a primitive hissing that distorted her features into a mask of disgust. "Awful, what these developers will do. You say she went to have it checked out?"

"Yeah, they say they can't make any promises about long-term effects, but she seems all right for now."

"And why didn't anyone call me?"

"I guess didn't want to disturb your sleep."

"Who sleeps anymore? I've got too many kids and grandkids to worry about. And just when the girl was beginning to get some backbone, too. If I'd have been there, I would've taken those snakes out of action the first time around."

Jared looked at the old lady in disbelief. Her eyes were bright bits of colored glass caught in fold after fold of wrinkles. How did a person keep that spark after so many years of living, staying in the same place while watching everything change shape around her?

"I don't know what's wrong with you young people. Looks like you're so busy blogging your guts out and posting to YouTube that you can't grasp a situation when you're actually in one."

"You saw the film?'

"I caught it on one of the girls' phones—not bad for a trailer. And my daughter looks darn righteous, like one of those Old Testament prophets."

"Thanks. Maybe I should pick up these cookies?"

"Don't tell anyone, but I had to get three boxes from the bakery. Looks like no one turns on their stove anymore. I heard one gal on television say that she turned off the gas on her stove so she could keep her sweaters in the oven."

Jared knelt on the floor and picked up the cookies—snickerdoodles, from the look of them. They were puffy on the top, thick on the bottom, gave off a scent of vanilla and cinnamon, left a residue of butter in his palm.

"Anyway, there's more where those came from. People don't want to bake at home, but these businesses are pretty anxious to donate for publicity. Where have those dogs got to? I'm surprised they haven't snapped all this up by now."

"They're at the vet's," Jared said. "Injured in action."

"I hope they're all right. Sally sure loves those animals—does more for them than some folks do for their children."

Mayweather looked to see if this was a deliberate slight, but it didn't appear to be. Lorraine had now picked one of the last remaining cookies from the box, broke it in two, and sniffed at both halves before biting into one. "Not bad, though they've gone a little wild with the vanilla bean. Want to try?"

Mayweather accepted the other half, bit into its surprisingly soft center,

"Now, tell me, Mr. Videographer, what are you doing with my daughter?"

The cookie dissolved on his tongue, and there was a medicinal aftertaste that he didn't care for—vanilla in the raw? Or had his taste buds just been depolarized by the Tasers? "How do you want me to answer that question?"

"I don't know, honey; take your time."

"I'm just a casual guy, you know, and Sally's got her life going on. Maybe she wants a little recreation."

"Believe me, that girl has had her recreation and then some."

"Well, OK then. I think I'll go get my pants."

Upstairs, Mayweather collapsed back onto the bed, chewed on a nail for comfort, cupped a hand over his crotch. He stared at the skylight in the ceiling, revealing the same patch of sky that Mason had seen before him—a snatch of blue heaven on the sly. Was this it, the blunt end of his cut-rate hero's journey, as far as he'd ever get from home? Where had he been going, anyway? He couldn't remember. The taste in his mouth turned bitter as undercooked Brussels sprouts. He felt a stab in his temple, then closed his eyes and slept for maybe ten minutes by Sally's clock, felt much better, then got up and dressed.

When he came back downstairs with his pants on, his mother had arrived, and she and Lorraine were cleaning up the living room together, Deirdre on her knees scrubbing the carpet with a sponge and Lorraine wielding the mysterious vacuum attachment to reach underneath the dust ruffle of the sofa.

27

Back at the truck, I'm shaking so hard I can barely work the clutch, but I'm determined to get home to Boonslick and check on my dogs before I collapse into a much-needed nap. As I pull onto the interstate, I feel my heart rattling—or is it my tires? I can't tell the difference between my body and my truck at this point—they're both just hard-used vehicles to get me where I'm going. It's not as if I really expected Eric to drop his professional caution and go after Bailey for me. And I'm reasonably sure that he'll be able to get my job back. But this rehearsal of our mutual past is humiliating, to say the least. I never thought I'd have to ask him for another favor again. I remember the rage that propelled me from my relatively successful career in Jeff City all the way back to the Boonslick backwoods. I didn't want to be a mistress, and I didn't want to be a wife. I didn't want to remain an assistant and I didn't want to become a manager. I didn't want to steal something on the sly and I didn't want to take my gratification like medicine measured out a drop at a time until it lost all appeal. I was determined, finally, to leave bureaucracy and deception behind forever and live the rest of my days as honestly as I could. Even then, I let him visit me five times; five times I opened the door, five times I unlocked the liquor cabinet, five times I pulled back the covers and let my body go where my head could not follow. On each occasion, I woke up the next day with a hangover and a raw cervix hanging there inside me like a sore tonsil waiting to be taken out. And that last time, it was Mayweather, appalled by the baby seat in Eric's car, who convinced me that I was slowly compromising myself into the ground.

Now I have to laugh at the puritanical impulse of youth. Mayweather, who counseled Ellen to get an abortion instead of taking the risk of fatherhood. Mayweather, who fell right into adultery as if it were just a particularly comfortable seat at the movies. Mayweather, who broke his word more frequently than he broke wind.

And yet, if I can't trust him, I might as well give up on trusting anyone. The traffic on the interstate is brutal, bumper-to-bumper gridlock. It's lunchtime and people are scrambling to maneuver their cars toward some sexual assignation, dentist appointment, or fast food meal. It occurs to me to wonder whether Eric scheduled our meeting for the lunch hour because he thought we were going to take a break to recreate old times. Worse, I wonder if I might have considered the possibility myself, if it weren't for my injuries. The road is lined with chain stores and gas stations, the only signs of nature these fraying and yellowed margins of lawn between parking lots. Across the way, the cupola of the capitol building sits like a huge egg half-buried in the detritus of the city, challenging justice to ever be born from it. The sun strikes the traffic so hard it looks like it could spark a fire, turning the whole roadway into a sea of molten metal ready to be recast. The thought is oddly appealing, as if I could perform a controlled burn on all of civilization instead of just a given field in the woods. And even though it's a temperate fall day, the greenhouse effect of the windshield is so intense that I roll down the windows, smell the exhaust, which ignites a coil of nausea deep in my gut, then roll the windows up again and turn on the air conditioning. I can feel my heart now—definitely faster than my engine. The sweat gathers in mineral pools on my skin, not a cool feminine spritz of moisture, but a thick sweat, heavy with the oil of living. My hands vibrate on the steering wheel, and my head feels as if some muscular giant were squeezing it between his palms. A line of tension goes from my ring finger right into my chest and settles there in a deep cramp. Is this a full-blown cardiac incident, I wonder, or just a run-of-the-mill panic attack? Since I haven't experienced either, I don't have much to go on. Still, I figure I need to get off the road as soon as I can.

At the same time, I am suddenly desperate to get to my dogs. When I visited at 9:30, Rye was alert and licking his hind leg, then practically knocked over the cage trying to get to me. But Di was despondent, barely conscious, and just whimpered when I opened the cage door to pet her through the bars. The vet wanted to keep her a few hours longer, and I thought it would be better to leave Rye there to keep her company. Why didn't I cancel my appointment with Eric and stay with them? It's not as if I couldn't just shoot the guy an e-mail and arrive at the same result. But no, I wanted to see him, apparently, to feel the excitement of his presence, to have him see me and admire the hearty woodswoman I'd made of my former neurotic self.

As I inch toward the exit, I tell myself the vet is the best place for Di, anyway. At home, she'd have Mayweather filming her and feeding her forbidden lunch meat, his ring tone constantly going off, radio blasting Boonslick Country. What is he doing there, anyway, I think. Did I actually invite him to stay? It is probably the least I could do, after having shot him in the belly, involved him in a criminal action, and corrupted his youth. My right arm feels numb and I can sense the truck dragging to the left. I over-correct and run over onto the shoulder, veer into a ditch and quickly throw on the flashers and the emergency brake. If I'm going to die, I'm not going to do it in my vehicle and I'm not going to do it in a crowd.

I open the door with my left hand and limp around the truck to the roadside. At least here at the exit there is some vegetation, the dry stalks of sunflowers, a small honey locust, and the blasted orange bells of trumpet creepers. As a pet owner, I'm accustomed to searching these islands of green where a dog can take his time to sniff and pee. But now it's me, not my animals, who needs a resting place. I make it to the tree, drop my body onto the earth, and close my eyes. I can feel the ground vibrating from the traffic of the interstate; I can smell the coppery corpses of dried leaves, the savor of dried sap, the nutrients in the earth. It is cool out here, cooler than I remember from this morning, and a breeze plays over my face. At the moment, it's the only thing I have to hold onto, and even that's rapidly passing me by. Only thirty miles from home, and I might as well be a continent away. Why did I have to rush out of the house this morning instead of going back to bed to recover like a responsible person? It's Lorraine coming out in me I suppose. By the time I'm sixty, I'll be a raging extrovert. But I'm never going to be sixty, I think; I may not even make it to forty-six. I could almost accept the idea of my own imminent demise if I could just make it home first.

I hold my breath, waiting for the next onslaught of pain. But it tricks me by skipping a beat, and until that moment, I hadn't recognized how much I was counting on those regular spasms to keep me centered. In the interim, I reach out and pick up one of the wilted trumpet creepers on the ground, its texture smooth as a shred of balloon, an internal organ, or one of your flimsier items of lingerie. I lift it to my nose and smell the orange heat of summer, a feminine odor, sharp citrus and bruised fruit.

Maybe I am not going to die after all. Maybe I should take measures to save myself. I think of my cell phone where I left it in my purse on the car seat. I'm in civilian uniform so infrequently that I can never get used to carrying a purse. How ridiculous to die just because I can't train myself to switch out the contents of my pants pockets. And then just as I'm thinking of it, the phone goes off in my head. I answer and to my surprise it's Mason, calling from Glacier National Park, he says, to ask if I can give him a reference. Sure, I tell him; send me the appropriate information and I'll get off an e-mail later today. But don't they think it will be a little suspicious coming from his ex?

"No," he said, "A good report from your ex-wife is about as rare as a black orchid."

His voice is shaded and kind, a respite from the sound of traffic and the buzz of Eric's office. I wonder if this is a sign that he is the man I was supposed to die with, and now I've screwed it up so badly that I'm forced to enact a long-distance deathbed scene.

"Tell me," I ask him. "Is it as rugged as they say?"

"You have no idea, sweetheart."

I picture the waterfalls spouting and steaming. I imagine the wildflowers, a slightly different variety than ours: Indian paintbrush, monkey flower and bear grass, the cannabis with an exotic pungent tang.

"You're not coming back, are you?"

"I wasn't there for a long time, Sally, and you didn't seem to mind."

"I was ...," I say, grasping for an explanation, and then wonder what I was doing myself. It was like Mason was my cover. As long as he was with me, I wouldn't have to get together with anyone else and I wouldn't have to be alone. He felt so much guilt over his first wife's fatal OD that I knew he would never hurt me, would never betray me, would never take anything away from me. But he wouldn't really go past a certain point with me either. His kindness was a coat that protected me from the wear of the weather. Now that I've stripped myself of it, I can feel the cold and rain again.

"Give my love to Di," Mason says. "She's got a rough road."

Why only Di? I think. Rye was always his favorite, the adventurous one with the speckled gums and comical face, always dumping the trash or attacking a muskrat, while Di was more the faithful companion, the first one to greet him at the door, the last one to stay sitting at his feet into the small hours of each morning until he finally decided to pack up his catalogs and almanacs and come to bed.

The connection begins to break up, crackling sheets of static, big eruptions of brute noise, patches of the purest silence, other voices on the line. When I listen closely, it seems like I recognize some of them: Lorraine's self-satisfied cackle, Chaz's polished vowel tones, Etta's silver laughter, Mayweather's provocative drawl. I can't hear what any of them are saying, can only make out a few words of advice or encouragement about the roll call up yonder, the credits rolling, the final score. If I have to go now, lying in this green and verdant ditch at the side of the road in a blasted capital city, it's good to know that I'm not exactly alone.

28

After an hour alone with two mothers, Sally's and his own, Mayweather was anxious for his host's return. Deirdre had taken one look at his Taser wounds and insisted on treating them with iodine, so that he now had two big red patches of war paint on his belly, sticky against his shirt. She reminded him of his several trips to the emergency room, stitches on his head at two, his right foot at seven, a sprained ankle at nine, and a broken collarbone at sixteen. "And I thought you were through with all that," she said. "Looks like you still need your mother after all." Watching her, Mayweather couldn't stand to remind her that he hadn't required her assistance last night, or in Chicago, either. But he did have to admit that being accident prone wasn't something he seemed likely to outgrow.

It was getting on for two p.m.; surely Sally had seen to the business in Jeff City by now. He hated to think what could be keeping her: a three-martini lunch at that bogus Italian hangout, a flat tire, a bit of backsliding in a back room. Lorraine, satisfied with the housework, put together a lunch of scrambled egg sandwiches and tomato soup. Since her daughter wasn't available, Lorraine informed Mayweather she would be taking him along on her on her day's errands instead: a trip to the veterans' hospital, a drive by the bakery to beg for more cookies, a visit to Chaz at the roller rink. After all, a lady of her age shouldn't be expected to ride around alone.

Mayweather, his tongue coated with a cheese rind slime and his head shooting auras, tried to plead injuries. He assured Lorraine that Sally would be home any minute, but the old lady said she was through waiting on anything good to come out of Jeff City. Meanwhile, Mayweather's mom Deirdre was expected back at the real estate office. She kissed him on the cheek and told him she didn't care where he was sleeping, but he ought to come home for dinner once in a while.

Lorraine's car, a long sedan so old it had neither a CD player nor a cupholder, creaked and bobbled when Mayweather settled his weight in the passenger side and rested a can of restorative soda on his knee.

"I'd let you drive," she said with a wink as she passed him her cane. "But I heard a rumor that you were on the drugs."

"Aw, don't let that stop you. Aren't all you AARP types constantly hopped up on the prescription goodies?"

Lorraine smiled, a secretive sliver of merriment in the midst of her wrinkles. "Privilege of age," she said, jerking onto the country road without ceremony, then flipping on the radio, the dial already set, Mayweather noticed, to Boonslick Country. Her driving was a little wobbly at the curves, but not incompetent otherwise. The inside of the vehicle smelled of horehound cough drops and pecan pie. Maybe this wouldn't be so bad after all. Besides, if he had to see Chaz, he'd just as soon have Lorraine as a buffer. Now if he could only stave off the migraine, he'd be fine. He concentrated on Lorraine's profile, the cheeks full and the lips drawn in with pinprick tucks. The wrinkles hung down her face in furrows, the skin so desiccated that it seemed to have been transformed into something more resilient than flesh, like a rind, the rind of a hedge apple maybe, with tiny knots where the skin crinkled into stars. She was wearing an American flag jersey and a pleated blue skirt, tiny Christmas tree earrings in her ears and a big turquoise cross hanging halfway down her chest. Her legs were so short that she had to keep her seat pressed right up to the steering wheel, and Mayweather, reclining, looked as if he was all the way in the back seat by himself

They just listened to the radio for a bit—Hank Williams shading into Taylor Swift. Mayweather felt the tide in his head receding, and was able to watch the scenery as they passed.

"I had three kids by the time I was your age," Lorraine said, as if continuing a conversation she'd already started without him. "And by the time I was Sally's age, one of them was long gone."

Mayweather, not knowing how to reply, remained silent and took a sip of soda, which washed all the way back to his jaw with an astringent surge.

"Something is wrong with you young people these days. You go so long without anything ever happening to you that you forget you are even struggling in this mortal coil."

He almost laughed at the idea that nothing had happened to him. He'd been to the emergency room half a dozen times, for fuck's sake, had relations with dozens of women, left home, gone broke, authored a corpus of incomplete and unmarketable art films, fathered a child. He wasn't even thirty and he wondered what was left for him to do.

"Mortal coil. What is that, anyway, some kind of contraceptive device?" he said.

"Oh, I know they teach you sex ed all right," Lorraine said sharply. "But that's not much good if you don't understand the rest of it. When do you ever get your death ed, is what I want to know."

Death ed? Who's dying? Mayweather thought. Not him, not Sally, not even Lorraine, who looked healthier than some of the young girls on the team in spite of her flesh-colored hearing aids and mottled skin. Then he remembered Sally's younger sister, who had been killed in a car accident all those years ago. According to Sally, her mom spent more time mourning this lost girl than tending to her other kids and grandkids combined. Death ed. What would they teach in that class, anyway? Forms of burial, varieties of disease, religious dogma regarding reincarnation, the resurrection of the body, the indestructibility of the soul? Jared thought of the prayer service and of Gabriella lying unconscious on her bed. He remembered how, back in the day, they used to make death masks of corpses, then later, after the technology developed, the bereaved commissioned somber daguerreotypes of the newly departed.

"Turn around," he said. "We have to go back for my camera."

And so Lorraine turned into the lot of the feed store, turned the sedan around, and went back the way they'd come, spraying gravel.

At the hospital, he hardly recognized Gabriella's room. Every available space was covered with flowers, mostly geraniums and mums, the smells of pepper and honey running rampant. Even the bed itself had a small quilted coverlet over the thin regulation blanket. Jewel-colored saints cards were fanned out on the dinner tray as if someone were using them to read tarot, and a gaudy papier-mâché cross hung on the wall—Jesus as piñata, Jared thought, always up in the air and getting batted around.

Two of the girls from the Boonslick Bombers, Raven Pillage and Britney Spearhead, were actually present, and the Bombers' merch was spread about the room: coffee mugs and banners, a couple of key rings attached to the shade, Gigi Haddist's jersey hanging prominently on the coat rack, as if the very sight of it would encourage her to stand up and skate. Jared was pleased to see that Britney had made it through last night's adventures and wondered who had brought her home at the end of the day.

Raven sat in a chair by Gabriella's bed and stroked the girl's head, which gleamed blue-black under the fluorescent lights, rich with the oils of three days' sweat. Reenie wasn't dressed up for once and appeared oddly childish in her corduroy jeans and pink sweatshirt, no makeup, her braids unbound and her coppery brown hair hanging down her back in glittery coils reminiscent of some abrasive copper scrub. Gabriella herself looked more relaxed and feminine than she ever had when she was on her feet. Her face, formerly guarded and inexpressive, now looked soft and meditative, as if she were dreaming of a lasting peace. But from Mayweather's vantage point at the foot of the bed, he could see that the purple nail polish was peeling off her toes and black hairs were growing on her calves and ankles. Could he get that on film? Should he?

Lorraine greeted Gabriella's mother Mrs. Hernandez like a long-lost daughter, and even spoke, Mayweather noticed, a few words of Spanish to her in a steep Missouri accent. The mother was prettier than Gabriella, with large eyes and tiny features, but lacked the bold profile that made Gabriella a standout on film. Her red windbreaker was stretched out on the back of a chair, and her T-shirt was stained with sweat, one yellow dribble of mustard over the left breast. She smelled of coffee and stomach acid; it had been a long three days. Limping back to her chair by the window, as if her foot had fallen asleep with all the waiting, she showed Lorraine the pillowcase she was embroidering, an American flag with an oddly Mexican design, the red stripes woven out of roses, the stars not stars at all but doves with their wings spread, about to take flight. Mayweather couldn't help but notice there were only about a dozen of them left.

The two women became involved in examining the work and Mayweather took the opportunity to take his camera out of its case and tentatively begin filming. The mechanism was alive in his hands; he could feel its hum persistent as the heart of a small bird or cat and its warm familiar lens extended like a muzzle. He lifted the instrument to his face and his eyes grew wise with knowledge; through the lens, the world was smaller, he knew, but also more meaningful, as if by framing it he was able to grasp the sum of its immensity. He was almost waiting for someone to stop him, but everyone was so occupied, Reenie with Gabriella, Lorraine with Gabriella's mother, Britney with her own narrow face, which she was patiently making up in the glow of a compact mirror, that they hardly seemed aware of his presence. So he went ahead and got it all—the jersey and the flowers, the embroidery and the saint cards, the Boonslick Bombers banners in the background of the gaudy cross.

He held his camera down to his side, however, when he saw Reenie pick up Gabriella's hand and uncurl the fingers, like you would open the clenched fist of an infant. Then she lifted the hand to her mouth and placed a kiss on the palm and let the fingers close again, pressing the fist together with unnecessary force. What was he seeing, he asked himself, then remembered a few shots from the earlier film, Gabriella yanking up Reenie's butt pad, Raven in a huddle, pressing her forehead into Gigi's brow and leaning there, hovering, for uninterrupted seconds of film. Well, the girls were supposed to look bisexual out there, after all, if only to stimulate the at-home viewer into shelling out the cover charge. Jared, who, unlike many of the male viewers, had actually experienced the reality of a ménage à trois, had to admit it was not as pleasant as he expected, like two girlfriends giggling over him in middle school, more attuned to one another than to himself.

Still, here was something between the women that was not for public consumption. How could he get it on film without spoiling it? The nurse arrived and shoved Reenie out of the way with a move that wouldn't disgrace a blocker out on the rink. She pulled the covers back, disconnected the IV, and prepared to turn Gabriella over, explaining that she needed to do this to prevent bedsores, commenting all the while on Gabriella's weight, really considerable for such a fit-looking gal.

"That's all muscle, ma'am." Reenie said. "Muscle weights more than fat."

"Well, muscle sure don't last long in a coma," the nurse said as she arranged the gown around Gabriella's hips, for modesty's sake.

Mayweather offered to help and the nurse said she wouldn't turn him down. He set the camera on the tray table still running and slid his arm under Gabriella's shoulders. She smelled of sweat and antiseptic, mixed into a sweet medicinal mulch, and he was frightened by the complete yielding of all that muscle, a solid weight unlike any female body he had ever lifted. Her hair tickled his ear, surprisingly coarse, and he saw a few dark hairs over her lip that she must have kept in check when she was conscious. Meanwhile, the nurse was lifting Gabriella's thighs. As she did, Jared saw a red spot on the bed; at first, he thought he was hallucinating, spots forming in front of his eyes due to the migraine aura. But no, it was an actual smear, the color of a candied apple. Maybe Gabriella had suffered internal injuries that the doctors had missed: a ruptured spleen, a perforated bowel. The red stain stood stalwart on the sheet, refusing to disappear. It was not, as he had first thought, a solid color but a base of gleaming marinara with clots of darker blood mixed in, almost black, seeds caught up in the flow. Smelling the clay and mud of Gabriella's body, he thought of the abortion he had recommended, the afterbirth he had never seen.

"Lord God, the gal's got the curse," the nurse said. "We sure don't see much of this here at the vets'."

So Gabriella was still bleeding, after all that bodybuilding and war-making. Mayweather had to admire the persistence of femininity, if nothing else.

Gabriella's mother stepped up to the bed, crying, and wiped at the stain with a striped hospital towel. Then she held the cloth up to her face, sniffed it in as if she were smelling the perfume of a cut flower, and began to cry, emitting harsh grinding sounds that threatened to choke her. Lorraine put her hand on the woman's back, and the nurse signaled Mayweather to set Gabriella down again so she could call for a gurney and clean the bed.

Meanwhile, Mrs. Hernandez leaned down toward her daughter and murmured some syllables of Spanish in her ear.

On the tray table, Mayweather's abandoned camera was still running, its familiar faint breathing a strange form of mourning as it mingled with the mother's words.

29

The next thing I know I am in a stranger's minivan and headed for another hospital. I don't know how or why this women picked me up; she is so petite and well-groomed, her short dark hair cut and styled to resemble a Victorian upsweep without the burden of the heavy bun. Her dog, on the other hand, is large and dirty, a blue tick hound if I'm not mistaken, at least fifty pounds, with a mottled coat of every color between blue and gray. His coltish legs and big paws give him a juvenile appearance, whatever his age may be, and the brown eyes and limp ears evoke the soulful look of a beagle without the exaggerated droopiness. He lies beside me in the middle seat and rests his nose on my thigh, as if to encourage me. I am half recovered and too embarrassed to sprawl across the seat, but not energetic enough to sit up straight, either. I pet the dog—called Lex, the woman says—and think of Diana, still at the vet's, with only Rye to keep her company. Is she holding out for me? I pet Lex almost unconsciously, as if he were my own, and notice how soft his fur is, thinner and finer than the coat of a Lab—his smell keener, with more clay and less smoke.

The woman drives somewhat recklessly, throwing elbows like a pro, making calls on her cell phone, and sipping from a cup of off-brand coffee. Between calls, she looks into the rearview mirror to ask me how I am, raising her eyes as if talking to an absent God. You can tell she is accustomed to using the mirror for this purpose, and the accumulation of comic books, plastic gadgets, sweatshirts, bats, pads, and balls attests to the presence of multiple children in her life. Although I am already well acquainted with Lex, who accepts me as if I were an old friend, I still know nothing about this Good Samaritan who found me at the side of the road and somehow dragged me into her vehicle. She hasn't even told me her own name yet. She has, however, called ahead to the hospital to get a good start on my admission process. Because believe her, she's done her time in the emergency room and knows her way around an insurance form. Am I hot? Am I cold? Would it help to listen to the radio? We're nearly there, probably five more minutes, tops. The traffic has dissipated somewhat and I suppose that means the lunch hour is over, and the commuters, finding themselves well fed, their cavities filled or their orgasms released, are now settled comfortably back at their desks, freeing up the highway for my more pressing needs.

I look at the sympathetic hound beside me and try to assess what they are. Have I experienced a seizure, a delayed response to being tazed? Or am I becoming a hysteric in my old age? I continue to pet Lex, just to make contact with something solid, and watch my wedding band as it disappears and rematerializes in his fur. I know now that the cell phone never left my truck and that I couldn't have actually talked with Mason, unless I believe that I have developed powers of transmission through the electrical intervention of the Tasers or that I am receiving signals through my wedding band. Still, I can't believe that the vision granted to me was so pedestrian that, instead of commanding me to build a monument or start a religion, it merely directed me to write a recommendation for one of the many departed lovers who are no longer in my life.

I pull my hand up and examine it, the strong, tanned and speckled back, tendons taut over the knuckles, a suggestion of blue branching veins and a slight webbing of wrinkles that shows only when I tense my fingers. Then I turn the whole thing over to reassure myself with the long lifeline on my open palm, a deep cut that extends in a curve all the way down to the wrist. I pull at my wedding band and see the pale half-inch of skin underneath, damp with sweat and as wrinkled as if it has been submerged in water. The gold band catches at the knuckle, but I manage to wrestle it off anyway and stow it away in the front pocket of pants. Why was I wearing it, anyway? Oh, I remember, to remind me to keep my hands to myself.

"So, Sally, any relatives I should call for you? Husband? Parents? Kids?"

I am of an age, I realize, when any arrangement is possible: still young enough for living and lively parents, old enough that I might have several exes or grown kids.

"We should probably call my mother."

"So you've from the area?"

"Boonslick," I say, anxious to distinguish myself from Jeff City and its ilk. "I was in an accident last night and I guess I'm not fully recovered yet."

"Oh. What happened?"

Too tired to come up with a story, whether fabricated or fairly accurate, I just say that I was exposed to electric shock and don't know yet whether there will be any lasting consequences.

In the rearview mirror, the woman looks as if she's putting the pieces together, her light eyebrows raised. "My cousin got hit by lightning a few years back. She's basically fine, but she can't smell anything to save her soul. Doesn't seem to make much difference, but to tell the truth, sometimes her cooking tastes a little off."

I tell the woman Lorraine's number and she dials it up while I wait, counting the beats it will take my mother to locate her purse and retrieve the phone from its depths. When she finally answers, I can hear the relief in my driver's voice; even a Samaritan doesn't want to take complete responsibility. "Mrs. LaChance, my name is Vivian Scott, I don't want to alarm you, but I have your daughter Sally here in my car. I picked her up by the side of Route Sixty-Three in Jefferson City. She looked like she had a spell of some kind. She seems OK now, but I'm taking her to the hospital just to get it checked out."

Lorraine's voice is so loud I can hear her response from the back seat, something involving the Lord's name only just saved, by a certain pious tone, from being taken in vain. Vivian hands the phone back to me, a hot pink number that looks more like a makeup case than a telecommunications device, and I hold it up to my ear.

"Sally, is that you? Are you still breathing?"

"I got a little overheated on the road."

"What are you doing out there, anyway? Your videographer tells me you were in a tussle last night."

"It was those polluters again, Mom. I've got to get some help."

"Honey, I don't believe there's any help worth having over there in Jeff City."

"To tell you the truth, I'm about to come to the same conclusion."

"Hold on, Sally. I'll be there in twenty minutes. Oh, and I've got your friend with me. Mayfield, is it? He's helping me out with the prayer service since you disappeared on me. One of us can pick up your truck and drive it home."

I hand the breathing phone back to Vivian, and settle back against Lex with relief.

Once we get to the hospital, I am sorry to leave him, but Vivian pats his back efficiently, tells him to wait, rolls down the windows, and helps me out the other door without so much as a backward look. After checking me in at the desk, she tells me she has to hurry off to pick up her youngest at nursery school.

"Don't worry, Sally. You're looking much better. You've even got the color back in your cheeks." And she is bold enough to touch the side of my face before she speeds off through the automatic doors, walking out of my life before I can even think of the words to thank her.

I am admitted within a few minutes, due to Vivian's fore-thought or the time of day. After going through the usual routine, the doctor, a man of retirement age with thick white eyebrows, black glasses, and large shaking hands, tells me he isn't sure what happened, but I appear to be fine, my heart rate checks out, my eyes are clear, my blood pressure is normal, my pulse is steady, my reflexes are strong. He offers, on little provocation, to prescribe me medication for panic attacks. I notice that the name he mentions is familiar, the same prod-uct recommended to me for depression, premenstrual tension, perimenopause, irritability, and stress. Soon, it seems, we will be able to medicate the pain of womanhood out of existence; a good deal easier, I suppose, than making space for women's pain in the post-industrial world. I take a pass and promise to go home and rest up with some green tea instead and he says that's not a bad idea.

While I'm getting dressed, there's a knock at the door and my mother appears, followed by Mayweather in the same ragged jeans he's been wearing for days, a look of fear on his face.

"It's just one hospital after another with you young people,"

Lorraine says. "I can hardly get the taste of formaldehyde out of my mouth."

"The doctor says I'm fine," I tell her. "I'd just as soon get out of here as quick as possible."

"Good thing, too. I've been missing your help."

We get into Lorraine's old Ford, me in the passenger seat and Mayweather in the back with the box of vigil candles and the cane. I am able to direct her, without too much trouble, to the exit where I had planned to make my last stand. There's my green truck, a bag of dry dog food in the bed, and the logo of the State Parks on the door. I can even see the depression in the grass where I was lying, a sad little nest of trampled weeds.

"Do you even have a license?" I ask Mayweather and he pulls a stash of folded bills from his back pocket, unwinds a rubber band, and reveals the familiar Missouri license with a photo of a younger Mayweather, beardless and breathless, looking at the camera as if he can hardly sit still.

"Is it current?"

"We've got until November. Think we can make it home by then?"

In the car, I wipe some dog hairs off the upholstery and settle into an unfamiliar spot in the passenger seat. Mayweather, meanwhile, is adjusting the driver's side, giving himself more room.

"Actually, we don't know that you are in any better shape than me."

"Shut up and let the boy drive," Lorraine yells from her car and takes off at an indecent speed.

Now Mayweather has moved on to the dash, looking as serious as a pilot checking the control panel. He flicks off the air conditioning and gives me a questioning look, but it's only when he finds that I have the radio set to NPR that he is actually provoked into reprimanding me.

He turns the engine on, shifts into gear with a jerk, and pulls onto the entrance ramp. I hadn't noticed that the ride was so rough. Maybe it is just my fragile, post-panic state, but I think I can feel each lump and irregularity in the asphalt beneath me. Or maybe the state's infrastructure is in worse shape than I think.

After a while, the cars thin out and I can see a few goldenrods still blooming on the side of the road, most of the trees yellow and red with a few evergreens mixed in, the billboards advertising reversible vasectomies, ninety-eight-dollar dentures, compassionate medical care, and an angry god, depicted, in this case, by a crazed hillbilly taking a whip to the horses of the apocalypse and shouting via a caption in gothic script, "Don't make me come down there and tell you one more time."

"You know, we could turn around and just keep going south," Mayweather says, now comfortable enough to reach across the gearshift and rest a hand on my thigh.

"What's south?" The hand is achingly heavy on the velvet of my trousers, and I wish I had worn clothing of a texture more unpleasant to the touch.

"Hell, I don't know, Texas, Florida, the Gulf of Mexico, the Keys."

"You're sure you don't want to head up to New York?"

"No ma'am. Even Chicago was too far north for me."

"What would we do in Florida?"

"I don't know, get a day job in the tourist industry and spend our nights drinking and screwing on the beach."

"Sounds romantic, but I don't know that I could stand the black flies."

"Come on, what else do you have to do? You just lost your job, right, and Mason's not coming back anytime soon. Chaz is about to sell the roller rink and then Reenie's going to go to law school for sure. Your mom has your brother to look after her. Besides, wouldn't it feel good to just pull the rug out from everyone, now that they're so sure they've got you tacked down to the floor for good?"

A pulse twitches at my neck. Should I concentrate on the insult or the invitation? The speech sounds oddly familiar, and I remember Chaz's obnoxious appeal, as he pitched his cable show to me.

"Are you saying I have nothing better to do?"

Jared takes his eyes off the highway, looks at my face, and moves his hand farther up my thigh. At least he knows it's a trick question.

"I'm just saying we could disappear together, and no one would be able to say anything." Instead of waiting for my answer, he takes the exit and barrels onto the ramp.

"You're not just stopping for gas, I guess."

"No, let's go back and take Sixty-Three down to Memphis."

He pulls back onto the highway, going in the other direction. The road opens in front of me and I can almost smell the brine of the ocean. Down there, everything flattens out; the horizon goes pastel as a baby blanket, and there is no underbrush to speak of. I wonder if I'm really ready for all that clarity, not to mention Mayweather twenty-four/seven and a constant channel of sexual current that makes my skin ache. I think about my mom. I think about my dogs. I think about my A-frame swallowed up by the forest like an abandoned castle in a fairytale.

But if he expects me to raise a fuss and rap his knuckles, he is sadly mistaken. I should try to enjoy being kidnapped by a strapping young man, full of piss and invention, even if it's only a short-lived little fantasy and I have to pay for the gas myself.

"Isn't there anything you'd regret leaving behind?" I ask.

He flicks his eyes back to the road and assumes a noncommittal expression. "You mean the dirty limestone cliffs of Boonslick? Boonslick Country radio, free Mexican buffet at the Naughty Pine on Thursday nights, a cold brew in the Karst, sweet home-grown weed that's never known the hand of the middle man, a clear shot of a deer or wild turkey practically any time you like?"

"Well, I have to admit, that's all worth missing, but I had someone else in mind."

"Shit. Think I want to stay around and watch the girl get corrupted?"

"Either that, or she's going to grow up without your influence."

Mayweather looks, for one second, as if he's going to cry, his hazel eyes magnified by moisture and his forehead crumpling up to show me where the wrinkles will eventually form. I'm almost relieved when his face turns red and assumes an expression of anger instead. "It's that asshole, isn't it, the one with the baby seat and the Godfather suspenders. That's why you're so excited about going back and sucking up to the man."

"Well, he did tell me he'd get me my job back," I say, happy that I have one thing going for me at least.

"Hard to commute if you're living in Florida."

"That's what I'm thinking."

"Sally, that guy is rock-bottom rot-gut. Didn't you get enough of him the first three hundred times around?"

I feel the truck pick up speed and want to tell him that over seventy, things get a little shaky, but I can see by looking at his Adam's apple that it's not the best moment. "I am just trying to keep my job," I say. "Something you obviously know nothing about."

"Yeah, well I'm sorry if I'm not willing to sell my soul to pay the devil."

"Didn't you crawl back to Chaz? Didn't you outsource your own daughter, for God's sake?"

"Don't talk to me about Etta. You don't have the right."

"Come on, Jared. I know Etta better than you do. At least, I see her once a week. What have you spent, maybe four hours in the girl's company since she was born? Let's see, that's about an hour a year. Are you sure you can live with that type of commitment?"

The tires screech and Jared knocks us down to fifty in a single slam of the breaks. I jolt forward with the force, and he holds his arm out in front of me to break my motion. We've both gone beyond our comfort level here and there's no telling where it will end.

"If you were a guy, you know, I'd have to hit you."

"Go ahead," I say. "I'm unarmed. But you might want to pull off the road first."

He punches the dashboard with his right hand, punches it repeatedly while imploring Jesus to fuck him, until I can feel the burn on my own knuckles and the irritation in my throat. Then he places both hands back on the steering wheel and looks straight ahead, without blinking, his face stiff and his hair hanging in a matted hank over his brow.

"Even if you can't be bothered to go back for your daughter, we still have to go back for my dogs," I say, not sure why I have to get in this last dig.

Still, I am surprised when Jared pulls off the highway again and drives me back to Boonslick without another word, the radio off for once, and the silence blooming between us.

30

At the vet's, Mayweather was tempted to hitch back to town and let Sally deal with the fallout on her own. After the way she'd treated him, he was certainly entitled. But then he wondered where he would hitch to, figured it would be Sally's place, anyway, and decided to save himself the drama. Besides, looking over at her, he saw that she'd turned pale and her face was stretched out into a blank stare. She was in love with those dogs, took them everywhere, and granted them more space in her bed than she was willing to allow the occasional overnight guest.

"I should have never gone in today," she said "I should have stayed in town to be available."

"The guy told you to leave them, didn't he?"

"Since when are you a fan of blind obedience?" she asked, in a sharp tone that made him realize she didn't want him to try to defend her.

The office was spacious, with long sectional sofas made of the same plastic as the booths in fast food venues, and the smell overwhelmed his senses: ammonia, dry feed, antiseptic, pee. The five or six animals in the waiting room skittered over the floor, their toenails clattering on the tile. A German shepherd barked steadily, without much conviction, and a hamster rolled around in a wire ball-shaped cage on the floor, at one point coming so close to Jared's red cowboy boot that he had to give it a gentle surreptitious kick to get it going in the right direction again.

When they got into the examination room, a bony man in mint-green scrubs brought Rye in on his leash, and the dog jumped all over Sally, his speckled tongue hanging out of his mouth, his paws resting possessively against her chest. Jared had to admire the bronze coat, turning smoky over the head and ears, the thick neck and the muscular haunches. But when they brought in Di, she was unsteady on her feet, her hindquarters drooping, so disoriented that she knocked into the leg of the examination table. Sally immediately knelt down on the ground, petting the huddled dog with a slow heavy stroke from the back of her ears to her tail. Jared had a kinesthetic memory of that motion on his own side, from his hip to his knee and back again, slowing all his vital functions until his migraine rolled over and lay immobilized, still pulsing but passive in his head. Di's fur was darker than Rye's, almost black, and Sally's pale hair against the animal made a contrast that cut into Mayweather's gut even as it attracted his eye. A yellow leaf on the black pavement. A field of wheat against the night sky.

"Tell you the truth, Diana's not doing so well," the vet said. "But there's not much more I can do for the little girl."

"Can I take her home, then?" Sally asked, and the vet said yes, it would probably be best. She pulled a treat from her pocket and tried to feed it to the resting animal, but Di turned away, her nose pushed down between her paws. Rye, attracted by the promise of food, was there quick enough, and Sally reluctantly gave him the liver snap she had offered to Di, then pulled another one out of her pocket, all the while exclaiming about its deliciousness and pretending to eat it herself. But Di only looked up sadly and put her head on Sally's knee.

When they left, Sally insisted on getting Di in the cab of the truck where there was hardly room for her. For a minute, Jared was convinced Sally was about to ask him to get out and walk home. But she managed to arrange Di in the well beneath her feet and then draw her own legs up into the seat. When he looked back through the rearview, Jared could see Rye sitting in his old spot, his ears blown back in the wind and his mouth open in what had to be the canine equivalent of a smile.

At the A-frame, Sally didn't even appear to notice that someone had cleaned up the evidence of the previous night's attack. She coaxed Diana up the steps and onto the bed and then tore off her outer layer of clothing, curled around the animal in her underwear as if she could save Diana with her body heat alone. Jared stood bedside for several moments, uncertain of his course. Then he took off his clothes, too, threw his arm around Sally, felt her body shake with inaudible sobs, and smelled the scent of fear coming from her armpits, wild onion and chives. It soothed him somehow, and he slept, his face in her hair, only awakening to the landline screaming in agony. Something about it struck Jared as crude and archaic, a cry that shouldn't be sounded except by an ambulance or tornado siren, and he had to crawl over Rye, who had come to join the pileup, to get to the source of the noise. As he picked up, he saw the sun shining through the window with a virile glare and realized that it was now probably twenty-four hours since he'd made and posted his film. Afternoon again, and the world had turned over one more time, getting him that much closer to where he was going. Who would know that Sally was home at this hour, anyway? Unless it was the user from Jeff City, calling back for more of the same. Sally, of course, was the only woman in the post-millennial world with no caller ID; no wonder she was less than selective.

The voice on the other line was rugged, but more confused than authoritative. "Have I reached the residence of Sally LaChance?"

"What's the matter; you didn't expect her to have company?"

"This is Guy Dempsey. I wonder if I can talk to Sally."

Jared, unpracticed in diplomacy, nevertheless recognized the name of Sally's boss. "Listen, dude, she is in no mood. I mean, you already pink-slipped her, isn't that enough damage for one day?"

"There's been a new development."

"What, you got a clue and realized she's the only one out there with any balls?"

"I don't know who you are, son, but I'm calling to talk to Sally. Do your friend a favor and hand off the phone before you get her fired again."

So Sally was being reinstated out at the park? Jared held the phone over his shoulder and looked at her sleeping with one arm around her dog. He couldn't bear to wake her up, even with good news. But Sally turned over, dragged herself up onto her elbow, and took the phone from his hand. Then Rye stood, too, getting his tail entangled with the phone cord so that Jared had to stand there unwinding him—why bother with a cord in this day and age? He was too afraid to take a close look at Di, who lay huddled at the other side of the bed, half-covered by a white flannel sheet, not moving at all.

"Ranger LaChance here," Sally said. "Who's asking?" But then she was silent for several minutes, lying propped up on one elbow and turned away from him, her hair pushed to one side, so that one white shoulder was exposed in its slender black bra strap. The long muscular cheeks of her ass were barely obscured by the triangle patch of her silky blue panties. *What kind of underwear was that?* Mayweather wondered. He couldn't remember seeing Sally wear anything quite so suggestive. Above and beneath the silk, the Taser marks were clearly visible, somehow fiercer than his own wounds, and he pushed up one panel to view the damage at closer range.

Sally immediately shrieked in the voice of a much younger woman. "Sorry," she said. "Looks like I've got a raccoon in the house. Is that good luck or bad? I can't remember."

She turned around and grimaced at Mayweather. Did this mean he was supposed to leave the room? He found his jeans on the floor and pulled them on slowly, trying to delay as long as possible so that he'd be able to pick up the gist of the conversation. The denim was stiff with the grime of three days. He could go downstairs and continue working on his film, he supposed, but there wasn't much of a point, unless he could imagine a time when he would actually be allowed to show it. So instead of leaving the area, he went into the bathroom and peed loudly, leaving the door open and hoping that old Guy could hear him. Then he decided to take a tour through the medicine cabinet— ibuprofen, iodine, witch hazel, eye drops, deodorant—nothing scary about that, but not much scope for recreational misapplication either. In the bedroom, Sally still wasn't talking, only saying *yes* and *no* and *I think that's accurate*, like a girl being asked to the prom. The conversation went on so long that Jared was driven out of boredom to take a shower.

Sally's water pressure was something fierce, but the narrow shower head didn't allow for much coverage, so he had to take on the body parts one at a time, grimy hands, matted chest hair, sticky balls. In his navel, he found a nest of lint the color of his T-shirt and wondered how long it had been since he had even connected with his own belly button. He eyed the irregular-shaped natural sponge in the wire rack under the showerhead, but then rejected the idea, thinking it was perhaps reserved for something of a sexual nature. The real challenge was the hair. He attacked it with fury. He found two ticks and more tangles than he could count, so that he had to use about a fifth of the bottle of coconut cream rinse just to get a comb through the mess. Then he stepped out of the shower feeling five pounds lighter. The steam covered the mirror, and so he could imagine anything he liked as he toweled off his damp torso and his dripping legs. Ony then did he realize he had nothing to wear. Maybe Mason had left some clothes behind. True, Jared was significantly taller and larger around the middle. But he could probably still work himself into a pair of the guy's sweats. He started to wrap the towel around his waist, then, deciding there was no need, used it to clear the mirror and then wrapped it around his head instead. He was still a good-looking guy, he thought, in spite of the gut and the stubble, his curved cock—which he now considered a sexual asset—half erect and his face almost feminine under the towel.

Just as he was digging around in a drawer for a pair of nail clippers, there was a cry from the next room. Maybe Sally was finally giving her boss an earful. But when he reached the bedroom, he saw that the phone was back in its cradle and Sally was lying over her dog, crying and groaning, high and low pitches he had never heard from her before. The sound filled him with fear. If Di was merely in trouble, Sally would be on the phone or in the truck with her on the way to the animal hospital. He froze in position. Was this a private moment, something he shouldn't witness, much less interrupt? He stood there for maybe two minutes, listening to Sally's sobs accelerate, and looking down at his own body, the damp brown curls of pubic hair and the rapidly retracting pink cock, the long thighs, the toenails ragged and yellow against the blue-and-maroon rug.

Sally's cries were now like a siren in the house, filling him with panic. He had to do something, anything, to stop the sound, so he crawled over the bed to reach her, put one hand on her back and the other on Di, and he felt something leave his body. The dog was warm to the touch, but there was no movement. He tried to feel for a heartbeat, but he couldn't tell whether the steady hard rhythm was coming from Di or Sally or himself. He saw that Sally's face was entirely wet, mascara smudged in dark spokes around her eyes and tears collecting at the base of her throat, welling up there between the sharp and intricate bones of her neck. By now, Rye had returned to the room, and leaped up on the bed, too, pushing at Mayweather's elbow. He took his hand away to let the dog in between them, and Sally called out again, as if by letting go, he had caused another rupture.

"She's gone," Sally said, laying her hand on Rye's head, "She's gone, boy. I used her and I didn't protect her and now she's gone."

All Mayweather could do was put his arm around Sally and sit there petting the dead animal. They both rubbed at the coarse smooth fur, moistened with tears and gleaming like the pelt of a seal. The coat gave up its musky scent and the rhythm became hypnotic, so that Di seemed to grow and loosen under their hands, and something escaped from them—the last thin layer of civilization. Mayweather felt his ribs ache, not with hunger or discomfort or even lust—but an unrecognizable emotion, horrible and irresistible, one he feared he would never be able to drink away.

31

When I know that Di is gone, my lungs collapse and I feel as if I am drowning inside my own body. This is what happens: You exploit a creature and you kill it, you abuse your position and you lose it, you play with a man long enough and he loses his capacity for anything other than play. How can I have reached this advanced age and still not understand the consequences of my actions? Di's face is relaxed and she is resting in the familiar position, head tucked into her paws and cocked sideways. Her dark glossy ears turn down so sharply that the fold appears white under the lights, slight and precise as the line between life and death. I pull in a deep breath and another—inhaling the scent of her coat, its smoky sweetness like a poison inside me, searing my internal organs and softening me up for my own death. Here it is, the pain I had hoped to never feel again after Sharee died and left me to climb up into adulthood on my own. I have somehow managed to avoid it until now, holding myself in reserve, minimizing my impact, cutting my losses, but it's there waiting for me just the same, having gathered weight and force in the interim. I take another breath and let it hit me. Now the grief crashes into my solar plexus and I realize that I've been waiting for it all along. Di investigating a turtle as it tucks its head back into the painted shell, Di pawing at a frog in the creek, Di leaping over a fallen tree, her underbelly showing and her ears on the fly. The dog is a natural predator, I have to remind myself, and Di herself was always sly as a panther, but in my imagination now she is a lamb—a black sheep, I guess you'd say—cruelly misled by her shepherd.

Rye licks my face, his saliva mingling with my tears, and then turns to Di and rests his head on her back, the bronze coiled into the black like the yin and yang. When Mason left, I couldn't bear to part the two of them, but now the matter is out of my hands, and I need to find a way to keep them separate in my mind, life and death, male and female, present and past.

Mayweather says he'll help me bury the little girl, when I'm ready, and I immediately think of the Karst, the place she loved the most, and where I started bringing her when she was only six weeks old so she and Rye could go off leash while I worked. But if I buried a corpse in a state park, that would make me no better than the polluters, dumping onto public land. This thought sends me into another volley of tears because I can't bear to think of Di—my best thing—as a piece of refuse to be gotten rid of. Something in me wants to keep her intact, or at the very least preserve those hard parts of her—the strong white teeth, the curved black claws—that might survive this dissolution and provide me with some pure, inviolable proof of her existence. I think of stories about people who've had their pets stuffed and mounted in their living rooms and shiver at my own fetishism. If I wronged Di in life, at least I want to do right by her in death.

Watching Mayweather pet her behind the ears and lift the flaps to examine their fine construction, I feel my spine crawl and realize that I need to put her back into the earth as soon as possible, to preserve her from being looked at, to prevent her from losing her wholeness and becoming a piece or garbage and a thing. I unhook her collar, my fingers trembling at the touch of her fur, and drop the red leather band to the floor, where its buckle clinks on impact and echoes over the wooden boards. Where is she? She is not mine anymore. I have to give her back, but to whom, I wonder? To the forest, to her species, to the ecosystem, to God, whoever he or she may be? It is hard to let Di go where I cannot lead her, although, come to think of it, maybe I'd be better off following, since I seem to have lost my own sense of direction in the rough and tumble of life. I can still feel her pulling on the leash, my right arm stiff with the pressure, and wonder what surprises she is already discovering in the life up ahead.

The temptation is so strong that it is a physical longing; maybe I have had all I can really taste of this life and the only joys left to me are those hidden in the beyond. But there is Mayweather, after all, pulling my other arm, and Rye licking my hand, and I have to come back to life again, if only for long enough to bury my dead.

I direct Mayweather to the shed where Mason has left all manner of gardening implements. There are two shovels leaning against the wall and out of courtesy I give Mayweather the newer one. Without speaking, we go out beyond the grapevines, where the yard touches the forest. There is a huge, old sycamore spreading its white arms. Its leaves, each as large as the face of a small child, are yellow in some spots and orange in others, revealing the uneven distribution of the sun's favors, and the bark of its trunk is peeling in gray patches, bone-white wood underneath. This is the spot where I used to come to lay out a blanket and read while Rye and Di lolled in the grass beside me, always there at my side whenever I needed to touch down for a dose of physical sensation. Mayweather digs and I dig and we don't speak at all. The ground is soft enough, but we keep running into roots, so that twice we have to give up and try again elsewhere. I am happy that, by some odd circumstance, Mayweather seems to understand my desire for silence. I can hear his shovel cut into the earth and then the rustle of the loosened dirt. I can hear the birds, who won't stop singing for anything, and the wind, whose pressure on my forehead is now the only pleasure I can remember of life. My hand is stiff on the rusty handle of the shovel, though God knows I do enough manual labor to have calluses on my hands. The beauty of the fall day seems like an affront to me; the hole deepens and widens and I have no desire to get to the bottom of it at all.

But when we are about five feet down, we go upstairs for Diana. I wrap her in my red bedspread, which I know I won't be able to use again, and Mayweather carries her down the stairs, me following behind with a bone and a chew toy. Rye, who has been standing guard by her all this time, is right at my heels, and I hear him padding behind me on the stairs. As Mayweather lowers Di's body into the hole, I regret that she can't rustle around in there and get herself comfortable.

Mayweather meets my eyes, then bends down and picks up a handful of dirt and pours it into my open hand. I smell its nutrients, the iron and the clay, the loam and residue of vegetation, earthworms, roots, mushrooms, shit. Then I throw it down onto the body, grateful that Diana is so dark that the earth blends into her fur. After that, we work for maybe fifteen minutes covering her up and I dread the moment when we will be finished and have to walk away from the task. What will I do next? Because there will have to be one step and then another. A minute and another minute, leading me further and further away from this last point of contact. I look at Mayweather and wonder if he's ever lost anything so precious. Not yet, I tell myself, but it will happen soon enough.

As we are walking back to the house, Rye starts to bark, his voice high and sharp, as if he's sighting his prey. We see a police car pull up to the house. The passenger gets out, a portly man of middle age, then the driver, a somewhat younger woman with shoulder-length hair, both vaguely familiar in their blue-gray uniforms. I suppose they are here to get our statement. We round the corner of the house without speaking to get a better look, and when the man hears us, he puts a hand on his hip and draws out a gun—or rather, a Taser—the same weapon responsible for Diana's death and the multiple puncture wounds on my ass. I startle and give a shout. Mayweather puts a hand on my shoulder and raises his other arm in a gesture of surrender. We see the laser beam light up and its red gleam part the air between us, but the guy realizes that we are no threat and reinserts the weapon into his belt.

"Sally LaChance?" he says. "Officers Tork and Denton here. We need to talk with you about the attacks."

"Yes, I'm Sally. Are the weapons really necessary?" I say. I am sure I have seen this man at a meeting of some sort. His nose has a flat spot on the end, like it's pushed against a piece of glass, and his dark hair comes down low over his forehead even though it is cut quite short. His face suggests a primitive type of intimacy and I can't remember whether I like what I've seen of him in action.

"I hear you had some visitors last night."

Rye hasn't stopped barking, and although he's generally friendly with people, after the events of the past twenty-four hours, I can't depend entirely on his good nature, so I crouch down to hold him by the collar. I can't lose him, too, not now. It is in this awkward position that I try to engage the cop in conversation and get him to tell me what he knows.

"I hope you got a real good look at them over there in police custody," I say.

The man shakes his head. "Bailed out by their employer this morning."

My throat clenches and I have to stifle a curse. Now I can be looking for them to return, I guess I will have to watch my back until the situation is resolved.

The policewoman looks Mayweather up and down. She is one of those pretty petite types, whose beauty hardens and solidifies with age, so that she looks like a jacked-up prom queen even at thirty-eight. Her hair is sprayed into an aggressive mahogany wedge and her face is colored with the familiar markings of her tribe. "This your boyfriend?" she says. "We heard you lost it and tazed him during the attack." Her tone is flatly flirtatious. "You plan on bringing charges against your sugar mama here?"

Mayweather, stumped, just plays with the tie of his sweatpants, as if this basic mastery will give him the confidence to move onto Gordian knots of more perplexing dimensions. What on earth is he wearing? I realize that he's found some of Mason's clothes, an old Incredible String Band T-shirt that stretches to ghostly thinness over his belly and a pair of slate blue sweatpants that barely cover his calves. If I'm his sugar mama, I should attempt to keep him in better style. But seeing Mason's clothes, I'm reminded of his growing operation out on the sun porch. I've hardly been out there since he left and I can't exactly remember what he's left behind—enough to incriminate me, surely, although probably not enough to nail me as a supplier on a major scale.

"While you're thinking about it, why don't we take a look at the scene of the crime?"

I open the front door and stand outside waiting for them to enter. I notice that the man wipes his feet on the mat, but the woman doesn't. She immediately starts looking around the house, stunned, I'm sure, at the spare—maybe even grim—surroundings, a woman's house without a woman's touch, unless it is that of Lorraine, who did insist on contributing dust ruffles and curtains.

My first thought is to get Rye behind a closed door where he will be safe and so I excuse myself and take him upstairs into the bedroom, away from the action. My next move should be to go out to check the sun porch, but I find myself lingering on the stairs, waiting for Rye to stop barking. I am close enough to hear Mayweather keeping up his end of the conversation. He's telling them about his night of drinking, then coming into the house to find some sort of struggle going on. "At first I thought it was consensual," he says. "But then I saw they were actually torturing her. These guys were brutal. If you don't believe me, just take a look at her ass."

Consensual? Maybe if Mayweather's mind wasn't always tuned in to the sex channel, he would have responded sooner. Maybe Di would still be alive.

"We'll get to that later," the policeman, Tork, I think it is, says, his voice assuming a more personal tone. "People tell us you are a videographer?"

"Yeah, where'd you hear that?"

"Some of the gals on the Boonslick Bombers were pretty impressed with your YouTube," Officer Denton tells him, and I think I hear the slightest smudge of a Southern accent on her vowels, hinting of dirtier things to come. "They gave us the link, but then by the time we surfed it up to take a look, the site had disappeared."

"Why's that, son? Why'd you take your film off the YouTube?"

"I'm not sure the world's ready for my aesthetic," Mayweather says.

"It wouldn't have anything to do with incriminating content?"

"Jared, look at me, " Office Denton says. "Did anyone pressure you to destroy your film?" The word "pressure" gets hit hard and drawled on; I don't know how much more of this he can take.

"I didn't destroy it," Mayweather says. "I'm keeping it for

future reference. But it's not for sale. A work of the imagination cannot be assigned a definite dollar value."

"Oh, we don't want to buy the film, son. We're law enforcement. We don't deal with currency. If we need something to promote the cause of justice we just search and seize the property, understood?"

This is the point where I'm compelled to intervene, even though, who knows, maybe Mayweather's interaction with the lady cop is actually consensual, given his obvious attraction to female authority. Should I attempt to make a sweep of the sunroom first? I probably wouldn't be able to destroy much evidence before they come looking for me. Besides, if it's only the film they're after, they may stop at the computer downstairs. I look at my hand and see that there is a smear of dirt on the palm, a thin layer of black under the thumbnail. There's dark hair on my shirt, too—and I pull it off, rub it between my fingers feeling its coarse texture, still so palpable, as strong as a bit of fishing line or a misplaced pubic hair. So this last bit of Di is still with me—her strength, her courage, her loyalty, her stealth. I lift the hair to it to my lips, blow on it, and watch it float out over the banister before I take a breath and follow it down the stairs.

32

Mayweather stood by the computer, considering his options. His father had instilled him with a deep distrust of the law, Johnny Law, in all his stiff pretension, the ultimate antithesis of pussy. And Jared's own experience confirmed that the straightest among us were often those most capable of violence, psychic and otherwise. Still, he wasn't without fond memories of Boonslick's finest, whom he would often encounter in the downtown diner after closing time, and who had on occasion entertained him with some choice stories about the local characters. The two specimens before him seemed slightly more congenial than the usual run of cops, the man low-key, the woman good-looking and casual. But the guy had certainly whipped out his Taser without much provocation. And the thought that they could simply take away his means of production filled him with a rage that sang through his cortex and threatened to instigate neural insurrection. The computer, in its electric blue casing, was so close that he could almost touch it, and he was stronger than either cop, he was sure, though remembering the Taser, he had to second guess himself.

"You folks ever hear of artistic license?" he said. "That film is a work of art, not the tape off some surveillance camera. In other words, it doesn't represent unmediated reality, and you can't use it as evidence without employing some kind of contextualizing lens."

Then Sally appeared at the foot of the stairs, her hair standing up with electricity and her eyes enflamed.

"Excuse me, sir," she said to the male cop. "But you can't search me without probable cause."

The policewoman touched her hair and ran a hand around her belt, as if to evoke the privilege of a tight waistline. "If you're so innocent, what are you afraid of?"

"Losing my computer for a week while you case through my personal correspondence, for one."

"Yeah, that and losing artistic control of my project," Mayweather added.

Sally looked at him incredulously and then flicked her eye-lashes away.

"Tell you what," she said, her tone changing to a tightly controlled rationality. "Maybe you can just wait until we talk to someone at the courthouse. I have the feeling that you were sent here on a false pretext."

"Are you or are you not Sally LaChance, female, forty-five years of age, twelve-twenty Karst Road?"

Sally looked, for a moment, as if she did not recognize her own vital statistics and then admitted that she was in fact the woman named.

"Then just plant your butt on the sofa and sit out the hot flash, why don't you, while we do what we need to do?"

"I'm not going to stand around biting my tongue while my house is illegally seized and searched. I'm the one who's just been attacked in my own home and now you come after me?"

"I said, sit down. You sure don't follow directions, do you?"

"That's because in real life, I am the one slinging the gun."

"That's what I hear. So how do you like having the piece waved around in your own face, huh?" The woman pulled out her gun. "You're just lucky we don't make you disrobe and search your person, too."

Sally backed away but still did not sit, her hands clenched in her pockets and a nerve pulsing in her forehead.

Mayweather, usually the loose cannon himself, now found himself in the odd position of trying to contain Sally. If she lost it with these cops, she might never get her job back and then where would they be? Thinking of this, he remembered that she had never gotten around to telling him about her conversation with Guy Dempsey. What had they been talking about on the phone for so long? Had she gotten the chance of a reprieve? If so, this incident might queer the deal for good. He put his hand on her shoulder and kneaded the back of her neck, which was oddly cold to the touch.

"I said, sit. You don't want to know what they do to women your age in prison."

She did not seem, on further consideration, like such a companionable gal. Mayweather wondered why she would show this much animosity toward a stranger. What did she care if Sally had held up and humiliated those polluters? Or was it something about Sally herself that set the woman off, some animal smell of sex and rebellion? Mayweather had never considered it, but Sally didn't have much to do with women of her own age, only those younger and older. And she was hardly the type to fall in line with any female protocol.

"Now you are threatening me with prison?" Sally said.

"Just sit down, girlfriend, and let me do my job."

Mayweather finally pulled her down onto the sofa with him and she didn't offer any resistance.

As the woman argued with Sally, the other cop went about systematically unplugging the wires of the computer. It looked forlorn, there in its electric blue casing, bereft of connection. Jared had heard of the police keeping confiscated computers for weeks and months; he wondered if he would even have the will to continue work on his roller derby extravaganza once he finally got it back—if in fact he ever did. Now he wished he had kept the film up on YouTube, so that he could retrieve it. When the male officer was done, he picked the computer up and carried it out of the room under one arm. Jared had a muscle memory of removing Diana from the premises, probably less than an hour before, the odd unwieldy weight of a body no longer animated by life. The computer and the camera were almost living beings for Jared, he thought, their steady breath a constant accompaniment, a sound so close to silence that it blended into his own chaos and calmed his mind.

As the computer left the room, he felt a searing pain his gut, as if a section of his own intestine had been cut out and carried off the premises.

Sally gripped his knee hard, her strength a reminder of her athleticism in bed and on the job.

But with the other cop out of the room, the lady cop became even more aggressive, getting down in Sally's face and insisting, now she was finally sitting, that she should stand up and allow herself to be searched.

Sally stood and spread her limbs in exaggerated compliance, her legs straddling a throw rug and her arms raised out to her sides as if she were lifting weights or holding up the pillars of the house. Jared thought of her lying in bed, taking up all the space possible, and admired the way in which she made a gesture of submission look like a fuck-you all the same. The cop ran her hands up and down Sally's sides, then made a show of grabbing her boobs and shoving them upward, as if they were hanging so low she might find something hiding underneath. "If you're going to rob the cradle, girlfriend, maybe you should at least invest in a good supportive bra."

Then she motioned for Mayweather to stand up, too.

"Now let's see what your sweetie is packing."

Her hands on his hips were tiny and expert; she smelled of some citrus perfume spiked with clove, and as she neared his crotch. Mayweather couldn't stop himself from wondering how she would look naked. He imagined big pliable breasts and stingy blue-rimmed nipples, pubes groomed as relentlessly as her head—perhaps even sprayed with some sort of mousse or shellac. It was a long time since he had contemplated a hate fuck, and it was strangely invigorating, if not entirely admirable. She leaned down in front of him and patted up his inseams. He hadn't bothered to put on underwear after his shower and Mason's tight but unstructured sweatpants offered little support for rising erection. She eyed the rise in the soft cotton with suspicion.

"Hey, this is business, mister. No fun and games with me."

Mayweather willed himself into a neutral state as she waved her gun at both of them and had them sit back down on the sofa.

When the policeman reentered the room, Officer Denton informed him that she was headed upstairs for a quick once -over of the premises.

Officer Tork had raised a sweat with just the slight effort, sat down in the chair across from them and took off his hat. His hair was damp and he smelled of meat and mustard.

"Whew, I should get my partner here to do the heavy lifting. She's the one always running off to the gym."

"They have you doing a lot of seizures lately?" Sally asked. "I heard they lost their computer over at the mosque, too."

"Oh, that was FBI, nothing to do with our operation. You know, people are just getting nervous with these terror alerts and all, crime on the rise, even here in Boonslick. You've got the gangs coming in from KC and St. Louis. Then you've got the meth labs coming up from the country. We asked the city for more officers, but we got this Taser program instead. Got to protect yourself, you know. You remember that poor girl—don't you?—maybe three years out of college, the sweetest gal on the force—got shot in the face last spring just stopping some guy for speeding. Terrible, terrible."

"You weren't out at the Karst recently, weren't you?" Sally said, her voice clearing up like a birdsong after a storm.

"We have our prayer breakfast out there every spring. It's a real pretty park you've got there. Too bad you can't get along with the neighbors."

They could hear the policewoman rustling around overhead. She opened the door to the bedroom and Rye started barking again. There was a stomp, then a thud and then another. Furniture being knocked over? Drawers being dumped?

Sally sat up straighter next to Jared and he could almost feel her spine rising to it full length. "What do you mean?"

"All this bad blood between you and Kevin Bailey. Why don't you just make a deal and get the funds to fix the place up?"

"Have you been in communication with Mr. Bailey?"

The man moved his hat around in his lap, like he had something larger than an erection to hide. "Look, Mrs. LaChance, I am just a public servant carrying out his mission. I'm sure your property will be returned to you in a timely matter."

"It better be, Officer Tork, or you will be hearing from my attorney."

When the policewoman came down, Rye trailing at her heels, her face was radiant with triumph, and she had, in her hand, a maroon velvet bag embroidered with dragons. Jared recognized the packaging. Inside, were two Ben Wa balls on a string, like jingle bells or the clackers little kids played in schoolyard tournaments. Although the use to which Sally put these items was slightly more exotic, they still seemed somehow indigenous, the logical extension of sexuality that was more mysterious than obscene.

"What are these?" the policewoman said, pouring them out in her hand and letting one dangle. "Some of those geisha balls?"

"I don't think they're illegal." Sally said. "At least not yet."

"They're evidence all the same," she said, squeezing them in her fist.

Sally shrugged. "Sure, take them and try them out if you you're curious. But I sure won't be wanting them back after that."

The male officer stood and brushed dog hairs off his pant legs. "We will be in touch about your computer, Ms. LaChance," he said. "And think about that option I was mentioned. There's no reason for you to make yourself into a martyr just because of a little litter under the bridge."

Once they were gone, Sally started pacing the room, as if gathering momentum for her next move. Several times, Mayweather found himself directly in her path, and had to grab her shoulders to steer her away. Then, when the police car was safely down the drive, she ran up the stairs, taking two steps at a time and he went up after her.

The bedroom was trashed, drawers dumped, dressers cleared off, clothes thrown off their hangers, the wicker basket of colored condoms dumped on the bed, and green-and white striped toothpaste squeezed out onto the sheets, with some kind of powder sprinkled over that. Talcum powder? Foot powder? Roach powder? Mayweather had no idea. But looking at the mess, he couldn't help but think of the clogged creek with its beaver dam of detritus.

"I suppose you'll be wanting a shot of that," he said.

"That is, if they didn't take your camera, too," she said, nodding. "Well, at least they never thought to look in the sunroom." She walked across the hall and opened the door, so that the light shot out and blinded them both. The long table, so lush with green weed only a few months previous, was now bare except for three orange plastic planters, the soil dried to a clay-like substance and the plants inside withered to brownish gray fronds.

Could it be that she hadn't even looked in here since Mason left? Mayweather couldn't imagine having access and then not even bothering to check it out.

"Looks like he tried to leave you a couple plants for personal use."

"Yeah, thanks Mason, wherever you are. Thanks to your generosity, I could have been charged with possession along with everything else."

"What are you going to do?"

"Call my lawyer. Call my lawyer, lodge a complaint, hold a prayer service."

"I'm right behind you," Mayweather said, but not without stopping to break off a section of one of the plants and hold the desiccated leaf to his nose. The smell was diluted with ash and decay, but he chewed a bit anyway, just on the chance that it was still potent.

33

It's almost four-thirty and I don't know if I have any chance of reaching my lawyer before quitting time. Paul Dodd, the guy who arranged my no-fault divorce from Mason, is a local figure of some renown. He's a bachelor in his forties: tall, dapper, completely bald, with a sartorial bent toward the spotted and striped, who seems more intent on making the scene than making a killing. He is the new version, I suppose, of that small-town attorney who appears in all the Southern movies of the fifties and sixties. Paul is to be found everywhere: at the farmer's market, in the coffee shops, at the various concerts and lectures held by the university, in the antiquarian book and vintage vinyl stores, at local fundraisers for the March of Dimes and Quantrill Creek. More than once, Lorraine has suggested Paul as a possible romantic interest for me, which is not out of the question, I suppose, except for the fact that I am not interested. Although Paul is intelligent and attractive, neither a bully nor a bore, there is something monkish about him, as if he has dedicated himself to the life of the city and has no energy left for a life of his own.

I ring him up and get the answering machine, leave my message and then start to fume, with no one to blame but myself. I have waited too long and now I can't afford to wait any longer. I should have called earlier, before the police arrived. I should have called this morning about the break-in, or even the day before, about my initial encounter with the polluters. I have been too busy reacting to make any kind of plan for myself. But it has only been three days and surely I can still catch up. If I had any gumption at all, I would at least have acquired the cell phone number of my lawyer and potential romantic counterpart. Then I remember Paul can usually be found at Boonslick Tavern, where he often eats dinner before making his evening rounds or simply going back home to drink and read. I am sure I have enough intuition left to locate the man without technological aid.

I give Rye a slab of lunch meat, find a few toys, and place them near him on the sofa, then relent, and decide it is too cruel to leave him alone in the house this soon after Diana's death. He can always sit in the truck or roam the woods through the prayer service. It will be dark in less than two hours and I am due at the Karst before then. No time to change, no time to think about the evening's events. Something in me is attentive enough to remind Mayweather to bring his sweatshirt and to switch out my overshirt for a lined denim jacket. Maybe I will have the gospel lady say a prayer for Di's soul, while she's at it. Looking out the window, I feel that Diana is still nearby; I see three red leaves fall, one by one, from the maple in the front yard, like time marking its territory. Now I am that much closer to death, and Di is that much further away from the moment of departure.

Outside, the temperature has dropped over ten degrees. It is that season of the year when, although you might be actually sweat inside your car at high noon, you will be forced to wear a jacket to sit out on the deck after dark. The clouds are massing overhead, and the light filtering in around them has the eerie quality of a photo in an illustrated Bible. I am reminded suddenly that they are actually 3-D entities, not just images projected onto the blue. There is a smell of minerals in the air, a heavy humidity, and the birds are chirping in anticipation. If it rains, I know Lorraine will find a way to blame me.

Mayweather offers to drive, perhaps because he thinks I'm too sore or sorrowful to do so, or maybe just because the power of the wheels has gone to his head. At any rate, I am happy to let him take over temporarily. Why not? I can definitely use the time to think. Half of the trees in the woods are still green and will probably stay that way until their leaves drop off with frost. But there are plenty of orange and red oaks and maples along the way. Even the trailing stalks of the elderberries have turned a bright abrasive maroon like stems of ripe rhubarb. Normally, this is my favorite time of year, the moment when everything shows its colors, gives off its smell, when you can finally tell where the bird's nests have been all through the thick and leafy seasons. But this year is different. The changing leaves offer little solace, and I feel more bone than blood in my heart. Looking back, I see Rye's ears blow back in the wind, his mouth open. If he can survive this, so can I.

"This Dodd, your lawyer, can you trust the guy?" Mayweather asks.

"As much as you can trust anyone," I say. "I'm sure you've seen his name. He's the one who's always got some case against Red Rock Insurance or the university or Three-M."

"And does he ever win?"

"Sometimes," I say. "All I can tell you is, he comes dressed to kill."

"So you say he handles domestic?"

"You have a secret marriage you forgot to tell me about?"

Mayweather slows down for a stop sign and slips his hand between my legs, as if to warm it there. "Actually, I was thinking about some kind of custody deal."

My throat dips in on itself. He is moving more quickly than I thought, and I can barely keep up. "You mean you want me to adopt you?"

"Etta, Etta! If there's DNA evidence that I'm the biological father, what are my legal rights?"

"Are you sure you're ready to get into that?"

"You think Ellen would agree to the test?"

"Slow down, Jared. You need to try persuasion before you take to the law."

"Yeah, I see where that's gotten you," he said. The woods were giving way to the subdivisions, the shabbier ones on my side of town that blur the line between duplexes and condos. When I reach this point in my drive, my chest clenches up, as I prepare myself to encounter civilization.

"What did Dempsey say about your job, anyway?" Mayweather asks.

"He said I might be able to hold onto it, but only if I make my peace with Bailey and the authorities."

Mayweather lets out a whistle and takes the turn into town. "Good luck with that. Man, that lady cop was seriously wack."

"I thought she was going to beat on me with those Ben Wa balls. You have to wonder why anyone wants to be a cop." Somehow the invasion is just now hitting me. I don't know which is worse, a break-in by criminals or a thorough trashing by the police.

"Well, why did you, Ranger?"

"Me, I'm only law enforcement by extension. I'm actually in it for the trees."

"Tell me you didn't like busting those guys' balls."

I smile, and find myself surprised that I still have the ability. "Maybe I got a little thrill out of it at first, but it sure isn't worth the repercussions."

At my direction, Mayweather pulls into a parking lot by the

bank, with spots after five. It's 4:58, by my watch, so it looks like we're safe. As we walk along the sidewalk, Mayweather in his red boots and short sweatpants, and me in my denim jacket and velvet jeans, I find myself wondering, for the first time, how we look to passersby. A drug dealer and his client? A college kid and his mom? Due to his lack of personal grooming, Mayweather can look both older and younger than his actual age: a weathered slacker or a derelict adolescent, while I have largely disappeared into the category of the well preserved and middle-aged. Still, we don't attract an unusual amount of attention as we go through the thick oak double doors of Boonslick Tavern. The place has high ceilings, potted plants, gleaming wood surfaces, and a long bar with a gold-flecked mirror and brass fittings. I can't help but think it looks like a joint I used to frequent in Jeff City. It's that type you will find here, too—people on their way over from the courthouse, college kids with their parents, the local Muleskinners, the Catholic Bible Study Group. The hostess appears in front of us in a red pantsuit, much makeup, and *I Dream of Jeannie* curls. She glares at Jared, and for one moment, I think she's going to evoke the dress code, maybe make him put on a jacket or tie. Then I realize that this dining requirement disappeared years ago, so there is no longer any official means of telling a potential patron that he looks like a bum. She settles for a scowl and a good look up and down his torso: the purple hoodie, the Incredible String Band T-shirt, the sweatpants that end mid-calf as if they are tucked into the boots. Then she takes a look at me, decides that I am paying, and seats us anyway.

In the dining room, I spot Paul Dodd sitting in the corner with a book spread open on the table in front of him. You might expect some legal tome, but I know him well enough to anticipate that it will be a classic Southern novel or a contemporary pop psychology bestseller. Sure enough, he has made his way half through Eudora Welty's *The Optimist's Daughter*, looking so attentive that you might think he is searching its pages for a precedent. He wears a nubby gray-green jacket and a tie patterned with fleur-de-lis. His bare head, articulated with subtle bumps and depressions, glows in the low light of the dining room, and the roast chicken dinner before him looks like a still life of an old master. He tilts the glass in his hand—bourbon, I'm guessing—but makes no move to take a sip. I glance at the menu, order a local beer on tap—for courage—and a reuben sandwich for sustenance. I only hope he doesn't leave before I am able to make contact.

Mayweather, meanwhile, is building a pyramid with packages of creamer. Do I dare take my eyes off him? I guess I have to leave him to take his chances with the waitress on his own.

I walk over to Paul, wait for him to register my presence.

He looks up, his solitude dissolving and the social being reforming itself as I watch: his gray eyes sharpening, his dimples flaring, his lips pressing together into a professional smile.

"Afternoon, Sally."

"Hello, Paul. Just wondering, are you still my lawyer?"

"Last I heard you could use someone good."

"Are you rushing off after dinner? I mean, maybe when you've finished, you could join us for dessert."

He looks at his watch, an antique item with Roman numerals to match his suit. "Looks like I may be able to squeeze in a few minutes before my next appointment. I can't resist the storyline."

"That's not the worst of it. Just thirty minutes ago, I was illegally searched and seized by the police."

"Just now? Did they offer any justification?" I can see his interest picking up, his eyes coming into deeper focus. "Give me a few minutes and I'll finish up here." He pushes his book away and starts to make serious inroads on his chicken.

When I go back to the table, Mayweather has his camera out and is reviewing his footage.

"So what's the guy say?"

"He's willing to hear me out, anyway."

I stare at him and wonder what he is thinking about Etta. Can he possibly imagine he can take care of her for even brief periods of custody? He downs his beer and I sip at mine, get foam on my lip, and wipe it off with a napkin. I don't have the energy to speak, so he just passes me the video camera frozen on the frame of my trashed bedroom and my brain freezes with rage. Is there nowhere I can count on being left alone?

Paul is at our table before the food arrives. He sets his book down on the empty chair next to me and holds his hand out to Mayweather.

"Paul Dodd. Good to meet you."

Jared looks puzzled, but shakes Paul's hand and mumbles his own name.

I'm surprised that Paul questions Mayweather first, takes a look at the film, shakes his head in disgust, then brushes down the narrow lapels of his jacket, and pushes his coffee aside. "I hate to say it, but we've been seeing a lot of these searches lately. Your situation is more complicated than most and you've got a bit more standing in the community than the usual run of petty drug dealers and meth addicts. So it might be a good opportunity to test the waters with a civil liberties case."

I shiver at the thought of a long drawn-out court case: paperwork, indecision, legal fees. But at least it would be a high-minded response to the assault charge that is surely coming my way. In moral terms, two wrongs don't make a right, but in the legal system, they just might cancel each other out and result in a clean slate and an only partially smudged reputation.

"What kind of legal team do you think Bailey has assembled?" he asks.

"What can I say? I've never even met the guy."

Here Mayweather surprises me by interrupting. "Well, I bumped into him last night and he tried to buy my film. But I wouldn't sell. That's why they called the cops on us."

"You think Bailey sent the police?" Paul asks, his eyelids oddly steady, as if he could put off blinking indefinitely.

"One of the cops, Officer Tork, did mention his name," I say, wondering if this Bailey can be so all-powerful as that. My Internet search had yielded little more than a few places of business and a city council report.

"Let me tell you what, Sally, I've been working this county for twenty years and I've never seen such an incursion into the rights of private citizens. We've got a number of people, the police just enter and exit their homes like bus stations. Because the precinct has the idea that once you are associated with a crime of any type, even bouncing a check or violating a traffic law, you are always open to probable cause."

While he's talking, a dark shape appears in my peripheral vision. Perhaps it's Diana still floating in the ether around me, hovering between this world and the next? I try to keep this thought at bay, to concentrate on what Paul is saying, the intent gray eyes, the clean-shaven upper lip, the wavy wrinkles in the skeptical brow.

But the shape keeps coming toward me, and eventually I have to turn, if only to ward it off.

It's not a specter, though, just a man in a black dress shirt with a silver stripe running through it, the sleeves pushed up to reveal buff forearms covered in dark curly hairs. Chaz sits down without preamble, puts his elbows on the table, leans into me in a mist of musk and sandalwood, and takes a sip of my beer.

"Hold on," I say, grabbing the glass away. "This is a private consultation."

"Ask me if I'm here to help," Chaz says, slipping his cell phone out of his pocket and sliding it across the table.

"Mr. Enright, good to see you. I got your text." Paul reaches across the table to shake Chaz's hand and my view is blocked by the conjoining of the two men, the bare forearm and the nubby sleeve, the receding hairline and the bald head.

So maybe I'm the third party after all. I look to Jared, to see what he's thinking, and realize that he's just staring at the phone because there's a photo of Etta on the screen. She's standing at the edge of the rink dressed in a Boonslick Bombers T-shirt and a black miniskirt with silver beading, the style and texture of an evening purse. Her hair is bound up in a high ballerina bun but just as many yellow curls are hanging down, clustered around her face, an oddly thin face for a child so young, the dimples no more than staple marks in the narrow cheeks, the sharp chin a provocation.

Surely it's not an accident that this just happens to be the image Chaz has dialed up on his screen.

Jared picks the phone up as if hypnotized and clicks on to another photo. But this is even worse, Etta bent down in an imitation of Reenie's starting position, squatting on the rink, her large hazel eyes level, fixed ahead on the track's curve.

He clicks to the next picture and the next, his Adam's apple pulsing, his elbow vibrating on the table. Chaz watches with amusement, still sipping on my beer. Then, as if some internal timer has gone off, he reaches across the table and holds out his hand.

"OK, jarhead, you got a good look. Why don't you give me my phone back?"

"Why don't you give my kid back?"

Jared makes as if to toss the phone to Chaz, and then throws it to me instead. I catch it without thinking and hold it up to the light. As I stare at Etta on the rink, I think I see a tear in her eye, but it's really only a glob of silver glitter stuck to her face in a beauty mark. Can we really be sure that she is suffering from the current arrangement, after all?

Paul just sits there, stirring more sugar into his coffee, taking it all in. "I wonder if we can get to the subject we came here to discuss. "

"And what's that?" I say. "I don't remember being invited."

"That's right, I'm going behind your back to save your ass because you won't do anything for yourself." He reaches over for my beer again, as if he's entitled, and I don't do anything to stop him.

In fact, I don't have a response of any kind, so I sit with the phone in my hand, its cool metal giving me some illusion of power.

"Did you think you were going to get out of this with just a couple of phone calls? Yeah, I know, I know, you used to ball the next director of Natural Resources and you think that gives you a leg up on the legal system, but guess what, the guy doesn't have smack to do with Boonslick. Sure, he can talk to Dempsey, but eventually Dempsey has to talk to the police."

"And the police are talking to Bailey, I take it."

Chaz nods, his eyes sliding over to Paul. "All of which will be resolved if we can just introduce a little diplomacy into the process. That's where Mr. Dodd here comes in. He's been able to finesse his way out of worse, isn't that right Paul?"

"Ms. LaChance, I think it's obvious to anyone who watched Mr. Mayweather's film that you were merely trying to protect the park. In addition to which, both invasions of your home were illegal, although it takes a fairly liberal jury to agree. Unless, of course, we are able to settle out of court."

"In the meantime, Mr. Bailey wants a public apology," Chaz says. "He'd like you to do it at the prayer service."

"Does he plan to have his goons apologize for breaking into my house and killing my dog?'

Chaz doesn't know about Di yet; I can see a flicker of sympathy move over his face and then drown in the general wash of cynicism.

"Look, those losers have a long haul in front of them. Don't worry about them. You're the one who can actually extricate yourself from this situation relatively unscathed."

But I know this isn't strictly true. Even if I do manage to keep my job and my savings, I still will have lost plenty: my dog, my integrity, the sense of personal righteousness that propels me through life, preventing me from indulging in self-pity or mooning over men. I look at Mayweather, staring dazed at the tablecloth, and realize that I will probably lose him, too, once the adventure of the past few days is over and there is no more spectacle to retain his attention.

As I am thinking this, the phone starts to vibrate in my hand, as if it's a living creature, its blind energy pulsing in my palm. "What about Etta?" I say.

"What do you have in mind?" Chaz asks, and I look to Mayweather

"I just want my daughter back," he repeats.

"One weekend a month," I say. "And some kind of summer holiday."

"You think the guy's dependable?"

"I'll vouch for it," I hear myself claim, though to tell the truth I have no idea. I look at the phone and see that it's showing Chaz's landline. "Anyway, maybe this is something you better discuss with your wife."

"As it happens, she's at the Empire, if you want to meet up there."

Mayweather looks toward me and I nod. I throw two twenties on the table, wrap my reuben in a napkin, and we walk out. As I cruise quickly along the street, I see that the leaves have blown off all the honey locusts, and the pods are lying on the sidewalk. In the ornamental planters by the curb, the coreopsis and blazing star have already given way to cold-weather plantings, dark pansies and fraying bouquets of purple winter cabbage that can last out the mild Missouri winter. The sky is opaque, mother-of-pearl, just a tint of pink hinting at the sunset to come, and there is a pine scent of rain in the air. The streets are lined with cars, and on the sidewalks men and women in suits and upscale sportswear mingle with kids in college sweatshirts, mothers in jogging gear pushing their high-tech strollers along. It's the fifteen-minute rush hour in Boonslick, a time when I try my best to be off the streets and safely ensconced in the woods. But today, there's no avoiding it, so I put my head down and aim straight for the truck, where Rye is waiting patiently, standing even, as if he sensed my arrival when I was still halfway down the street.

I climb onto the truck bed, happy that I'm still in my boots, and tear apart the oily Reuben to share it with him. I'm surprised by my urgency, as if I haven't eaten for weeks. The tinny meat and pickled cabbage are sharp against the creamy dressing, and my stomach growls, just waiting for the nourishment to reach my gullet. I have lived my life hungry, I think, not by necessity, but only because I couldn't imagine any other way to keep my independence except by going without. Should I comply with Bailey's wishes and give the public apology he demands? I certainly don't believe I should go to jail, or even pay extensive damages, for what I have done. But when it comes right down to it, I actually am sorry; the incident has cost me headache and heartache and even I know that I jumped the line.

Beside me, Rye has finished his half and is begging for more. I split the last bit, give him his share, and pet his chest as he bolts it down so that I can feel the food pass into his body. His slick fur tickles my chin, and I think I would rather just stay here with him than drive out to the Empire.

But now Mayweather is waiting for me, humming a syncopated country tune.

When I go to get in on the driver's side, I see that he's beaten me to it. I guess he's finally built up the momentum to act on his own.

"So, you're really going to do this?" I say.

"I thought it was your idea. Getting cold feet, Ranger?"

We drive out of the District and into public housing, where we pass Chaz on his bicycle, his butt raised off the seat and his aggressive profile pointed down toward the handlebars. Mayweather swerves a little too close and I feel his satisfaction in the power differential. Now we're on top for once, elevated in the truck of the cab. Now we're the ones who're moving faster, even if we're propelled by something beyond our own strength.

Chaz gives us the finger as we surge ahead. It's not a race, but it feels like one as we pass out of the residential area and into the industrial space of the city's seedy perimeter. The car lots and pawnshops seem smaller and shabbier, with letters missing from their signs. And overnight, it seems, the few trees in the area have lost their leaves and now stand naked at the side of the road. Meanwhile, a stiff breeze is blowing, stirring up trash and spraying a filigree of golden leaves across our field of vision.

The Empire emerges at the intersection, its patriotic colors hot on the horizon, like a disco sunset. It's the prettiest thing in sight, but it pales in comparison to the rink I remember from my childhood—pink and purple, fluorescent with neon and frigid with excess air conditioning. Come to think of it, maybe the Empire was shabby even then, but I was too naive to know it.

Sure enough, there's a realtor's sign posted out front. So Chaz wasn't bluffing about selling the building off.

An Anheuser Busch truck sits in the middle of the lot with a dozen vehicles parked around it. I recognize the red Jeep Wrangler my brother bought Reenie for her graduation, a skull and crossbones hanging from its rearview mirror.

Jared parks right next to it and bursts out of the cab.

But I'm not too anxious to go inside. So I let Rye out of the truck bed and take him down the alley to pee. As he does his business, I survey the graffiti, which has grown more explicitly political since my time: "Jessica is baller. I don't want to die for A-Rack in the desert. Queers for Peace. Skate punks shit skinheads. Keep your sand niggers off my beach. Jesus came to save your ass so pull your pants up and repent." Even out here, it's impossible to escape the barrage of troubles. My head throbs with the weight of them, and I wonder how I can feel entitled to claim my own bit of happiness, snapping it away from the world like a hungry beast.

Then I hear Mayweather following me down the alley.

"Go in already," I say, turning to see him in his purple hoodie with the orange cross painted on the front, his short blue sweatpants, and his red boots. Even dressed like a clown, he has an arrogance that I want to shatter. "Haven't I done enough?"

"I don't know if I can hack it without you."

"Jared," I say, "She's already four. Maybe you can usually get the girls to wait for you. Maybe you can get Ellen to wait for you. Maybe you can even get me to wait for you if you're willing to try. But Etta's already growing up without you. She's not going to wait until you're ready to be a dad."

He looks at his boots and Rye drags me farther down the alley. Something of interest must be up ahead. The smells of stale beer and strange piss, the promise of rotting fast food and dead vermin, the decay of autumn that somehow fills the animal brain with the hope of spring.

"All right, all right. I'm right behind you," I shout. The sound echoes in the narrow alley and I hear my own voice from a distance, as if it is my sister's and not my own.

34

Sally's voice, normally a rich alto crackling with sex and humor like a worn piece of leather or a good country song, now rose and frightened Mayweather with its urgency. Could she have been harboring expectations all along? He retraced his steps, the meetings at the Karst, the run-in with the boyfriend from Jeff City, the entanglement with Mason and his daughter, the scene with Ellen, the long absence while he tried his fortunes in Chicago, the trip down to Meramec Caverns in the spring. Never had he promised Sally anything, and never had she asked for any type of reassurance. There was, between them, a constant light tension of not knowing, a suspension of assumptions that kept both of them buoyant and light on their feet. He did not want to lose that bounce. He did not want to sink into dependency, no matter how comfortable. He stared down the alley and heard the wind singing at the other end, pulled his sweatshirt tight around his ribs, and felt his camera weighing on his chest. What if he did get some kind of custody agreement to see Etta on a regular basis? Where would he keep her? In his mother's house? In Sally's A-frame? In his own place, something compact and squalid like the garage apartment he'd rented for three years before moving to Chicago? That was highly unlikely. He might as well imagine the two of them inhabiting a fairly tale or nursery rhyme. He put her in a pumpkin shell. And there he kept her very well.

The thought, which should be depressing, was oddly pleasing to Mayweather, as he pictured Etta in her brown ribbons and golden curls, nested inside a glorious orange throne of living vegetation. He was so absorbed that he almost bumped into the deliveryman steering an empty gurney through the foyer. The Busch drone nodded and averted his eyes, as if he had just performed some shady operation, and Sally pulled Mayweather closer to her side.

Reenie greeted them in the snack shop, where she wearing an unfamiliar costume and unpacking a box of merch. "New uniforms, you like?" The colors were the same, but the ragged edges had been hemmed and the result was something like the uniform of a fifties carhop. All of the nostalgia and none of the punk.

Reenie turned and pulled up her skirt to reveal her name in red sequins on her skinny rump.

Mayweather could only stare. He was grateful for Sally, who fussed around Reenie, lifting a braid so she could read the "Busch Bombers" insignia on the pocket of her shirt.

"If we're going to make the break, we need a sponsor."

"If Chaz sells the rink, you're going to need a place to skate." Sally said. "But don't let me stop you from dreaming."

The other Bombers sat around on the benches or cruised the rink while the lone male ref stood next to the lockers kicking a hacky sack.

Mayweather found Ellen leaning against the barrier in street clothes, a red blouse and a skirt short enough to raise his blood pressure. If Chaz sold the rink, would Ellen quit the team? He leaned in so close that her hair tickled his nostril and he got a whiff of her sandalwood perfume. "Got a minute, pretty lady? I need to talk about Etta."

"Out there," Ellen said, pointing toward the rink where the little girl was skating between Marilyn Monsoon and Britney Spearhead. Her sequined costume made her look like a baton twirler as she passed back and forth under the blue and red lights. Her lashes were thick with mascara and her blond hair had been sprayed into a horrific static wave.

"All grown up, don't you think?"

"What, are you entering her in a beauty contest?"

"I should consider it."

Mayweather felt the blood beating in his forehead and his fingers curling into a fist. He thought of Ellen's nude photo on Chaz's screensaver. He thought of Sally hypnotized by that snake in Jeff City. He remembered Baily's threat against his mom. All the women he knew trapped inside power's glossy grid.

But getting angry hadn't worked for him yet. So he just swallowed his rage and kept on talking.

"Listen, what would you think about shared custody?"

"And will she be staying with you at Sally's?" He could hear the slightest tinge of jealousy in her voice, distrust mixed with flirtation, and he remembered her burnt-orange heat in bed.

"Too soon to tell," he said, maintaining his focus at some cost to his pride. "I'll figure out something."

He could sense her impatience. Hell, he was impatient with himself. How long would he keep circling the rink, he wondered. He had tried to get away, tried to push off on his own, and found himself stranded at the edge of the world, where his reality thinned out to his few physical needs and his fewer acquaintances and his art had stalled, pristine and hypnotic but without momentum. Was it just a question of money? Money appeared to seek Chaz out just for the pleasure of attaching to him, but Mayweather, like his father before him, repelled the green stuff with an almost chemical predictability. Perhaps it would help if he got a job, Jared thought, a real one, and not just a freelance assignment with a dubious friend. He went over the possibilities, considered the dignity of the bartender, the humility of the doctor, Bailey's calloused hands around his neck. What was Mayweather suited for, after all? At twenty-nine, he had worked hard to rid himself of any marketable skills, and had become one pure purple pulse of chaos and negativity.

Before he could elaborate further, Chaz swept in the door, followed by Lorraine, who hobbled over to Sally and nudged her daughter with her cane.

Mayweather calculated that he had less than a minute to convey his urgency to Ellen.

"Please," he said, moving his face close to hers and breathing in her ear. "Do it for the team."

She lowered her lashes, and for one melting second, he thought he had convinced her. Then she opened her eyes as wide as a doll's and reminded him of the many times he'd disappointed her.

She was still at it when Chaz came up behind him, kneading his shoulder with one hand and Ellen's with the other.

"Jarhead unveil his master plan? What do you think?"

Mayweather waited for the deluge to resume, the accumulated weight of his betrayals, shortcomings, fuckups, and ill-conceived stunts all redounding with a vengeance on his poor migraine-addled head.

But he was saved by the voice coming from the loudspeaker. A soothing voice with deep pockets of humor and a suggestive lilt. It was Sally, who'd climbed into the emcee booth and was speaking into the mic. "Testing. one-two-three. Testing. Attention, Boonslick Bombers or Busch Bombers or whatever you call yourselves these days. I have an important announcement for you. Lorraine just came back from the vets all hopped up on sugar and good news. She tells me that Gabriella has recovered consciousness. Gigi Haddist is with us again!"

A shout went up from the benches as the rest of the Bombers streamed into the rink and began skating. Britney lifted Etta onto her shoulders and Reenie weaved in and out of the pack, waving a pair of panties above her head. Mayweather, caught off guard, nevertheless had the wits to turn on his camera.

Maybe he'd never have the opportunity to complete his film. But here it was, the last scene, bringing the whole sequence into visibility again.

Lorraine stumbled into the rink and lifted her cane above her head, as if directing the action. Chaz pumped his fist and hooted along.

This was the visual Mayweather wanted. It was almost too much. His chest cramped with recognition. Then, when he was sure he had everything, he saw Sally descending, her hair flying and her face stained blue as a Bollywood Shiva under the revolving lights.

They walked to the truck with her hand in his, Rye's leash getting intertwined between them, and then drove out toward the Karst without speaking. The wind had picked up again and leaves blew across the road in front of them. Many of the trees had emptied out, their bare branches now holding nothing but sky and the clouds moved quickly against weather the color of aluminum siding. Mayweather felt the chill of winter in his light jacket. He did not want to let go of Sally's hand, not even when she shifted gears, and had to finally force himself to give up his grip and grab onto his own knee instead. The cab of the truck smelled of antifreeze and electricity, or maybe it was his own migraine aura coming on. He closed his eyes and saw the pulse of purple there, the reverse image of the sun, and the wheeling pieces of reality looking for a place to land. Was it Sally he wanted or was it only the thing she was leading him toward? He could not tell the difference anymore, so he opened his eyes and tried to keep a sharp lookout.

At the Karst, the cars stretched for half a mile down the gravel road, and Sally slowed down, remarking on the turnout. She backed into the reserved employee space, released Rye, and walked straight into the woods, with Mayweather walking beside her on the narrow trail so that they nearly touched at the shoulder. He could hear rustlings in the underbrush beside them, as if invisible ghosts were following along. A vine hung down, twisted like a rope. A brown leaf, raised on its five points, scuttled across their path. In a patch on the ground, there was a nest of black walnuts the size of ben wa balls, looking as if they had been charred in a fire. The mushrooms were out in force, strange white-and-orange polyps like sea anemones or underwater sponges. He had his camera on by now, of course; he was falling behind. How could he just pass it all by without recording anything? Even in winter, there was plenty to see. He stopped to review the film he had just taken, puzzled again by the disparity between what he observed and what he had actually recorded, the mushrooms dimmer, the trees smaller, Sally's face completely obscured by shadow, the green field of tall grass burning orange with the reflection of the setting sun. It amazed him that people considered film to be a documentary art, that anyone would consider it reliable as evidence. For him, there was an immense distance between the eye and the lens. In order to attempt the translation, you had to see into the background, visualize the various objects turning in space, anticipate their movement toward some imagined endpoint, take a deep breath and shoot into the future of the frame.

He leaned in over a half-rotted hedge apple and saw, behind it, a pair of dark brown loafers. His lens moved up the leg and torso, until the face emerged, in front of a stand of red sumac, a familiar face, ghostly tracks of braces and one dark eyebrow interrupted by a scar.

Bailey kicked at the hedge apple and grinned. "I guess you got my message. Maybe I wasn't clear enough the first time. See, I really did want that film."

Mayweather could hear the rustlings and murmurings of the crowd in the clearing up ahead. He guessed that Sally was probably already out there, conferring with Lorraine, and was glad that she didn't have to encounter Bailey in the flesh.

"Too bad you didn't feel up to cooperating," the developer continued.

Mayweather turned off his camera, as if to protect it, and fitted it back inside the case.

Meanwhile, Bailey put his hands in the pockets of his brown bomber jacket and rocked a bit on his feet. "Tell you what, I'll give you another opportunity. I've got some unrest out there in the Maple Leaf subdivision. Foreclosures, gang violence, drug wars. There are some rough characters squatting right in our construction zone, stealing pipe. I'd give you four hundred bucks a week to go over there and keep a look out, do some surveillance, keep a watch on my investment."

"What's the matter with the rest of your guys?"

"We had to halt construction. The market isn't as buoyant as expected and I had to let some of them go."

Mayweather looked behind him and saw a crowd coming up the trail, a group of bikers in their leather paraphernalia, one of whom he recognized as a girl from the team. He waited for long enough to let them pass, then turned back to Bailey. "Why would you want to hire me, dude? I just kicked your butt."

"Looked to me like I kicked your ass right out of the club. But you did do well enough to make an impression."

"So, let me get this straight. You want to pay me to be a watch-man-slash-bouncer-slash-videographer for your subdivision."

"Free rent thrown in. I've got a couple units open. Tell you what, you can even take your pick of the lot."

"What does it matter?" Mayweather said. "They all look the same." But he began to imagine: a yard for Etta, a room of her own, a space for a studio, more space than he'd ever be able to afford, even after years of legitimate labor. A few more people up the trail, a whole family, including two grade-schoolers and a granny in a puffy coat. Mayweather stepped aside, for the sake of politeness, and found himself standing closer to Bailey than he'd like, breathing in his spicy scent of sawdust and Mexican beer.

Bailey leaned in and whispered in his ear, even though there was no need. "Plus, if it means anything to you, I can get you back your film."

Mayweather stood, feeling a pinprick of mist on his face. He didn't know where he was anymore, in the rink or the bar or the Karst. Everywhere he went he was tempted with favors he could never repay.

"You're like I was, Jared. No cash, no connections, no fucking father to build you up or bail you out. Tell you what, though, that's the real advantage you've got over these hometown mama's boys. They've got the sweet stuff, sure, the cars and clothes and country clubs and computers. But what does it to matter to you? You got your own balls in your hand and that's more than most guys can say for themselves in the end."

Mayweather winced, feeling his anatomy dissected. Was it

really enough to possess yourself? Or was that an illusion, too? A childish pretense of autonomy in a society that was nothing but an endless daisy chain of favors and deals?

There was a warmth behind Mayweather like a fire at his back and he felt Sally's hand on his shoulder.

"What are you doing here, Bailey?" she said. "You suddenly get the urge to pray?" Mayweather had no idea how she recognized the guy, since as far as he knew, they'd never met.

"Public land, public use: Isn't that your motto, Ranger? With that philosophy, you can hardly keep me out, no matter what you think of me."

"As long as you behave."

"Didn't I make my point yet, lady? I've got it covered—the police, the court, the Natural Resources. Hell, even the ministers and priests in town line up for me to tuck bills into their G-strings."

"I'm still on duty," Sally said. "So I'll thank you to treat me like legitimate law enforcement."

"That's right. You're here to make your apology. What do you have to say for yourself?"

"Wait and see. In the meantime, you better keep your feet on the trail. It's not too late in the season for a little poison ivy. We've got a particularly vicious strain."

Down the path, he could see a group of three women in hijabs and long coats. their bright robes floating over the brown and red leaves, placards under their arms, serious faces turned toward one another, deep in conversation. Just before they passed, one woman's veil caught on a shrub and she froze in her tracks, her neck tensing, and took two steps back. Then the woman next to her moved out of position, patiently disentangling the blue cloth from the branch. Jared pulled out his camera to track the visual. By the time he turned back again, Bailey was gone, and Sally was greeting the women, admiring their placards and shaking their hands.

He had missed his opportunity, he thought, looking back toward the clearing, where Bailey's bomber jacket was disappearing in the foliage. But just as he was about to put his camera up again, he saw a shape running down the path—a figure in red boots and an orange jacket, blond curls on the fly. I'll get her, he thought, or at least I'll get what I can, as he filmed Etta moving toward him, seeming to change and grow as she approached, her features coming into focus, more advanced, more evolved, more adult with each movement, until he saw his own unfinished face trapped in the viewfinder.

35

Mayweather's face, emerging from behind his camera, looks numb, and I wonder what it is that Bailey has said to him. As I watch, Etta crashes into his knees and he lifts her up, swings her around by the wrists, and sets her lightly back on the ground. I am standing, talking to the women from the mosque, and can't quite make out what Etta's saying, but I'm willing to bet my last month's salary that she's begging him to repeat the move. The woman in the blue veil, the imam's niece, tells me that she is becoming more concerned about the FBI investigation. Yesterday, her father was called in for an interview, at which point he learned that their landline had been tapped.

"Now we are trying to think of everyone we talked to from home, and what we could have said to them," she tells me, her young face parted with a single deep wrinkle between the eyebrows.

"That is worrisome," I say, thinking of my own recent troubles and watching as Mayweather swings Etta around again.

"So you see why it's even more important for us to keep a positive image in the community."

I look at her standing between her two friends and think of the

Three Wise Men in their robes. How could any image be more positive? And yet, I am in no position to grant her request and sanitize the roller derby, rename Gigi Haddist on her hospital bed, or ban all comic references to a tragic war. All I can think to do is to ask her to join in the prayer service and contribute her own religious perspective.

"There is no God but God," she says, bowing her head, and shifting her prayer mat under her arm as I try to puzzle out whether this is a refusal or an agreement. "We are sorry for your skater's troubles."

More people move up the trail—bikers in their Harley jackets, kids in college sweatshirts, adults in work clothes—and I lose sight of Mayweather in the crowd. I try to stay focused on the conversation at hand, taking the elbow of the women in blue and guiding her slightly off the path, to where a stand of red sumac provides some cover. She jostles against me, crouching a bit, no doubt afraid of being caught by her veil again.

The sun is coming down on the forest, the denuded branches revisited with color—brutal pink and acid orange layered like a psychedelic parfait in the sky. This is the most difficult time of the day for me. I never fear the sun, even as I age, because I prize the clarity that daylight brings, and the dark, with its blessed blunting of sharp contours, is a comfort to me. But dusk fills me with apprehension. Have I done enough during the day? Will I be able to sleep through till morning? Can I reach that black border of night before dissolving into the despair of my indeterminate state? This sunset is worst than most, because it reminds me that I will have to decide, in a matter of minutes, what to do about my public apology. And now that I know Bailey is on site, the matter has become even more sensitive. Who knows, my attackers may be here as well, seeing as they have been so quickly released on bail.

Just as I am at my most vulnerable, I see Lorraine trekking up the path in a bright turquoise parka with braid and glitter rick-rack sewn into the seams. She seems to walk right through the last crack of light, an explorer on a strange planet, her cane lifted toward the sky for emphasis, making me think of Moses, who was denied entrance into the Holy Land for trying to beat water out of a rock instead of just speaking to it softly as the Lord commanded. Walking next to Lorraine is the individual I assume to be the evening's performer, perhaps the only person in the state who is more of a spectacle than my own mother. The woman, maybe ten years my senior, her asymmetrical gray braids woven together into a kind of a basket over her right shoulder, intertwined with beads and feathers, then narrowing again to a single tail twisted into her waistband, the tassel protruding like a trumpet from above her fanny pack. As if that isn't enough, she wears a knit hat with a large poppy on the brim, a white shirt, a red velvet cummerbund, and a long skirt that appears to be made of a quilt, the American flag prominent among the scraps from which it is sewn. She carries a composition book in her hand and a Bible tucked underneath her arm.

Is this really what Lorraine has come to? I can see the delight in her step; her hobble looks more and more like a joyful skip. Not only has she discovered someone whose grief is more gaudy than her own, she is now dragging this human apocalypse home for all her friends and family to see.

I cringe there are at the side of the path, waiting for her to recognize me, but she barrels on through, talking nonstop to the woman at her side, who remains silent, her eyes focused on the horizon ahead, as if she's already entered some kind of trance. I see that Ellen has joined Mayweather, and the two of them are walking along with Etta between them. The Muslim woman and her friends proceed up the path and I fall in behind them with

Chaz, who has dressed out for the event in real trousers and a wool jacket, the knot of his maroon tie just visible inside the lapels. The peaks in his hair are lying down flat and for once he looks his age, a respectable age for a man, just settling into the long virile stretch of midlife.

"After you," he says, touching my back with unearned authority.

"Why are you so damned happy and mysterious?"

"OK, to tell the truth, Bailey was one of the potential buyers I had in mind."

As he speaks, we round the corner into the clearing and my throat constricts. They've built up a bonfire in an undesignated area, its orange flames snapping maybe twelve feet into the air and its circumference as wide as the base of a prize oak tree. With so much happening, I neglected to come out here and see what they were planning. I know I should be irate, but I'm actually gratified: I'm anticipating doing a controlled burn here, anyway, and they're only given me a head start on the job. Still, I'm surprised that no one has objected, not even the police, who have pulled their car right into the tracks made by the polluters. Two familiar officers lean against the side of the car, their arms crossed.

"You would sell the Empire to Bailey? After all that you know about the guy?'

"Maybe the Empire has served its purpose. Think about it; aren't we all ready to move on?"

I feel the ground shift beneath me with the footfalls of the crowd, and my heart jerks, pulled up short like a fish on the line. How can I move on when there's nothing to move on to, when the past is closing up behind me is and the future is disappearing up ahead?

"Anyway, Bailey's pulled out already. I think the sticky construction bubble blew up in his face."

"So you're not going to sell the place after all?"

"As it happens, I have another buyer interested."

"Oh?" I say, running through the possibilities. If Eric is right, only the government will be buying in the next few months. Come to think of it, the Empire would make a decent VA post or benefits office, a city rec center or a transportation hub.

Chaz takes me by the shoulder as if offering to dance with me, his touch curiously cold, and draws my attention to the group around the fire. Some of the Bombers have gathered into a line with their arms around each other and are swaying to the music, which appears to come from a large rented speaker, now spewing forth Loretta Lynn's rendition of "May the Circle Be Unbroken," perhaps for Lorraine's benefit. Meanwhile, the rest of the crowd forms a ring around the pond, standing there among the molting cattails, as if they too have sprouted up along the banks. The cattails glow white in the dark and the fire ripples on the surface of the pond, causing me to remember Mayweather's trick photography by the bank of the stream.

"Sometimes the answer is closer than you think."

I go over the possibilities again, considering the alternatives. Of the Bombers, only Reenie comes from an upper- middle-class background, and I can hardly see my brother Trev investing in the enterprise that has caused him so much embarrassment and grief. Where is Reenie, anyway? I haven't seen her all evening, and the service is set to start in less than five minutes.

"You'll never guess," Chaz says.

"It isn't Reenie, is it?"

"You're warm but not hot."

"Who has the money to buy the Empire?"

"Let's see, maybe someone who has no faith in the stock market and wants a safe place to stash their life savings."

The answer is as plain as the look of superiority and satisfaction on Lorraine's face.

"You wouldn't let her do that, would you? Sink her life savings into some white elephant on the wrong side of town?"

"Look, I'm bleeding cash here. I've got to cut my losses."

"She was a school secretary, for God's sake. She doesn't have that kind of money."

"You'd be surprised what those Depression babies were able to save. Anyway, your brother's got the goods to back her up, doesn't he?"

"You're really that broke?" I say, looking at his wry and animated face, as if it will tell me anything about the state of his portfolio.

"I'm not one of those guys who's ashamed to cut back and adapt. That's why I am going to stay afloat. Listen, I think it's supposed to be a surprise, so don't mention anything until Lorraine brings it up."

"This means I don't have to apologize?

"You can do what you like regarding the lawsuit, but I'm personally out of Bailey's pocket. Anyway, looks like your mom can give you a job now."

I look out at the clearing and see Lorraine pacing back and forth in front of the assembled Bombers, trying to work them up with a megaphone and a cane. Meanwhile, her friend Mariah is silently staring into the fire, holding her hands out over the flames, and feeding in sticks from the woodpile. She lifts her skirt to warm her legs and I see that her tights are striped like candy canes, her combat boots clamped halfway up her calves. What would be worse, I wonder, working for Chaz or working for Lorraine? As happy as I am to have the Empire saved in some form or another, I am reluctant to become any more involved with its daily operations and hate to see Reenie's plans for law school further delayed. I worry about Lorraine losing her nest egg just to preserve a piece of her own usefulness and her daughter's memory, now rapidly disappearing from the consciousness and even the very architecture of the town. Still, come to think of it, the Empire is the only roller rink in Boonslick, so she'd have a monopoly in this expanding community of elementary school kids with fundraisers, middle-schoolers with nowhere to go and energy to burn. Perhaps it isn't such a bad investment after all, or at least no worse than anything else at the moment.

"Thanks but no thanks," I say as I leave him behind and move swiftly toward the fire, passing the police car and trying not to turn toward the officers, who appear to be the same ones who desecrated my home and taunted me with my own sex toys only hours before. Even though I turn the other cheek, it still burns in the chilly dusk, as if I can feel their disapproval on the side of my face.

As I move past, I see the signs people are holding up, "Medical Insurance for Athletes," "Boonslick Bloggers," "Clean Water, Clean Air, Clean House," "Hispanic Americans Are Patriots, Too," "Bring Them Home," "We All Live Downstream," "Veterans for Christ," "Arrest Police Brutality," "Respect Our Men & Women In Uniform," and "Stop Terror in Its Tracks." My friend the imam's niece is there, too, with her little group, holding up the familiar sign, "Make Hajj, not War."

Their causes, pressing and contradictory, crowd together in my chest, and I wonder how I can claim priority for my own case. No doubt even Bailey has his story, a narrative of bootstraps and spreadsheets, the rage of a small businessman against the government's machine. Or this is what I've been able to glean from my random search of the Internet, which will end, I suppose, by leaving no one to pass through life with his or her story unrecorded. Isn't this what we all wanted, our pictures flashed through the ether, our words reproduced endlessly, our actions amplified by mass consumption, everyone a celebrity of her own little demographic on the screen? I've spent the last half of my life courting anonymity, which, it turns, out, is the biggest luxury of all, and something that has finally eluded me. But since notoriety has come to seek me out, I might as well go forward and meet it. As I pass the pond on my right, the night scent rises up from the water, and I try to separate its components of must and spore and spawn. I look for a gap in the crowd where I can see through to the surface and there it is, an expanse of orange, reflecting the sun's glare, the wind producing a steady ripple running toward me, and the dried lotus pods lifting their heads above the fray.

Someone recognizes me and shouts out: "It's the Ranger." The voice is joined by other cries: "Fascist Slut!" "Keep your safety on, honey." "You go, girl." "You a mean rollerbitch, dawg." I hear one obscenity too many and peer into the crowd at my side, where my attackers have appeared, just at the spot where they were so recently pissing into the pond. The two of them stand there hulking together in their twin Carhartt jackets, hands on their belts, leering as if my rage makes me the subject of a dirty joke. I want to stop and respond; I even feel my hand inadvertently seek out my hip, where there is, of course, no gun, since I am dressed out as a civilian, and I brush against the nap of my velvet jeans instead, rubbing and rubbing, as if I can produce a weapon from the friction. But this is not the moment for retaliation anyway. I may not be a hero, but for this one week of my life, I seem to be the spot where all the loose cannons converge. I can feel the pressure on every side, as if my body is the only thing preventing some violent confrontation.

I approach the fire and a flame turns in my direction, the smoke insinuates itself into my eyes and I start to cry. I've cried so much in the past day that my eyeballs feel like they are turned outside in and I am looking directly into the foggy space of my own brain. I see Lorraine in a blur of bright turquoise. I see Mayweather behind Etta's red coat. I see Chaz, who hasn't left my side, it seems, and now appears as inseparable from me as my own evil. Here I am, unarmed and unprotected, ready for any random stranger to feed me to the flames.

36

Mayweather luxuriated in the pressure of Etta's back against his chest as he held her up to get a better look at the fire. Her heart beat very quickly, so quickly that it frightened him, and he wondered if there was something secretly wrong with her, some biological peculiarity that would require a heroic intervention on his part. He almost hoped so. He felt the need of a disaster to draw them together, a near miss to force his hand and bind him to her service for good. The air was pungent with smoke and leaves and the damp earth underfoot. In contrast, Etta herself smelled of Ellen's honeysuckle shampoo with some sharp curt little-girl scent emerging from underneath. She had her hair pulled up in doggy ears and her neck was exposed, so that he could see the down at the nape, blond as forsythia, and the pointed tuft of hair emerging from the bottom of her part, like a widow's peak in reverse. He wanted to touch this space, but felt it was too intimate, so just stared at it instead. As he did, his mind filled up with terror at his own wish. Etta didn't need a physical flaw; in spite of her beauty and the crass perfection of her image on Chaz's phone, she was actual after all, and that should be enough to allow him to love her without further proof of her mortality.

Etta lifted her hand and pointed to the crowd around the pond.

"Aunt Sally," she said, and there Sally was, striding past the assembled fans and protesters on her long legs, a movement calculated to suggest roundups and rodeos, though in reality, he knew, she was far more agile in the sack than in the saddle. What could she be thinking? As far as he could tell, she did not operate with any plan in mind, but only acted on inspiration from moment to moment. That accounted for the initial attack, of course, and the Taser incident too. But she had also managed to get Chaz to consider shared custody, and he wondered what he owed her for that.

Ellen touched his elbow and he jumped, almost spilling Etta onto the ground. In the near dark, she was even more gorgeous, her profile unlined like a slice of the moon, her breasts filling out her red coat and topping it off, too. Maybe he had loved her after all. Maybe Etta was not the waste product of a meaningless fuck but the rare flower of an evolutionary development.

"Are you really ready to take this on?" Ellen said, biting her lip to nip off a smile.

"Don't you trust me?"

Ellen laughed. "Where have I heard that before?'

"Yeah, but OK, you don't think I'm going to kidnap her or leave her at a bar or anything, do you?"

Ellen reached out for Etta's leg and turned up the cuff of her jeans. "I know you care about her," she said. "I just hope that you can get it together before you're too old to change."

"Was that the problem with us?" Jared asked. "You thought you were too outdated to keep up with me?"

"Jared, I'm sorry. You were the best thing in my life for a little while there. I don't regret anything, but there was, you know, just a part of me that wanted to see what I'd be like out on my own."

"And you didn't like that independent chick?"

"Let's face it, Jared. She was kind of a poser."

Sally poked her stick into the fire and hoisted it up again, flame tipping three separate branches. Fire was something that did not translate well into film, Mayweather remembered, because it was really more transparent than you realized, and even a great blazing bonfire like this one wouldn't look like much more than a few translucent orange streamers flapping in the wind. From the long central stalk of her stick, Sally lit the torches of the Boonslick Bombers, their team jerseys worn over leggings and hiking boots. The girls ran out and circled through the crowd, as gracefully as if they were still on skates, lighting up the vigil candles as they went, so that separate flames flitted up out of the night. Some of the assembled just held up their cell phones instead, until the whole clearing glowed. All those people holding their phones up like badges to the sky, Jared thought, letting the extraterrestrials know there was still hope for communication. Taser, cell phone, camera. How many ways to tap into another creature without ever touching? Mayweather, holding his daughter for the first time, knew that nothing would ever take the place of this fleshy contact. But just as he was getting comfortable standing there, Ellen started edging closer to the fire, as if drawn by some alien force and Etta pulled the cell phone out of his pocket and held it up in imitation of the adults around her. "Where's Daddy?" she said. "I want to call my Daddy." The words were like spitballs propelled directly into his face and he turned away from them, blinking. But how could you blame a four-year-old for repeating the lie that had been sold to her? How does anyone ever know their father except by rumor and hearsay? Maybe Jared himself would have been better off if he had been told a similar lie. Ellen finally quieted the little girl, saying the ceremony was about to begin; there was no time to make a call.

The Bald Knobber evangelist flapped her skirt, exposing the tops of her knee socks, and lifted her hands to the sky, shouted out some unrecognizable syllables and began to rock on her feet, pulling on the tag end of the incredible hemp heap of her hair, threatening to unravel it. Lorraine stood by tapping out the rhythm with her cane, as if she was receiving Morse code from the beyond. And the Bombers, who had returned to the fire, surrounded her, looking uncomfortable, before joining arms and swaying to the rough music of the evangelical ranting.

Then Sally's voice seemed to rise from within the sound, fuzzed with the intervention of the microphone, but warm and irregular with life. "Thank you for coming out to show your support for a fallen hero. Gabriella Hernandez is a warrior. She served her country in Iraq and lived to fight another day. Then she was taken down by a sports injury in a roller derby bout, where no one expected any danger. For three days Gabriella lay unconscious on her hospital bed. For three days her teammates kept vigil. Three days and her mother never left her side. But tonight I'm happy to report our prayers have been answered. I just received word that Gabriella recovered consciousness this afternoon." She paused and the crowd erupted, the woods echoing back their shouts and yodels, praise Allahs and amens.

"So now we don't have to pray for a miracle, friends. We only have to pray for the healing to take its natural course. I think we can all get behind that, in spite of our differences. Some of you are here to show your support for a veteran. Some are here to the bear witness to the joy of an athlete, an amateur female athlete who competes for no glory but the appreciation of her teammates. And some, I know, are here to protest. You don't like the Boonslick Bombers throwing around the fighting words of war, disrespecting the U.S. military or the Muslim faith. You don't agree with the glorification of violence. Or maybe you have an issue with the Boonslick Bombers' emcee, a lady who's been dishing out her own violence lately."

Here the crowd began to shout, but the words were difficult

to decipher: The Muslim women had taken out their prayer mats and unrolled them on the damp ground and now they were prostrated in what looked to Mayweather like an exotic yoga poses beneath their robes and veils, nothing but their hands visible.

Jared saw Sally through the lens, then zoomed in to watch her features unfolding so rapidly that he couldn't make out the emotions as they passed and the magnification itself was little more than a frustration. Why was it that he could never get Sally onto film? She was either too impassive or too agitated, her features turned inward or distorted with some outsize emotion, as they had been in the YouTube film. Where was the actual baseline of the face?

The shouting quieted down, the women speaking in tongues began to hum, and Sally went on. "For those of you who are dismayed by my actions, I have to say, I share your disbelief. I am just like you, trying to figure out how to defend myself and what I love without giving in to complete and total road rage. But we are not here to talk or to debate. We are here to pray."

And she set her stick down, and knelt onto the ground.

"Dear God or Goddess or Spirit of Life, I pray for the recovery of our fallen sister, Gabriella Hernandez. I pray that she will get up off her hospital bed and walk, and skate, and live to fight another day. I pray for our country, that it can retain its principles amid war and terror. I pray for this beautiful forest, that it will survive our era of greed. And I pray for myself because I gave in to anger when I should have exercised compassion instead."

Jared was confused; Sally wasn't supposed to pray; was Sally even religious? She certainly didn't drink or fuck like she was. Her head bent in submission and her hair covering her face, she reminded him of the scene in the A-frame, her neck and back bared to her attacker.

And then, as if called out from Jared's own memory, a figure appeared from behind the fire, a man with a long hunting rifle, which he pointed directly at Sally's bent head. "Now I got the gun, you stupid cunt," he said, in a nasal voice of triumph. His shape was vivid against the bright background of the fire, his body was long and agile in camouflage hunting gear, legs planted far apart, arm cocked to hold the rifle in position. "You think God hears the prayers of hos and bitches? Yeah, you destroy a man's pride, you destroy his life, and then you try to suck up to the Almighty and think he's going to forget all about it, just wipe the slate clean. What should I do with this bitch, Lord? Should I take her head off right away? "

Mayweather felt the fear flare up in his chest and his gut drop deep into the well of his being, a bottomless well, that went on and on past his own torso and into the damp ground beneath his feet.

"You take Etta," he whispered to Ellen, shifting the weight of the little girl. "Cover her up. Sit on her if you have to." But as he untwined Etta's arms from his, he felt his body shrink in protest, even his nerve endings aware that if things went badly, he might never touch his daughter again.

And the man continued to hold the gun to Sally's head, execution style. Jared could not see any movement, he could not see her face, or any indication of life. He felt shame at his relief, but he couldn't help thinking that as long as the man had the gun pointed at Sally, he could not fire it into the crowd, where Etta was hidden among the knees and sneakers.

But the man seemed more intent on talking than on taking action of any kind. He told about losing his job at Boeing Aircraft. He told about not being able to afford child support, watching his kids go without winter coats and school supplies, eating plain noodles for dinner every night. He talked about the job at Bailey's and then this cunt, this bitch, this piece of human shit who seemed to think that a few sticks out in the country were worth more than a man's dignity or a family's living. The police were right there, Jared thought, standing right there in plain sight leaning against the side of their patrol car; you'd think they would do something. You'd think they'd be good for something besides confiscating PCs and sex toys. But they appeared to be as hypnotized as everyone else. Surely, someone will have the wits to use those cell phones to call 911. He felt in his own pocket and fingered the keys inside the front pouch of his sweatshirt, producing a text by feel—

crkpt w/gun@Krst Prk

—and sent it off without looking. Beside him, Ellen had moved onto the ground and was holding Etta behind her. He could hear the little girl's whimpers, blending in with the sounds of owls and crickets, which didn't stop, he realized, even for the most horrific of human affairs.

Surely reinforcements would arrive soon—five minutes, eight? But that was far too long. The prick could kill Sally in the next thirty seconds if he wanted. The hand, the gun, the neck, the skull, the eye. It was all a matter of millimeters. And in the midst of his calculations, Jared remembered his hand meeting Sally's over Diana's body, the feel of death still so close it bloomed in the air between them, as if solemnizing some unspoken vow. But what? Fidelity, honesty, camaraderie, secrecy, the code of honor among adulterers and thieves? If he could only see Sally's face, he thought, then he might have some idea of what to do. He gauged the distance between himself and the fire—maybe forty feet. If he was able to crawl through the crowd, he might be able to evade detection. He crouched down and hit the ground with his hands and knees. The earth was still damp from the recent rains, and the grass had been tamped down by the feet of the crowd. Even so, the cold blades irritated the flesh of his knees through the thin cloth of Mason's old sweatpants as he made his way past boots and tennis shoes, the torn knees of jeans, the grommets of workpants, aggressive trouser pleats. He knew by instinct when he reached Chaz—still with the bike shoes, while wearing a suit even. Should he even bother stopping and asking him for help? He saw Chaz's hand hanging down by his side, the fingers rubbing against each other. It must kill him to just stand there, unable to intervene. A billow of nausea sloshed through Jared's guts and he remembered Etta back there in the crowd without either of her fathers to protect her. He had to trust Ellen; he had to trust her so he could trust himself.

Fear trilled inside his chest. At first, he thought it was his heart—a heart attack, a seizure?—then he realized that it was just his phone vibrating in the pocket of his sweatshirt. He sure as shit was not going to stop right in the middle of his rescue mission to play phone tag with the police. But although he hated to admit it, he could not ignore the mute appeal. He pulled the phone out of his pocket and found a text from Reenie:

"Gab up! Sal's fon off. R U On?"

Chaz, probably alerted by the light from the device, looked down and made huge eyes at Jared from under his thick brows and then glanced nonchalantly away, as if unwilling to acknowledge his own helplessness. For once in his overcommitted life, Chaz did not have a plan. Jared's throat dropped into his balls, and he didn't know whether to be relieved or disappointed. Because whatever the reason, he seemed to be the only person in the vast pack of paralyzed souls still capable of movement. So he put his phone back into his pocket and kept crawling toward the fire.

37

Here's what I think when I am down on the ground with a gun barrel pressed to my head: I haven't lived hard enough to die. I have spent too much energy defending my territory and not enough on making it yield—what? Happiness? Achievements? Children? Good works? What have I managed to do in forty-five years? Just survive, I guess, and avoid suffering—my own and that of those around me. Until these last few days, when I seem to have hunted up enough grief to last a lifetime, including the accumulated sorrows of these random men I encountered in the forest. This is the one, I know, who didn't show up at my house the other night, the one I humiliated so badly it took him this long to recover and retaliate. I recognize his voice, a gristly nasal whine with fat streaks of pure tenor. I recognize his anger—justified, I know—but weirdly self-righteous, as if I am some evil and implacable authority instead of just a poor civil servant trying to find her own way through the woods. What was the matter with me, anyway? Why didn't I simply hold the gun on the guys, make them pick up the trash, and leave it at that? What made me want to see my own impotence mirrored in the fear of a crew of disenfranchised workers with fewer options than myself? My back aches with old wounds and new, my face is pressed to the cold earth, the smell of damp grass and charred wood and mud, not just any mud, but the specific makeup of the Karst, its rich mix of mushrooms and black walnuts, hedge apples, dried sycamore leaves, cattails, pond scum, and chalk. I take in the scent like a tonic, as if it can restore me to my former self.

If the gunman does kill me, at least I will be reunited with Diana, I think, and wonder what makes me so sure that there is some life after this one. I am not a religious woman, but I am not a skeptic, either, and something about the way my dreams are set into the shallow soil of my waking life tells me that this life we're stuck in isn't the only reality in town. If I go now, no one will ever be able to fire me and kick me out of the Karst. Eric won't have to save me. Chaz won't have to torment me. My mother will be forced to mourn me along with my sister and Mayweather will never get the satisfaction of seeing me grow old.

Still, what will happen to the assembled crowd—my mother, Jared, Etta, the Bombers, and Boonslick's various protestors and well-wishers, every one of whom I have led to this spot as surely as if I dragged them here by force? Will the gunman, after dispatching me, turn and fire on them at random? Will I die with their deaths on my conscience, too? I close my eyes, which are so tender they feel bruised by the movement of the lashes. I taste the raw inside of my mouth, the sauerkraut from the Reuben sandwich mixed with the bitter bile of fear. And then, when I have shrunk my consciousness to a pinpoint of light, it implodes, and I see the roller rink restored to its former glory, the disco ball rolling like a huge shuddering eyeball, the lights laying down color as thick as tempera paint, and Sharee skating backward with a boy, his hair almost as long as hers, his narrow hips canted into the curve.

A little girl—surely Etta—is trailing along behind them, carrying a woven Easter basket and throwing long brown seed pods into their wake. And in the center of the rink is a round red screen–a drain of some kind, maybe, like the drain in a communal shower. I look closer and see that it is a huge dried lotus, a paper honeycomb with dark seeds inside. While I'm watching, a dragon pokes its head out of the opening and its wet webbed wings struggle to emerge from the lotus. Then, as if in response to the movement, the floor of the roller rink cracks like ice. It is ice, I realize, shattering into separate shards that don't break apart but that cohere to one another in defiance of all laws of physics and perspective.

No one seems to notice what has happened. Etta continues to scatter seedpods. Sharee puts her hand on the boy's ass. He licks a bit of glitter from her cheek. They veer toward the brink of the dragon's nest and skirt around its salamander head. Just then, Sharee turns the corner and I see the boy's face framed in her hair. It is Jared, without a hat, without a camera, without a gut, I think, but I would know him anywhere, his dark eyes taking in everything but what's right ahead of him. Will I have to lose both my sister and my sweetheart again? I feel my anger pulsing in my throat, a bitter ball of phlegm I cannot swallow

There is a sharp movement above me. If I'd going to act, it has to be now. I hear a clatter of metal, the scud of a body hitting the ground. Two bodies, not one, practically on top of me, so that I have to struggle to get out from underneath.

And when I look up, it really is Sharee running across the sodden ground, so fast I cannot see her features blurred in flight.

38

The man just stood there with his gun pointed to Sally's head, narrating her sins, her bitchiness, her barrenness, her bestiality. He kicked at her back and pushed her face to the ground. Mayweather felt the pressure of his own spine and lost his balance, over toppled by the weight of his gut, and fell forward so that his camera pressed painfully into his chest. The phone buzzed in his pocket again, a reminder of life outside the clearing, and he looked at it to see that Reenie, who'd gone to see Gabriella, was actually in the park, determined to deliver an update on her teammate's condition in person. He quickly composed the text.

"Stp wk-jb w/gn."

Would this mean anything at all to Reenie, who, in spite of her fascination with the law, had never encountered a criminal in her life? Well, he had done what he could, and had to continue on with his mission past Air Jordans and hiking boots and tasseled loafers. His gave way to a kind of tracking instinct, there close to the smell of damp earth and genitalia. It was a relief after all to know exactly what he had to do, no hesitations for once in his life. He was now so close that he could feel the heat from the fire, hear its branches cracking and its sap dripping and see the coffee or tobacco stains on the attacker's cuff, the cuff over the hand that held the gun aimed at Sally's unknowable head. Sally herself was completely immobile as if she were in a coma or trance, her hair hanging down over her face like the pale bare fronds of a willow in winter. Was something wrong with her—a heart attack, maybe, or another incident like the one in Jeff City? Or maybe she was just wily enough to play possum when necessary. He thought he saw her shoulder shift, as if readjusting an invisible burden, and the gunman responded, swinging his shoulder up so that the sweat flung off him and reached Jared there on the ground, a slimy feel like the track of a snail on his forehead.

But it wasn't Sally who had disturbed the gunman after all. Someone was running through the crowd. Jared could feel the ground pounding beneath him and the crowd jostling to readjust to the movement. A woman in sports sandals actually stepped on his hand and he let out a muffled groan. Reenie, he thought. It must be Reenie. The attacker lifted his gun toward the distraction and Mayweather visualized the distance between them, imagining the smudged imperfect reality before him broken apart and reassembled by the rough cut of time. He took a breath, clenched his calves, and rose up to jump the man, only certain that he'd survived his own idiocy when he heard the heavy camera knock against the gunman's skull.

Then, from his position on the ground, Mayweather heard the sound he never wanted to hear again—a whip parting the ether inside his head. For a moment, he could feel his limbs vibrating, his heart receding, but then he realized the agitation he felt was only the motion of the body thrashing beneath him. He himself had been spared. He quickly jumped up and looked around. The police had drawn close and Officer Tork was holding his Taser down to zap the gunman again, should he offer any resistance. The man himself was sprawled on the ground groaning and twitching, his piss mixed with ash. Jared didn't have the stomach to look, much less relish his victory. The police hadn't been waiting idly by after all. They must have been easing toward the fire from the other direction. Sally herself was already half up off the ground. Jared grabbed her elbow to help her to her feet and felt the heartbeat—slow in comparison to Etta's, but there all the same, some steady counter-rhythm that filled in the spaces of his own hesitation. He looked into her face and saw the clear profile, the narrow forehead smudged with dirt, the vivid blue-green eyes like cracked marbles in her head.

As he pressed her to him, Mayweather felt the outline of her ribcage, the pressure of her warm breasts, while over her shoulder, he watched the moon reframing itself inside the wide white branches of a sycamore, Britney propping her foot on a log to adjust her tights, Chaz lifting Etta up unharmed in his arms, Rye returning, ears and tail alert, from a romp in the forest, and the prayer lady poking relentlessly at the fire, which gave forth a bevy of stray sparks, bright as a swarm of fireflies released into the night. A horrible pain lodged in his chest, somewhere between his throat and his heart, like a big bite of sandwich caught in his windpipe, preventing him from speaking or breathing. Was this love? If so, it was more excruciating than any Etta James song had ever suggested.

Reenie had arrived now and Sally was hugging both of them at once, so that Jared found himself squeezed into an uncomfortable mix of limbs and tits and clashing perfumes, the contact only increasing his panic. He slid through and extricated himself, feeling the outlines of his body re-emerge in the reassuring chill of the night.

"I talked with Gabriella," Reenie said. "The doctor thinks she's going to have a complete recovery. They're going to start physical therapy right away."

"That's beautiful," Sally said. "Now you can both go back to school."

"Actually, I think I'm going to give it another season with the Boonslick Bombers. Lorraine claims she's going to buy the rink so we can all go in on shares. What do you think, can you do another year up in the booth?"

But before Sally could answer, Marilyn Monsoon and Annie Warhaul swooped in and lifted Reenie onto their shoulders, her skirt riding up over her butt pad, her curls gleaming like copper tubing under the glow of the moon.

And now Lorraine stood there in her place, her ancient face rough as karst in the firelight. "Sally, Sally. For a minute there, I thought I was going to have to take out that thug with my cane," she said, then looked over at Mayweather. "Lucky for him, your boyfriend got there first. Good show, Mr. Mayfield."

The two women embraced and Jared watched as Lorraine brushed Sally's hair away from her face, fussing and brushing with increasing force, as if she might finally reveal the daughter underneath. "Now maybe I can keep you a little longer, girl."

Sally began to cry and for the first time, Jared saw what she had looked like as a child—the plain good girl, the distraught preadolescent, the angry twenty-two-year-old with something to prove.

Rye bounded up to her, resting his paws on her chest, and Guy Dempsey appeared behind him, pardoning and excusing his way through the press of the Bombers, his left eye twitching violently, as if he had gotten a twig stuck in it. "Welcome back, Sally. You sure are one lucky camper. Looked like you were about to meet your reward."

"Don't worry, I'm not going to desert my post. Not unless I'm forced out of it."

"Oh, no worries on that score. I got an e-mail from Eric Gaines over in Natural Resources this afternoon, and he thinks he's figured out an angle on our public relations snafu. He just got the go-ahead for some public works projects and he thinks you'd be the ideal woman for the job."

"What job?" she asked, scratching Rye behind the ear.

"You know, interface with our contractors to get the best end of the deal."

She wrinkled her forehead. "Sounds more like a penance than a promotion." But her voice registered some of its old music, a cracked country melody with honey welling up in its seams.

"Well, you think about it, Sal. I hear Mr. Bailey here is raring to go." And there the asshole was, half hidden behind the blue veil of the pretty Muslim protester, bobbing his bullet head, hands tucked inside his bomber jacket and his teeth gritted into a huge industrial smile. Sally looked incredulous, but Guy pressed his hand to her shoulder as if to test the strength of her muscle or charge her up for future use.

Officer Denton cuffed the gunman, and her partner helped him up to his feet. His clothes and face were covered in ash, and when he spoke his voice was muffled, hoarse, his rage tamped down to an ember in his throat. "Stupid cunt," he said, turning toward Sally. "You're going to be in lawsuits until you're seventy."

Sally just ignored him and knelt down on one knee to pet Rye more thoroughly, setting her check against his neck so her pale hair shaded into the bronze of his coat. Looking up at Mayweather, she flashed him an expression of gratitude that quickly sharpened into a grin. "So sweetheart, you sorry you risked your life to save a stupid cunt with legal troubles?"

"Not yet," Mayweather said, feeling the strain in his windpipe and reaching down to touch Rye's coat for comfort. "But there's still a long stretch of sunlight up ahead." And as he spoke, he saw, out of the corner of his eye, the barest sliver of a future, some liminal phosphorescence that might, with any effort, coalesce into a fully formed scene. He began rearranging the pieces, a girl here, in summer or on the weekend, a short day of work, a long night of editing, a woman as salty in bed as she was in the forest, yellow in one corner, green in the other, some dark red cells that kept multiplying out of the frame, more than you wanted, more than you expected, more than you would ever need. He looked at Sally to see if she was following. No, he thought, the poor woman didn't know a thing about visions. He would have to make her see.

Acknowledgments

Thanks very much to Deb Brenegan, Rose Marie Kinder, and Phong Nguyen for their detailed commentary on this manuscript and for their support and encouragement.

Thanks also to Angela Burson, Greg Eltringham, Grant Gardner, Aaron Judlowe, Glynis Kinnan, Felicia (Whiskey ShinDig) Leach, Devoney (Stonecold Janeausten) Looser, and Megan McKinstry for extra-literary inspiration. Thanks to Lorrie Moore for choosing my story "Limestone Diner" for *Best American Short Stories* and thus encouraging me to continue writing about this cast of characters in Boonslick, Missouri.

I want to thank the University of Missouri for a generous research leave and the Columbia Public Library for its congenial study rooms, where I wrote much of this novel. Thanks also to the Viebranz Family, who sponsored my year as Viebranz Visting Writer at St. Lawrence University, and to the Saint Lawrence English Department for the warm environment in that cold place. I am grateful for residencies and fellowships at the Vermont Studio Center, Norton Island, and the Summer Literary Seminars in Vilnius.

Thanks to Mike Czyzniejewski at Moon City Press for his faith in this manuscript. Thanks to creative writing assistant Chris Bolinger George, who makes it possible for me to maintain my writing schedule in the midst of lively departmental activity. Thanks to my students at the University of Missouri, whose optimism has kept me focused on the open possibility of literature. Thanks to Noah Heringman and Mary Jo Neitz, colleagues who have inspired me through their intelligence and integrity. Thanks to my neighbors Amy and Tim Langen for their unwavering friendship. Thanks to Eileen and Scott Bjornstrom for keeping me grounded. Special thanks to Marly Swick for a literary friendship that has sustained me through many years.

Thanks to my parents, Frank and Linda Lewis, for a lifelong tutorial in politics and language, and to my sister, Terry Lee Hall, for her gifts of empathy and imagination. I thank my sons Eddie and Jude Barrett for their patience with my eccentricities. I eventually wrote a sports novel after all! Finally, thanks to Mike Barrett, who holds it all together with his immense reserves of energy, intellect, and joy.